Acclaim for internationally bestselling author

LISA JEWELL

and her captivating novels

THE HOUSE WE GREW UP IN

"A dramatic look at siblings, parents, and hoarding."

—*Redbook*

"Jewell cleverly frames the destruction of the Bird family."

—*Booklist*

"Jewell keeps the reader engrossed with her characters' winding, divergent paths."

—*Publishers Weekly*

"Jewell delivers with this latest tale of loneliness and the lure of beautiful things."

—*Kirkus Reviews*

"Lorrie is one of the most vivid—and co̶m̶p̶l̶e̶x̶ characters I've read in years."

—Jojo Moyes, *New*

"You'll be desperate to find out ̶.̶.̶.̶ ̶family up so badly."

—Sophie Kinsella, #1 *New York Times* bestselling author of *Shopaholic to the Stars*

"Prose so beautiful that it glitters on the page. . . . Unforgettable."

—Jo-Ann Mapson, author of *Owen's Daughter*

"Lisa Jewell's quixotic Bird family functions like an operatic ensemble—each voice distinct, each singing its heart out, seemingly oblivious to the others. Yet somehow by the end of this engrossing, beautifully crafted novel, their separate stories will draw them back together, reminding us that, however hard we struggle against them, family ties are not easily undone."

—Judith Ryan Hendricks, author of *Bread Alone*

"This richly rendered family saga is populated with such compelling characters and told in such luscious, insightful prose that a singular tragedy is made universally relatable."

—Jessie Sholl, author of *Dirty Secret*

"A gorgeous, powerful, affecting tale of a family both ordinary and extraordinary. . . . I'm afraid to say it made me neglect both my children and my husband. The Bird family might be dysfunctional, but I was strangely sorry to leave it."

—Anna Maxted, author of *Getting Over It*

BEFORE I MET YOU

"Jewell unfolds each detail . . . with impeccable timing."

—*Publishers Weekly*

"Jewell keeps the pace steady, the plot intriguing, and the characters highly relatable. Family dynamics, the search for love and personal meaning, and the simple yet evocative daily motions of each woman keep the pages turning."

—*Booklist*

"Heartbreakingly good."

—*Marie Claire* (UK)

THE MAKING OF US

"An engaging tale of choices made and not made, families lost and families gained, this should appeal to fans of Jewell's work as well as such authors as Jodi Picoult."

—*Booklist*

"Compelling and entertaining. . . . Jewell's moving novel immerses readers in the lives of these unique characters through the universal themes of family and a search for belonging."

—*Publishers Weekly*

"Odd and lovely. . . . Filled with heart and humor."

—*Kirkus Reviews*

"An irresistible read. . . . Anyone who has ever pondered the nature of family or imagined finding a long-lost sibling will be captivated."

—*Shelf Awareness*

AFTER THE PARTY

"Lisa Jewell's writing is like a big warm hug, and this book is a touching, insightful, and gripping story which I simply couldn't put down."

—Sophie Kinsella

"Flipping between their perspectives and illuminating their desires, fears, and sometimes clumsy actions, *After the Party* entertainingly marches its characters along the path to finally growing up."

—*Booklist*

"Jewell's easy prose and storytelling ability make for a pleasant trip. Engaging."

—*Kirkus Reviews*

"Jewell writes, as ever, with wit and verve."

—*Guardian* (UK)

THE HOUSE
WE GREW UP IN

A Novel

LISA JEWELL

ATRIA PAPERBACK

New York   London   Toronto   Sydney   New Delhi

ATRIA PAPERBACK
An Imprint of Simon & Schuster, Inc.
1230 Avenue of the Americas
New York, NY 10020

First Atria Paperback edition April 2015

ATRIA PAPERBACK and colophon are trademarks of Simon & Schuster, Inc.

For information about special discounts for bulk purchases, please contact Simon & Schuster Special Sales at 1-866-506-1949 or business@simonandschuster.com.

The Simon & Schuster Speakers Bureau can bring authors to your live event. For more information or to book an event, contact the Simon & Schuster Speakers Bureau at 1-866-248-3049 or visit our website at www.simonspeakers.com.

Interior design by Kyoko Watanabe

Manufactured in the United States of America

10 9 8 7 6 5 4 3 2 1

The Library of Congress has cataloged the hardcover edition as follows:

Jewell, Lisa.
  The house we grew up in / Lisa Jewell. — First Atria hardcover edition.
     pages cm
  1. Home—Fiction. 2. Family secrets—Fiction. 3. Brothers and sisters—Fiction. 4. Domestic fiction. I. Title.
  PR6060.E95H68 2014
  823'.914—dc23

                              2013025887

ISBN 978-1-4767-0299-5
ISBN 978-1-4767-7686-6 (pbk)
ISBN 978-1-4767-0301-5 (ebook)

*This book is dedicated to Guy and Celia Gordon,
with all my love*

THE HOUSE
WE GREW UP IN

1

Tuesday 2nd November 2010

Hi, Jim!

Well, I must say, I didn't think for a minute you'd be called something earthy like Jim! The Barbour and natty waistcoat in your profile photo make you look more like a Rupert or a Henry, something serious with two syllables, you know! And talking of syllables, and since you asked, no, I'm not really called Rainbowbelle. OF COURSE NOT! I'm called Lorelei and my name has three or four syllables, depending on how you say it. (My parents named us after mythical maidens. My sister is called Pandora. There was an Athena, but she was stillborn, so you know.) Anyway. Lor-a-lay-ee. Or Lor-a-lay. I'm not fussy really.

I'm sixty-five years old and I live in one of the prettiest villages in the Cotswolds in a big, crazy old house full of what I call TREASURES and what my children call CRAP. We are probably ALL right. ☺

I have four children. Megan is forty, Bethan is thirty-eight and the twins, Rory and Rhys, are thirty-five. Oh, and thanks mainly to the frantic reproduction of my eldest daughter I am a multiple grandmother too! Do you have any children? You didn't mention them so I assume not? People usually tell you about their children before anything else, right? I don't see them very much, unfortunately, they're all so busy, and I'm, well, I suppose you could say insular these days. I lost my partner about four years ago and things kind of unraveled from there, you might say.

Anyway, what can I tell you about me? I love nature, I love the countryside, I love children, I love to swim. I'm fit, for my age. I've kept my figure over the years, and am grateful for that. I see some women I've known for many years just turn to woolly mammoths once they pass menopause! And, as you can see from my picture, I've kept my hair long. Nothing ages a woman faster than a haircut!!

Anyway, that's enough about me. Tell me more about you! You say you're a widower. I'm very sorry to hear that. And whereabouts in the North do you live? I can see from your photo that you have a dog. That is a very beautiful retriever. What is it called? We had a dog when the children were growing up, but once they'd all gone, I could never quite see the point of animals.

I will see what I can do about photographs. I'm not really very techy beyond my laptop. But there must be something else I can send you. I'll check it out.

Well, thank you, Jim, for getting in touch. The Internet really is a marvelous thing, especially for old codgers like us, wouldn't you say? I'd be lost without it really. I'd love to hear back from you again, but please don't feel you have to, if you think I sound dreadful!!

Yours with best wishes,
Lorelei Bird

APRIL 2011

The damp heat came as a shock after the chill of the air-conditioning that had cooled the car for the last two hours. Meg slammed the door behind her, pushed up the sleeves of her cotton top, pulled down her sunglasses and stared at the house.

"Jesus Christ."

Molly joined her on the pavement, and gawped from behind lime-green Ray-Bans. "Oh, my God."

They stood together for a moment, side by side, the same height as each other now. Molly had caught up last summer, much to her delight. They now both stood at five foot eight. Molly long and lean as a fashion drawing, tanned legs in denim hot pants, honey-dusted hair bundled on top of her head in an artful pile, white Havaianas, a chambray shirt over a pink tank top, tiny ankles and wrists layered in friendship circlets and rubber bands. Meg, on the other hand, solid as a quarterback, sensible in three-quarter-length navy chinos and a Breton-striped long-sleeved top, a pair of silver-sequined FitFlops and a last-minute pedicure her only concession to the unseasonal heat wave. Mother and only daughter, in the late stages of a nightmarish, clichéd teenage disaster that had lasted more than three years. Almost friends now. Almost. Someone had once told Meg that you get your daughter back when she's nineteen. Only four more years to wait.

"This is worse than I thought. I mean, so much worse." Meg shook her head and took a tentative step towards the house. There it stood, brick for brick, exactly as it had been the day she was born, forty years earlier. Three low windows facing out onto the street; four windows above; two front doors, one at either end; on the right by the side entrance a plaque, made by a long-dead local craftsman, an oval with the words *The Bird House* painted on it and a pair of lovebirds with their beaks entwined. The green-painted gate to the left of the house that opened up onto a graveled path to the back door, the stickers in the windows declaring membership of Neighborhood Watch (whatever happened to Neighborhood Watch? Meg wondered idly), allegiance to the RSPB and an intolerance towards people selling door-to-door.

All there, just as it had been forever and ever.

Except . . .

"This is the worst house I've ever seen," said Molly. "It's worse than the ones on the TV shows."

"We haven't even been inside yet, Moll, hold that thought."

"And my nose too, right?"

"Yes, probably." She sighed.

The windows, which to her recollection had never been cleaned, were now so thick with grime that they were fully opaque. In fact, they were black. The pastel-yellow Gloucester brick was discolored and damaged. The green gate was hanging off its post by one solitary nail and the graveled pathway was piled high with random objects: two old pushchairs, a rusty bike, a dead Christmas tree in a broken pot, a box of magazines swollen and waterlogged to twice their original size.

The flat-fronted style of the house meant that it held most of its personality within and behind, but even on such scant display, it was clear that this house had a disease. The village had grown more and more gentrified over the decades, all the old houses scrubbed to a gleaming yellow, doors and window frames Farrow-&-Balled to the nth degree, and there, lodged between them, like a rotten tooth, sat the Bird House.

"God, it's so embarrassing," said Molly, pushing her Ray-

Bans into her hair and wrinkling her tiny nose. "What must everyone think?"

Meg raised her eyebrows. "Hmm," she said, "I'd say that judging by our local reputation this is probably no more than anyone in the village would expect. Come on then"—she smiled at her daughter, nervously—"let's go in, shall we? Get it over with?"

Molly smiled back grimly and nodded.

APRIL 1981

Megan pulled back the ivy and pushed her fingertips inside a small crevice in the wall.

"Got another one!" she shouted out to Bethan and the twins.

"Oh, well done, Meggy!" her mother called from the back step, where she stood in her strawberry-print apron watching proceedings with a contented smile. "Bravo!"

Megan pulled out the small foil-wrapped egg and dropped it into her basket. "It's pink!" she said pointedly to her younger sister.

"Don't care," said Bethan. "I've got three pink ones already."

Megan looked up at the sky; it was cloudless, densely blue, hot as July. Mum had said they needed to find their eggs quickly, otherwise they might melt. Her eyes scanned the gardens. She'd found all the eggs in the woodpile, gingerly plucking them from next to rubbery woodlice. There'd been more in the beds of daffodils and hyacinths that lined the pathways around the greenhouse and she'd come across a big gold one sitting in the branches of the cherry tree outside the kitchen door. She counted up her eggs and found she had twelve. Bethan and the twins were still searching close to the house, but Megan suspected that the top garden had been all but stripped of its eggy assets, so she skipped down the slate-covered steps to the lower garden. Suddenly the sounds of her siblings and her mother faded to a murmur. It was warmer down here, soft and hazy. The grass had stripes in it, from where Dad had mown it yesterday, this way and that, and little piles of shaggy grass trimmings already turning pale in the burning sun. A camellia bush, confused by the early summer, had already bloomed and spilled its fat blossoms onto the lawn, where they lay browning and sated, halfway to ugly. Megan headed to the lichen-spotted sundial in the middle of the lawn. Three more foil-wrapped eggs sat on top of it and she brushed them into her basket with the side of her hand.

She heard Bethan tripping down the steps behind her in her flamenco shoes. Megan turned and smiled. Sometimes when she looked at her little sister she felt overcome with love. Her worst enemy and her best friend.

Meg and Beth looked identical. They both had what her mother called the "Bird face." It was the same as her dad's and the same as her auntie Lorna's and the same as Granny Bird's. Apple cheeks, high foreheads, wide smiles. The only difference was that Megan's hair was brown and curly like Mum's, and Bethan's was straight and black like Dad's. Rory and Rhys, the twins, looked like their mum. They had "Douglas faces." Low foreheads, long noses, neat bee-stung lips, and narrow blue eyes peering curiously from behind curtains of long blond hair.

People always said, *"Oh, such lovely-looking children."* They said, *"You must be so proud, Mrs. Bird."* They said, *"What perfect angels."*

And Mum would say, *"You should see them when they're at home,"* and roll her eyes, with one hand running through Rory's hair, the other wrapped around Rhys's hand and her voice full of love.

"How many have you got?" Meg called out to her sister.

"Eleven. How about you?"

"Fifteen."

Their mother appeared at the bottom of the steps with the twins in tow. "The boys have got nine each, I think we're almost there," she said. "Think *yellow*," she added with an exaggerated wink. The boys let go of her hands and ran towards the slide at the bottom of the garden that had yellow handles. Bethan ran towards an upturned bucket that was actually orange. But Megan knew exactly where her mother meant. The Saint-John's-wort bush right in front of them. She walked towards it and let her eyes roam over the clouds of yellow flowers abuzz with fat bumblebees before they came to rest on a row of terra-cotta pots underneath, overflowing with eggs and small yellow puffball chicks with glued-on eyes. She was about to scoop up the eggs and chicks when her mother touched her on her shoulder, her soft dry hands firm against Meg's sun-freckled skin. "Share them," she whispered softly, "with the little ones. Make it fair."

Meg was about to complain but then she took a deep breath and nodded. "Here!" she called out to her siblings. "Look! There's millions."

All three hurtled to the Saint-John's-wort bush and their mother divided up the remaining eggs into four piles and handed them to each child in turn. "Already starting to melt," she said, licking some chocolate from the edge of her thumb, "better get them indoors."

The cool of the house was shocking after the heat outside. It draped itself over Meg's bare skin like a cold flannel. Dad was pouring juice into beakers at the kitchen table. The dog was dozing on the window seat. The yellow walls of the kitchen were entirely covered over with the children's art. Megan ran her finger along the edges of a drawing that she'd done when she was four. It always amazed her to think it had been stuck to the wall there, in the very same place, with the very same piece of Sellotape, for six whole years. She could barely remember being four. She certainly could not remember sitting and drawing this portrait entitled *megn and mumy,* composed of two string-legged people with crazy hair, split-in-half smiles and hands twice the size of their bodies, suspended in a gravity-free world of spiky blue trees and floating animals. The wall of art was a conversation piece for anyone coming into the house; it spanned all three walls, spread itself over cupboard doors, over door frames, around corners and even into the pantry. Dad would try and take some down occasionally, to *"update the wall"* as he'd put it. But Mum would just smile her naughty-little-girl smile and say, *"Over my dead body."* If Dad ever saw one of his children producing a piece of art he'd snatch it away the moment it was shown to him and say, *"That is so very beautiful that I shall have to put it in my special folder,"* and spirit it away somewhere (occasionally tucked inside his clothes) before Mum saw it and stuck it to the wall.

"Now," she said, pulling her tangly hair back into a ponytail and removing her apron, "you can eat all the eggs you like as long as you promise you'll still have room for lunch. And remember, keep the foils for the craft box!"

The "craft box" was another bugbear of Dad's. It had once been a small plastic toolbox neatly filled with sequins and pipe cleaners and sheets of gold leaf. Over the years it had expanded into an ever-growing family of giant plastic crates that lived in a big cupboard in the hall, filled with an impossible tangle of old string lengths, knots of wool, empty sweet wrappers, toilet-roll middles, old underwear cut into rags, packing chips and used wrapping paper. Megan didn't really do crafts anymore—she was nearly eleven now—and Bethan had never been as creative as her sister, while the boys of course would rather be roaming the gardens or charging about the house than sitting with a tube of Pritt and a handful of old ice-lolly sticks. No one really used the craft box anymore, but that didn't stop Lorelei constantly topping it up with all sorts of old junk.

She pulled the egg foils eagerly from the children now as they discarded them, smoothing them flat with her fingertips into delicate slivers, her face shining with satisfaction. "So pretty," she said, piling them together, "like little slices of rainbow. And of course, they will always make me think of today. This perfect day with my lovely children when the sun shone and shone and all was right with the world."

She looked at each child in turn and smiled her smile. She ran a hand over Rhys's hair and stroked it from his eyes. "My lovely children," she said again, her words encompassing all four of them, but her loving gaze fixed firmly upon her last-born child.

Rhys had been the smallest of all of Lorelei's babies. Megan and Bethan had both weighed over nine pounds. Rory had been the first twin out, weighing in at a healthy six pounds and fifteen ounces. And then, as her mother often recounted, out popped poor Rhys like a plucked quail, a little under four pounds, blue and wrinkled and just about able to breathe on his own. They'd put him under lights—or *lightly toasted him,* as Lorelei also often recounted—and declared him fit to go home only after three long days.

Lorelei still worried about him more than the other three. At just six years old he was smaller than Rory, smaller than most of the children in his class, with a pale complexion and a tendency to catch colds and tummy bugs. He clung to his mother whenever they were out in public, wailed like a baby when he got hurt and, unlike his brother, didn't like playing with other children. He seemed happy only when he was here, at home, brother on one side, mother on the other. Megan didn't know what to make of him. Sometimes she wished he'd never been born. Sometimes she really thought they'd be better off without him. He didn't "match." All the Birds were fun and gregarious, silly and bright. Rhys just dragged them down.

Megan unthinkingly squeezed her fist around the gold foil that she'd just unpeeled from the big egg she'd found in the cherry tree, and jumped slightly as her mother's hand slapped down against hers.

"Foil!" Lorelei cried. "Foil!"

She immediately let her fist fall open and her mother took the crumpled foil with a smile. "Thank you, darling," she said sweetly. She let her gaze fall on the foil and said, "Look at it, so pretty, so shiny, so . . . happy."

❧

The Easter holidays stretched out for another week. The heat wave continued and the Bird children came indoors only for beakers of juice, slices of bread and butter and desperately needed visits to the toilet.

Friends came and went, there was a day trip to the beach at Weston-super-Mare, and on the last weekend of the holidays they had a visit from Lorelei's sister Pandora and her two teenage sons. Dad filled the paddling pool and the adults drank glasses of Pimm's with fruit-shaped plastic ice cubes bobbing about in them. Megan's cousin Tom played David Bowie songs on his heavily stickered guitar. Rory burst the paddling pool with a stick and the water seeped heavily onto the lawn, leaving it waterlogged and boggy, and Dad said, "Well, that's that then." Lorelei scooped the floppy remains of the punctured pool into her arms like it was an injured child and carried it into the garage murmuring, "Dad'll fix it up." Dad said, "You and I both know that Dad won't fix it up. I have no idea how to fix paddling pools and I still haven't fixed the one that got burst last year." And Lorelei smiled and blew him a kiss across the garden.

Dad sighed and said, "Well. We now have *three* punctured paddling pools sitting in our garage—this house is just a dumping ground," and raised his eyebrows heavenwards.

Pandora smiled and said, "Just like our dad. He never could throw anything away."

Megan's other cousin Ben smiled and said, "Tell us again about what Lorelei used to collect when she was a child."

Pandora frowned and then smiled. "Autumn leaves. Ring pulls. Tags from new clothes. Cinema stubs. The silver foil from Mum's cigarette packets."

"And hair!" said Ben gleefully. "Don't forget the hair."

"Yes," said Pandora, "anytime anyone in our family had a haircut, Lorelei begged to keep it. She had a shopping bag full of it under her bed. It was quite gruesome."

The adults and teenagers laughed and Megan looked at them curiously. They'd had this conversation before—every time they were together, it sometimes seemed—and whenever she heard them talking about her mum like this it sounded different. The older she got the less she found it funny and the more she found it peculiar. Because she was now the age that her mother had been at the time of these strange childhood collections and she could no more imagine herself collecting old hair than she could asking to go to school on a Saturday.

"Are you laughing at me?" her mother asked good-naturedly as she returned from the garage.

"No, no, no!" said Ben. "Absolutely not. We're just talking about you affectionately."

"Hmm," said Lorelei, wiping her damp hands down the length of her long denim skirt. "I strongly suspect not."

And then she spread her arms upwards, revealing unshaved armpits of lush brown curls, and declared, "Look at that sky, just look at it. The blueness of it. Makes me want to snatch out handfuls of it and put it in my pockets."

Megan saw a look pass over her father's face at that moment. Love and worry. As though he was aching to say something unspeakable.

The look softened as Megan watched and then he smiled and said, "If my wife had her way, her pockets would be full of pieces of every single thing in the world."

"Oh, yes!" Lorelei beamed. "They would be. Totally and absolutely *bulging*."

᠂

Pandora had brought homemade butterfly cakes with fluffed-up cream and more tiny yellow chicks atop.

Lorelei served them in the garden with tea from a pot and scones and cream. There was more Pimm's and a plastic bowl of strawberries. The twins ran barefoot back and forth from the hosepipe to fill their water pistols, which, after countless tellings-off, they were using to squirt only each other. Tom and Ben had retired to the bottom of the garden to smoke cigarettes in the hammock and share secret jokes together. Megan and Bethan sat side by side, listening to the grown-ups talk.

When Megan herself was a grown-up and people came to ask about her childhood, it was afternoons such as these that would impel her to say, *"My childhood was perfect."*

And it was. Perfect.

They lived in a honey-colored house that sat hard up against the pavement of a picture-postcard Cotswolds village and stretched out beyond into three-quarters of an acre of rambling half-kempt gardens. Their mother was a beautiful hippy called Lorelei with long tangled hair and sparkling green eyes who treated her children like precious gems. Their father was a sweet gangly man called Colin, who still looked like a teenager with floppy hair and owlish round-framed glasses. They all attended the village school, they ate home-cooked meals together every night, their extended family was warm and clever; there was money for parties and new paddling pools, but not quite enough for foreign travel, but it didn't matter, because they lived in paradise. And even as a child, Megan knew this to be paradise. Because, she could see with hindsight, her mother told her so. Her mother existed entirely in the moment. And she made every moment sparkle. No one in Megan's family was ever allowed to forget how lucky they were. Not even for a second.

A cloud passed over the sun just then and Lorelei laughed and pointed and said, "Look! Look at that cloud! Isn't it wonderful? It looks *exactly* like an elephant!"

APRIL 2011

The keys were where Lorelei had always left them, under a cracked plant pot behind a water pipe beneath the kitchen window. Meg pulled them out and dusted the sticky cobwebs from her fingertips. "Yuck."

The house had been impenetrable by either of its front doors for many years now. The family had always come in and out through the kitchen door at the back and for the last few years Lorelei had been using both hallways at the front as bonus "storage areas."

"Right," Meg said, rejoining Molly by the back door, "let's go. Deep breath." She threw her daughter a brave smile and was gratified to see her smile reflected back at her.

"You okay, Mum?"

Meg nodded. Of course she was okay. Meg was always okay. Someone had to be and she'd been the one to draw that straw. "I'm fine, love, thank you."

Molly peered at her curiously and then took one of her hands in her own and squeezed it gently. Meg almost flinched at the tender power of it. Her daughter's touch. Until recently her last memory of her daughter's touch had been the sting of a palm across her cheek, the jab of toes against her shins, the drag of fingernails down her arm. It had been that bad. Truly. Everything she'd been warned of about teenage girls, squared and squared again. But lately, things had started to change. Lately, it seemed as though her daughter had started to like her again.

"Thank you, love," she said again.

"You know you can talk about it, don't you? You know I want to listen. I want to help. You've lost your mummy. If I lost my mummy, I'd . . ." Molly's eyes filled with tears and she smiled through them. "Oh, God, well, you know."

Meg laughed. "I know, baby, I know. But honestly. I'm good. Really."

Molly squeezed her hand one more time before letting it

go. She pulled in her breath theatrically and then nodded at the key in Meg's hand. Meg nodded back and fitted it into the lock. She turned the key. She opened the door.

MARCH 1986

The sky was dark with rain clouds and in the very far distance, thunder was starting to rumble. The York stone paving slabs were still stained charcoal gray from the last downpour and fat droplets of rain clung tremulously to the edges of leaves and spring blossoms. Behind the cloud was a strip of blue and there on the horizon, the faint beginnings of a rainbow. Lorelei stood barefoot just outside the kitchen door, wrapped in a long multi-colored angora cardigan. Her waist-length hair was twisted and held on her crown with three large tortoiseshell combs.

"Look, Meggy," she said, her head appearing around the door. "Look. A rainbow! Quick!"

Meg glanced up from her revision, spread before her on the kitchen table, and smiled encouragingly. "In a minute," she said.

"No!" cried her mother. "It'll be gone in a minute. Come and look now!"

Meg sighed and rested her pen on her notepad. "Okay," she said.

She joined her mother outside, feeling the wetness of the flagstones seeping through her sheepskin slippers.

"Beth!" her mother called back into the kitchen. "Boys! Come quickly!"

"They're watching telly," said Meg. "They won't be able to hear you."

"Go and get them, will you, darling?"

"They won't come."

"Of course they will. Quick, darling, run in and tell them."

Meg knew it was pointless to argue. She sighed again and headed towards the sitting room. Her three siblings sat in a row on the grubby sofa with the dog lying listlessly between them. They were watching *Saturday Superstore* and eating carrot sticks.

"Mum says there's a rainbow," she said defeatedly. "She wants you to go and look at it."

No one acknowledged her so she returned to her mother with the bad news.

Lorelei sighed melodramatically. "That's a terrible pity," she said. "And look"—she gestured at the sky—"now it's gone. Gone for good. Forever . . ." A small tear rolled down the side of her nose and she wiped it away with a bunched-up fist, the way a small child might do. "Such a pity," she murmured, "to miss a rainbow . . ." Then she forced her face into a smile and said, "Ah well, at least one of you saw it. You can always describe it to the others."

Meg smiled tightly. *As if,* she thought to herself, *as if I will sit with my siblings and regale them with descriptions of the red and the yellow and the pink and the green, the awe and the splendor of the purple and the orange and the blue, the miracle of distant prismatic stripes.* "Yes," she said. "Maybe, later."

∾

It was still raining the next day. Lorelei insisted on the egg hunt taking place regardless.

"Let's do it indoors, darling," Colin had suggested gently.

"No way, Jose!" Lorelei had countered. "Easter Sunday is egg hunt in the garden. Rain or no rain. Isn't that right, kiddies?"

Meg looked out towards the garden, through the rain-splattered panes of glass, and thought of her hair, lovingly back-combed that morning into a fat quiff and sprayed hard with Elnett. She thought of the muddy lawn and the cold, wet grass and her canvas pumps, and she thought of her drainpipe jeans that she'd had trouble squeezing into this morning, and the date she was going on next week, for which she planned on being able to wear said jeans, not to mention the troublesome spot forming on her chin.

The twins jumped into their Wellington boots and raincoats, while Lorelei ran around in the rain, planting her eggs in the garden. Meg watched her through the window. She looked like a wraith, long and lean, in a cream muslin smock, faded jeans, green Wellingtons and a floppy-brimmed straw hat, her long hair sticking wet to her back, her small breasts growing visible through the fabric of her top as it dampened. Her face was shining with joy as she hopped from spot to spot, plucking eggs from a straw basket held in the crook of her arm.

The boys stood in the doorway, bristling with anticipation. Just turned eleven years old they could still be held rapt by Lorelei with her enthusiasm and childlike charm. Her babies, still, just about.

"Ready, steady, *go!*" she called out a moment later, and the boys hared out onto the lawn, followed more sedately by Bethan in a pink polka-dot raincoat and rubber boots.

"Meggy?" Her mother stared at her curiously. "No eggs?"

"I'll leave them for the others," said Meg, hoping a suggestion of sibling-oriented kindness might prevent further urging.

"There's lots to go round. Tons and tons."

Meg shrugged. "I don't want my hair to get wet."

"Oh, for goodness' sake. That's no excuse. Put on a rain

cap, here . . ." She pulled a clear plastic hood from a drawer and forced it into Meg's hands.

Meg stared at it, aghast. "I'm not wearing that!"

"Why on earth not?"

"Because it's an old lady's hat."

"It is not! It's *my* hat!"

"Exactly."

Lorelei threw her head back and laughed hard. "Oh, darling," she said, "one day, God willing, you'll be forty too, and I promise you, you will not feel a day over eighteen. Not a day. Now put the hat on and come and have some fun with the little ones. Imagine," she said, her face turning serious for a moment, "imagine if something happened to one of us and there was no Easter egg hunt next year, imagine if everything stopped being perfect—you would wish so hard that you'd taken part today . . ."

Meg stared into the depths of her mother's eyes, the greeny-blue reservoirs of a million fervent emotions. They were set firm. She forced a smile and said, "Okay," dragging out the second syllable to demonstrate her sacrifice. She found eleven eggs that morning and gave them all to her siblings.

꙰

Pandora and her husband, Laurence, arrived at midday, without either of their now-grown-up sons but with a new puppy in tow. Shortly afterwards, Colin's sister Lorna turned up, with a carrier bag full of Easter eggs. Some neighbors were next to arrive, Bob and Jenny and their three young children. Lorelei roasted a leg of lamb in the Aga and served it with far too many honey-glazed carrots (*"Aren't they the most glorious shade of orange?"*) and not nearly enough roast potatoes. The children sat at a plastic picnic table at one end of the kitchen while the adults sat together around the antique pine table in the middle. Megan felt lost among the two parties, too old for the children, too young for the adults, not one person in the room to appreciate her perfectly applied eyeliner or her new Aran cardigan with leather buttons or the fact that she'd finally got down to eight and a half stone. She didn't like carrots and was toying with the idea of vegetarianism, so she picked daintily at the one roast potato she'd been allocated by her mother (*"family hold" back, darling!*) and stared through the window at the incessant rain, fantasizing about her escape.

Megan imagined it to be a glorious explosion of glass shards, as she slammed her fists through the invisible walls around her. She imagined fresh air and bright light and dizzying amounts of space. She saw a room with four flat bare walls, a square bed dressed in plain white sheets, a tall window hung with a simple pair of white curtains like the ones in Demi Moore's apartment in *St. Elmo's Fire*. She saw a shiny kitchen, gleaming pans, a white bathroom and a quiet man with clean fingernails and a silver guitar.

Then she looked around her own kitchen, at the fifteen years' worth of children's art lovingly hung and tacked and stuck to the walls, and the thought of escape soured in her heart. She left the children's table and went and sat herself on her father's knee at the grown-ups' table, hoping for a return of the sense of the sugary days of her childhood. He wrapped a gangly arm around her waist and Megan smiled across the table at her mother.

"You know, Lorrie," their neighbor Jenny was saying, "your kitchen really is the loveliest place to be on a grotty day like today."

Lorelei smiled and put an arm around her friend.

"No, it really is. So warm. So welcoming. If I ever found myself stranded on the side of a snowy mountain, freezing to death, I would probably hallucinate about this place. About Lorrie's lovely kitchen."

"Thank you," said Lorelei, kissing her on her cheek. "Meggy thinks the house is a mess, don't you, my darling?"

"It *is* a mess," she replied.

Lorelei laughed. "Diff'rent strokes for diff'rent folks, darling, isn't that right?"

Meg raised her eyebrows and rolled her eyes. "I just don't know why you have to keep so much stuff. I mean, I understand all this . . ." She gestured at the artwork. "But why, for example, do we have nineteen tea towels?"

Lorelei snorted. "We do not have nineteen tea towels."

"We absolutely *do* have nineteen tea towels, Mother. I counted them the other day. Just as an experiment. Look!" She leapt to her feet and yanked open a kitchen drawer. She pulled out examples and held them up as evidence. "We have tea towels with holes in them, tea towels with burn marks, stained tea towels, threadbare tea towels. But look! We also have brand-new tea towels—look, *nice* ones."

Pandora laughed. "I must confess, Lorrie, I bought you that one because I was a bit alarmed by the elderly appearance of the existing tea towels last time I came."

"Yet, still," Meg continued theatrically, warming to her theme, "do we throw the old ones away? No! We do not! We wash them and we dry them and then we *fold* them and we return them to this drawer which now has *nineteen tea towels* in it!"

"Well, darling," her mother replied drily, "I must say, given that you'll be sitting your O levels in less than three months,

I'd have thought you might have better things to do with your time than count tea towels."

"Please let me throw one away, Mother. Please. I beg of you. How about this one?" She held up a limp gray cloth with a rend running down the full length of it.

"No!" exclaimed Lorelei. "Absolutely not! It'll do for rags."

"Mother," said Megan in exasperation, "we have a black bag on the landing bulging at the seams with 'rags.' Which we never use. We do not need any more *rags*."

"Put it back," said her mother, her joyful eyes clouding over for a moment. "Please. Just put it back. I'll do a clear-out another day. When you're all back at school."

"But you won't, will you? You know that and I know that. If I came back here in ten years' time there'd be thirty tea towels in that drawer. *Including* this one." She hurled the tea towel down on her mother's lap.

"Oh, now, Megan, come on," said Jenny nervously. "Stop bullying lovely Mummy."

Meg sighed and groaned. She looked around and realized that everyone had stopped talking and that they were all staring at her with varying degrees of discomfort. Beth looked at her in an accusatory way from the other table and her father stared at his shoes. Then Meg looked at her mother again, who was smiling nervously and rubbing at the pointy nibs of her elbows.

"It's only tea towels," said Rhys.

"Yes," said Lorelei brightly. "That's exactly right, Rhys, it's only tea towels. Now, who's for more carrots? Absolutely heaps left!"

Megan went up to her room and listened to the Top 40 on Radio One, letting the clean, sweet melody of Simple Minds rub away her frayed nerves.

APRIL 2011

It was not a kitchen. Not in any traditional or easily recognizable way. It was a structure, a form, an entity, like the guts of a living creature. It was dark, eerily dark, no sense of the bright spring day outside, just a white stripe of light strafing through a gap in the piles in front of the windows. Meg felt around the wall to her left for the light switch. The lights did not come on. She was unsurprised. She switched her mobile phone to its torch function and swept the beam around the room.

"Sweet Jesus Christ."

Molly stood behind her mother, a hand clamped over her mouth, her darkly kohled eyes wide with horror. She grabbed Meg's arm with her other hand and gripped it.

Megan sighed. *"Oh, Mum."*

Molly relaxed her grip on her mother's arm and let her hand drop from her mouth. "I remember eating breakfast in here," she said. "There was a big table. There. With benches. And the cereal was in jars, over there, with cork lids. And there was a view, through the window. Of a tree . . ."

They both turned to look at the place where the windows had been. But it was hard to place them, behind the wall of things. It was disorienting. The house no longer made any sense.

Molly turned back to her mother. "How are we going to get through to the rest of the house?"

Meg sighed and swung the torch beam to the area at the back of the room that should, in theory, have contained a door leading to the hallway and the rest of the house. All that the beam picked out was more walls. Walls within walls. There was no sign of the back of the room and no immediate sense of how to locate it. But then the light picked up a gap, a foot wide. She shone the light down onto the floor and saw flagstones. The flagstones of her childhood. The only familiar feature so far.

"I think," she said, shining the light back onto the tiny gap, "we'll have to go this way."

"You're kidding me," said Molly.

"I'm afraid not."

"I'll have a panic attack if I have to go through there."

"Yes. Me too. Although, Christ, I'm not even sure I could squeeze through. I mean, look, it's so narrow."

"Well, I'm not going there on my own. No way."

Meg set her shoulders. She'd lost three stone six years ago—she was no longer a size sixteen—but still, she was a solid woman, not a waif like her mother and her teenage daughter. "Fine," she said, sucking in her stomach, "fine. I'll lead the way."

"Oh, Jesus," whimpered Molly, holding on to the back of Meg's T-shirt. "Mum, I'm scared."

"Don't be daft," said Meg, holding back her own primeval monsters. "There's nothing to be scared of. It's just Grandma's house. That's all."

"But we're the first people to set foot in here for years. I mean, shit, Mum, there could be anything in here. Rats! Mum, what about rats?!"

"It's going to be fine, love. There won't be any rats. Grandma didn't really eat at home, so there was nothing for them to dine on. Come on. Just hold on to me and breathe in."

The walls compressed Meg firmly from both sides. They felt solid and uniform against her body, but the light from her phone picked out details: a shirt cuff, a shred of netting, the corner of a book, the knot in the top of a black bag. All smoothed to a formless corridor by the passage of Lorelei's body over the countless days she'd lived here alone, refusing to accept visitors or help.

"You okay, love?" she whispered into the muffled darkness.

"Yes. I think so. Are we nearly there yet?"

Meg could feel her heart contracting and throbbing with a deep-seated sense of unease. "Pretty much," she replied cheerfully.

"What's at the other end?"

"Not sure yet. Hoping for a door."

The corridor turned through a forty-five-degree angle a moment later. She aimed the light ahead and saw an opening. "We're there," she said. "We've made it."

She expected a cool rush of light and freedom as she pulled her body from the claustrophobic crush of her mother's corridor; she expected to be able to shake out her bones and feel released. But she saw immediately that this corridor led directly into another one. The doorway from the back of the kitchen into the front hall was merely a pit stop. She suddenly saw the rest of this journey unfurl in her mind's eye. She saw herself squeezing through smaller and smaller apertures, into deeper and deeper corners of the house until she was squashed into a ball and unable to turn around. She swallowed back an urge to scream and said, "Right, well, at least it's not quite so dark in here." The window on the landing was only partially blocked, allowing a wash of dusty-blue light across the tops of the towers. At least here Meg could gain height and perspective. Ahead of her was the door into the snug, to the left the door into the living room and to the right the foot of the staircase. She only knew this from memory, because no such things were visible from where she stood. She'd been told that Lorelei had lived mainly in her bedroom, so she decided that they should aim to get there, that it was probably less cluttered (*Ha! Cluttered! What an entirely insufficient word that is*) than the rest of the house and that they were both less likely to die getting into it.

"Right," she said, encouraging her daughter. "Next one! Are you ready?"

Molly nodded uncertainly and grabbed the back of Meg's T-shirt again.

They slithered sideways through the tunnel, which, almost like a well-planned road system, had a junction halfway down where they turned right. Meg felt for the first runner with her toes and then gingerly walked up, subconsciously numbering them as she'd done countless times as a child. Eleven to the landing. Then a dogleg and another eight to the first floor.

As she emerged at the top of the stairs she turned to Molly and smiled. "It's quite bright up here," she said. "Look, the top of the landing window. You can see out into the garden." Molly stood at her side and they drank in the view from the window as if it were water in a desert. Dust motes sparkled in the midday sun like clouds of glitter. Furry cobwebs hung from the wooden beams in the ceiling and from the old paper light shades. It smelled mustier up here, meatier. Downstairs had carried a smell of dead paper and dust; here it smelled of old flesh and unwashed things.

Molly put her hand to her mouth again and shuddered. "Gross," she said. "It's just as well you can't actually smell these places on TV. No one would watch those shows other-wise. Seriously."

"It's not as bad as I thought it would be. Given how long she lived like this."

"It's disgusting."

Meg shrugged. She couldn't argue. "This is like hell."

"It's worse than hell."

"It's hell on actual earth."

There were no words. No language sufficient to convey this experience. For years Meg had lain in bed awake at night, imagining this, picturing it, hearing about it secondhand from social workers and the council: *"This could be the most extreme case of hoarding we have ever encountered. Her life is at risk, every moment of every day"*; listening to her mother on the phone playing it down: *"Oh, it's all such a fuss. Such a fuss about a few things. I'm all alone now. I can live how I choose."*

Meg would try to argue: *"You'll kill yourself. It'll bury you. They'll have to pull the house down to get your body out."*

And Lorelei would laugh lightly and say, *"That's fine with me."*

But none of her imaginings had brought her to this place, to the meaty stench and the Gothic horror of it.

A low corridor of objects brought them into Lorelei's bedroom. Meg remembered vividly the last time she'd been in her mother's bedroom. Six years ago. The last time she'd come for Easter. She'd arrived with Molly and the boys and found the house already halfway to the state it was in today. Her mother had been sitting in the middle of this room, hillocks of junk piled up around her, like a spider in the middle of its web, painting her toenails periwinkle and smiling at Meg as though all in the world was as it should be.

The memory brought a sudden lump to her throat.

She remembered how cross she'd felt to see her mother like that, buried up to her elegant neck in her own shit, letting her beautiful home fall into decay, cooking up yet more fodder for the neighbors to get into a sweaty lather about. She'd been so cross that she'd almost hated her.

But now, as she edged her way into the room, she saw the

armchair where her mother had been, a fat, flowery thing padded out with cheap cushions, tables at either side, holding bottles of nail polish, paperbacks, rice cakes, the oversized headphones she'd wear to listen to the radio, and instead of filth and junk, all she was aware of was the empty space at the center of it all.

Molly crunched uncertainly across a rocky pathway of scattered ephemera—empty packaging, discarded clothing, old newspapers—and joined her mother at the center of the room. "I remember her sitting there, when we came that time," she said breathlessly. "Right there. I was scared of her."

Meg turned to her daughter and said, "Scared? Really?"

"Yes," said Molly. "She just looked so bizarre, sitting there, so thin and scrawny, her eyes were kind of like, *wild*. She wasn't like anyone I'd ever seen before."

"Poor Mum." Meg sighed again. "Don't you remember the hot chocolate, though?"

Molly glanced at her blankly.

"She made you all hot chocolate. At bedtime. You were all so excited. Don't you remember?"

Molly shrugged. "No recollection at all," she said. "I just remember that." She pointed at the chair. "Her. There."

Meg felt overwhelmed with sadness.

"I still don't understand," said Molly. "I mean, you're like, just so normal. You're like the most normal person I've ever met. And you're such a clean freak and everything. How did *you* come from *this*?"

Meg shook her head. "Well, obviously it wasn't always like this. Once upon a time, Moll, this place was actually relatively normal."

"But your mum? Grandma? Was she ever normal?"

Meg smiled sadly. "Well," she said, "that's a good question.

And I think, with Mum, it really was all just a matter of degrees."

She took two more steps towards the armchair and touched it, with the very furthest tips of her fingers. And then, before her inner clean freak could tell her that she'd *catch fleas*, that she'd *never get the smell out*, that it was *filthy dirty* and *full of germs*, she lowered herself right into it, right into her mother's armchair. She let her head fall back against the graying upholstery and she looked up at Molly and she smiled. "Tiny, tiny little degrees."

2

Friday 5th November 2010

Hello again, Jim!

I am delighted to see that I didn't scare you off, and thank you
for your reply. It was fascinating to find out more about you,
and of course, I can see now that you would have started out
as a James. You look more like a James than a Jim, but I agree
that Jim is a much "friendlier" name—particularly up there
in Gateshead. You wouldn't want to stand out too much, I
suppose! Do you have a lovely accent? I don't have much of an
accent. I suppose you would say that I am "posh"! I was brought
up just outside Oxford, went to the local girls' grammar, Mum
and Dad were both writers, my father wrote about medicine,
my mother wrote about gardening. It was all very ramshackle
and left-wing middle class, nobody ever looked in a mirror,
nobody ever hoovered. But at the heart of it was a deep, deep
sadness. Probably about the baby, Athena. And other things
that happened. Things I can't really talk about. So even though
it should have been a happy childhood, it really wasn't. And
then they both died young, my parents, pretty much one after
the other. I was twenty when my father passed, twenty-three
when my mother did, and there was all this stuff, stuff we'd
never talked about. Stuff I really do rather wish we had talked

about. But you know what it's like when you're that age, you think you have all the time in the world, don't you? I would say I was rather a strange child, a bit like you say you were. I was very introverted and lived quite a colorful imaginary life. I collected things, obsessively, and wet the bed well into my early teens. I was almost feral in some ways. Quite wild yet also excruciatingly shy. I was forever being carted off to therapists but none of them had a clue. And then I left home at eighteen, went off to university, and I completely changed, blossomed into something quite different. It was as if my childhood had never happened, like I'd shed a skin. So there you go, that's me. Well, the early stages of me. And I suppose, in a way, it was having such an odd and uncomfortable childhood myself that made me so utterly, utterly determined to give my own children the best childhood possible.

It remains to be seen whether or not they would say that I succeeded.

So, tell me more about your son. Do you live with him? How old is he? What's his name? I'm glad you have a child. It will give us more to talk about.

Oh, BANGBANGBANG! The fireworks are starting already here in the village. I hope you're watching a lovely display somewhere, wrapped up warm and cozy. I'll be making do with listening to it, from here in my chair. I can't really find the motivation to get out there and stand about in the cold with a bunch of strangers!

All the very best to you, Jim, take care,
Lorelei

APRIL 1987

Bethan had grown breasts. Huge ones. Quite suddenly and as if from nowhere. One minute she'd been a bony little thing in a training bra from Woollies, the next she was off to the shops with Mum, looking for something in a 32C. Megan was both alarmed (her baby sister!) and jealous (her baby sister!) but mainly fascinated as Bethan now possessed the only substantial pair of breasts in the family.

"Let me see them," she badgered as Lorelei and Beth bustled into the house on a dry April afternoon halfway through the Easter holidays.

Beth looked embarrassed as Meg snatched the bag from her. "Ooh," she said, fingering the cream lace thing with its solid underwiring and its unlikely capacious cups. "Nice," she said, trying not to sound jealous. "Did you get anything else?"

"No," said Beth, snatching back the bra and shoving it into the carrier bag before one of her little brothers saw it.

"I did, though!" said Lorelei, her high cheekbones flushed pink, her green eyes flashing with something chemical and profound. "Look! There's a new shop open in town. What was it called, Beth?"

Beth rolled her eyes and said, "Poundstretcher."

"Yes! Poundstretcher! Everything's a pound. Can you imagine? Look!"

She emptied a bulging carrier bag onto the tabletop and let her eyes roam over her booty with a hunger and a joy that were almost tangible.

"Look!" she said. "Hangers. Ten for a pound. Aren't they lovely? I just loved the colors, especially this blue one. And pan scourers, a pound for twenty . . ."

Meg too stared at the items on the tabletop and said, "Why have you bought three packs?"

Her mother's smile froze for a split second. Then she laughed and said, "Always good to have stockpiles."

"Oh, yes," said Meg, "just think how smug we'll be when we're living in a postapocalyptic wilderness and we're the only family in the village with *pan scourers*."

Meg saw Beth's face cloud over then and noticed a tiny, barely perceptible shake of her head. She tutted loudly and said, "Sixty pan scourers, Beth. We have sixty pan scourers."

Beth smiled apologetically and Lorelei stood there, her shoulders slightly slumped, the light gone from her eyes. "Why do you always have to spoil everything, Meggy? Why?" Her eyes filled with tears and she hurriedly returned her treasures to the carrier before leaving the room.

"What?" snapped Meg, looking at Beth's accusing face.

"Oh, come on, why d'you have to be so hard on her?"

"Don't you see," Meg hissed, "it's because of you lot, everyone in this fucking family, that she is the way she is. You encourage her!"

"But what does it matter?" said Beth. "Who cares if we've got too many pan scourers? Who cares if funny things make her happy? Why does it bother you so much?"

"Because," she began, the rage starting to separate in her mind into manageable chunks of theory, "because I think she's ill."

Beth laughed. And then stopped dramatically. "Ill?"

"Yes," said Meg. "Mentally. Ill in the head."

"Oh, don't be so ridiculous."

"I'm not being ridiculous. I mean it. All this—all these collections and obsessions with colors and tea towels and . . . and *rainbows*."

Beth shrugged.

"And think of what she was like when she was a child. You know, collecting *hair*. Everyone acts like that's normal. It's not normal. It's crazy."

"What are you two whispering about?" asked Rory, passing them in the hallway, his long blond hair hanging into his eyes, long skinny legs like his dad's in baggy jeans, the best-looking boy in his class, *apparently*. Not that he was interested in what the girls in his class thought of him yet. He was only twelve.

"Nothing," snapped Meg.

"You're talking about the pan scourers, aren't you?"

Meg said nothing. Beth said, "Don't you start."

"I'm not starting anything," he said nonchalantly. "I think it's great. You can never have too many pan scourers."

"Where's Rhys?" asked Beth, delicately changing the subject.

"Outside," said Rory. "Staring."

The three children laughed at the predictability of this reply. Megan looked from Beth to Rory, her siblings, and, for their many differences, her soul mates. And then she thought of Rhys; tiny, unknowable, inexplicable Rhys, lying in the garden, staring into empty blueness, all alone. She thought, for a moment, of going out to find him, to ask him what he was thinking about. But then the phone rang in the hall, and it was Andrew Smart wanting to take her to a gig on Saturday night, and no sooner had it arrived than the thought faded from her consciousness.

Easter Sunday dawned warm and gold. Meg's eyes struggled to open against the dazzling morning sun. Her radio alarm told her it was only 8:29. She stopped struggling to open her eyes and let them fall closed again. As she waited for sleep to return, her thoughts reeled through the pleasing events of the previous night: the screech of tires on tarmac as Andrew Smart and his friend Nick pulled up outside the house to collect her, the metallic smell of vodka in a hip flask being passed back and forth between the three of them, the sun setting behind the tall trees as the countryside flashed past in a copper-hued blur, Andrew Smart's fingers absentmindedly tickling the small of her neck, the wonderful grown-up easy sense of it being no big deal, the feeling of escape from the house and the village, the buzzing queue wrapped tantalizingly around the venue, the smell of congealed beer, the feel of strangers' clammy T-shirts against her bare skin, Andrew's arm across her shoulder, the music, the roll and swell of the mosh pit and then the cool air on her flesh as they drove home again, too fast, down winding roads, spiky shadows of trees thrown across the road by the headlights, and then a quick kiss, on the lips, outside her house. Nothing more—it hadn't been a date, not in that sense. Nick had watched fondly from the backseat and said, "Aah, sweet." Andrew had thrown a rolled-up paper bag at him and Meg had slipped from the car and into the dark of the sleeping house, light as air, smelling of other people's cigarette smoke, smiling.

She'd jumped when she'd seen him sitting there.

"Rhys! Shit, you scared the crap out of me. What are you doing up so late?"

He was sitting at the kitchen table, his blond hair lank around his face. His hands were spread open on the tabletop, bathed in bluish light from the moon through the window. He shrugged. "Couldn't sleep," he said.

Meg frowned. "Couldn't you, you know, like, read a book or something?" she asked.

He shrugged and pulled his open hands into fists.

"Come on," she said. "I'm too wired to sleep, come and watch some telly with me." The living room was dark, apart from the embers in the fire basket. The remnants of her parents' evening were still strewn about the room: two empty wineglasses, a jar of olives, the *Mail*, slippers and a cookbook held open at a recipe for chicken Marsala. The sofa still bore the imprints of both parents and the dog. No cushions had been plumped, no debris removed, as though they had faded away rather than actively gone to bed.

It was the end of some film, an old-fashioned American thing with women with flicked hair and men in nonsensical flared trousers, and a plinky-plonky soundtrack. Megan brought through a carton of orange juice and two beakers.

"Meggy!" She heard her father's reedy voice emanate from somewhere above. "Is that you?"

"Yes."

"Just checking. Sleep tight, darling."

"You too, Dad."

Meg and Rhys looked at each other and smiled. "How long had you been sitting there?" said Meg.

Rhys shrugged again. "Dunno."

"Do you do that often?"

"Not really."

"What were you thinking about?"

"Not much."

An American lady on the TV was shouting at an American man who was wearing aviator glasses and a gold necklace. They were standing underneath a palm tree.

Usually Meg would have given up at this point. But her mind was soft with vodka and music and the first tentative outposts of falling in love, so she moved closer to her brother and stared at him thoughtfully and said, "Are you happy, Rhys?"

He looked at her sideways. "Of course I am."

"Is school all right?"

"Yeah, it's fine."

She paused, then continued. "It's just, you know, Rory seems to have made so many friends already, but you—"

"There's more to life than friends," he snapped back.

Megan nodded. "Of course," she said, "but is there anyone at school, anyone who you hang out with, you know, at lunchtime and stuff?"

"Sure," he said. "Loads of people."

"Are people kind to you?"

Rhys spun round and fixed her with a black look. "Let's just watch the film, shall we?" he said.

"I don't want to watch the film. I want to talk to you. I never talk to you."

"Talking's overrated."

"How can you say that?"

He turned away from her then and rearranged himself on the sofa.

Megan stared at him for a moment, at the delicate set of his features, his sinewy arms hanging from a baggy gray T-shirt, his sharp kneecaps pushing through the denim of his unfashionable jeans. He seemed so angry, so sad.

She sighed and when the film finished five minutes later, she ran her hand gently over the crown of Rhys's head and made her way upstairs to bed without saying good night.

⌒

When Megan finally arose, two hours after first waking up, she found her mother in the kitchen in rose-print pajamas, her long hair twisted into a bun.

"Oh, good"—she beamed—"you're up! Bob and Jenny are

sending their little ones over in half an hour for an egg hunt. I need your help."

"The gig was fantastic, thanks for asking," Meg replied. "Andrew Smart kissed me on the lips and we've arranged to go out again on Thursday."

Her mother blinked at her in surprise. "Oh," she said vaguely, "good! That's good then?"

"Of course it's good. Not that I expect you to care when there's *vitally* important things like *egg hunts* to arrange."

"Oh, Meggy." Her mother folded her arms together and pouted. "No one's saying it's *vitally* important, it's just, this is us! The Birds. This is what we do. Easter Sunday. Rain or shine. It's a tradition."

"Yes, but, Mum, your youngest children are now twelve years old. It's a tradition that needs to *end*."

"Nonsense."

"I mean, Bob and Jenny have got their own garden. Why can't they do their *own* egg hunt? For their *own* children?"

Her mother's eyes started to brim with tears. "Because," she said, "we've better nooks and crannies in our garden. They're all laid to lawn next door . . . you know, very flat . . ."

Megan nodded sagely. "Oh, yes," she said. "Very flat. Poor wee things."

"So—" Her mother ignored the sarcasm and brightened herself. "I need to go up and dress myself. Can I leave you to open the packets?"

Megan sighed. "Yes. Sure."

"Good." Lorelei beamed. "Thank you, darling girl."

Bob and Jenny and their three children arrived at just after eleven a.m. Rory and Rhys agreed to join in with the little ones and by eleven thirty all the eggs had been found. Lorelei's eyes shone with a mixture of satisfaction and, Megan couldn't help but notice, a hint of panic as the children handed the eggs to their mother to save for "after lunch."

"Don't forget to save the foils," she trilled. "All such lovely, lovely colors!"

Megan tutted and said something mean about her mother under her breath, which thankfully she didn't hear.

"Such a shame you can't stay for lunch," said Lorelei as their neighbors made their farewells half an hour later.

"Yes, well, Bob's mother's over from Ireland so it's a big clan reunion."

Pandora was in the Bahamas with Laurence, and Lorna was in Devon with friends. For the first time in living memory the Bird family were alone on Easter Sunday.

"So," said Colin, closing his cutlery together and scrunching up his paper napkin after lunch, "I've had an idea. Slightly crazy. But listen . . . how about next Easter, since it might well be the last Easter everyone's still at home, we go away somewhere? We haven't been away as a family since before the twins were born. There's some amazingly cheap package deals around these days. And I've always wanted to go to Greece."

Megan could feel Lorelei's expression change without even looking at her. It was like an ice floe passing through the room, steady and foreboding.

She laughed first, as Megan had suspected she might, a menacingly girlish sound. And then she said, "What a silly idea, Colin. How on earth could we afford to go away, with four children?"

"Well," said Colin, beginning, rather nervously, to stack together dirty plates, "I was thinking, with the girls growing up now, we don't really need the big car anymore. I mean, when was the last time all six of us went anywhere together? So we could sell it—"

"Oh, come on," snorted Lorelei. "Who on earth would buy our dirty, disgusting old car?"

"We could sell it to the Millers," he continued patiently. "They're expecting their fourth child any day. They've offered fifteen hundred for it."

"Ha!" said Lorelei. "More money than sense, those Millers."

"And then, if we've only got the one car, we won't need the double garage anymore. And I was just talking to Bob and he said he'd buy the other half of our garage off us for five grand . . ."

Megan had not drawn breath for almost thirty seconds, watching this almost comically doomed conversation unfold.

"Five grand! Ha! Ridiculous."

"Well, yes, but he wants to build an extension at the back and use the garage as a workshop, so it's worth it for them."

"But all our *things*. I mean, we have so much stuff stored in there."

"Well, yes, indeed we do. Like several burst paddling pools, my sweetheart. It's overdue a clear-out."

In the absence of anything logical to say, Lorelei merely flapped her bony hands about and said, "Oh, it's all just silly. And a package deal to Greece sounds quite ghastly."

Colin smiled gently and turned his gaze to his four children. "Kids? What do you think? Easter in the sun? Calamari and chips for lunch? Swimming pools with slides? On-site *disco*?" He aimed this last at Megan and Bethan.

Lorelei laughed again, that high-pitched schoolgirl thing she did. "Ha! Sounds like *someone's* been doing their homework."

"Just some brochures," said Colin, "from the agents on the high road. Want to have a look?" He smiled and glanced at each child in turn.

"Oh, Colin, honestly," said Lorelei, piling up the plates from her side of the table. "This really is about the silliest plan I've ever heard. And even if we can afford it—and who's to say that the Millers and Bob won't change their minds, leaving us with a stonking great unpaid debt to some tacky holiday company—if it's going to be our last Easter altogether, then it has to be here! At the Bird House. Isn't that right, kiddos?"

A terrible silence fell upon the table. Rory cast his gaze down to his lap. Bethan nibbled her fingernails and Rhys stared at the ceiling. Megan looked intently through the kitchen window at a magpie bouncing on the branches of a tree outside, and tried not to read too much symbolism into its presence at this precise moment.

"*I'd* like to go away," said Megan, taking the lead as the firstborn child. "I mean, I know I'll always be able to come back here as the years go by, but once I leave home, who knows if we'll ever get the chance to go on holiday together again?" She shrugged and left her words hanging.

There was a small shard of silence, during which Colin nodded encouragingly and Lorelei raised her eyebrows exasperatedly.

"What about you?" he asked Beth.

She smiled apologetically and said, "I want to do whatever everyone else wants to do."

"Rory?"

"Cool," said Rory. "Yeah. Brilliant." Then he looked slightly embarrassed by his betrayal and turned away.

"Rhys?"

Rhys blushed and shrugged. "Don't mind," he said almost silently.

"Well, there you go," said Lorelei triumphantly, holding

the pile of plates out in front of herself. "Looks like nobody's particularly interested. And I'm sure we can think of better things to spend all that money on. I mean, Meggy will be off to college next September. That'll be an expensive enterprise."

Colin frowned and said, "You know my mother's offered to help us out with all that, so that's not an issue, darling."

"Well," she said, landing the pile of plates into the butler's sink with a deafening clatter, "I still don't see the point of spending all that money on a holiday that nobody's really interested in."

Meg stared at the shape of her mother, rigid and too thin, at the kitchen sink, her shoulder blades protruding through the chambray cotton of her smocked tunic, and she swallowed the urge to walk over to her and hit her with her cutlery, hard, around the back of the head. Instead she inhaled and said, "Erm, I think I recall saying that *I* wanted to go, Mother?"

"And me," said Rory.

Lorelei's shoulders slumped and she sighed. And then, very slowly and deliberately, she left the kitchen, sobbing quietly under her breath.

~

On July 25 that same year, while Lorelei was out at the shops, and Megan was violently kissing Andrew Smart on a blanket in a field in the middle of nowhere, and the twins and Bethan were alone in the house, two sixteen-year-old boys wearing hooded jackets broke in and took, after a leisurely exploration, the video player, two television sets, a watch, some jewelry, and a leg of lamb and a joint of beef from the chest freezer in the utility room. They did all of this without disturbing any of the three children in the house, and it was only when they let the kitchen door bang shut behind them that Rhys peered over his window ledge just in time to see them running down the garden path and onto the street. He rushed then to a window overlooking the street and saw them pile into a matte black Ford Escort and screech away through the village, whooping and hollering through the opened windows as though they thought they were in Harlem.

Rhys found the whole episode thrilling beyond words. He called 999 before he even told the others, for fear that someone else would want to do it. And for a few days afterwards he dined out on the whole episode, to the point of being boring. But Lorelei couldn't see the harmless drama of the thing. She could only see it as, in her own melodramatic words, *"a violation akin to rape."* She kept stalking desolately round the house, peering into corners and touching things. And at the merest sound of footsteps on the pavement outside the window, or the whine of a car driving too fast, or the rumble of a car driving too slow, or the crack of a twig under the paws of a squirrel, or the rustle of leaves in a soft breeze, Lorelei would gasp and run to the nearest window, her arms wrapped defensively around herself.

"They were only kids," Megan would say, "just a pair of spotty dweebs."

But Lorelei would not be assuaged.

"Well, *you* can all go to Greece next year," she said self-righteously, "but I'm going to stay here to protect our home."

So of course, nobody went to Greece.

APRIL 2011

Meg's phone rang. She picked it up from the arm of Lorelei's chair, expecting it to be Bill telling her that he and the boys had checked in, that everything was going to plan. But it was an unknown number. She stared at it for a moment.

"Who is it?" asked Molly, anxiously nibbling a fingernail.

"Don't put your fingers in your mouth," hissed Meg. "Seriously, you have no idea what you've been touching."

Molly let her finger drop from her mouth and wiped it absentmindedly against the denim of her hot pants.

"Who is it?" she asked again.

Meg pressed Decline. "Unknown," she said. "I'm not sure I can face talking to a normal human being right now. Maybe they'll leave a voice mail."

"You look weird sitting there," said Molly.

"I *feel* weird sitting here."

"Can I have a go?"

"Sure." Meg stood up and eased herself into a corner to let Molly sit down.

Molly leaned her head gingerly against the back of the armchair and rested her delicate hands upon the arms. She looked up at her mum. "So this was, like, where she spent all her time? Just here. In this chair?"

"Pretty much. According to the social worker, she went into the village a couple of times a week, had something to eat, chatted to the neighbors, went to the charity shop, bought a paper or two. Sometimes she went for a swim at the pool in town, mainly so she could have a shower, I suppose. And every weekend she'd get in the car and go to the cash-and-carry to *pick up some bits*." She groaned under her breath. *Pick up some bits*. Infuriating, ridiculous woman. "And then she'd get home, push her way through meters of pitch-black corridors and emerge up here, like a rat out of a drain cover."

"Oh, don't talk about rats."

"And God knows what she did then." Meg looked about

her for any evidence of activities. She saw her mother's laptop; it was tiny, state-of-the-art, must have cost a fortune. She had no idea where it had come from. She knew that her mother, despite her twin loves of the Internet and shopping, had never developed an Internet shopping habit, mainly because it would have taken her too long to get to the front door to collect any packages. So she must have bought this in a shop. She could not picture her mother in a shop, buying a laptop. But still, there it sat, covered in a thin layer of dust, untouched for the four days since Lorelei's death. There'd been talk of an online lover. A man in Gateshead called Jim whom she'd never actually met, but with whom, she'd declared dramatically, she was *crazy in love*. It sounded, from what Meg had managed to glean from between her mother's very skewed conversational lines, as though Jim might have issues of his own. She wondered if Jim knew about Lorelei's death. And then she realized that of course he didn't. He probably thought he'd been dumped. Dumped by Lorelei from the Cotswolds. Without so much as a by-your-leave.

Poor Jim.

Her phone rang again. Still Unknown. This time she pressed Answer.

"Hello?"

"Meg?"

Meg's flesh wriggled slightly at the familiar tone of the caller's voice. "Yes, speaking."

"It's me. Beth."

Meg breathed once down the line, and then twice.

"Hello?"

Meg hung up.

MARCH 1991

Megan and Beth sat side by side in a subterranean concrete room off Shaftesbury Avenue. The room was a bar called Freuds; someone had told Megan that it was *the* place to be and it was certainly unlike anywhere she'd been before. *Industrial* was the word. Unfinished walls, beaten copper bar, Cubist seating, chalked lists on blackboards, everything very dark and very uncomfortable.

It was hard to concentrate on her sister sitting hunched up beside her, sipping a 7Up through a black straw, because there was a constant overwhelming sense that something terribly exciting was about to happen over her shoulder. It wasn't, of course. Everyone else here was just like her: twentysomething, office worker, new in town, earning peanuts, looking for love, expecting everything to be a lot more exciting than it actually was.

Megan felt proud to sit here with Beth. Her little sister was a full two inches taller than her and, she imagined, a full double take more beautiful. Not that Megan was plain. Megan was far from plain. But Bethan was the one with the long mane of sleek black hair and the kissable mouth and the blushing cheeks and the legs that spoke their own language. And the boobs. Bethan was the one with the boobs. Someone once said to Megan that sisters always feel more beautiful when they're together and, ever since, Megan had found it to be true. Without Beth, Meg felt reasonable; with her she felt exceptional.

Beth was dressed in black. Black jeans. Black angora cardigan with the sleeves pushed up her arms. Black lace tank top. Black ribbon in her black hair.

"Remember your polka-dot raincoat?" said Megan, returning to the place they always came back to eventually, their shared childhood.

"The pink one? How could I forget! It was literally the most important thing in the world to me. She's still got it, you know."

Meg groaned and said, "Of course she has. I think that could probably apply to any random item of clothing you care to mention."

"So," said her sister, her expression growing serious, "are you coming?"

Meg groaned. Easter weekend. She'd told her mother she'd let her know, that she wasn't sure what her plans were yet, and her mother had tried to sound as though she didn't mind either way—even though it would be the first Easter Megan hadn't spent at home and therefore something that Lorelei would find traumatic even to contemplate. "I don't know," she said. "It's such a long way."

"I know," said Beth, "but please come. It'll be shit if you're not there."

"No, it won't," scoffed Meg. "It'll just be exactly the same as it is every single year except with one less person around the table."

"Yes, exactly. And you're the only normal person in the family."

"Dad?"

"Well, yeah, just about, although I think that twenty-five years living with Mum are finally starting to grind him down. He doesn't seem quite himself lately."

"What do you mean?"

"I don't know. He just seems distracted. And thin. He looks very thin."

Megan considered her father, all six foot one of him, his floppy hair, his pixie face, his almost absurd patience with his highly strung, immature wife. He could not afford to be distracted or thin. He needed to be solid and sensible and fully engaged or the whole structure of things would just come apart.

"How are the twins?"

"Hmm."

"Hmm?"

"Oh, they're fine. But Rory's got some rather dodgy new friends."

"Hasn't he *always* had dodgy friends?"

"Well, yes, but these are slightly dodgier than the last lot."

"Drugs?"

Beth shrugged. "Probably."

"Oh, God." Megan dragged her hands through her brown curls. "And what about Rhys?"

"Rhys is Rhys. No dodgy friends. No friends at all from what I can see. He just sits in his room listening to grunge music, very loud, until really late."

"That boy does not get enough sleep."

"No, I know, and it's affecting his schoolwork. You know, Rory can just flip through his revision in half an hour and he's done, but Rhys needs to really concentrate and because he doesn't really sleep, well, Dad thinks he's going to fail all his GCSEs. And he's just a bit, you know, weird."

"What, weirder than usual, you mean?"

"Yeah, a little bit. He got hauled in front of the head teacher at school the other day for hanging around the girls' changing room."

"No!"

"Yes. It was horrible. We only found out about it because

Dad knows the geography teacher and it was all round the school. And they couldn't prove he'd done it so he wasn't punished, but now apparently all the girls hate him and call him a creep and a pervert." She shuddered lightly. "It's horrible," she said, almost silently.

"Christ," said Meg. "What does Mum say?"

"Oh, well, you know, she's taken his side obviously, closed ranks completely, her precious baby, etc., etc. And as she says, there is no proof, just one girl's word against his. But to be absolutely honest"—she paused and lowered her voice—"it really wouldn't surprise me if it was true. He's the oddest boy I know."

"Come down and live with me," said Megan, suddenly fearful for her softhearted younger sister, who had barely spent a night away from home since the day she was born, and who tiptoed around the characters in her house as if they were the leading men and woman and she was just a lowly extra. "Come and live in London. Seriously. There's space for another bed in my room, we could split the bills and everything. I could ask around for you for a job at my place—they've always got vacancies."

Beth smiled. "Yeah," she said, "right."

"What?"

"Can you imagine me telling Mum that?"

"Why not?"

"Because—" Her sister looked flustered for a second. "I don't know," she said. She smiled. "Maybe I could."

"Of course you could! You finish college in June. You'll be a qualified secretary. London will be your oyster."

Beth's face went from uncertain to quietly excited. "Yes," she said. "I mean, it would be fun, wouldn't it?"

Megan nodded. "Ten different types of fun."

"And Mum would still have the twins . . ."

"Stop worrying about Mum!"

"I know, I know. You're right. I just can't help it sometimes."

"You need this," said Meg. "You need to get away from her. From all of it. It'll swallow you whole otherwise. I mean it. It really will. And you won't even realize it's happening until it's too late."

⟡

Two days later Beth returned home from London. The Bird House sat quiet and dusty, filled with sunlight and distant sounds. She rested her weekend case at the foot of the stairs and called out once or twice. No one replied and she presumed herself alone. She felt coated with the grime of the big city. Although she'd had a shower in Megan's immaculate little en suite shower room just that morning, she couldn't shake the feeling of it all over her skin. She made herself a mug of tea and took it up to her room. She stood for a while in the middle, imagining herself not in it anymore, imagining herself instead in her sister's room in Wood Green with its high ceilings and its views over a parade of shops, its shared kitchen and flatmates from foreign countries.

It didn't seem possible, although in every practical way of course, it was. She went to her window and took in the view across the rambling gardens, down to the old green hammock at the far end and the fields beyond. Memories fluttered about her mind, of days that had passed and died and were never to return. But when she turned her thoughts to the future there was nothing there, just space. She sighed and sat on the window ledge, pondering her lack of ambition, of forward propulsion. She'd only signed up for the secretarial course because the college was ten minutes away and she knew she

49

wouldn't muck it up. She assumed that at some point soon she would probably end up being a secretary. But through fatalism rather than design.

She began to take off her clothes, feeling the sweet release of her breasts from the ill-fitting bra she'd been wearing since Friday morning. She looked at her body in the foxed mirror inside her wardrobe. She saw the loveliness of it and blanched slightly, thinking of the things she hadn't told Meg in the bar that night. The looks from her brother. The sense of someone outside the bathroom door.

She'd watched Rory become interested in women, but with him it had been like the unfurling of a bud: something natural, inevitable, almost adorable, something separate, entirely unconnected to her. But with Rhys it was like a dark shadow spilling over everything he touched. Including her.

She wrapped her body in a towel, tucked her hair inside a shower cap and made towards the bathroom. A strange sound made her stop outside the door of her parents' bedroom.

"Mum?"

She clutched her towel closer to her chest and gently pushed at the door. Rhys was lying in his parents' bed, the satin eiderdown pulled up to his armpits, naked as far as Beth could tell, staring straight at her.

"Jesus," he said, surprised to see her, "when did you get home?"

She held the door half against herself, shielding her body from his strange, angry gaze.

"About ten minutes ago," she said. "What are you doing, Rhys?"

He shrugged. "Sleeping."

"But why are you sleeping in Mum and Dad's bed?"

"Electric blanket."

She nodded, once, but then grimaced at him. "It's sixteen degrees out there. What do you need an electric blanket for?"

He shrugged. "I like it."

She nodded again. "Why are you naked?"

"I'm not," he said, flipping back the eiderdown to reveal his pale body, in underpants that were too large for him.

She turned away and grimaced. "Fine," she said. "I'm going to have a shower."

"How was London?" he asked before she could go.

"It was good."

He nodded. She moved her gaze away from his body again and said, "Anyway."

"How was Meg?"

"Fine," she said, "she's fine." She wanted to go now. She did not want to have a conversation with her brother lying there in his parents' bed in his underpants. She locked the bathroom door behind her and leaned against it for a moment, listening to his footsteps passing down the corridor towards the bathroom. They slowed down outside the door and she heard his breath. And then she heard him turn and leave, and the gentle click of his bedroom door closing behind him.

∾

Meg did come home for Easter. She slept on a mattress on Beth's floor because her own bedroom, since her last visit, had been rendered virtually uninhabitable by yet more towers of paperbacks and boxes of household goods bought in bulk from a cash-and-carry that Lorelei had recently signed up to.

"It's not that bad," said Lorelei, peering around the door over Meg's shoulder. "Plenty of room for you."

"Not that bad?" repeated Meg. "Jesus. Mother. Why are

51

you stockpiling"—she brought her gaze down to the box nearest her feet—"insect repellent?"

Her mother rolled her eyes. "We live in the countryside,"
she said pointedly, as though Megan were no longer a member of this exclusive country-dwelling club. "We get a lot of
insects."

"I mean, this is a fire hazard, isn't it? Can you imagine that
lot going up? It would blow the roof off the house. Jesus!"

"It's economics, darling," her mother replied, all singsong
disingenuousness. "Saving the family *money*."

"Well, yes, but the family won't actually *need* any money if
we all burn to death in a massive fireball."

"I get through a lot of it!" her mother snapped. "And there
won't be any fire."

"Mum, this whole house is a fire hazard. It's fifty percent
paper."

Her mother tutted. "You know," she said, "it's quite interesting to me that I am perfectly happy living in this house until
you come home and start criticizing everything."

"That's because I'm objective, Mother. I see things that you
lot don't. I see what you're doing here."

"And what exactly am I doing here, Megan, apart from
looking after everybody and doing the best job I possibly can
to look after our lovely house?"

Megan didn't bother to reply. It would have been too cruel.

⌒

Bob and Jenny had moved out the previous summer, and
the house next door was now inhabited by a young couple
with a baby who'd swapped a flat in Clapham for the picture-
postcard Cotswolds cottage. They were called Vicky and Tim
and their baby was called Madeleine, and of course Lorelei

had invited them over for Easter lunch. Megan could only imagine that the invitation had taken them unawares, leaving them no time to form a polite excuse. She could see it with her mind's eye, Vicky stuttering and clutching her throat and saying, "Er, oh, well, yes, that would be *lovely*," with a terrible fake smile and a gulp. The baby was only six months old but still Lorelei planted her foil-wrapped eggs and brought out the battered wicker baskets and they all followed Vicky and Tim and the baby round the garden, trilling and oohing every time somebody found one, the baby in her mother's arms looking entirely nonplussed.

The lamb was cooked and carved; the eggs were eaten; the foils were smoothed out, commented upon and put aside; the sun shone; there were too many carrots, not enough potatoes; the yellow walls ached under the weight of children's art; the conversation sagged under the strain of nobody really knowing what to say anymore; and Megan wished she'd stayed in London. At four o'clock Vicky and Tim took their sleeping baby back home to bed and then, rather surprisingly, Vicky reappeared five minutes later with a bottle of Beaujolais and she and Lorelei secreted themselves away in the snug, where they sat and drank and laughed and talked for a full three hours.

Meg and Beth raised their eyebrows at each other as the sound of raucous laughter drifted from the window into the garden, where they sat together in the last rays of the evening sun.

"Well," said Beth, "not *everybody* thinks Mum's as awful as you do, you know."

"I don't think she's awful. I just think she's ill."

Beth tutted. "She's eccentric, that's all."

"Hmm."

"Well, she is," laughed Beth. "Honestly. She's a sweet-heart—so much energy, so much character. She means well."

"She does *not* mean well. You know she hasn't asked me one single question about my job since I got back. Hasn't even noticed my haircut."

"Maybe she's cross with you for leaving home."

"Well, that's not normal, is it? What sort of mother gets cross with a twenty-year-old for leaving home?"

"Okay, maybe not leaving home as such, but living in London."

"What's London got to do with it? Half the teenagers in this village end up living in London. It's what *normal* people do. And what about Rhys?"

"What about Rhys?"

"Well, she just seems to have given up on him. She didn't even make him come down for lunch. It's like she doesn't care."

"She did try, I heard her. He just refused to come down."

"Well, if that was my child I would not be able to sit at that table with those virtual strangers going *'tralalala, egg hunt, egg hunt,'* like there was nothing wrong. I would have dragged him down. I mean, he hasn't even eaten anything. And it's"—she glanced at her watch—"it's nearly seven o'clock. It's nearly seven o'clock and she's sitting in there, getting pissed with some woman she barely knows, and her son has been on his own all day and she hasn't even been to check on him." She got crossly to her feet and headed indoors. "I'm going to make him a sandwich," she said.

She piled offcuts of cold lamb and mint sauce between two fat slices of bloomer and smothered it with Hellmann's, then found a bag of crisps and a can of Coke and grouped them all together on a tray. She felt furious to be mothering her little brother while his real mother sat drinking red wine, delighting in the attention of a new and unsuspecting admirer. As she made her way through the house she cringed at the cardboard boxes that lined each and every part of the staircase and hallway, the piles of unopened post, the paintings waiting to be hung and the unwashed laundry. Everything was half-way to being where it needed to be, everything was a work in progress, with no systems, no logic, no sense of organization about any of it. Everyone who came here—including Tim and Vicky—gushed and cooed about the charm of the place—*"It's so cozy! So welcoming!"*—but they did not see the truth, that this house was the work of a disordered mind and all the enablers she lived with.

Megan paused for a moment on the landing and watched the birds in the trees outside: a cluster of tits and sparrows, all jostling about for space. She put the tray down on the window ledge and sat. From below she could hear her mother and her new friend squawking and shrieking and from above she could hear Alice in Chains blasting from her brother's room in the eaves. But outside there were only the sounds of nature: the trilling of the tiny birds, the rumble of a distant tractor heading back after a day in the fields, a dog barking somewhere out of sight. She inhaled deeply, holding it in. She missed this when she was in London; not this mad, claustrophobic house and its piles of stuff, not her crazy mother or her passive father, her troubled brothers and her too-nice sister, but this—the peace and the purity of life outside these windows. She breathed it in again and held it inside her for a beat. And then she picked up the tray and carried it up the eight steps that took her to the door of her baby brother's bedroom. Eight small steps between *now* and *then*. Between what she knew and what she'd grow to wish she'd never known. Between the past and the future, between a small moment of peacefulness and the worst moment of her life. When her brother didn't open the door on the fourth knock, Megan felt a tightness in her gut, an overwhelming wave of foreboding. She put the tray down on the floor and kicked the door in. It gave way relatively easily under her amateur karate kick, just a badly screwed-in bolt (fixed by Rhys himself because Lorelei didn't believe in children having locks on their rooms) on the back of the door.

The music was so loud that Megan could feel it through her feet, through the ancient, buckled floorboards hammered in place three hundred years ago by craftsmen who would not know what to make of this cacophony, who would imagine it to be some business of the devil. And there he was. Her baby brother. The one she'd never felt fitted in. The one she resented and failed to bond with. The small one. The worrisome one. The one she couldn't talk to. There he was, hanging by his thin, pale neck from the beams high above his single bed, long dead by the look of him, his protruded tongue swollen and obscene, the crotch of his jeans stained wet, his eyes wide open.

3

Wednesday 24th November 2010

Hi, Jim!

Can you believe this weather! They've put out flood alerts in some parts of the county! What's it like in Gateshead? I always check the forecast now for you when I listen to the weather, it looks like you're ankle-deep too. Yuck! Luckily we're not in a vulnerable area, and there's never (FINGERS CROSSED!) been flooding here. My God, just the thought of this house going under, with all my things in it, argh! I have an awful lot of newspapers (oh dear, does that make me sound like a mad old hag?!) and they would swell up, wouldn't they, like a cork, plug me in here? Oh, anyway, not worth thinking about, I suppose.

   I was so sorry to hear about your son. Bloody bloody hell, Jim. So awful, even if he had been a drug addict for all those years. Thirty-one is absolutely FAR TOO YOUNG, and the old cliché about parents outliving their children is one of the truest. It subverts the order of everything and nothing ever makes sense again, does it? And you see, I should know. Because, since we're becoming so intimate, so quickly, I feel able to tell you this now, and I have lost a son, too. My baby one. Little Rhys. He died just after his sixteenth birthday. He hanged himself, in his own bedroom. On Easter Sunday.

Sorry. I had to take a break there. You know, I've never really spoken about it to anyone. But then I never met anyone who'd lost a son too (apart from my husband of course but that's different, isn't it?). I did such a good job of dealing with it at the time that I was always too utterly terrified to pick at the scab, as it were. Do you understand what I mean? I don't really expect you to. I suspect you were more "normal" about it all, thrashed about and screamed and wailed, etc.? Anyway, so, yes, there you are, we have even more in common than we first thought. And in case you're wondering, no, Rhys left no note, no explanation. It's an infinite mystery. A terrible mystery. Although . . . well, I've never told anyone this before, Jim, but I think I know why he killed himself. And I've never told anyone, because he would have hated anyone to know. And so would I. But anyway! Can't go spouting all my deepest secrets too soon, you'll run screaming for the hills!!!

So, on to less grisly things. Are you interested at all in horoscopes? In case you are, I'm a Cancerian. I would say I'm very typical—home-loving, nurturing, sensitive, creative, etc., etc. How about you, Jim? What star sign are you? I'm guessing at . . . VIRGO!! Am I right?!

All the very best,
Lorelei
xx

APRIL 2011

"So did Grandma, like, *sleep* here, too?" said Molly, stroking the lumpy arms of the chair.

Meg glanced around the room. Lorelei's bed was entirely buried beneath a landfill of clothes and bags. There was a duvet on the floor at the foot of the chair, patterned with fuchsia and lavender stripes, and a matching pillow. "I suppose she must have," she replied.

"God."

Meg nodded. If there was one luxury that Meg never took for granted, it was the sensation of lying herself down at the end of every day upon a king-sized mattress, stretching out her limbs, stroking the soles of her feet against the silky bedsheets (laundered, pressed, sprayed with expensive scented water, changed every five days and not a moment longer), kissing her pillow, submitting to it all. When she saw homeless people it was that, more than the constant threat of violence that they lived with, the poverty and the loneliness, that made her heart bleed for them. *No bed.* And here had been her own mother, in a five-bedroom house, curling herself up every night, small and tight, her back a crooked arch, her neck a cricked right angle, in this shabby, lumpy chair, the same chair she'd sat in all day. Never lying flat. Never stretching out. *My God*, she thought, *did she really hate herself that much?*

"Come on," she said, "let's go and see what else has been going on up here." She put out a hand to help Molly out of the sagging pit of the armchair.

"Can we see your room?"

Meg grunted. There hadn't been a "your room" since roughly a week after she'd left home at the age of twenty. Her mother had turned it over to junk storage even before Meg's first visit home.

"For what it's worth," she replied.

Meg turned left out of Lorelei's room and forced her way through another junk-filled corridor to the door of her former bedroom. She pushed at it and then turned to Molly and grimaced. "Jesus Christ," she said. "I think this one might actually be totally blocked up."

"Let me try." Molly pressed her slight body to the door. She pushed against it with her back, with each side, and then with her arms. She turned to Meg. "It's blocked," she said. "How is that even possible? I mean, how did she get that stuff in when you can't even open the door?"

Meg shrugged. "None of this really stands up to any kind of right-thinking analysis. None of it. Your grandma was a very strange woman."

"Which one was Beth's room?"

"Round here," said Meg, "round this corner." She felt her way with her hands, trailing her fingertips against the damp wallpaper. Laura Ashley's finest, pale-green leaves against a magnolia background, still bearing the marks of the childhoods lived here—felt-tip trails, half-ripped stickers—and there, Beth's door, still with its plastic plaque bought from a gift shop in Weston-super-Mare. BETH'S ROOM. They'd each had one. Both the girls. Meg still remembered the excitement as they spun the carousel around and found that *yes*! There was a *Megan*! (Although no Rory and no Rhys, but the twins had been too small to feel hard done by.) They'd stuck them to their doors with sticky felt pads. Meg had eventually taken hers off, at some point during her teenage years, and it had broken apart in her hands. She'd tipped it into a bin, never thought of it again. Until now. A sudden, searing reminder that they'd *once been happy*. All of them. Even Rhys.

Impossible, she thought. *Impossible*.

Beth had never taken her plaque down, stuck in the past as she'd been for so long, half-formed and amorphous, like an embryo in a jar. The door was half-open and peering through the gap Meg saw, without much surprise, more generic, formless piles. The curtains across the window were drawn and dirty, drooping from the runner at one side, letting in a half-moon of daylight. Beth's wardrobe sat to the left of the door. Its doors were wide open, revealing Beth's clothes: her old clothes, the clothes she'd worn when she was still a person who made sense to Meg. When she was still her sister.

Meg's phone rang again. She looked at the display. BILL. Thank God.

"Hello, darling."

"We're here!"

"Oh, good!" said Meg, crossing one thing off her list of dread fears. The other half of her family had failed to die in a plane crash on an Air France flight from Gatwick to Bern. "How was the flight?"

"It was good, great."

"How are the boys?"

"Boys!" she heard her husband call out. "Mummy wants to know how you are!"

Meg smiled as she heard the oddly high-pitched sound of her three boys loudly exclaiming that they were well.

"Bit of a scene at outsize items," Bill was saying. "Only three pairs of skis came through. Had to hang around for half an hour. Had to, you know, *shout* at people."

"Oh, God, not at Swiss people. You shouldn't do that, you know? They don't like it."

Bill laughed. Meg's heart calmed at the sound of it. How far away it all seemed now: soft, warm, shouty Bill, her three wild, red-haired boys with their freckles and their hugs, the whiteness and glare of a Swiss airport, four immaculately packed suitcases full of clothes that smelled like home. *Her* home.

"Do you want to talk to Daddy?" Meg mouthed to Molly. Molly shrugged and then said, "Yeah, all right."

"Molly wants to say hello. Hold on, hold on. No, I'll tell you later, yes, we're here. I'll tell you everything later. Love you. Love you all. I'll call you when Molly and I get to the hotel. Yes. Yes. Love you. Bye."

She passed her phone to Molly and felt shocked by the transition from one world to another, from cleanliness and love and chaos, to dirt and loneliness and death. Her ears rang and the silence ate her up. Not just the silence of the countryside, but the unsettling muffled silence of this house, where every wall was buffered and every surface was covered. The muted silence of a pillow over your head.

APRIL 1995

An alarm wailed from somewhere. It was not an alarm that Megan recognized. Hers made a high-pitched buzz. This was more of a drone. She opened her eyes and forced them to focus. Boxes. Dozens of boxes. A bedsheet pinned over the window because they didn't yet have curtains. A large beveled mirror that was not hers, balanced against the far wall, in which was visible a tableau of two people on a brand-new divan bed, one sitting up, looking back at her, the other still asleep. The person looking back at her was disheveled and confused. Megan flattened down her hair and yawned.

The droning alarm seemed to grow louder as it went on. It was not her alarm. It was his. Bill's. She nudged the man sleeping by her side and said, "Bill. Wake up. Your alarm's going off. You need to unpack it and turn it off."

Bill opened one eye and then closed it again. He smiled and snuggled himself into Megan's rounded tummy.

"Bill!" she said again. "It's driving me nuts! Please do something!"

He groaned and unpeeled himself from her body. "Are you sure it's mine?" he asked raspily.

"Yes. Of course it's yours. I'd know if it was mine. I'm amazed you don't recognize it."

"I'm pretty sure mine's set to radio," he said. "I've definitely never heard it buzz before."

He swung his legs out of the bed and Meg watched him stumble, naked, through the city of unopened boxes that surrounded the bed. She smiled at him in amusement as he put his ear to each box in turn.

"You look completely mad," she said.

"I'm sure I do," he replied. "You could help, if you wanted."

Meg threw back the duvet and pointed at her swollen belly. "I am exempt from everything for the next two and a half months."

"Everything?"

"Yes," she said. "Absolutely everything."

The baby was not planned. Definitely not. She was only twenty-four. She and Bill had only been together for six months. It was ridiculous.

But Megan had always wanted a big family. At least four. Getting an early start was a good thing.

And from the moment she'd seen the test results held in her shaking hand in a toilet cubicle at work, it had felt right. Meg wasn't a young twenty-four. She'd partied hard throughout her teenage years, had two long-term relationships and ten previous lovers. She'd experimented with drugs and decided she preferred alcohol. She'd drunk herself sick and decided she preferred moderation. She could cook a roast dinner, write to her bank manager, maintain her own car and drive on motorways. She had no overdraft and most of her friends were older than her. And then there was Bill.

Bill was thirty-two. Bill ran an art gallery. He had an ex-wife. And a mortgage. He was losing his hair.

In some contexts, twenty-four sounded young to have a child. But in the context of Meg and Bill, it was just perfect. So Bill had sold his little post-divorce love shack with blood-red walls and zebra-print furniture above a barber's on Chalk Farm Road and bought them a two-bedroom flat in Tufnell Park with a garden. He'd done this unquestioningly and happily. And this morning, a bright Easter Sunday morning, they were waking up there together for the very first time.

Bill stood up triumphantly. "Aha," he said, in a stupid Russian accent. "I have located the device. I have thirty seconds to dismantle it before it detonates." He peeled the tape from the box and plucked the clock from it. "There," he said, hitting a button and bringing instant peace and quiet to the room that rang out like a high-pitched chime. "Sorry about that."

Meg smiled. "Not your fault," she said.

"Ha, there you go. You see, my ex-wife would have told me that it *was* my fault. You are so wonderfully sane and reasonable. Please don't ever change."

Megan loved it when Bill mentioned his ex-wife because he never had a good word about her. Megan had never met her, but in her head she looked like Cruella de Vil. Her name was Michelle. She'd married her boss and lived in Spain and was of little consequence in Megan's world.

The phone rang and Bill and Meg looked at each other. "Our first phone call!" she said, leaning across him to reach it. "And I bet I know who it'll be."

"Happy Easter!"

"Happy Easter," replied Meg, leaning back into the pillows and cupping the phone into the crook of her neck. *It's Beth,* she mouthed at Bill, who nodded knowingly and headed to the bathroom. "How are you?"

"Fine!" said Beth in her singsong voice, a vaguely irritating facsimile of their mother's. "How are you?"

"We are absolutely fine," said Meg, stroking her big bump and stretching out her toes.

"How did the move go?"

"Brilliant," said Meg. "I just sat on my big fat bum and let everyone do everything. Now we've just got to unpack. Hang some curtains. Mow the lawn. Take up the carpets. Sand the floorboards. Redecorate. And have a baby."

"Oh, I can't wait to see you all," said Beth longingly.

"Well, you know, *anytime,*" Meg replied drily. Beth was becoming as difficult to pry out of the Bird House as her mother.

"Yes! Yes. Maybe next month."

"Yes," repeated Megan, "maybe next month. How's Mum?"

"She's good. You know. Do you want to talk to her?"

Meg sighed. "Yeah," she said. "Okay. Put her on."

The phone line sounded muffled for a moment and she could hear her mother through the flesh of Beth's hand, complaining gently about something, but then a moment later she came on the line.

"Hello, darling!"

"Hello, Mum."

"Happy Easter! We're just about to head into the garden for the egg hunt. Maddy's here. And little Sophie. And Vicky, of course. Say hello, Vicky!"

Meg rolled her eyes and heard Vicky in the background

calling out, "Hello Meggy!" In the aftermath of the terrible Easter of 1991, Lorelei and Vicky had become inseparable. It turned out that Vicky's first boyfriend had hanged himself at the age of eighteen, so they had more in common than a taste for Cotswolds houses. According to Beth, Vicky "popped over" every day at about ten thirty with her two little ones and would then spend the rest of the day at Lorelei's, giggling with her over Chardonnay when the sun went over the yardarm and not leaving until she heard her husband's car pulling up on the pavement outside, at which point she would hastily down the last dregs of her wine and head next door to greet him.

"It's nice," Beth would say. "*I'm glad she's got a friend.*"

And Meg would say, "It's just fucking weird, if you ask me." Which Beth hadn't.

"When are you going to see Rhys?" she asked impatiently.

"Oh," said her mother, "well, now, I'm not sure we'll have time today, will we?" She asked this supposedly of the other people in the room with her, not of Megan lying prone in her new bed in Tufnell Park.

"Can you put Beth back on for me?"

"Okay, darling." Her mother sounded relieved and happy to end the conversation with her eldest child.

"Beth!" Meg snapped as her sister came back on the line. "What's going on? Why isn't Mum going to see Rhys?"

Beth sighed. "I don't know. She says she's moving on."

"Moving on! It's only been four years. You don't 'move on' from visiting your son's grave on the anniversary of his death."

"Well," ventured her sister nervously, "you're not going to see him either, are you?"

"No," snapped Meg, "of course I'm not! I'm nearly seven months pregnant, a hundred miles away, and I've just moved into a new flat. I would love to be going to see Rhys. I've been to see Rhys every chance I've had these past four years. Please tell me Dad and Rory are going?"

There was a brief silence on the end of the line, long enough to alert Megan that all was far from well at the Bird House. "Tell me, Beth, tell me the rest of you are going?"

"Well, the thing is, Dad's not here."

"Where is he?"

"I don't know."

"And Rory?"

"I don't think he came home last night. As far as I know."

Meg groaned. "You're all fucking useless," she yelled. "The whole fucking lot of you."

And then she hung up.

≈

He bought her an egg. Just a cheap one. Purple foil and full of chocolate buttons. And then he pulled some daffodils from a well-stocked bed outside someone's house. The sun was high and bright and it felt like the beginning of everything. For the first time in his life, Rory Bird was in love.

Her name was Kayleigh and she was waiting for him now, in her bedsit. He'd met her three nights ago at his local pub. She was the cousin of one of his mates, just moved across to England; two years older than him, bleached-blond hair cut into a bob, Irish accent, her own guitar, a tattoo on her left breast and a livid scar on her wrist that she said she'd tell him about one day, when she "trusted him."

He hadn't left her side since that night, until now. She'd sent him out for milk and cigarettes and now he walked fast through the morning streets of Cirencester, desperate and aching to get back to her. It was the strangest feeling. In fact, just feeling anything at all was strange. He'd been numb for the past four years.

"I'm back!" he called out, taking the steps two at a time to the front door.

She was still in bed, lying stretched out and naked. Her flesh was deathly white, her eyes fixed on a tiny portable TV on the chest of drawers at the foot of the bed. She smiled at him and arranged herself onto her elbow. "I missed you," she said.

He grinned at her and pulled the egg and the daffodils from his carrier bag.

"Happy Easter," he said, joining her on the bed and presenting them to her.

"Oh, you sweet fool," she said, taking the egg and sniffing the daffodils. "I didn't have you down as the religious type."

"What's religion got to do with Easter eggs?"

"Everything, where I come from." She smiled and started to take apart the packaging. "I'd love a cup of tea," she said, "to go with my, you know, *nonreligious* chocolate egg."

He cupped her face with his hand and kissed her on her soft lips. "Coming right up."

She pulled the egg out of the box and unwrapped it. Rory watched her and resisted the temptation to say, "*Save the foil.*" He smiled at the thought and Kayleigh glanced at him affectionately and said, "What are you smiling at?"

He said, "Nothing. Just . . ." They'd talked about his mother, about his family, about Rhys. Of course they had. You don't go falling in love with people unless you've talked about the things that matter. "My mum's always had this thing about foils. Every Easter, it was always, you know, '*Save the foils! Save the foils!*'"

"Your mum sounds like a fruit."

He grimaced and filled the kettle from the tap. "Yeah," he said absentmindedly, "she is a bit. A lovely fruit, though."

"I'd love to meet her. One day."

"You can meet her today," he said rashly. "If you want."

She laughed. "Nah. Thanks all the same, though."

He nodded, relieved. This was just for him. He wanted to keep it to himself for as long as he possibly could. But even so, it felt wrong not being at home today. Megan wasn't coming back for Easter—she was moving house or something—and Dad was on one of his mysterious "writing courses," so it would just be Mum and Beth and the stalker woman from next door. Mum had insisted that Easter would be what Easter always had been, a day for fun and chocolate and lamb and family. She'd said, "Rhys wouldn't want to have spoiled Easter for everyone. Rhys would want it to carry on."

Rory had no idea what Rhys was thinking that day, but he didn't suppose for a second that it had anything to do with what might happen on Easter day after he'd gone. The little fucker hadn't even left a note. He supposed there might have been a clue in the lyrics of the Alice in Chains song he'd left playing on repeat, but Rory was buggered if he knew what it was. He'd given up having a clue what made his twin brother tick a long time before he killed himself.

"Mmm." Kayleigh sank her teeth into a splinter of chocolate and let her eyes roll back into their sockets. "Yum yum." You could tell by looking at Kayleigh that she didn't really eat much chocolate. She was the type of person who forgot to eat, who had toast for dinner, who would lose weight absentmindedly. "Want some?" She waved the egg at him.

"No, thanks," he replied. He suspected that he might never eat an Easter egg again. The particular flavor of chocolate molded into a thin curve—and it did absolutely have its own unique taste—would always throw him into some Proustian hellhole of bad associations.

"Will you do something for me?" he asked nervously. "Today?"

She narrowed her eyes at him. "That totally depends," she began, "on what it involves."

"Will you come to his grave with me?"

"Your brother?"

He nodded.

"You want me to come to your brother's grave with you, on the anniversary of his death?"

He nodded again. "I mean, sorry, I know it's macabre, I know you never met him, I know it's a big deal, it's—"

"I would love to come with you," she said simply. "It would be an honor."

～

The graveyard was canopied with pink and white cherry blossoms. The sky was cobalt blue. The sun was warm. Kayleigh wore a black vest, ripped jeans, Ray-Bans and a somber expression. She held Rory's arm in its crook with one hand, and with her other she held a small posy of wildflowers she'd pulled from the nooks and crannies of the cemetery. She appeared to be in her element.

"This takes me back," she sighed, looking around herself as they walked towards the dark corner where the incinerated remains of Rory's brother had been interred almost four years ago. She sighed and Rory felt impelled to say, "Back to what?"

"Oh, nothing. You know, just *death*. My granny. My granddaddy. The lady who lived next door who got hit by a chimney stack." She sighed dramatically and Rory tried not to think too deeply on her rather tenuous allusions to a shared experience. For all her wan melodrama and mysterious scars, it struck

Rory momentarily that maybe she was putting it all on a bit. Which oddly enough made him love her all the more. He squeezed her hand in his and said, "This is it."

A small slab of granite marked the spot. It was carved with the words:

RHYS ARTHUR BIRD
1ST MARCH 1975—31ST MARCH 1991
SWEET SIXTEEN FOREVER

Lorelei had chosen the wording without consulting anyone in the family. Rory had always thought it was stupid. There had been nothing "sweet" about Rhys. Rhys had been all vinegar and angst. All "It's not fair" and "It wasn't me" and "Fuck off and leave me alone."

They'd begun to grow apart when they moved on to the big school. Before that they'd always been in the same class and a kind of intimacy had been forced upon them. But then they were put in separate classes and, to put it bluntly, Rory was in the cool class and Rhys was in the nerdy class and Rory didn't really want to cross over. He had it good where he was. All the prettiest girls were in his class, guys he was still friends with even now. His kind of people, basically. For the first time in his life he'd had some distance from Rhys and suddenly he'd been able to see his brother objectively. And objectively, he was a loser.

None of which meant to say that he hadn't loved him desperately, passionately. And none of which meant to say that Rory didn't miss his little brother with an agonizing ache every minute of every day. His twin. They'd shared a womb, then a bed, then a room. He would never be closer to another person, not as long as he lived. But still. He was weird. Had been. Weird. And Rory wasn't weird. And that, frankly, was life.

"So, that's your birthday, is it? March the first?"

He nodded.

"You're a Pisces?"

He nodded again.

"Me too," she said, falling to her haunches in front of Rhys's grave. "Were you similar then, the two of you?"

He shrugged and sank down to her level. "Not really. We used to be, when we were little, but then we kind of grew apart."

"I heard about that kind of thing before," said Kayleigh. "Girl twins, though, it was. Inseparable when they were wee, worst of enemies now they're grown. So sad, you know?"

"Sad is an understatement."

"Yeah."

They sat side by side on the grass bank. It was still so warm. It reminded Rory of an Easter day years ago, when they were about five or six and it had been hot enough for a paddling pool and water pistols. It felt, in retrospect, and possibly not entirely accurately, like the last really happy Easter at home. The last Easter before Megan had got all grown-up and stroppy, when it hadn't rained, when Ben and Tom had still been young enough to come too, when his mum and dad had seemed as if they liked each other, before that woman from next door had come and taken over everything. And before, of course, Rhys had spoiled Easter forever.

Rory felt a roll of anger thunder through him and he breathed it in hard.

"So," said Kayleigh, putting together a spliff on the shelf of her bony kneecaps. "What about the rest of the family? Don't you usually all come together?"

He sighed. "There's no such thing as 'usual' in my family," he said. "Not anymore. Rhys kind of stopped 'usual' in its tracks."

Kayleigh nodded knowingly. Rory could tell she wasn't used to being upstaged in matters of tragedy and life experience. He could also tell that she was gripped by it all. But far too cool to show it.

"You know, when my granddad died my granny wore black for the rest of her life. Proper mourning she went into, you know. The Widow Doherty, that's what everyone called her. Went to his grave every day, polished it all up, fresh flowers. The works. It was almost like it was her job, you know, her professional occupation . . ."

She trailed off and they both stared for a moment at the unkempt grave. "So his actual anniversary," she said, "it was two weeks ago?"

"Yeah, but we always come on Easter Sunday, feels like an anniversary, not just an arbitrary date. You know."

"Well," she said pointedly, "doesn't look like anyone came to see him on the thirty-first either." She finished making the spliff and then she lit it, held in the corner of her mouth, her eyes slanted against the first rush of smoke. She passed the spliff to Rory, got to her feet, pulled the dead flowers from the grave and arranged the meadow flowers in their place. She brushed some dirt away with the palms of her hands and then wiped them clean against her black vest.

"Have you got a tissue?" she asked, turning back to Rory.

"Er"—he patted himself through his clothes—"er, yeah, actually, I do." It was a paper napkin from Spudulike. He had no idea how it had got into the pocket of his jeans, which spoke many volumes about the nature of his existence in recent years. She used the napkin to polish up the dull granite of the headstone, until it shone. Then she sat down next to Rory on the grass bank and took the spliff back from him.

"There you go," she said. "That's a whole lot better."

Rory turned and glanced at her from the corner of his eye. He was struck, as he'd been roughly every thirty seconds since the first time he laid eyes on her in the pub three days ago, by her extreme and almost vulgar beauty, but now he was struck by something else. She loved him. He could see it. It was blinding and incredible.

He stared at her in wonder and awe.

"What?" she said.

"Nothing." He smiled.

"Not nothing," she said. "Why are you staring at me like that?"

He touched the ends of her home-cut hair with his fingertips and then stroked the dip of her cheekbone. "Because I love you," he said.

"Oh, you daft bastard."

"And you love me."

She put her hand to her throat and looked at him in fake horror. "Outrageous!" she squeaked.

"But true."

She dropped her hand from her throat and let her shoulders go soft and then she held his hand against her cheek and said, "You got me."

He smiled and brought her to him, pressed his lips up against hers. "Forever and ever," he said.

"Forever and ever."

∽

He took her home the following week.

It was a moment he'd been both looking forward to and

dreading. Looking forward to bringing these two enormously important elements of his life together, dreading the shock of objectivity that this would bring about. He did not want to know what Kayleigh looked like to a person who was not insanely in love with her. And he did not want to know how his family and their peculiar home would appear to someone who had not grown up there and seen how things had come to be that way. He could feel excuses forming in his subconscious already. *I know she looks a bit rough, but she's a sweetheart, I promise you. I know my mum seems a bit distracted and disengaged but she really loves us underneath it all. I know our house looks like a tip but it's actually quite clean.*

It was the last day of the school holidays and Vicky was there with her little ones. *Of course.* She came upon them in the hallway, all bouncy dyed-blond hair and scrubbed cheeks, wide hips in stretchy jeans and huge piles of breast under a too-tight T-shirt.

"Rory! Hello, stranger. We've missed you."

She kissed him extravagantly on both cheeks, swathing him in a blanket of milky perfume. She peered at Kayleigh standing behind him, her hands stuffed into the pockets of a tight denim jacket, thin blue-white legs dangling from a matching miniskirt, chewing a piece of gum and looking for all the world like a call girl he'd just plucked off a street corner.

"You must be Kayleigh!" she tweeted. "I'm Vicky. Hello! Come through. We're all in the kitchen. Making banana cake. Bit of a mess, I'm afraid."

Rory and Kayleigh exchanged a look and followed her into the kitchen. He'd already warned her about the ever-present Vicky.

"Hi, Mum." He kissed his mother on the cheek and she smiled delightedly.

"Hello, darling boy," she said, gripping his arm and looking into his eyes, searching for some kind of change in him. "And this," she said, "this must be . . ." She'd forgotten her name. Either by pure scattiness or deep-seated lack of interest.

"Kayleigh," he said, taking his girlfriend's hand and leading her forwards. "This is Kayleigh. Kayleigh, this is my mum, Lorelei."

"Call me Lorrie! Everyone just calls me Lorrie."

This wasn't quite true. Vicky called her Lorrie. Everyone else called her Mum. Or Lorelei.

"Lovely to meet you," said Kayleigh, her hands still tucked firmly inside her jacket pockets. Rory watched his mother's face as she took in the detail of his rough-and-ready love. She looked at first surprised and then mildly amused. "Likewise," she said, and turned away to assist one of Vicky's small daughters with slicing an overripe banana with a blunt knife. Rory blanched. It had been a slight. Barely perceptible, but without a doubt, a slight. He hoped to God that Kayleigh hadn't noticed.

"Wow," said Kayleigh, "look at all of this! It's totally crazy." She was standing in the center of the room, staring wide-eyed and gorgeous at the walls of artwork. "Is this all your stuff?" she asked Rory.

He laughed. "No, not just mine. All of us. All four of us."

"Oh, look." She stepped forward to examine a picture of a Dalek, collaged over with pieces of tinfoil and old buttons, the word *ekstminat* written below and the words *rory bird* above. "Look what you made, you little cutie-pie!" She pulled him towards her by the crook of his arm and leaned into his body. "I had no idea you were an *artist*." He smiled at her and Lorelei turned and said, "They all are. All my children. Natural artists." Rory saw her clock Kayleigh standing up against him and witnessed a cloud of something fearful pass across her eyes.

"Can I get you a drink, Kayleigh?" said Vicky, plugging the gap in Lorelei's hostessing duties.

"Sure," she said, "that'd be nice. Do you have any juice?"

"Just Ribena, I'm afraid," Vicky replied apologetically.

"I love Ribena." Kayleigh beamed, snapping her gum between her teeth.

Vicky beamed back at her and poured her out a glass. "So," she said, passing it to her. "You're Irish?"

"How'd you guess?"

Vicky's smile faltered for a second while her brain played catch-up with Kayleigh's humor. Then she said, "Ha, ha!" and blushed. "Whereabouts are you from?" she continued.

"I'm from County Clare." Kayleigh pulled the gum from her mouth and dropped it into the waste-paper bin. "Been here for less than a month. It's all taking a bit of getting used to, to be honest."

"Oh," said Vicky with widening eyes, "yes. I'm sure it is. And what brought you here then?"

Kayleigh noisily gulped down half her Ribena and then wiped her mouth. "Too many enemies," she said, "back home. Everyone hated me. Fancied a fresh start."

Vicky stared at her uncertainly, clearly having no idea what to make of her. She laughed again and then looked blank.

"And what about you, what's your story then?"

Vicky's face softened as some kind of normal order was applied to the conversation. "Well, the usual story, brought up in the countryside, ran away to the city, fell in love in the city, had a baby in the city, decided to bring the baby up in the countryside."

Kayleigh looked at her blankly. Clearly *not* a story she'd heard before. "And Rory tells me you've all but *moved in*."

Rory stiffened and threw Kayleigh a look.

Vicky laughed. "Well, not strictly true, y'know. More, I think, found a new friend."

"What's wrong with your own house, then?"

Rory clutched his forehead and dropped his head. He'd half known this would happen, but hadn't been expecting it to happen quite so soon.

"Well, there's nothing wrong with my house. It's just, when you've got small children it's nice to get out of the house with them, you know. Can make you go a bit screwy being stuck in your own house all day. And I know, well, at least I *think*, Lorrie enjoys the company. Wouldn't you say, Lorrie?"

Lorelei looked up from the mixing bowl she was helping one of the children to stir cake mix into and said, "Hmm?"

"I was just saying to Kayleigh, I think you like the company, you know, when I bring the little ones over."

"Oh, yes," said Lorelei, stroking the child's hair. "Yes, I certainly do. Don't know where I'd be without them. I'd be lost. Completely lost."

"Oh, well then," said Kayleigh, "that's nice." Her face spoke volumes, but no one was looking apart from Rory. "Oh," she said busily, as if she'd just remembered something, "by the way, me and Rory, we went to visit Rhys at Easter. You know, at the cemetery."

Lorelei's shoulder twitched slightly but she didn't turn round.

"That's nice," said Vicky brightly.

"Yeah," Kayleigh continued. "We had a bit of a tidy-up, you know, said a little prayer, left some flowers. It was a bit sad looking, you know, looked like no one had been there for a while . . ."

"Well," said Vicky, her voice pitched at a new place, no

longer bright and shiny, but deep and forbidding. "It's hard for Lorrie. It's hard for all of us." She forced a sour smile.

"Yes," said Kayleigh in a voice full of fake empathy, "I'm sure that's true. I'm sure it is. So," she said brightly, changing the subject, "you have a beautiful house. It reminds me of my own home, except"—she laughed in anticipation of her next comment—"my own mother is an anal retentive, you know, the house is like an actual operating theater, not a speck of dust anywhere. And everything put away, mugs snatched away before you've had the last sip out of them." She tutted good-humoredly and then stared round the room again. "This," she said, "is quite the opposite. You have a lot of stuff, Lorrie."

"Yes," said Vicky, interjecting again. "Lorrie likes shopping."

"Wow," said Kayleigh. "You know, I don't think I can recall ever seeing so many plates in one home before."

Rory looked at the shelves hanging heaving and bowed from the kitchen walls. His eyes roamed over the dinner plates: he estimated around a hundred. Then he looked at the bowls: teetering arrangements in every color of the rainbow, melamine, china, clay, beautiful in some ways, but obviously, it was now clear to him, completely excessive. There were three shelves of colorful tumblers and glasses that caught the afternoon light like votives, and more shelves loaded down with pitchers, jugs, vases, pots, tins, jars, platters, gravy boats and condiment sets. It occurred to Rory suddenly that there were ten different salt-and-pepper mills. And, he suspected, more buried away in the cupboards.

"Can I see the rest?"

Vicky looked at Lorelei, who appeared to be either ignoring Kayleigh or oblivious to her, and said, "I'm sure that'll be fine, won't it, Lorrie?"

"What's that?"

"Kayleigh wants to see the rest of the house."

Lorelei beamed, showing all her unkempt teeth, and said, "Of course! Excuse the mess, though!" She had cake mix smeared across her cheek and looked slightly unhinged.

"Christ," said Kayleigh, following Rory through the house, "this place is pure *chaos*. How can you all live like this?"

Rory looked around and sighed. The delicate, tissue-thin layers of his own lack of objectivity were being ripped apart, just as he'd known they would be.

"You get used to it," he said, stepping over a pile of bin bags marked "For Oxfam," which had been sitting at the bottom of the stairs for roughly two years.

"I mean, that's not to say it's without its charms," she continued, taking his hand and stepping over the bin bags herself. "It's a lovely house. But you know, it's kind of nuts. Wouldn't you say?"

"My mum," he began, not quite knowing where he was about to head, "she's kind of excessively nostalgic, you know, sentimental. Always has been. It's like she's scared that if she lets go of things, she'll never think of them again. And that if she never thinks of them again then they were just kind of *worthless*."

"Hmm," said Kayleigh, joining him at the top of the first flight of stairs, "and yet . . ." She stopped and looked pensive.

"And yet what?"

"Well, and yet she doesn't come to visit the grave of her beautiful dead son on the anniversary of his death."

The words hung there in the space between them, like a bullet suspended on its trajectory. They both turned to look through the window on the half landing at the gardens beyond.

"Pretty," said Kayleigh, cupping the glass with the side of her hand and peering through it. "Very pretty."

Rory showed her his bedroom, his parents' room, Beth's room, Megan's room, now turned into a storage space for piles and piles of books and paperwork. And then she said, "Will you show me his room? Rhys's room?"

Rory shuddered. He never went into Rhys's room. He shrugged. "Sure," he said, "if you want."

He stood just on the threshold and watched Kayleigh walk in.

"Are you coming?" she said.

He shook his head and she threw him a tender look.

"Come on," she said, "it's just a room."

He shook his head again and smiled.

She stopped in the middle of the room and looked up. "So this is where it happened, yeah?"

He nodded and smiled, embarrassed. He'd never had this conversation before.

"Jesus," she said, staring at the beams overhead, "how fucking tragic. Did he leave a note?"

"No, no note. No clues. Nothing. Selfish bastard."

"God, that really is, you know. Ultimately selfish."

Rory smiled with relief. It was the first time he'd ever said that out loud, and the first person he'd said it to had agreed with him.

"But you know, it's a sickness, right?" she continued. "You can't try and pin logic and rationality onto the thing. It's gone way beyond that by the time someone sticks their neck in a rope."

"Yeah," said Rory, "I know that. I do know that." He sighed. Four years he'd spent wondering what had really happened in this room when they were both sixteen and he still had not even half an answer.

"So, who was it that found him? Was it you?"

"No. It was Meg."

"Aah, the infamous Meg. How old was she when that happened, then?"

"She was twenty."

"Christ above, what a holy mess." She left the room and joined him on the landing outside Rhys's room.

"It was best it was her. She's the sanest one in the family. It might have tipped anyone else over the edge. But Meg's handled it really well."

Kayleigh raised an over-plucked eyebrow at him and said, "Well, she doesn't seem the only one who's handled it well."

He threw her a questioning look and then said, "Aah," as realization of her meaning dawned. His mother. He opened his mouth to defend her and then closed it. There was no point. You couldn't explain his mother in mere words. You had to live his mother, breathe his mother. And even then she didn't always make sense. "Come on then," he said, putting his arm around Kayleigh's shoulders, "let's go and look at the gardens, shall we?"

∽

They had sex up against the wall at the very bottom end of the garden. It was easy, logistically, given the length of her skirt. A sheep approached from the neighboring field to see what they were doing. Kayleigh laughed and called out, "Fancy a threesome, sheepy?" And then she laughed again and said, "You'd have to give yer arse a clean first, though, it's terribly shitty." They both laughed, and Rory thought he'd never known it was all right to laugh during sex; he'd always thought it was supposed to be serious. They hung together in the hammock after, sharing a spliff, their legs entangled. They could hear Vicky's children laughing and shrieking nearer the house and Rory felt the roughness of the smoke inside his lungs and the stickiness inside his jeans and the love of the woman in his arms, and he smiled. His childhood was behind him. Kayleigh had walked into his childhood home an hour and a half ago and untied all the ribbons that had held him to this place for so long.

"We should go away," he said suddenly.

She laughed. "Like where?"

"I don't know," he said breathlessly. "I've never been any-where. I haven't even got a passport."

She looked at him agog and laughed again. "You're kid-ding me."

He shook his head. "None of us have."

"But that's . . ." She paused to find the right word. "That's *diabolical.*"

He shrugged and then he laughed. "Nearly went to Greece once."

"You *nearly* went to Greece." She rolled her eyes. "Good *God!*"

"I wanna get a passport," he said, sitting upright and grasp-ing her hands in his. "I want to go somewhere, with you."

She smiled. "That's a superb plan, it really is, but neither of us has two pennies to rub together."

"I can get hold of money."

She eyed him suspiciously. "How?"

"I don't know," he said. "I'll sell something. I'll ask my dad if I can borrow some. I'll get a job. I'll do all three. Seriously. I want to go somewhere. I really, really want to go somewhere!" And then, unexpectedly and overwhelmingly, Rory began to cry. He cried for his lost brother, his mad mother, his distant father, his sweet sisters. But mainly he cried for himself, for all the time he'd spent in stasis waiting to want to go.

Kayleigh held him in her skinny arms and kissed the top

of his head and told him that everything was going to be okay. And he believed her.

⌖

A week later Lorelei stood with her hands against her hips in the middle of Megan's old room, looking from one side to the other. "Gosh," she said, "now. Well . . . this is tricky."

Rory groaned. Here was a woman with ten salt-and-pepper sets, a woman who had kept every last mark on paper made by four different children over the course of fifteen years or more, a woman who never threw away anything colorful, eye-catching or shiny, a woman who bulk-bought cleaning products and household gadgetry, a woman who accumulated stuff on a grand, almost baroque scale, yet she could not locate a simple birth certificate.

"But, Mum, I don't understand, how can you lose a birth certificate?"

"I haven't *lost* it, darling, I just haven't found it yet! Just give me a minute. *Please.*"

Lorelei now referred to Meg's old room as her office. It was not an office. It was a room of piles. Mainly paperback books that Lorelei picked up at charity shops and jumble sales and never got around to reading (she didn't sit still for long enough to read a book), and filing boxes and lever-arch folders and wallet folders and piles and piles of loose, unfettered paperwork that made Rory feel dizzy just looking at it, trying to imagine what lay within. Meg's bed itself was now invisible, swamped by piles of old coats and bin bags full of clothes headed vaguely, unconvincingly, towards charity shops. Meg's old dressing table, a piece of furniture that had once been her pride and joy, white with a triptych mirror and gilt edging (Rory seemed to recall it had been a special birthday present or a reward for doing something brilliant at school), was now in use as Lorelei's desk, and again, virtually invisible under more piles of paperwork, random selections of stuffed animals, snow globes, mugs, paperweights and for some unknown reason, a pile of deflated pink balloons still tied with curled nylon ribbon.

A couple of years back Lorelei had bought two filing cabinets from Ryman, with which to apply some order to her paper, yet these were now so overstuffed that the drawers hung open, spewing out their contents.

"I mean, how the hell do you ever find anything in here? It's a nightmare."

"Oh, I know." Lorelei dragged a bony hand through her still-long hair and sighed. "I'm going to sort it out. Vicky says she'll help me."

"When?"

"Oh, I don't know. There never seems to be enough time."

"That's ridiculous, Mum, of course there's time. You don't work, all your children are grown-up . . ."

"Yes, well, there's the little ones. They're so time-consuming."

"They're not your little ones. They're not your responsibility. They're Vicky's. Just ask them not to come over for a few days. You'd easily get this room sorted. I can help you . . . I mean, for example, this pile of old magazines, we could get rid of this right now, eh?"

"Well, yes, of course we could. Except we'd have to search through it first, to make sure there's nothing important buried away between them."

"Like your children's birth certificates, you mean?"

"Precisely, darling." She sounded almost relieved. "Do you see? Do you see my problem?"

Rory nodded. He saw many problems. "Right—" He clapped his hands together. "Let's start looking, shall we?"

His mother smiled apologetically. "Maybe we should wait for Daddy to get home."

Rory groaned. "No, Mum," he said, "I need it now. I need to get my application off, like, yesterday. We've booked our flights. We're going in two months."

"Going?" she said absentmindedly.

"Spain. I told you. Me and Kayleigh. Going to Spain, for a month."

"Oh, yes, of course." She tutted loudly.

"Why are you tutting?"

"Oh"—she wrapped her hand around the back of her neck—"I just don't get it. I don't understand what the attraction is. *Going away*." She tutted again and laughed under her breath, as if *going away* was some kind of oddball pastime.

"Everyone does it, you know? It's perfectly normal."

"Oh, I *know* that, silly. Of course it's normal. It's just, when you've got this"—she gestured around her—"and that"—she gestured at the window—"and all the people you love, why would you want to go anywhere else? All that faffing, and packing and unpacking and sleeping in a strange bed and not seeing the people you know when you go to the shops . . ." She shuddered delicately. Then she looked around the room again and said, "Well, darling, you're welcome to see what you can unearth in here, but frankly, I'd rather wait for Daddy. He's much more organized than me. And you know, it might not even be in here. It could be anywhere. Anywhere at all. And I really need to get back to the little ones now. We're making pasta necklaces."

Her body language was all directed away from Rory and away from this hellhole of a room. He was about to move out of the way to let her pass when he felt something rise up through him, a question he'd never realized he wanted to ask before, but one that suddenly felt like the most important question in the world.

"Why do you never want to talk about the past?"

"What?"

"You. You never talk about the past. Or the future."

"I live in the moment, darling, didn't you know that? It's the secret of true happiness."

"Yes, but . . ." He paused. "But you're not happy."

"Not happy?" She blinked at him with her big owlish eyes.

"No. Not happy."

"What on earth are you talking about, darling? I'm deliriously happy."

"How can you be?" he asked, a hint of anger in his voice. "How can you be happy?"

"Because of everything I have. All my blessings."

"But . . . *Rhys.*"

Her smile froze.

"He was your baby. Your special one. You didn't cry at his funeral. You don't visit his grave. You don't even have any photos of him on display. It's like . . . it's like he never existed."

She narrowed her eyes at him and growled. "This is *her*, isn't it? This is that girl."

"Kayleigh?"

"Yes, her. She's changed you."

"Yes, she has. For the better."

"No, I mean, she's made you hard, like her."

"She's not hard."

"Oh, darling, sweetie-boy, of course she is."

"What, because of the way she looks, you mean?"

"Well, partly, yes, but it's her aura, too. She has no soft edges. None at all. Vicky noticed that, too . . ."

"Urgh," said Rory. "Vicky, Vicky, bloody fucking *Vicky.*"

"Darling, horrible language. I thought we were having a civilized chat. Don't be base. I assume that's more of *her* influence."

"No. I've always used bad language. Just not in front of you. Because I had too much respect for you."

"And now?"

He shrugged. "I can't respect someone who doesn't respect the memory of her dead child."

She looked at him then, a terrible haunted look, a look that Rory would never forget as long as he lived, and said, "Don't you *ever* talk to me like that again."

For a moment he thought she was going to slap him. But she didn't. Instead she shoved him roughly out of her way and left the room.

⌒

Rory's dad found the birth certificate two days later. It was in a carrier bag full of disposable bendy straws in fluorescent colors that Lorelei had bought in bulk from Poundstretcher. The receipt in the bag was from 1989. "Oh!" she'd exclaimed with pleasure, taking the straws from her husband. "I was wondering what had happened to those. The little ones will *love* them."

All four birth certificates were together, in a pale-blue folder marked "Kiddies." There were other things in the folder: medical papers about the first few days of Rhys's life, GP certificates, notes on vaccinations and four little plastic wrist bracelets with the words "Baby Bird" on them, which struck Rory as rather charming.

His father suggested they meet in the pub. Said he could do with a change of scenery. Rory had never been to a pub with his dad before. He'd never even considered the possibility.

"Well," said Colin, handing him the certificate, "I'm really, really happy you're doing this. It's been a long time coming. I feel like we've all been set in aspic these past years, pickling ourselves in grief. And Mum would never let us go away when you were all young, so, good on you."

"Remember Greece?" said Rory, picking up his pint.

His dad laughed drily and rolled his eyes. "How could I forget? It took me years to get up the nerve to suggest it in the first place. Then those bloody burglars . . ."

"Mum hates her," he replied.

"Who? Kayleigh?"

Rory nodded.

"Oh, I doubt it," Colin said dismissively. "I doubt it very much. She just resents you spreading your wings, finding charms outside her tightly controlled little world. And she finds it easier to blame that on an outsider."

Rory nodded again. He was probably right. "Do *you* like her?" he said.

"I barely know her."

"No. I know. But from what you've seen?"

His father narrowed his eyes at him and took off his glasses. "I think," he began, rubbing the lenses of his glasses against the hem of his shirt, "that she is just what you need. Right now. But . . ."

"What?"

"But maybe not what you need for the rest of your life?"

"Why not?"

"Because she's a drama queen. And drama queens are difficult to live with. They don't want a quiet life. You'll be left gasping in her wake . . ."

Rory absorbed this pronouncement. There was something thrilling about the concept of gasping in someone's wake—it sounded better than being "set in aspic" or "pickled in grief" at least.

"What was Mum like, when you met her?"

Colin replaced his glasses, picked up his glass of wine and smiled. "Incredible," he said. "Joyful. Glamorous. She looked like a model, hair down to her waist. Always smiling. Hundreds of friends. Always dancing, turning somersaults, doing cartwheels, hair everywhere, laughing, vibrant. It was like going out with . . . with *summer*."

Rory had stopped breathing. His father's face was candescent. He'd never seen him look like that before.

"And then," Colin continued, "well, you know, babies, more babies—it takes the edge off a bit."

"She thinks she's still happy, you know?"

"I know."

"Even though Rhys is dead."

His father sighed. "I know."

"What are we going to do about it?"

Colin looked at him curiously. "I have no idea. How the hell do you help someone who insists on believing that she's happy?" He blew out his cheeks and sighed again. "To be honest, to be totally and *entirely* honest"—he paused, then looked Rory directly in the eye—"I've kind of given up."

He glanced away then, quickly, but not too fast for Rory to see the look of guilt and regret that passed across his face.

✑

Colin drove them both to the airport two months later. Lorelei had said she was far too busy to come. Rory hadn't even wanted to know why. She'd hugged him hard the last time he'd seen her and told him to have an incredible time, that she loved him, that she'd miss him, that she couldn't wait to hear all about his adventures. It had been a perfectly reasonable enactment of a mother-and-son farewell scenario. Any casual onlooker would have sighed and found it charming. But Rory had felt the distance in her body language, the need to be getting on with something else, to be elsewhere, otherwise occupied. *Hurry up*, said her body language, *hurry up and go*.

Kayleigh and Colin were sitting in the front of the car chatting about Andalusia, Kayleigh flicking through her *Rough Guide*, pointing things out to him. Her hair was short now, and white-blond. She looked like a beautiful little boy. From behind, it occurred to him in an uncomfortable wave of realization, she looked like Rhys.

He turned his gaze to the window and watched the countryside pass him by. It was high summer. The world was vivid green, with wide stripes of yellow where the rape fields grew. Everything was so familiar to him: the soft butterscotch of the Gloucestershire bricks, the evocative names of the villages, the peaty smell of the air, the solid feel of British tarmac beneath the tires of his father's car. It was all he'd ever known.

"Oh, by the way"—his father turned to address him—"don't forget to call on your mother's birthday, will you? And Beth's, too, if you can remember."

"Oh, God, yeah, when is that?"

"July the nineteenth. She'll be twenty-three."

"Poor Beth," Rory sighed, under his breath.

"What's that?" said Kayleigh, picking up on the tiny, rising bubble of family discord.

"Oh, nothing," he said. "Just feel sorry for her. Stuck at home on her own for her birthday. Seems a bit of a pitiful way to turn twenty-three, that's all."

"I'm going to be twenty-three next year," said Kayleigh,

"and I've been living away from home since I was sixteen. She needs to cut the apron strings. You know what I mean?"

"And remember to give us a phone number. So we can let you know when Meg's baby comes."

"I'm pretty sure there won't be a phone there," said Kayleigh. "I kind of think that's supposed to be the idea. You know, a retreat."

They were going to stay with a guy called Ken to whom Kayleigh had lost her virginity when she was seventeen and he was forty-nine. She'd met him at a festival in Limerick and stayed in touch with him. She referred to him, rather charmingly, as her "pen pal." He now lived in a kind of informal commune in Andalusia with three girlfriends, some goats, some donkeys and half a dozen children. He sounded both hideous and mesmerizing in equal measure. But he was giving them free board and lodgings in return for some light farming, building, decorating and child care, and given that Rory had exactly £200 to last him the month, it was an offer he couldn't reasonably refuse.

"Are you still in love with him?" he'd asked.

Kayleigh had thrown him a withering look and said, *"Are you mad, Rory Bird? You think I would take you across the world with me to stay with a man I'm in love with? What kind of a person do you think I am? I may be a lot of things, but a polygamist is not one of them."* Which was kind of reassuring to hear.

"Well, then," said Colin, "be sure to get to a phone if you can around about the due date. Meg will be livid if you don't get in touch somehow."

"Leave it with me, Colin," said Kayleigh, gently touching his arm. "I'll make sure your son does all the right things. I promise you that."

Colin turned and smiled at her and said, "Good girl."

Rory still saw ghostly little Rhyses everywhere. He could barely remember Rhys as a teenager, but he vividly remembered him at nine, freewheeling down this hill on his BMX. He remembered Rhys at six trying to keep up with him as they chased through those woods together looking for the wild pigs that someone at school had said they'd seen there. He saw Rhys sitting on the steps with him outside the chemist on the High Street with his chin on his hands, waiting for Mum and the girls to come out with bags of things that were of no interest to either of them. And he remembered Rhys sitting there, in the boot of the hatchback where he always wanted to sit, facing backwards, his legs stretched out and the dog in his lap.

And now Rory was going somewhere that Rhys had never been. He wondered if the ghosts would follow him there. And if they didn't, he wondered if he would miss them.

4

APRIL 2011

Rhys's room was just as it always had been.

The sheer volume of empty space before her almost took Meg's breath away.

"My God," she muttered, "she kept it. She kept it as it was."

"That's freaky," said Molly. "Totally."

"It really is. I mean, how could she have controlled her impulses? It's like, I don't know, if she could stop herself hoarding in this room, why couldn't she stop herself doing it in the others? If she could control part of herself, then why not the rest?"

The ancient floorboards creaked and complained beneath their feet. Rhys's bed sat stripped bare in the far corner; his wardrobe was empty, his desk piled with just a few objects: an encyclopedia, a pot of pens, some folders, deodorant in a rusting nineties-designed aerosol can. There was his stereo, a huge thing, designed for CDs and records, that had never heard of MP3s or iTunes. And posters on the walls. Dozens of them. Pearl Jam. Nirvana. NWA. Alice in Chains. Courtney Love.

"It's, like, a museum of the nineties," said Molly.

Meg nodded and smiled. It was. Untouched, just clothes and bedding taken out. Everything else as it had been that day, when she'd put down that tray of food and kicked down the door. She ran her hand around the inside of the door and felt it there, the lock still hanging off the door by uprooted nails.

"And is that where he, you know, did it?" Molly nodded towards the buttress beams in the high ceiling.

"Yeah," said Meg.

"With rope?"

"Yes. A very long piece of rope."

"Where'd he get it?"

"What?"

"The rope. Where did he get a very long piece of rope?"

"Christ. I don't know."

"What, like, the village rope shop or something?"

Meg threw her daughter a look of only half-formed outrage.

"And how did he get it up there?" She nodded again at the beams.

"It was there," said Meg, the image coming to her, clear as the present moment. She pointed to a lower section of the beam. "He stood on a chair. That chair."

Molly paced across the room, her arms outstretched. She put a hand on the chair and said, "Same age as me. Nearly." She let her hand fall from the chair and turned to her mother. "Isn't that crazy? He was the same age as me. I mean, what was he like? Would I have liked him?"

Meg smiled sadly. "No," she said. "You wouldn't have liked him. You would have called him sad and a loser, and you'd have stood and stared at him pityingly every time he walked past you at school. Assuming you'd even noticed his existence in the first place, that is."

Molly looked affronted for a moment and then her face softened. "That's really tragic."

"I know. He was really tragic. *It* was. I remember when Alfie started secondary school, God, I was terrified for him."

"What about me?"

"You? Well, I knew you'd be fine. Alpha female that you are. That you have *always* been. But Alfie reminds me sometimes of Rhys. So quiet, you know, so few friends. And that was when it all went wrong for Rhys, the day he started at the big school. That was the beginning of the end . . ."

"But Alfie was fine."

"Yes, Alfie was fine." Meg smiled. "Is fine."

"Best boy out there." Molly blushed.

Meg gazed at her in surprise. "Really? You think that?"

"Well. Yeah. Alfie rocks. He's brilliant."

Meg's stomach rolled pleasantly. "Good," she said. "I like that very much."

She absorbed the wonder of Molly's pronouncement, took it as a compliment on her parenting, on her mothering, as a certificate of excellence. But then she felt her pride fade away at the thought that if Rhys had had a big sister like Molly, maybe he would have thought he was worth more than sixteen years of life.

Her phone rang again and she sighed. It was Unknown again. It might be her. But then again, it might be any number of people who needed to talk to her in the wake of the death of the county's worst hoarder. She inhaled. "Hello."

"Meg, please, it's me. Please don't hang up."

Meg waited just one beat, listened to the sound of her sister's urgent, panicked breath down the line, and then she ended the call.

MARCH 1997

Beth collapsed into the sofa and caught her breath.

"You're a natural," said Meg, scooping wooden blocks back into a drawstring bag.

"I'm absolutely *not*," she replied. "I have no idea how you do it. And in your condition." She pointed at the enormous bump straining the fabric of Meg's T-shirt.

"Well," said Meg, pulling herself with some effort to a standing position and throwing the bag of bricks into a plastic crate, "it's not as if I have a lot of choice."

"Sit down, for God's sake," urged Beth, patting the cushion next to her.

"Not quite yet, I'm afraid. I've got a wash to hang out. And a shirt to iron. And *then* I can sit down. Here—" She threw Beth the remote control. "Enjoy."

Beth watched Meg leave the room. From behind you could not see her bump. She was all out the front. But it was obvious from the ducklike roll of her gait that she was heavily, urgently pregnant. Her second baby had been due four days ago. Beth had come down to help out with Molly while Meg was having the baby. But the baby was still not here and now Beth was rather concerned that she was not going to make it home for Easter. Rory and Kayleigh were still living in Spain. Their one-month holiday had extended itself into several months and they'd been living on a hippy commune with this guy called Ken for nearly two years now. Having made it home for Easter last year with baby Molly in tow, Meg and Bill were once more out of commission due to reasons of imminent confinement, and Dad was going to be away on business. Again. So it all came down to Beth. She'd promised her mum that she'd be there. And she had no intention of letting her down. *Good old Beth.*

She heard the key turn in the lock and stiffened slightly. She touched her hair and cleared her throat. Then she rearranged her legs, crossed them, then uncrossed them again.

"Hi," she said as Bill walked into the room, all thick, shaggy hair, trendy trainers and soft, smiling, careworn face.

"Hi, there, Beth," he said, dropping a flight bag onto the dining table and flicking through a pile of letters. "Where's Meg?"

"She's hanging up wash. And ironing a shirt."

Bill grimaced. "She's a lunatic," he said. "What the fuck is she doing ironing shirts in her condition?"

"You know Meg. Never could sit still."

"Well, yes," he said absentmindedly, sliding his finger under the flap of an envelope, "but sometimes you really do just have to." He looked up and glanced around. "Molly gone to bed?"

Beth nodded.

"Oh." He sounded disappointed. "Must be later than I thought. Might just go in and have a look at her."

"No, you won't!" they heard Meg call through from the kitchen. "You'll wake her up!"

He smiled indulgently. "No," he called back, "I won't wake her up, darling. I promise you."

"Well," Meg called back, "if you wake her up, then you have to get her back to sleep."

"Deal," said Bill, throwing Beth a conspiratorial smile that turned her stomach to milk. Then he put down the letters and headed back into the hallway.

Beth let herself relax. It was terrible. Truly, truly terrible. This crush on Meg's partner. It had come from nowhere. From out of the blue. For two years he had been just "Bill."

Just this nice bloke who lived with her sister. Just this amiable, fluffy-haired guy with an easy smile and twinkling eyes. She was sure the change had come from him. She was sure he'd started it. She hadn't even packed any pretty clothes to come down to stay. If she'd already suspected she had feelings, however subliminal, for him, she'd have packed something nice to wear. Pretty pajamas. That kind of thing. But she hadn't. So clearly *this*, whatever *this* was, had not been started by her. No. It was him. It was the way he looked at her, this complicity that had developed between the two of them. He and Beth against Meg. Sort of. Vaguely. I mean, it was clear to Beth, *blindingly* clear, that Bill adored Meg. He adored Meg and he adored Molly and he adored his flat and his family and his life. But still, there was something there when he looked at her. Something that had definitely not been there before. And, Beth was pretty certain, that thing was sex.

∾

Meg went into labor very early the following morning. Meg and Bill left Beth at home with a still-sleeping Molly and instructions for how to get her to her childminder at nine a.m. It was the first time Beth had been alone in their flat. She sat at the breakfast bar in her ugly pajamas and sipped at a cup of tea and stared at the clock on the kitchen wall as it ticked over from 6:32 to 6:33. It was so quiet. She thought about phoning home, to let her mother know what was going on, but then she envisaged her mother's slightly panicky journey from deepest sleep to the phone that sat on the landing and she knew, anyway, that her mother would have only the most passing interest in something that might not, in theory, happen for another two or more days and would probably be a bit cross about being woken up. So she decided to wait until nine o'clock or until there was some news, whichever came first.

In the meantime, she stared around the silent kitchen, taking in the details she hadn't picked up on before, when the place was full of Meg and Bill and Molly and all their loud distractions. It was built into the corner of a large living room from shiny white units with brushed steel handles. There was not a fingerprint or a splash of dirt on anything. A small collage of neatly arranged family photographs hung on the wall in a white frame; a glass vase of yellow gerbera daisies sat on the immaculate windowsill; knives, forks and spoons all sat in soldierlike rows in the cutlery drawer; and there were exactly eight white plates, eight white bowls, eight white side plates, eight white egg cups and one salt-and-pepper cellar. Even in a state of labor, Megan had left the house pristine: fluffed cushions, tidied toys, remote controls neatly arranged in a row on the clutter-free coffee table, clean shoes set in straight pairs in the hallway, a wash hung to dry on a plastic dryer, coats hung in size order from pegs on the wall, not a speck of dust anywhere, not even on picture rails, not even on lightbulbs.

Like a show home.

Lorelei would hate it.

Beth sighed and carefully, almost reverently, placed her teacup in the showroom-shiny dishwasher. Then she tiptoed to the door of Molly's little room and peered in. It was as immaculate as the rest of Meg's flat. The only thing in the room that lacked order was Molly herself, buried within her little duvet, which she had gathered around herself in twisted clumps. Her reddish-brown hair was tangled over her face and across her mouth and one of her plump arms was dangled through the bars of her cot, her fat fingers trailing against the unstained cream carpet. Beth felt overwhelmed for a moment with love for her niece and her insistence on subverting the lines of Meg's strictly ordered world. *Good girl,* she thought, *good girl.*

Not that Beth blamed Meg in the slightest for being the way she was. How could she be otherwise, given how much she'd always railed against her mother's ways? But a little bit of give, a little bit of flexibility, wouldn't have gone amiss. She saw it in Bill's glances sometimes, little twitches of his eyebrows, little half-formed smiles or grimaces. Bill hadn't signed up for this. He hadn't signed up for not being able to kick off his trainers and drop the remote control absentmindedly down the side of the sofa. He hadn't signed up for there being a right way and a wrong way to hang up a tea towel or open a carton of orange juice. He hadn't signed up for tiny aggressive handheld vacuum cleaners that sucked away crumbs before he'd even noticed them, and newspapers being folded away and disposed of before he'd even read them, and half-eaten packets of cookies being thrown away because a new packet had been purchased. He really, really hadn't. But he was a good sport. He didn't like it, but he put up with it. Because Meg was Meg and he loved her.

She tiptoed away from Molly's room and then peered into the tiny little box room that had once been an office and now housed a shelving unit full of carefully arranged baby accoutrements: a pile of tiny nappies, already out of their packets and stacked just so; a pile of ice-white muslin squares and nipple pads and Babygros and soft animals and jars of cream and fluffy towels. They didn't know what they were having, a strangely laissez-faire attitude, mainly down to Bill, who would clearly appreciate a few more surprises in his life. Everyone thought it would be a boy. Just because everyone always thought it would be a boy. But Beth thought it would be another girl. She could see it in the extra bloom on Meg's skin.

The clock ticked round to 6:37. Beth decided to take a very quick shower. The only shower in the flat was in the en suite to Meg and Bill's room so she hadn't used it before. She took the soft blue towel that had been left folded just so for her at the foot of the little put-you-up bed in the box room, and she checked once more on Molly, and then she walked through Meg and Bill's bedroom—bed made, slippers in pairs, coordinated cushions—and into their shower room. She showered fast, mainly because she didn't want Molly to wake up and find herself alone, but also because she felt she shouldn't be in here, in their little sanctuary, in the place where Bill and Megan took their clothes off, in the place where they brushed their teeth together every night and had private conversations and made plans for their future. She didn't use any of their products for fear of messing anything up, and after her shower she sprayed the inside of the cubicle with the spray that had been left for that purpose, and she cleared all the glass walls with the window scraper, and then she wrapped her blue towel about herself and dashed back to the little box room, where she dressed and put on a tiny bit of makeup.

It was now almost seven a.m. She wondered if they were at the hospital yet. She wondered what they were doing. She wondered how this day was going to pan out. She wondered how the next few days would pan out. The baby would be in a Moses basket in their room at first and Meg had said she could stay in the box room as long as she liked. In fact she'd said, *"Please stay, please, I need you!"*

But there was Easter to think about, and Mum. There was also the lack of space in this tiny flat and the stress of living with a newborn, and more than any of that there was this *thing* between herself and Bill. If the baby came home tomorrow, she could stay another twenty-four hours and then still be home in time for Easter lunch. Beth knew on a fundamental level that her sister needed her more than her mother did. She knew that Easter lunch was not as important, in the scheme of things, as spending time with her new niece or nephew, but the sheer, ground-in pull of it, of her mother's emotional neediness, was virtually impossible for her to ignore.

"Mama?" said a small voice in the hall outside her room. "Mama?"

"Hello, sweetie." She quickly got to her feet and went to Molly.

"Where Mama?"

She looked disheveled, almost Neanderthal. Her hair was a puffball of knotted curls and her cheeks were blotchy with sleep.

"How did you get out of your cot, sweetie?"

"Mama?"

"Mama's gone to have the baby. To the hospital. With Daddy."

"Mama have a baby?" she asked thoughtfully.

"Yes. At the hospital."

"Beth make a toast?"

"Yes!" Beth breathed a sigh of relief that the news had not been met with tears or anxiety. "Beth make a toast. Come on, sweetie." She took her niece's small hand in hers and led her to the kitchen, where she sat her in her high chair. Molly looked just like Meg, just like her, just like Dad and Auntie Lorna. She had the Bird face. It still took Beth by surprise that this child existed. It felt like only a few minutes ago that they had all been children themselves. And in fact, in most respects, Beth still was. She still lived at home, she still slept in a single bed, she still used the same face flannel and stared at the same face in the same mirror in the same bathroom. She still had breakfast with her mum and dad every morning and drove her dad's car and ate food bought and prepared by her parents. She was, to all intents and purposes, seventeen years old. Except she wasn't. She was twenty-four. A twenty-four-year-old woman. In July she would be twenty-five.

She had no idea why she was still at home. She had a boyfriend. They'd been together for four years. His name was Simon and he was doing a masters in combined science in York. She only saw him every fortnight or so and even then he was too distracted and stressed to contemplate having conversations about their future. Not that she wanted to have conversations about their future. She didn't know what she wanted yet. She didn't have a clue. She'd done a secretarial course just under six years ago. She could type a letter in a minute and a half and take down a garbled conversation in shorthand and program a word processor to print addresses onto envelopes. She was working for a local building company as PA to the managing director. Her boss said she was the best secretary he'd ever had and had given her three pay raises already. She was great looking (other people told her that all the time, complete strangers sometimes), she was young, she was hardworking and bright and conscientious and yet . . .

She gazed again upon her niece, chasing a slippery piece of banana around the tray of her high chair with one chubby finger. The child that her sister and her partner had made together; that her sister had grown in her body, in her womb, had pushed out and fed and nurtured and got to the age of nearly two without any harm coming to her, whilst simultaneously washing lots of clothes and plumping lots of cushions and buying lots of fresh fruit and working part-time in a school and making a whole other baby. She couldn't, she just couldn't, imagine any of it. How did a human make all those decisions? All the big ones, and all the little ones? How would you know you were doing it right? How could you trust yourself? Beth did not trust herself in the slightest. She felt much safer bobbing about in the same patterns and the same places with the same people.

She thought back to the year Rhys had died. She remembered sitting in a weird wine bar near Covent Garden with Megan, before Meg had met Bill, when she was eighteen and Meg was twenty and they were both still vaguely on a par with each other. And she remembered Meg suggesting that she could come and live in London with her. Come and share her bedroom. She'd been half-tempted. It had seemed a soft entry into the world of grown-up-ness. Her sister there by her side to hold her hand. But then Rhys had done what Rhys had done and how could she? How could she have left them all there? And so she had stayed. And stayed. And stayed. And the only mistake she was currently in danger of making, she realized, was the mistake of leaving it all far too late.

⟨◇⟩

Meg was at a hospital called the Whittington in Highgate. It was big and Victorian and scary looking and it was hard to believe that something as wholesome and cheerful as the arrival of newborn babies was happening within its moldering walls.

Beth was directed to a laboring room (which put her in mind of a room full of men in dungarees with pitchforks and chisels and sweaty backs), where she found Meg and Bill flicking through magazines and eating tortilla chips.

"Was she all right?" asked Meg, the minute Beth walked into the room.

"Absolutely fine. Honestly. She is one cool customer. She didn't even say good-bye."

"Oh, thank God," said Meg, holding her hand against her chest. "That's the first time anyone apart from me or Bill has ever dropped her off—I thought she might freak out a bit."

"No, she's been a little angel. Ate all her breakfast, let me change her nappy, wasn't *too* keen on getting into her pram but we managed it in the end." Beth beamed. She was feeling strangely powerful. She had not only cared for her niece single-handedly, she had also successfully navigated the streets of a frankly rather terrifying inner London neighborhood with a child in a pram and then found her way, using public transport, to the hospital.

"How are you?" she asked, her eyes directed at Meg's stomach.

"Well, apparently I'm only five centimeters dilated and my contractions have slowed right down, so looks like we might be here for the long haul."

"The childminder lady . . ."

"Danielle?"

"Yes, that one, she said Molly can stay extra hours. She said she can keep her until six if you like?"

Meg smiled. "Oh," she said happily, "that's great. I love that woman. Have you told Mum?"

Beth gasped. "Oh, God," she said, "I'm really sorry! I completely forgot. I was going to do it earlier, but I didn't want to wake her, and then Molly woke up and it was all so busy just getting her ready and everything and—"

Meg rolled her eyes and sighed. "My family is unbelievable," she said. "Completely."

"There's pay phones round the corner. I'll go and call her now."

Bill counted some coins out of the pocket of his jeans and gave Beth a complicitous smile that made her catch her breath.

But there was no reply at home and Beth went back to Meg's room.

"You know," said Meg, "in other families, in *normal* families, the mother would have been here right now, holding my hand, helping out. And please, God, don't think I'm not grateful to you, because I really, really am, but you shouldn't have to be doing this. You have your own life to live. My mother should be here. And if she can't be here she should be on the phone every hour asking for news. You know, she has not called me *once* since my due date, not once, since *argh, Jesus, argh!*" She clutched the sides of the bed and sat up rigidly, her teeth clenched together and her eyes screwed shut. Bill jumped to his feet and took her hand. "Another one?" he asked.

"*Argh!*" replied Meg. "Jesus *Christ!*"

Beth stared at her older sister through wide circles of eyes. She'd never seen another human being make that face before, or the noise that came with it. It was *horrible*.

"Shall I call the nurse?" she asked, edging towards the door.

Meg relaxed the rictus mask of her face and said, "No, don't be daft. It's just a contraction. I'll be fine."

A contraction, thought Beth, *what is a contraction?* It was a word that meant nothing to her beyond a vague association with the mechanics of childbirth.

"What does it feel like?" she asked.

"It feels," began Meg, "like a gigantic metal fist squeezing and twisting and pulling all your internal organs until you think you're about to pass out. It is the most revolting feeling imaginable. And you know, as much as I think our mother is completely and utterly useless in almost every respect, I will always have the greatest admiration for the fact that when she had the twins she had to do this twice. In the *same day.*"

Beth smiled. Meg had said the same thing last time, after

Molly was born, and had been terrified during both pregnancies that the sonographer was going to point out two babies on the screen.

"Coming up for six years," she said, her thoughts turning to Rhys. "I can't quite believe it."

Meg nodded. "Twenty-two," she sighed. "I wonder what he'd be doing now . . ."

"Rhys?" asked Bill, looking over the top of his magazine. They nodded.

"Poor soul," he said.

"Has Mum been to his grave lately?" asked Meg.

Beth bit her lip and shook her head.

"You?"

She shrugged. She kept meaning to. "Not really."

"Not really? I mean, you either have, or you haven't."

"Well, in which case, no, I haven't."

"Oh, God, Beth—"

"I know," she interjected defensively. "It's just, it's so scary there. I don't like going on my own. I always feel like I'm going to get raped or something."

"Can't you go with Dad?"

"I suppose. It's just, he's hardly ever around. And when he is he's just kind of . . . *busy.*"

"Busy doing *what?*"

"Oh, God, I don't know, just doing stuff. Writing his memoirs, apparently, though I've never seen anything he's written. And catching up on correspondence. Anything to keep him away from Mum and Vicky." She sighed. She hated talking about home. It made it sound all wrong, whereas, when she was there, living there, just getting on with her life, it all felt perfectly reasonable.

But Beth was spared the trouble of taking this conversation

to its uncomfortable extrapolation by the onset of another contraction and the sight of her big sister throwing herself back against the pillows and screaming, "*Jesus* fucking Christ-ing bollocks, let me die."

◇

Meg was still having irregular contractions by the time Beth had to leave the hospital to collect Molly from the childminder. There was talk of doing something to get them coming more frequently, to *move labor along*. But it seemed to Beth that the baby was not coming any time soon and that she would be required to stay overnight with Molly and repeat all of today's processes over again tomorrow. Which was fine.

She had finally got through to Lorelei at about midday, who had said, "Oh, how marvelous, tell her I'll be keeping my fingers crossed for her all day. And Vicky will too, won't you, Vee?"

She'd heard Vicky chirrup something affirmative in the background and made a mental note not to share Vicky's best wishes with her sister. "Well, I'd better be off, darling," her mother had said a moment later. "Time to collect Sophie from nursery. And then we're taking her to get new shoes. Let me know the minute there's any news, though, won't you, darling? And big hugs to Meggy and Bill."

It had been as if she'd called to tell her that Meg's car was in for an MOT or that her cat was having an operation, but she'd dismissed the thought before it grew roots. It was just her mother's way. Lorelei filled her head with the things closest to her, the here and now, not the over there and then. It was how she was. It didn't mean she was a bad person. But still, Beth had waited a count of five or so minutes before returning to Meg's bedside, where she'd slapped a joyful smile on her face and said nothing about new shoes for Sophie.

She took Molly to a playground on the way home. An old lady admired the little girl and said, "She looks just like you." And Beth smiled and said, "She's not mine, actually. She's my niece. I'm just looking after her, while my sister's in hospital having the second baby."

The old lady smiled back and said, "You'll have your own one day then?"

And Beth's smile stretched out uncomfortably and she said, "Yes, I'm sure I will. Yes. I'm one of four, so you know . . ."

"Yes. When you come from a big family, you want it for yourself, don't you? But you shouldn't wait too long, not if you want your children to be close to their cousins."

She said this sternly, with a hint of insight, as if she *knew*. As if she'd looked at Beth and seen inside her soul, seen a clear line to her future. But then her smile softened and she said, "But you're still young. No rush really, is there, dear?"

Beth laughed nervously, politely. "No," she said, "no rush at all." But she knew that there was. And it had nothing to do with babies. Before she could even begin to think about babies she first had to find her way to the starting blocks of life.

She was reading *Bridget Jones's Diary*. She'd found it on her sister's alphabetically ordered bookshelves. It had been published the year before and everyone had been talking about it and telling her she should read it, but Beth didn't really read. Usually she watched TV with her mum until she was so tired she could barely speak and then she flopped into bed. But Molly was finally asleep in her cot after a long and rather disordered evening, and there was no one to watch TV with. Hence the book. It was quite funny, although she found it hard to relate to all the talk of weight gain (she never gained weight) and drinking (she never drank) and mad, mouthy girlfriends (she had no mad, mouthy girlfriends). But she was enjoying the bits about the heroine's crush on an unsuitable older man.

Although, no, she would not call what she was experiencing a *crush*, no, it was not a crush, it was a . . . *frisson*. Just a sort of electrical thing, invisible to the naked eye, like a trip wire. It was in the way he looked at her when there was no reason to be looking at her. The way he grasped her by the waist when he hugged her hello and good-bye. And she still hadn't decided whether she was flattered or appalled.

She was going to turn down the corner of the page and then realized that bent corners were probably on Meg's long list of Minor Domestic Misdemeanors, so she inserted a hair clip instead and was about to turn off the bedside lamp when she heard a sound that made her heart beat violently. It was the front door. She heard it first open, and then click shut, very gently. She held her breath and put a hand over her racing heart. She envisaged gangsters, she envisaged knives and guns. She envisaged being gang-raped and brutally murdered. She envisaged all the things that she never worried about when she was at home in the Cotswolds. She did not belong here, in the city. It was not the place for her. She wanted to go home, home to the country, to her safe cozy room in her parents' safe cozy house. Why did Meg live here? Why had she had children here, in this terrible place? She glanced around the room, looking for something heavy, or sharp, or both. But all she could see was nappies and plush bears. She gulped back a strangled cry and was about to start whimpering when she heard a man clear his throat outside her bedroom door.

Bill.

She breathed out and smiled.

She opened her door and peered out into the hallway. Bill was unzipping his jacket. He turned at the sound of her and his face softened and he said, "Hi, sorry, did I wake you?"

She said, "No, not at all. I was awake. I thought you were burglars."

"Burglars, plural?"

"Yes, a whole gang of them."

He smiled. "Sorry. I'm clearly not as light footed as I thought I was."

"So," she said, "any news?"

"Well, if you call a nine-pound-nine-ounce baby boy with bright red hair 'news,' then yes, we have news."

Beth squealed and then covered her mouth with her hands. Then, unable to find a less noisy alternative, she skipped across the hallway and threw herself into Bill's embrace. "Oh, wow," she whispered loudly into his ear, "wow. *Congratulations!* A boy. Amazing."

He didn't caress her waist this time. He didn't hold on to her for that split second longer than necessary. There was nothing within their embrace beyond mutual delight. He had, of course, just watched his beloved wife push an enormous baby out of herself.

"Come and have a drink with me," he said, glancing towards the living room.

She nodded and smiled and followed him through. She sat cross-legged on the sofa while Bill found something in the fridge for them to drink.

"Is she okay? Are they both okay?"

He smiled and said, "They are both absolutely fine. Once the contractions started to regulate it all happened really quickly. Bam bam bam, he virtually popped out like a champagne cork. Talking of which"—he waved a green bottle at her—"this has been sitting in the fridge waiting for a special occasion since Molly was born. What do you think?"

Her instinct was to say no. She was virtually teetotal. It would go straight to her head and then she'd have to go to bed and it would be completely wasted on her. But on the other hand . . . a boy. Safely delivered. It would be churlish not to.

"I think that's a lovely idea. Just a glass, though. Maybe we can save the rest for Meg tomorrow?"

"Good thinking," said Bill. "I should probably take it easy too. Big day tomorrow."

"When is she allowed home?"

"First thing, I reckon. We were waiting for the pediatrician, but she never came. So I decided I'd come back and get some decent kip before the onslaught begins. Again . . ." He smiled wryly.

"Easier second time round, though? You know what you're doing."

He raised an eyebrow at her sardonically. "You reckon?"

He brought the bottle and two glasses over and sat down next to her on the sofa.

"I called your mum, told her the news."

"Oh," said Beth, "good. Was she suitably thrilled?"

He shrugged. "She was reasonably delighted, I suppose. Said something about some three-packs of Babygros she'd seen last week and how she'd bought them in pink *and* in blue just in case and how she'll hold on to the pink ones just in case, and maybe get some more and blah, blah, blah. Though she did perk up a bit when I told her what we were calling him."

"So what's my nephew going to be called?"

"Alfie," replied Bill. "Or Alfred Rhys Liddington Bird, if we're being more formal."

"Oh," said Beth softly. "That's lovely. Mum must have been thrilled. And Dad. *Alfred Rhys . . .*" She tasted the name on her tongue. For a moment she felt envious that Meg had got in there first, had the baby boy to replace the one they'd lost, got to give him that name, got to make everyone smile and feel better for a moment. She smiled sadly. "It's a gorgeous name," she said. "Really gorgeous. And where did the red hair come from?"

"Well," said Bill, putting his hand up, "that'll be my lot. I'm the only one without red hair in my family. Seriously. When I was growing up I felt like the Steve Martin character in that film—what's it called?—where he's the only white kid in the family. *The Jerk*. Yeah. My mum's auburn, my dad's carrot and my brothers are both flame red. So"—he shrugged—"there was always a danger this might happen."

"I love red hair," said Beth. "I can't wait to see him."

He passed her a glass of champagne and picked up another one for himself. "To Alfie—" he started.

"And to Megan," Beth finished.

"Absolutely!" he said, blowing out his cheeks in a suggestion of awe at Meg's recent exertions. "To remarkable Megan."

"And to you," said Beth, for reasons she could not quite explain.

"Ha, not sure what I've done to deserve a toast."

"Well, you know, it's what you did nine months ago . . ."

He laughed out loud and raised his glass and said, "Oh, well, yes, of course. To my amazing ability to impregnate fertile women. Cheers!"

Beth laughed too. She felt both embarrassed and delighted.

"And to you, a big thank-you for today, for taking care of Moll, holding the fort and keeping the place up to your sister's unfeasibly high standards."

"Oh, God, don't," said Beth. "It's been hell. Every time

Molly touches something or moves something I'm in a total state of terror in case I put it back in the wrong place or the wrong way up. I have to keep making mental notes of where things go."

He laughed again. "Oh, yes, that all sounds very familiar. Although she'll probably cut you some slack, what with you being her sister and all."

"I've definitely inherited more of Mum's approach to housekeeping."

"Ah," said Bill, "you're a bit of a hoarder, too, are you?"

"Well, no, no. Not in that way. I don't really buy much stuff. Or collect things, like my mum does. But then again, I don't really throw stuff out either. I don't organize stuff. It's all just in a jumble. Nothing matches. I mean, you can probably tell from the way I dress that I'm not really that fussed about . . . well, you know, being just so."

"I love the way you dress," said Bill, a little too fast.

"Oh," said Beth, "thank you."

"Yes, you always look very feminine."

"Oh," she said again, "I never really thought . . . I mean, I just kind of throw stuff together really, stuff I like. It's . . ."

"Organic," he finished for her.

"I suppose." She found herself mentally picturing Megan then, in one of her impeccably put-together outfits, usually trousers to cover her heavy knees, black and gray and white and cream, slightly masculine tailoring for her job at the school, softer for at home, jeans and T-shirts that flattered her athletic top half, her small breasts and narrow waist. The T-shirts always looked brand-new, mainly because she ironed them (Beth had joyfully shared this tidbit with her mother when she'd returned from her first visit to Meg's flat, just before Molly was born. *"She irons T-shirts! And knickers! No, I'm not joking. She irons everything!"*), and her jeans were always sparkling indigo without a hint of a worn patch or frayed edge. Meg always looked shower-fresh, salon-fresh, boutique-fresh, she always smelled of soap (because she was always washing her hands) and the expensive perfume she bought for herself from Space NK. Her fingernails were always snipped and scrubbed, her trainers always clean and fragrant. She was the kind of statuesque, immaculate, capable woman who without even opening her mouth managed to intimidate every other woman in her vicinity. Beth had been in her shadow all her life. She enjoyed being in her shadow. She'd never wanted the spotlight. It didn't suit her. Beth let Meg and her mother do all the loud, look-at-me grandstanding, while she and her dad quietly got on with things without making any fuss. It was the way it worked. It was fine.

But Beth could feel a strange subtle shift inside herself, like the imperceptible movement of tectonic plates. Just a millimeter here and there. Just enough to open her mind to the possibility of more. More life, more love, more attention.

She smiled at Bill. "I mean," she continued, slightly ingen-uously, "I just don't think about clothes too much. You know. It's not a priority for me. As long as it's relatively clean and not completely out of fashion I don't really care where it came from and whether it, you know, whether it *matches my T-shirt*."

"I know," said Bill, just as she'd known he would, "and that's something I really, really like about you. You're just so very . . . *natural*."

⟡

Bethan got back to the Bird House at midday on Easter Sunday. She had two whole rolls of film in her bag that she would take to Boots on Tuesday to have developed, full of photos of

Molly and Megan and Bill and gorgeous fat Alfie with his thick shock of red hair and his air of vague surprise.

Bill had brought Meg and Alfie home from the hospital the morning after she and Bill had drank champagne together. Meg had looked shell-shocked and jubilant with her huge new baby at her breast and her stomach a punctured barrage balloon beneath her striped Lycra tunic top. Molly had been wide-eyed and horrified, but then lost interest very quickly and insisted on Beth taking her for a round of mini croquet in the back garden. And then they had settled down into a lovely unit of four. Two parents, two children, everything fresh and new and exciting. Beth had quickly felt surplus to requirements and booked her train ticket home with a sense of relief. At Meg's insistence Bill had taken her to the train station, and their conversation had been gentle and bland. Apart from a splinter of a moment just as she was getting out of the car, when he'd said, *"We'll miss you."* She'd said, *"No you won't, you've got each other."* And he'd said, *"Well, yes, but it's always nice having you around."* And it had been somewhere between avuncular and pensive with a delicate lace of flirtation around the edges. She'd ignored it and gone, marched into the train station without looking backwards. But the thought of it had rested in her consciousness like a warm, seductive hand the whole way back to the village.

Vicky was in the garden with the girls. She was blowing bubbles for them from a plastic bottle and they were chasing them around with their arms in the air. She kept their hair short; Bethan had never found out why. They wore cords and stripy jumpers and blue Wellington boots and looked like two small boys. Vicky herself was dressed in one of her stretchy dresses in a bold tribal print that she bought from a catalog that seemed to sell nothing but clothes in bold tribal prints for extroverted ladies who were a bit overweight and shouldn't really wear bold tribal prints but didn't care and wore them anyway. Her thick blond hair was cut into a harsh jaw-length bob and was starting to look faded and gray in the brash midday sun. Her breasts were swinging from side to side as she ran girlishly around in circles with her bottle of bubbles. She beamed at the sight of Bethan and said, "Hurrah! You're home!"

She greeted Beth with one of her pungently perfumed embraces and said, "Girls! Girls! Look who's here. Beth's home."

The girls waved shyly at Beth. Maddy showed her her stash of pastel-colored chocolate eggs and Beth noticed that she had a preponderance of pink. "Do you like pink, Maddy?" she asked.

And Maddy nodded and said, "Pink is my favorite color."

"Yes," said Sophie, "and pink is not my favorite color. My favorite color is *blue*."

"Oh, yes," said Beth, peering into Sophie's basket, "so it is. Well, that works out very nicely then, doesn't it?" She smiled tightly and felt herself swimming through a sudden wave of sickening emotion. She remembered herself at Maddy's age, full of unquestioning love for her family, for the world around her, for pink eggs and pink raincoats and pink icing. She remembered how she had adored her big sister, envied the curl in her hair and her strong physique and her authoritative position within the family, closer in age to Bethan but almost on a par with her mother and father. She closed her eyes against the wave and found herself outside Rhys's bedroom, six years ago today, Easter Sunday. She saw her father trying to locate the volume button on Rhys's stereo, pulling at his thin hair with his hands, saying, *"How the fuck do you turn this thing off?"* The first time Beth had ever heard her father use bad language. And then the silence when he finally turned it off and the unearthly creak of the rope swinging against the beams, her mother standing on her tiptoes on a chair, frantically pulling at the knot in the rope with her long, sinewy fingers, Megan trying to help by pushing against his bare feet from below. She remembered her own fingers twisted around the door frame, holding on to it to stop herself from falling. And Vicky, behind her, this stranger with her musty aroma and her sour-wine breath and her meaty arms and her kind words, saying, *"Come away, come away with me, lovely. Let's go."* And turning to look at this woman whom she had only just met for the first time today and saying, *"Okay, thank you."* And turning just one time to see all three of them, Mum, Dad and Meg, finally bring the tiny body down and onto the floor, where it landed with a soft thud, and there was Rory, bounding up the stairs behind them shouting, *"What? What? What's happening?"* And Vicky saying, *"Come with us, sweetheart, come with us."* Which of course he didn't, and the last thing that Beth remembered as she started down the stairs with Vicky's arm heavy upon her shoulder was the sound of Rory seeing his brother dead on his bedroom floor, the excruciated roar of indignation and fury, of impotent incomprehension.

She put her hand against Sophie's soft urchin cut and stroked it. "Lucky you two," she said, in a voice fissured with repressed tears. "Having each other. Having it all to look forward to. Lucky girls." She turned to Vicky and smiled tightly at her. "Where's Mum?" she said. She hoped for one foolish split second that Vicky would say, *"She's gone to see Rhys."*

But she didn't. Of course.

She said, "She's gone to get more carrots. She said there weren't enough." She rolled her eyes then, affectionately. "She should be back any minute."

"And where's Dad?"

"Oh, he and Tim have gone down to the pub, for the usual pre-lunch pint or two. I suspect they'll be back in a minute, too."

Beth looked at her curiously. There was a brittleness to her voice. A narrowness to her eyes. Her usual solid demeanor seemed shaky. It was almost, Beth mused, as though she was lying.

But the possibility didn't linger long. Why would she be lying? And what would she be lying about? A second later Vicky rallied and said, "Wonderful news about the baby. So exciting."

And there followed a fairly high-pitched exchange about the red hair and the size of him, the shock of his being a boy, the joy of his being given the name Rhys and the possibility of sibling rivalry; and then Mum came home and then Tim and Dad came home and before too long, the lamb was on the table, the carrots were buttered, the red wine was uncorked and it was Easter.

Again.

Beth toyed with the idea of raising her glass, of proposing a toast to Rhys. She grasped her glass between her fingertips and took a breath. She heard herself saying the words, repeated them to herself over and over again. She pretended to be Megan. Megan would just say it. She would just do it. Megan wouldn't even pause to draw breath.

But the more she thought about it the less able she felt to do it. She couldn't be the one to bring him up today, to change the atmosphere, to make everyone feel uncomfortable. Raising a toast to Rhys was the job of an adult. And Beth was not yet an adult. So she relaxed her grip on the glass stem, smiled and instead raised a toast to Alfie Rhys Liddington Bird.

5

APRIL 2011

"What about Rory?" said Molly, sitting on the edge of Rhys's bed, clutching the thin, stained mattress with her fingers. "What did he think, when Rhys died? I mean, he was his, like, twin. He must have been devastated."

"He was very angry," said Meg. "Very, very cross. He cried. A lot. But always with this face like thunder. Always with these red cheeks and these eyes full of rage. Like he wanted to hit someone. I kept my distance, to be honest. And he just kind of retreated into his friendships. His friends had always been more important to him than his family. His friends were his life."

"And then he met Kayleigh?"

"Yeah. Then he met Kayleigh."

Molly rolled her eyes. "And the rest is history."

"Oh, yes," Meg agreed. "It certainly is."

"Do you think he'll come? Now he knows your mum's dead?"

Meg shrugged. It had taken days to track him down. Her calls and e-mails had ricocheted halfway around Asia, from Thailand to Vietnam, the Philippines to Indonesia, until she'd finally cornered him in an Internet café in Chiang Mai, where they'd had a very surreal Skype conversation. The webcam kept tilting up so that Rory's face would slide down the screen until she was talking to the top of his baseball cap, then she'd tell him to push it back up and it would slide down again. A small cross man on the monitor behind him was shouting at someone else on Skype and the Internet connection had cut out completely just as she'd finally asked him if he was coming home. He'd looked brown and thin and feral. His accent had been hard to place, somewhere between Essex and LA. He had been shifty and unlovable. A stranger to her. A stranger to her family. "Christ knows," said Megan. "I've offered to pay for his flight. Who knows? Who cares?"

"I care," said Molly, swinging her long legs. "I'd like to meet him."

Meg thought of the life-raddled man on her computer screen two nights ago and shook her head. "I'm not sure you would, darling."

"But he's my uncle. I'm, like, nearly sixteen and I've never met him."

"Well, you have met him, actually. Once. When you were about three or four. When Alfie was a baby. Here. You met him here."

"Are you sure?"

"Ha! Of course I'm sure! I'm totally sure. There's no way I would forget it. Because it was the last time I ever saw him."

APRIL 1999

Vicky pulled the curtains apart and smiled. "Darling," she said, glancing at the slumbering figure in the bed, "it's gorgeous out. Absolutely beautiful."

Lorelei opened one heavy eyelid and peered over the top of

the bedspread. "In a minute, Vick. Not yet." Then she closed her eyes and turned over.

Vicky gazed at her for a moment. Her beauty. Her love. She still couldn't quite believe that she had her. That after all those years of aching and wanting and desiring, Lorrie was now hers and hers alone. That she got to wake up with her in the mornings, lie down next to her at night. That they were one. Lorrie and Vicky. Vicky and Lorelei.

Lorrie's waist-length hair, streaked with gray and almost gray, was spread about her head on the pillow, one long, chiseled arm hanging over the edge of the bed, her bony shoulders in the strappy, silky stuff she wore to bed. Who would have guessed, during all those years of not knowing, of yearnful wondering, that Lorrie Bird wore such things in her bed. Peach and ivory, lace and silk, tiny pearly buttons and flibberty ribbons. All wasted on her great lanky nonsense of a husband.

Vicky had seen it, from the very first moment she stepped into their house. The pair of them had that look about them: ashen, cloistered, given-up. And that was before their boy had done what their boy had done and made sure that they would never again feel comfortable laying a hand on each other in this house.

And Vicky had known, from the very first moment she set foot in this house, that this was where she belonged, in this charming mayhem, with this charming, peculiar woman with her heaps and piles and color and passion. Nobody appreciated her. Her older daughter, Megan, so stern and unyielding, so resolute in her disdain for her mother and everything that mattered to her. Rory, unfocused and footloose, disloyal and uninterested, off with his hard-faced Irish princess without a backwards glance. He never called, except to ask for money.

And even lovely Beth, pretty little thing, soft and pliable, she was only here because she didn't have the guts to be anywhere else. Because she felt like the last guest at an unsuccessful party, too guilt-ridden to leave.

Vicky loved them all, she did, almost as though they were her own. But she hated them too, for the lack of love they showed their mother, the looks they threw each other over her head, behind her back, the whispers and the conspiratorial giggles. She'd felt so desperately sorry for Lorrie, stranded in the middle of it all, looking for rainbows and seeing only disparagement and scorn.

It was just over two years ago, their first kiss.

It happened when Beth went down to London to stay with Meg, when Alfie was born. She'd dropped Sophie at nursery, picked up some Danish pastries from Sainsbury's like she did every Tuesday—pecan for Lorrie, raisins for herself—and let herself in with the key that Lorrie had given her many years earlier. There they were, just the two of them and an empty house (Colin had been somewhere else, who knows where else—Lorrie had stopped wondering a long time ago); they sat in the garden in the spring sunshine, drinking tea from mugs, admiring the new blossoms, discussing the children—her children, Lorrie's children—as they always did, and Lorrie had begun to cry. It was perhaps strange that after all these years of admiring Lorrie's joyful outlook, her sunny demeanor, her ability to skim across the grimy surface of life looking only for the bits that sparkled, she should desire her more than anything for her tears. She'd put an arm across her shoulder, as she would do for any soul who cried in her company, and Lorrie had flopped her head against Vicky's soft bosom and there it had been, something Vicky had forgotten about in all these years of marriage and men and mothering and being what everyone thought she should be. There it was again, like a lovely forgotten object found at the back of a drawer.

Lorrie had been surprisingly unsurprised. The timing had clearly been impeccable—Vicky could no longer even remember why she had been crying and neither could Lorrie. All they could remember now of that afternoon was the delight of finding each other at last.

Well, it was hard to imagine now, two years later, how awful it had all been at the time, telling Tim, telling Colin, telling the children (only the big children—the little children would work it out for themselves sooner or later). Oh, the screaming and the terrible rage-filled voices, the tangible distaste, the venom, the rawness of it all. Awful. Beyond awful. Tim lived in the next village now in a little two-bed cottage. He still didn't talk to Vicky at handovers. *"You are dead to me."* He'd really said that to her. The way someone in *EastEnders* might do. Vicky had never suspected him of being so theatrical. Colin had been an easier proposition. He'd left Lorrie years ago, in reality, and he'd made a show of being terribly cross, but really Vicky thought he'd been relieved. He still lived in the house—they put in a partition wall and a separate front door (the house had originally been two cottages, so it had been easy enough to do)—and he came and went, civil enough.

But Bethan, wide-eyed little Bethan, well, she had thrown up. Not metaphorically, but really, genuinely, spat up some regurgitated food into the sink. Quite revolting, really, but also terribly sad. A grown woman of, what, twenty-five, twenty-six, she'd been at the time? Still so firmly battened down to the floor of her childhood that she would physically evacuate her stomach at the suggestion of her mother having a female lover. Not that Vicky would ever say that to Beth. She always trod very carefully around her, tried to respect her sensitive nature, make it as tolerable as possible for her to live with them. No PDAs. No overt shows of the way she felt about Lorrie. Just business as usual so far as was reasonably possible.

But here, in the sanctuary of their room (yes, the room that Lorrie had once shared with Colin, the very bed that she had slept in with Colin, but it seemed an irrelevance to both of them, it was just furniture, after all), they could be exactly what they were. Without shame or embarrassment. Vicky and Lorelei. Lorrie and Vicky. She sat down upon the edge of the bed and she kissed her beloved softly against her lips.

～

The last Easter Sunday of the millennium held secrets. Secrets and surprises. Vicky was keeping them as little gifts for Lorrie. The first secret was on its way, right about—she checked her watch again—right about *now*. Pandora in a rental car, direct from the airport, a surprise visit from her home in Corfu, with Ben and Ben's son Oscar in tow. The second secret was still unconfirmed. It was nigh on impossible communicating with the weird house in Andalusia, the strange man called Ken who occasionally answered a phone at the bar at the end of his dirt track and promised, unconvincingly, to get a message back to Rory and Kayleigh, who had a modem that appeared to run on donkey pee or some such, as reliable as it was. (*"I sent you an e-mail on Wednesday. Did you get it?" "No, our modem's been a bit temperamental."*) But, all being well, Rory and Kayleigh were also heading back home. Who knew what time they were due. Vicky certainly didn't. Meg and Bill were already here. They'd arrived last night and were staying next door with Colin. Vicky didn't blame them. Less clutter in his place, a big room with four beds in it and its own en suite bathroom, perfect for a family. Nothing personal, Vicky knew that. Meg, being the oldest and the most pragmatic of the Bird children, had no issue with Vicky and Lorrie being together. Once she'd ascertained that her father was not about to fall apart like an over-baked pie crust, she'd been fine about it. Vicky suspected that Megan thought she was a good thing, a force for the good. What was it she'd said? Yes, that's right, she'd said, *"I'm glad she's with someone who cares about her."*

Precisely.

Colin had not been a bad husband, he'd not been a drinker or a liar or a fighter or a controller, but neither, it had to be said, had he really cared a terrible lot.

Vicky could hear the little ones next door, through the thin partition wall. Somebody was having a tantrum. She could not make out the details of it, but the general shape was that of apoplectic rage. It sounded like Alfie. She smiled, not smugly, but with some satisfaction that she had passed through that phase. Her girls were eight and nearly six. She was in the gentle stage of the parenting journey known as "middle childhood." Her children were solid, predictable, safe. They didn't scare her anymore as they had when they were small, when there had been the ever-present fear of a public tantrum, a broken night, a dash off a curb, an unannounced bowel movement in a public pool. And neither were there the fears to come: the failed exams, the bad friends, the late nights and the journeys home in unlicensed taxis. Here she could exhale for a while, pause to admire the view, think fondly of her babies but know that she would never have to go back there again.

Poor Meg, still at the starting posts. Grumpy, bossy Molly, hyper Alfie and now another one on the way; a veritable baby machine, a glutton for punishment. She heard the front door of Colin's cottage open and close and then she heard small fists on their door. She checked the time again. It was 7:25.

Her girls were still fast asleep. Good sleepers, her girls. No, she wouldn't want to go back there again, not for all the chocolate in Belgium.

She pulled on a smile and opened the door. "Hello, sweethearts," she cooed, clocking Meg's thunderous face behind them, "have you come for your breakfast? I've got strawberry yogurts—are they allowed yogurts?" It was always best to check, especially, Vicky had found, with Megan, who had some very hard-and-fast rules about the contents of her children's stomachs.

"Perfect," said Meg, grimacing. "Anything. Just please, would you mind keeping an eye on them for a few minutes while I try and have a lie-down?"

The smile froze on Vicky's face. *What about Bill,* she thought but did not ask, *what about your partner? Or your father? Or have they both died in their sleep?* She kept the smile in place—it was *vital* that she remain utterly charming at all times when it came to her dealings with Lorrie's family—and said, "Absolutely! Of course. Come in, lovely little people, come in." And she thought, but did not say, *And please do not wake up my big, proper slumbering children who, left to their own devices, might well sleep through until nine o'clock, giving me another hour and a half to prepare for the massive family reunion which I have so rashly chosen to undertake this afternoon.* Meg's little ones were still in their pajamas, Alfie's rather soiled already with something garden related, Molly in lovely, and very expensive-looking, white cotton things with lace edging. Alfie's eyes were red-rimmed from his recent tantrum and Molly was looking thoroughly unimpressed with her lot. Meg was wearing a stretchy maternity top that had clearly seen her through both previous pregnancies, and leggings that showed the solid set of her long but rather shapeless legs. Her brown hair was cut shorter than she'd ever had it before and her eyes were dull with sleepless-ness. "Thank you, Vick," she said. "I really, really appreciate it. I'll be back in an hour."

"No, no," said Vicky. "Longer. As long as you need. Go. We're fine."

Alfie raced through the house and out towards the garden. Molly looked at her mournfully with those big blue eyes of hers. Then she looked pleadingly at her mother. "I also have chocolate spread," Vicky said, not making eye contact with Meg, not giving her the opportunity to grimly pronounce, *"Actually, I don't let them eat sugary spreads—here's a pot of organic sprout paste."* "You can have it on toast, or even"—she smiled playfully—"on a crumpet!"

Molly's demeanor softened—so easily bought—and Vicky led her by her small, eager hand towards the kitchen.

⇍

Molly's mouth loosened with every nibble of chocolate-covered toast. Vicky had made herself a slice too and they sat side by side outside the kitchen door watching Alfie forage for snails, quite companionably, almost as though sharing a bottle of rosé.

"So," said Vicky, "are you looking forward to your new brother or sister?"

Molly wrinkled up her pretty little face, considered the question for a while and said, "No, not really."

"Oh, dear," said Vicky. "Why's that?"

Molly shrugged, tiny shoulders going up and down in their sockets. "Don't know. I just am not looking forward to it. I've already got a brother."

"Well, yes," said Vicky empathetically, "one brother proba-bly is more than enough."

Molly nodded and ate some more toast. She had a chocolate-spread crescent bisecting her mouth, which looked incongruous against her serious expression. "Why is Nana's house so messy?" she asked after a moment.

Vicky smiled. "Ah, well, you see, your nana is a very special lady—she is really quite magical, you know—and when she looks at the world she sees it in a very special way, like it's a party bag, or a toy shop, and she likes to keep bits of it. And she feels sad when she throws things away."

Molly nodded again. "My mummy throws away *everything*." She said this with a roll of the eyes.

"Yes, so I hear."

"Really," she emphasized, "*everything*. It's really annoying."

"Oh," said Vicky, "I can imagine."

"But," said Molly thoughtfully, "I *think* I prefer it living in a house that is tidy than in a house which is untidy. Like Nana's house."

"Oh," said Vicky, with a hint of sadness, "well, everyone is different. Some people like a lot of things around them, and some people like it all put away."

"I think," said Molly, "that I would like it all put away. But not *thrown* away. When I am a grown-up I will be tidy, but I will not throw things away. Especially not my *toys*."

"That," said Vicky, "sounds like a very good compromise. Very sensible indeed."

⌒

Vicky had not been to Meg's house. Lorrie still refused to spend a night away from home even twelve years after the burglary. But she had heard much about it from Beth. She had heard about the sparkling antibacterial surfaces and the cupboard full of sprays, the storage boxes labeled with stickers and the multitude of coasters. It was obvious to Vicky that Meg's fastidiousness was not a genetically inherited trait, but a direct reaction to the way she felt about her mother. Meg was disgusted by her mother, despised her childlike ways, her dreamy outlook, her love of stuff and things and bits and bobs. All the things that Vicky loved about her. Living with Lorrie was like living with a person formed from your favorite grandmother and the kooky girl in the sixth form and the teacher who let you off homework because it was her birthday. It was like living with all the best and most colorful people you'd ever known all rolled up into one. But then, Vicky had always liked weird people. She'd always happily made conversation with drunks on the tube, chatted to the strange man at the party whom everyone else was avoiding, befriended confused old ladies at bus stops and got to know the homeless guy with the voices in his head who sat outside her office. Nothing fazed her. She was utterly fearless. The only person who scared her was Meg.

Meg terrified her.

Vicky was forty-five.

Meg was twenty-eight.

They were both tall women, five foot eight, and big boned. They both had loud voices and strong opinions. They were both matriarchal and bossy.

But still. When Vicky was with Meg she felt like a shrimp.

Absolutely ridiculous.

That fear was currently manifesting itself into a frantic dash for a wet cloth at the sound of Meg at the front door, and a rather rough-handed removal of the chocolate smile from Molly's face. Meg had taken precisely the hour she'd said she wanted, not a minute more, not a minute less. Vicky could hardly see the point of asking for time for a nap if you were just going to lie there watching the clock.

"Come in, come in!"

Vicky stationed the little ones in front of a *Teletubbies* video in the sitting room. Megan seemed momentarily vexed about this, then looked very tired and resigned, left them to it and followed Vicky back into the kitchen.

Everyone else was still asleep: Lorrie, the girls and Bethan. So, until one of them surfaced, it was just the two of them. Vicky and Meg. She made a fresh pot of tea and opened a packet of croissants.

Megan peered suspiciously at them.

"When were they bought?"

Vicky smiled patiently. Meg always thought that everything in this house was past its sell-by date, festering with unseen mold, wriggling with invisible mealworms, noxious with lethal bacteria. "Yesterday," she replied genially.

Meg nodded and picked one up.

"This house . . ." she began, looking about herself awkwardly. "Christ. It gets worse every time I come."

"Well," said Vicky, in the smoothest voice she could arrange for herself. "It's since the house was split. You know. We've less space now and you know your mother, she just won't countenance . . ." She trailed off, feeling her customary surge of loyalty bubble to the top. "Although, I must say, in her defense, she has let a few bags of stuff go. Recently. A load of clothes. To the charity shop." She rubbed nervously at her elbows. Of course, she wasn't being quite honest. She'd done it herself, while Lorrie was at a doctor's appointment for her alopecia (a bald spot the size of a ten-pence piece that had appeared virtually overnight on her crown). And she'd felt so terribly nervous doing it, as though she were committing some dreadful crime, as though there were a dozen surveillance cameras focused in on her, beaming her activities directly into Lorrie's head. Possibly through the bald patch.

What had it been in the end? A sweater, a scarf, some old work shirts of Colin's and a pile of really, really unreadable-looking paperbacks. Not a lot. But as much as she thought she might be able to get away with.

"Well," said Meg, "that's better than nothing, I suppose. And how is she? Generally?" Meg pulled down the cuffs of her maternity top and smoothed her brown curls behind her ears, which were decorated with small and annoyingly discreet diamond studs.

Vicky, still unshowered, still in her banana-print pajamas and matching yellow hair, nodded enthusiastically and said, "Marvelous. Really."

"She looked very thin last night," said Meg, pulling shreds off her croissant and depositing them delicately into her mouth. "And what's with this bald patch?"

"Oh, gosh," said Vicky, "I don't know. It's just one of those things, isn't it? You know, it's been a hell of a couple of years for her, all in all."

"She's been through worse."

This was a pointed comment. Meg had never forgiven Lorrie for not being more upset about Rhys. And Vicky really couldn't blame her. It was the one thing, really, of all the odd things about Lorrie, that she absolutely couldn't get to grips with. She'd been there. That evening. Oh, even now, eight years later, she couldn't think about it without being there, you know, actually properly *being there*. She could taste her red-wine breath and feel the dizzy splendor of intimacy, her and Lorrie in the snug, by the fire, putting the world to rights. She felt a kind of retrospective guilt that she had not said to her new friend, "Where's your youngest? I'd love to meet him," that she had not been interested in the person missing from the lunch table. But that was only now, now that she knew them all, now that this was her family and this house her home. At the time, why should she have cared?

And even now, she could feel the pit of her stomach contract and expand, contract and expand at the memory of the wee thing, hanging like a forgotten Christmas decoration from his bedroom ceiling, the panicky feeling that she must get the others away, back down the stairs, back to their perfect childhoods. And the sudden, gruesome exhumation of the buried memory, her first love—not a boyfriend as she'd told them at the time, because she didn't yet know them and she wanted them to think of her as conventional, but a girl called Hazel with blue eyes and black hair who couldn't quite come to terms with everyone hating her for being gay.

It was a baptism of fire, the quickest journey into the inner world of another family it was possible to imagine. One moment she was just the woman next door, the next she was a central component of their personal history. Awful, the whole thing, just absolutely awful. And she had waited for Lorrie to do what she herself imagined she would do if one of her lovely children had taken their own life; she waited for her to lose the plot, to scream and grieve and kick and scratch and cry and die a little. But she never did. She just kind of *got on with it*. Eerie. Unsettling. But also, maybe, depending on your outlook, utterly utterly marvelous.

Vicky still hadn't quite decided.

She nodded thoughtfully at Meg's last comment. As much as she liked to argue with her on most matters, on this point she really could not.

"I still think she needs some help," Meg continued. "Honestly. It's been going on too long now. She needs some therapy. She needs to talk to somebody. She's fifty-three. She's still relatively young. She's got another thirty, forty years to go, God willing, and I can only see all this"—she gestured aggressively at the space around her (even the kitchen was now beginning to show the signs of Lorrie's rampant over-shopping and refusal to throw anything away)—"getting worse. And as for the Rhys thing. I mean, that's the sort of thing that can give you cancer, you know, sitting on a wound like that, not *dealing* with it . . ."

"Morning, girls!" She was standing right behind them. She didn't question the tail end of the conversation she absolutely must have picked up on. She just smiled and rubbed Vicky's hair. Maddy and Sophie appeared behind her, bleary-eyed and tangle-haired. Lorrie picked up a mug; began to fill it with tea from the pot; pouted childishly when it ran out halfway through; waited for Vicky to get up, refill the kettle and put it on to boil; and then she turned to the girls and said, as she had every single Easter morning since Vicky had known her and, she was sure, for the many years before, "So, who's looking forward to an egg hunt?"

∽

Rory and Kayleigh arrived shortly after ten. They were staying in Cirencester with Kayleigh's cousin, the cousin who'd originally introduced them to each other all those years ago. The only room that was free at the Bird House was Rhys's old room and no one slept in there. Not ever. It was for the best, anyway, Vicky felt. The first and only time that Lorelei had met Kayleigh had been nothing but awkward; Lorrie didn't like her and frankly, Vicky didn't like her either. And who knows what state Rory would be in now, after four years in that weird commune.

He sat now, in the kitchen, with his arm around his mother. He looked, of course, very brown. Brown as a berry, as her mother always used to say, although Vicky had never actually seen a berry that was brown. He had turned lean and sinewy and had three tattoos at various junctures up his right arm. His teeth needed attention. He had taken to chewing tobacco, like a hoary old cowboy. And drinking fifty-peseta red wine from unlabeled bottles, like a hoary old Spaniard. But his hair, it was a dream. The constant sun had turned his hair back to its childhood flaxen.

"He's a regular golden boy," Kayleigh said, playfully rubbing his brilliant mop. "You should only see the fuss they make of him out there. I think they think he's a film star, you know, the reincarnation of Robert Redford." She arched her eyebrows sardonically.

Kayleigh herself looked well. She'd grown her hair long again; it was halfway down her back and dyed scarlet. She had a suggestion of a tan, though it was clear that her skin didn't quite have the gumption to go properly brown, and she seemed well fed, or, at least, better fed than she had been four years ago. She wore a faded Lycra dress and heavy boots and had a tattoo on her right arm that directly matched one of Rory's. (Vicky had not the slightest idea what it was supposed to be; nobody had roses anymore, or anchors, it was all Sanskrit this and Celtic the other.)

It had been just as Vicky had hoped it would be, like something from a TV show, when Lorrie had seen her boy standing there in the hallway half an hour ago, with a bunch of daffs and a Black Magic egg the size of a head.

Meg and Bill and the little ones were next door, variously having naps and late showers. Colin was in the garden clearing cobwebs in advance of the egg hunt (Maddy had a phobia of cobwebs) and Beth was sitting next to Vicky, with Sophie on her lap, smiling dreamily at her prodigal brother. The oven was heating up, the lamb was on the counter draped over with stems of rosemary from the garden, the pastel-colored eggs were in a bowl ready to be distributed, the sun was fighting its way through some dense black cloud. The scene was almost set for the first proper Bird family Easter lunch, since, well, since Rhys had died.

"So," said Lorrie, smiling up at her boy with sparkling eyes, "what are your plans, you two? Are you back for good?"

Rory and Kayleigh exchanged a look. Clearly there was some contention here.

"For now," said Rory.

"Well," Kayleigh interjected, "for a little while. Maybe a week or two."

"Maybe longer . . ."

"Maybe. And then . . ." She shrugged. *"Who knows."*

"Well, we do *kind* of know . . ."

The sound of Meg and her family arriving saved them the effort of trying to find an account they could both agree upon of their short-term plans. But Vicky already had half an idea. It was in the way Kayleigh was tearing at the skin around her fingernails, the new bloom upon her skin.

"Hello, hello!" She got to her feet to greet Bill, whom she had not yet seen this morning. She loved Bill. He was the type of man she'd like for one of her daughters. Solid and fun and just sexy enough. He flirted with Vicky, in that way that men felt they could now they knew she wasn't going to take it seriously. They were cut from the same cloth, Vicky and Bill; no-nonsense, loud, warm, family-minded and up for a laugh. They always got along.

He was wearing one of his trademark brightly colored polo shirts with the striped collar, 501s, trainers. His hair was still wet from the shower and he had Alfie in his arms, facing outwards, the way Vicky had noticed that men always held their babies, like football trophies, for the world to admire.

"Good morning, everybody!" he boomed in his public-school accent roughened up from his years dealing with artists in edgy corners of London.

Meg came in behind him, holding a bag full of Easter eggs and wearing bunny ears. Her mouth opened wide at the sight of her little brother at the table and she squealed, dropped the bag of eggs, darted around the table and threw herself at him. Vicky's heart sang a little song. Families should always be together, she thought, especially families who'd been through what this one had been through.

"Bill," called Meg, holding Rory's hands in hers. "Bill! This is Rory! Look. It's actually, really Rory. Molly! This is your uncle, this is Uncle Rory. You know, from Spain."

"Uncle Rory," said Rory, looking slightly puzzled by the concept.

"Makes you sound like an old perv," said Kayleigh. "'Come on, sit on Uncle Rory's lap, little one, I've something in my pocket for you.'" She acted this out in the voice of an elderly man.

Vicky laughed out loud. She felt she had to, as she knew nobody else would.

Molly looked at Rory, aghast, and hid her face between Bill's solid thighs. Rory laughed. "Look what you've done now, Kayleigh," he teased.

"It's probably for the best," she jested, "you know, in the long term. What with your being a pedophile an' all."

Vicky laughed again, so loud that she almost made herself jump.

"Kayleigh," said Rory, taking her hand in his, "this is my big sister, Meg."

"I have heard a lot about you," said Kayleigh, not rising to greet Meg, but absentmindedly putting out a limp-wristed hand as though handing a soiled stocking to a housemaid.

"Likewise," said Meg, taking the hand firmly and smiling slightly—it had to be said—imperiously.

Vicky held her breath. Meg and Kayleigh. The queen bees. This was a match worth watching.

"And look at the size of you!" said Kayleigh, eyeing Megan's bump with a strangely hungry look. "You are the ship in full sail, you really are."

Meg squeezed in next to Rory, and Vicky saw Bethan move along to make space for Bill on her side of the table, smiling shyly at him. Bill leaned across the table with his hand extended. Rory met him halfway. "Nice to meet you at last," said Bill. "After all these years."

"Same here," said Rory. "We just missed each other, didn't we, back in, when was it . . . ?"

"Ninety-five," said Meg. "Nineteen ninety-five. Just before Molly was born. You went then." She smiled tightly and continued, "*Literally* three weeks before my due date."

Kayleigh pulled a face. "Uh-oh," she said, "we're in trouble."

Meg laughed. "Hardly," she scoffed. "It was just a pity, that was all, to have missed the birth of your first niece by three weeks."

"Ah, well," said Kayleigh, answering once again for her boyfriend, "you know, they're all very dinky when they're new, all little tiny teeny, but they're much more interesting at this age. Big girls are much more interesting than boring little babies. All boring little babies do is piss and shit 'n' scream. Isn't that right, Molly?"

Molly stared at her and then stared at her mother for direction, which did not come. Meg had been rendered speechless.

"Ah, bless her," said Kayleigh, "she's adorable. Isn't she, Rory?"

Meg's face softened and Rory nodded and Vicky felt it was time to gently prise the conversational reins from between Kayleigh's fingers.

"So," she said brightly, slapping her hands down upon her lap. "Who's ready for an egg hunt, then?"

Across the table she caught Lorrie's eye. There was a hint of dark resentment there. Vicky caught her breath. She'd gone too far, she'd crossed a line. It was always such a blasted balancing act with Lorrie, between caring for her, picking up the slack and disempowering her, and she was *always always* getting it wrong. "Lorrie," she soothed, "darling. Egg-hunt time! Over to you."

Lorrie's dark look diminished and she smiled girlishly, delightedly. *Clap clap* went her long bony hands, *clap clap*, and there it was, sunshine, literally, not figuratively; the sun appearing from behind the thick wall of cloud, casting its good mood across the room, across the family, across Easter.

৵

Beth lay in the hammock, contemplating her feet. She had never before thought of her feet as alluring in any way. In fact, she'd never really thought about her feet at all. They had just lived quietly on the ends of her legs, a narrow size six, slightly sinewy, sometimes with colored nails, sometimes not. But she looked at her feet now and tried to see what he saw, tried to see them as objects of sensual, remarkable erogenousness. He had told her that her feet were beautiful. And maybe they were. She wanted to believe every word he said.

She turned her head to look up towards the house. She could hear the clatter of things being put into the dishwasher, other things being placed on shelves, children fighting, adults laughing. She heard her mother call out, "Oh, Meg, it was nothing like that, nothing at all!" She heard the back door opening and closing and then she heard the sound of Bill's voice. She heard him say, "I'm off for a smoke, Meg, keep the kids away." She smiled. Bill's children didn't know he smoked.

She looked up again, into the sky. It was lilac, veined with jet trails and wisps of cloud. Then she peered down, into her dress, plucked at the top of her bra, gazed at her breasts. Her lovely firm, youthful breasts (he'd told her that too). She thought of the way he grabbed them as though they were handfuls of dough, the way he licked them and cupped them and held himself between them. She shuddered slightly, with a kind of awful disgust. And then she heard his feet against the grass, soft and strong, and there he was, standing alongside her, pulling a pack of Camels from the back pocket of his jeans. He offered the pack to her, silently, with one eyebrow raised.

She plucked one out and let him pull her to a sitting position.

"Well," he said, lowering himself gently down alongside her. "That was . . . *different.*"

"Kayleigh, you mean?"

"Christ above, what a piece of work."

Beth laughed. "She is that."

"Poor Rory," he sighed, lighting Beth's cigarette for her. "She's got his balls in a vise."

Beth smiled and didn't say, *"Haven't they all?"*

They smoked their cigarettes in silence for a while, enjoying the proximity of each other's bodies, knowing that there was nothing more for them here than this, smoking cigarettes, chatting in the dusk. There were other places for the rest of it. This was not one of those places.

"He's very different, isn't he?" said Bill, bending down to

grind his cigarette out in the grass. "Different to the rest of you?"

Beth put her hand up the back of his T-shirt and ran it up and down the small of his back, his satin skin, the points of his spine. He arched against her touch.

"We're *all* different to the rest of us," she said. "We're like a badly planned dinner party." She turned her fingertips into claws and scratched at his skin.

"Ooh, yes," he said, "just there, just *there*, no, there, there, up a bit, just to the left, to the right, back to the middle, ooh, yeah, yeah, right there, *right there!*"

Back-scratching was one of their things. Along with foot-kissing and breast-licking and a special position that they honestly believed they must have invented because they'd been through the Kama Sutra more than once and failed to find it. Beth had always thought she didn't like sex. Bill was doing everything in his power to prove to her that she did. She was still only half convinced. She still couldn't really work out what the point of it was. But it made Bill happy and as long as she was making Bill happy, Beth was happy.

Beth quickly snatched her hand from under his T-shirt at the sound of a voice in the top garden. They both sat straight-backed, unnatural.

It was Vicky.

She smiled when she saw them there. "Hello, you two!" she boomed, zipped up snugly inside a purple Boden body-warmer, her strong arms swinging at her sides. "What on earth are you doing out here in the half dark?"

"We're *dissecting*," said Bill.

Vicky looked from Bill to Beth and then back again. Beth gulped and felt her skin prickle all over with guilt. Bill was so good at this, so blasé.

"She's a pill, all right," said Vicky, leaning against a tree trunk and tucking her hands into her pockets. "She just told me that I'm not really a lesbian."

"What!"

"Yes, and—I will not attempt to do this in her accent—she said, 'You've just decided to be gay because you wanted your feet under the table here.'" Vicky hooted loudly. "Outrageous! The girl doesn't know the first thing about me."

Beth smiled tightly. She had no idea if Vicky was a real lesbian or not, and she was still too uncomfortable sitting here, squashed up against her sister's partner, in a hammock, in the dark, even to begin to join in this conversation.

"What the fuck is a 'real lesbian' anyway?" said Bill. "It's all shades of gray."

"Well, yes," agreed Vicky, "exactly. Who's to say? I mean, would you decree that a person was not a 'proper' heterosexual because they'd once had a crush on the head girl?" She tutted and sighed. "Well, anyway, all I can say is that I'm jolly glad she's not a permanent fixture. She adds a certain color but with a rather bad flavor, if you see what I mean." She pulled her hands out of her pockets and slapped them against her legs. "Well, I'd better get back inside, make sure Lorrie's okay. Are you coming in?"

She glanced again from one to the other, and then up to the darkening sky. A look passed across her eyes, as though she were doing long division in her head. Beth flinched.

"Not yet, Vick," said Bill. "In a minute."

"Okay, good." She smiled. "Yes, see you both in a minute." They sat and watched her march back up the garden towards the house.

"She knows," said Beth, pulling herself off the hammock and scrabbling to her feet.

"Don't be nuts," said Bill, lying down in the space she'd vacated, tucking his hands behind his head and staring up into the sky, where the stars were slowly starting to reveal themselves like shadows on a Polaroid. "Course she doesn't."

"Seriously," she said, "the way she looked at us just now. Didn't you see? She knows. She totally knows. Or *suspects*."

Bill shrugged. "And?"

She put her hands against her hips and stared at him, questioningly.

"Well, if she *suspects*, then what's she going to do? Unless she actually catches us *in the act*, she can suspect as much as she likes."

"You are so ridiculously cool, Mr. Liddington. I honestly have no idea how you do it. It's scary."

"It's genetic," he replied. "Runs in the family."

"How do you do it? How do you go home to her and pretend that you've just been working late? If I had to lie to someone all the time like that . . ." She shuddered. The sun had disappeared now, behind the horizon, taking the last caress of warmth with it. "I'm going in," she said, feeling suddenly cross with him. She couldn't find a specific reason for her annoyance, it just sat there on her chest like a heavy book.

"What's the matter?" he called out after her.

"Shh," she hissed.

"What?" he called, quietly this time.

"Nothing, nothing."

She strode up the lawn, towards the glowing lights of the house. On the grass in front of the house, her mother was doing a cartwheel. Her long graying hair swept the tips of the grass as she turned. When she righted herself she saw Beth and she smiled. From this distance, in this light, she looked all of fourteen.

"Where on earth have you been, darling?" she asked.

"Having a cigarette," she replied breathlessly. "With Bill." Not a lie. Entirely and completely the truth, in fact.

"I still can't believe that you took up smoking at the age of twenty-six." Lorelei said this sadly.

Beth smiled. "I know," she said, "I'm such an idiot. I'll give it up soon. I promise."

"Easier said than done," said a voice behind her. She jumped. She'd thought she and her mother were alone out here. Kayleigh sat on her haunches on the bottom of the slide, staring at Beth through narrowed, inquiring eyes. "A bad habit. A *very* bad habit. You need to stop that. *Right now*." She threw her a penetrating look of understanding.

"Do you hear what I said?" she continued. "You need to stop that. Right now. Knock it on the head. For the sake of everybody."

Beth gulped and nodded. "Yes," she said, her voice as solid as she could make it. "Yes. I hear you. And I will."

"Good," said Kayleigh.

"Kayleigh is absolutely right," interjected Lorelei innocently. "Thank you, Kayleigh. Do you smoke?"

Kayleigh pulled herself to her feet and smiled. "No," she said, "not right now I don't. But I have done. So I know"—she looked at Beth again—"how difficult it is to give up."

Beth nodded and turned away. She pushed her way into the kitchen, ignored the scene of social gaiety spread out before her: Colin, Pandora, Meg and Ben loud and exuberant over a bottle of red wine, elbows on the table, scraped-out pudding bowls waiting to be cleared, small children in pajamas darting about like fish, Rory at the sink washing up and laughing at something someone had just said; she ignored it all and she ran to her room. Still her room. Twenty-six years old and still here. The only time she wasn't here was when she was there. In London. Having sex with Bill in his office at the gallery. Eating dinner with Bill in unfashionable restaurants where he wouldn't see anyone he knew. Having sex with Bill in the toilets of unfashionable restaurants. Bill was a family man. There were no overnights, no waking up together—he was unassailable on that point. He slept in his own bed, woke up with his own wife. He'd pick up a taxi, drop Beth off at the station for the last train, take it on home. A five-hour round trip for two hours of him.

How do people do this? she thought to herself. And the world seemed to be full of people doing this. Every time you switched on the TV or opened a newspaper, someone was having an affair with a married man. They all made it look so easy. Bill made it look so easy. It was not easy. And now this: Kayleigh. She threw herself back onto her bed and mouthed the word *Fuck*. Then she mouthed it again. *"Fuck fuck fuck fuck fuck."* Silently. There were too many people in this house, too many pairs of ears. She punched the mattress with both her fists.

Jesus.

Kayleigh, there, in the dark, listening. Knowing. This woman she knew nothing about. Would she tell Rory? Would she tell Meg? It had been worded as a friendly warning, not a threat. How much had she actually heard anyway? Beth couldn't remember what they'd said. She knew she'd been whispering, but Bill was incapable of whispering. What had he said? She flinched as she remembered that he'd used the words *in the act*.

If she stopped now, right now, it would be almost as if it had never happened. They'd only been doing this, this affair thing, for a couple of months. She'd only had sex with him a handful of times. If they could stop it now, grow a thick layer of skin over the memory of it . . . there was no paper trail, no physical evidence, they could pretend it had never happened. No one would get hurt.

But she already knew she couldn't do that.

She couldn't stop now. After all, they'd only just begun.

6

Wednesday 1st December 2010

Dear Jim,

Oh, gosh, I have to tell you that I have not thought about Christmas at all. No. I would say that I tend to float rather aimlessly through the days and months these days. Like a child's lost balloon. Towards the horizon. Never to be seen again. Ha, ha! My children all live too far away. (And of course, I could go and stay with them but I think I've mentioned before my rather silly fear of spending a night away from home. The last time I slept in a bed that was not mine was at the hospice, in the closing days and nights of my partner's life. Before that it was the night after the twins were born. And before that it was, GOD, before any of the children were born, I suppose. So, yes, I am rather stuck here now. And happily so!) My parents, as I mentioned, are long gone, my sister lives in Corfu, so that's it. I'm Norma no-mates! Having said that, my partner's children still live locally, the youngest in particular is quite fond of me, so I may receive an invitation yet. But frankly, Jim, I really don't care much either way. It's just another day to me now. They all are. I hope that doesn't make me sound like an awful old misery-bags! I'm really not. Honestly. Considering some of the things I've lived through, considering my circumstances, I'm really rather a jolly person! And what about you? How will you spend Christmas Day? Do you have any family locally? Any friends? Or maybe you'll have lunch at your pub? I must say, I do like the sound of your pub. I feel I've made a mistake in my life not finding myself a nice local watering hole, somewhere cozy to go and see friends and have a glass of wine, get me out of the house every day! But I think that boat has sailed. The pubs round here these days are all ghastly gastropubs now, all posh Londoners and their loud conversations and silly great cars. And half the time there isn't anywhere to sit and have a drink if a drink's what you want.

Anyway, I should get out more, that's beyond question. But the older I get, the more time passes, the less I feel like there's anything for me out there. It feels like it all belongs to other people, you know, the grubby little face at the window of the smart restaurant. That's how it appears to me. And here, in my home, with my things, I'm the Queen! In my palace! I belong. Aah . . . ? ☺

Anyway, I guess at our age, we're all a bit odd, aren't we? How's your dog's leg, by the way? I do hope she's recovering well from the operation.

All best love,
Lorrie xxx

APRIL 2011

"How come you've got a signal in here?" said Molly, waving her phone around, pointing it towards the window.

"No idea," said Meg. "Let's go, shall we. Let's go and check into the hotel."

"Oh, yes, please!"

The hotel had been half the lure to get Molly up here. She hated skiing and had been angling to stay in London with her best friend, Georgia, instead. Meg had not been happy about the prospect of worrying about her teenage daughter for fourteen days and fourteen nights and had been playing mental tug-of-war with herself over whether or not Molly was ready to be left. Then they'd had the phone call about Lorelei, and Bill had said he'd take the boys skiing on his own and Molly had said, "Hmm, I'm not sure," when Meg had asked her if she'd come with her, so Meg had found the cutest, plushest, bijouest little boutique hotel on the Mr. and Mrs. Smith website and said, "Look, I'll be staying here, are you sure you don't want to come?" and Molly had said, "Cool! Yes! I'll come with you!"

Molly had always loved what she used to call when she was small "fancy hotels." When she was eight she'd had it all decided that she would be a hotelier when she grew up. She would draw intricate sketches of her hotel; there would be real palm trees in the bedrooms and buttons you pressed to get champagne out of the walls and a menu for choosing the exact color of bath towel you required. Nowadays her ambitions lay in "something to do with television, maybe producing or directing or something. You know."

The journey back through the house, like all return journeys, felt shorter and less convoluted; the sense of knowing how long the tunnels were and where they ended up was reassuring and for a moment, Meg could almost feel the security that her mother would have felt, passing about here in the warm corridors of her self-created warren.

Meg locked the back door behind them and tucked the key into her pocket. She regarded the door pensively for a moment and then turned to greet the outdoors, this sweet expanse of space with its smell of air and its noises of traffic and everything being as it should be. Molly waved her phone about again and said, "Still no signal."

"I'm sure you'll pick one up, once we're on the road."

Meg was quite glad there was no signal. With a signal Molly would be lost to her, the car would be filled with the teeth-achingly irritating noise of not-that-bright teenage girls talking rubbish to each other, or the sound of text messages pinging back and forth every ten seconds. Without a signal they could sit, side by side, appreciate the scenery and maybe even talk.

Meg started the engine and Molly stared at the house through her Ray-Bans. "So weird," she said. "Just to think, you lived there, all of you, you were all just, like, normal kids, going to school and stuff, having friends and then, one by one you all left her and she died, you know, completely alone in, like, the Worst House in Britain, or whatever." She shook her head solemnly. "Weird," she said again. "I mean, can you imagine that happening to us? Like, seriously? All four of us just leaving you there and all falling out with each other and Dad going off with some crazy woman and you just going completely mental and not letting anyone in and building, like, *tunnels*, out of, like, *newspapers*. Think of our house. Our lovely house, with all its lovely things in it and yeah, okay, it's a bit too tidy for my liking, but, you know, it's a really nice house, and we all live there and we're so happy and everything. And when I'm an adult I want to see my brothers all the time, you know, I want to go to their houses and stuff and have my kids play with their kids. I mean, you haven't seen your brother and sister for, like, *five years*. Your actual brother and sister. Who you used to live with. And see every day. I mean, I just don't get it. How can things go, like"—she turned to stare at Meg with wide blue eyes—"so *wrong?*"

Meg flicked on her indicator and glanced in the wing mirror, her hands balanced on the steering wheel. "Sometimes, darling," she began, pulling the people carrier out into the road, "I simply do not have an answer."

APRIL 2000

Meg squirted sun cream onto her fingertips and slicked it over the limbs, shoulders, noses and knees of the three small children lined up before her by the pool. Molly received the application of sun cream as if it were an expensive spa treatment. She stood straight and solid, fingers splayed out, eyes closed, turning on command. Alfie received it more like a spiteful punishment, wriggling and grimacing and wailing, "Why, Mummy? Why?" Stanley, the baby (walking, already, at ten months! That had not been the plan when they'd booked this holiday six months ago. He was supposed to have been a baby still, portable and immobile, not this toy-sized human running about in proper leather shoes), took it more as a game, smiling coquettishly at his mother as he tried to avoid her touch.

Three children down the line, a four-year-old, a just-three-year-old, a very-nearly-one-year-old, Meg was military when it came to this kind of thing. Bill, the self-appointed civilian, lay across from them prone on a lounger, holding a paperback spread wide open above his face to keep out the fierce rays of the Greek sun.

"Need any help?" he said, at the precise moment that she had screwed the lid back onto the tube of sun cream. She smiled bittersweetly at him and said, "No, darling, I'm fine, you just relax."

He knew she was being facetious but he also knew that if he wanted to be able to carry on lying there reading a book, he should not acknowledge this.

"Can I swim now?" asked Molly.

"No, darling," said Meg, "you have to wait for the cream to absorb."

Molly tutted and rolled her eyes. "How long will that take?"

Meg smiled wearily. "About ten minutes."

Molly tutted and rolled her eyes again.

Meg crouched by the side of the pool and dunked Alfie and Stanley's inflated armbands into the water, then she squashed them up their arms. "Right," she said, "let's all have an ice cream. By the time you've eaten the ice cream it'll be okay to go in the pool. Okay?"

They all nodded, three small heads, the pale-brown curls of her daughter and the amber-red helmets of her sons.

"Can I have some money?" she turned to ask Bill.

"Hmm?" He looked up at her from his paperback as though he'd just that minute remembered she was there.

"Some money. I need some money. For ice creams."

"Oh, yes, sure. In my shorts pocket, over there."

She pulled a handful of coins from the warm depths of Bill's empty shorts and took the children to the kiosk on the other side of the resort pool.

"Can you get me an espresso?"

Meg gazed at him in awe. They needed to work on this, she mused, they needed to acknowledge the fact that they had three children, that there was not a network of fairies and elves fluttering around behind the scenes getting everything done as Bill appeared to believe there was, and work out some kind of timetable. Some kind of schedule so that Meg could maybe, just maybe, read a book, too.

The choosing of ice creams turned them briefly into a small circus. Molly couldn't decide and became very cross with Meg about it, Alfie decided too soon and changed his mind the moment Meg had pulled the wrapper off, and Stanley dropped his on the floor and screamed. A woman appeared behind them in the queue, a serene creature in a white dress, tailed by two immaculate sylphlike daughters, all blond, all legs. Meg glanced briefly at them, then at her raggle-taggle mismatch of screaming infants, Molly in last year's chlorine-stained swimsuit because they hadn't started selling swimwear in the shops yet, the boys in cheap blue things from Woolworths, freckled backs and chocolate-smeared faces. She thought of herself, a size fourteen to sixteen now. *Fourteen to sixteen.* And all on her hips and thighs, not an extra ounce on her boobs. She thought of her unwaxed bikini line (she simply had not had the time, she'd had to shave instead and had given herself a rash), her sensible swimsuit, her latest, not entirely successful haircut (she'd had the baby on her lap and hadn't been concentrating on what the hairdresser was saying—it was very short). She thought of the past five sleepless nights all squashed into what had laughably been described as a "family" suite but was in fact a normal hotel room with a travel cot and two camp beds packed into it.

And then she smiled tightly at the mother behind her and said, "Sorry about this traveling circus, we'll be out of your way any minute."

The blond mother with her feline features and long hair and finely turned ankles smiled and said, "Don't worry, it's fine, we've all been there."

And Meg laughed drily and thought, *No, we haven't. Or, if we have, some of us have taken a very different route through it.*

She collected Stanley into her arms and helped him hold

his replacement ice cream. He was slick with sun cream and she almost lost him through the space between her arms. But somehow she managed to keep hold of both him and his ice cream and she carried them and Bill's fucking espresso back past the pool, past the sun loungers full of people lying down, reading books and sipping cocktails and, more gallingly than anything, sleeping. *Bastards.*

She landed in an ungainly way on her sun lounger, the combined weight of herself and her hefty infant almost folding the thing up in half. Molly had finally settled—much to Meg's distaste, but really, if there was one thing that Meg had learned about dealing with children it was how to pick your battles—upon a lurid green thing in a paper tube that she did not know how to operate.

"Mummy," she whined, "I can't open it. Mummy!"

Meg dropped the tiny cup of espresso loudly and pointedly on the table between their loungers and snatched the thing from Molly's hand, hissing, "For God's sake, give it to me."

Bill looked at her reproachfully.

"What?" she snapped.

He put down his paperback—*finally*—and stared at Meg as though appalled by her.

"Come on," he beseeched, "we're supposed to be on holiday. Can't you just relax a little?"

He said this in his "nice Bill" voice. The voice he used to remind her that he, at least, was still the Good Guy he used to be. Even if she was no longer the Lovely Girl.

"No," she said quietly, "I can't relax. How can I?"

Bill looked at the three children, now arranged quietly and happily in a row before him, eating their ice creams. "Just enjoy them," he said. "They won't be little for long. Hands up, who's having the best holiday ever?"

All three put their hands in the air. Then Molly put hers down and said, "Actually, this isn't the best holiday ever."

"Really?" said Bill. "Right, so which holiday was?"

"The one we haven't had yet," she replied, looking pleased with herself for saying something unexpected. Bill and Meg looked at each other over their children and laughed.

"Oh, yes," said Bill, "I like your attitude, Molly-Moo. I like your attitude very much."

He stroked her hair and picked up his espresso. He smiled at Meg. "I love you," he said pointedly.

Meg smiled back. "I love you, too."

"Come on then." He jumped to his feet, showing off his nearing-middle-aged but still passably fit body in baggy surfer shorts. Having children had closed the age gap between them. These days Meg often felt as though she was the older one. Twenty-nine going on thirty-nine. "Who's coming for a swim?"

They followed him excitedly, jumping up and down, squealing. He took the boys by a hand each and bounced them as they walked, their tiny weightless bodies fluttering at his sides. They disappeared behind a palm tree and then reappeared at the shallow end. Meg watched them keenly, enjoying them from a distance, a little bit worried that Bill would get distracted by the boys and let Molly drown, but swollen with pride for them all. How could she have felt that flicker of shame just now at the ice-cream kiosk? *Look at them,* she thought, *look at my lovely babies. Look at my handsome man.*

She saw the elegant blonde with the slender preteens. She was rubbing cream into the younger one's back. There was no man. Single mum. Doing it all by herself. No one to share a carafe of wine with on the balcony after the children were asleep. Meg smiled. She was feeling better by the minute.

She heard Bill's phone vibrating and traced the noise to the other pocket of his empty shorts. She pulled out the phone and saw the name BETH. She smiled—her baby sister—and then she frowned. Why was she calling Bill's phone?

"Hello?"

"Oh, hi, Meg, it's me."

"Yes, I know it's you, your name came up on Bill's phone."

"Oh," said Beth, "that's useful. I was calling to speak to you, actually."

"Oh, right, how come you didn't call my phone then?"

"Oh, er, Bill said to use his, he'd got a better rate on international calls or something."

"He told you that? When?"

"The other day. I called you at home. When you were out."

"Did you?"

"Yes. Anyway. How are you?"

Meg passed the phone to her other ear and narrowed her eyes across the pool. Bill was plunging the baby under the water and then bringing him back up again. Stanley was thoroughly enjoying himself but Meg could hardly bear to watch.

"We're fine, thank you. Having a lovely time."

"How's the weather?"

"Scorchio."

"The kids?"

"Having the time of their lives."

"Good." Meg could hear a hint of sadness in her sister's voice. "That's good."

"So . . . ?"

"Oh, yes, I was just calling because it's Easter Sunday."

"Oh, shit, really, is it?" Meg felt her stomach turn with anger at herself. She had forgotten. For the first time in nine years, she had forgotten the anniversary of her brother's death. "Oh,

Christ, yes, of course it is. It's just, you know, out here, you kind of forget what day of the week it is."

"Yes, I know, I know. It's easy to do."

"It's no excuse. I'm cross with myself. I'm as bad as Mum."

"Don't be stupid. Of course you're not. And it's fine. You've remembered now."

"Only because you reminded me. Are you going to the grave?"

"Yes," said Beth. "Me, Dad and Vicky are going later, after lunch."

"Mum?"

"No." She pulled out the vowel in the word to express the inevitability. "She says she's going to 'think about him' instead."

Meg sighed. It was barely worth talking about anymore.

"Anyone coming over today?"

"No," said Beth, "just us. Dad. The girls." She sighed. "I wish you were going to be here."

"Yes, well, I was going to say 'me too,' but really, how over-due is this Greek holiday?" She laughed and Beth laughed too.

"I know," she said. "It's just, it's so weird here now. Every-thing's so different. I hate it here sometimes, I really do . . ."

Meg took a deep breath. She could hear tears in her sister's voice. She could also see Molly running towards her, looking aggrieved about something.

"Mummy! Alfie pushed me and Daddy said it wasn't his fault and it *was* his fault, he did it on *purpose* and everyone always thinks everything is *my fault*." Meg nestled the phone between her shoulder and her ear and opened her arms to her firstborn.

"I'm going to be twenty-eight this year. I haven't got a boy-friend. I haven't got a flat. I haven't even got a best friend. I feel like such a failure."

"Oh, that's ridiculous, Beth. Come on! You're the best PA in the county. You're beautiful, you're—"

"Look, Mummy, look! I've got a hurt where Alfie pushed me, look, I need a plaster!"

She kissed the hurt absentmindedly and squeezed Molly to her and moved the phone once again to the other ear.

"Well, yes, but don't you think, at nearly thirty, there should be more to life than being a good secretary and being pretty? I just feel so trapped, Meggy. I feel like Gulliver, tied down all over with tiny little ropes, like they're all so tiny, but there's so many of them that I can't move. Do you know what I mean? And most of them are in my own head, because . . ."

"Come in the pool, Mummy. Please come in the pool with me. I don't want to be in the pool with Daddy. I don't like Daddy. I like you. Please, Mummy. Please!"

". . . really, there's no reason why I couldn't have been like you, is there? Why I couldn't have moved out, got married, done something with my life."

"Please, Mummy, please, Mummy, now, Mummy, *now, Mummy.*"

"Okay!" she shouted. "Okay!"

"What?"

"Not you, Beth. Not you. Molly. She wants me to take her into the pool. Sorry."

Beth sighed. "Don't be sorry. It's my fault, I'm sorry. I shouldn't be bugging you on your holiday. I shouldn't be loading you down with all my stupid problems."

"I'll call you back," she said, "in a few minutes. Okay?"

"No," said Beth, "you don't need to. Really. I'll be fine. It's just, you know, Easter. Getting older. I'm probably just having a—what is it they call it?—a quarter-life crisis."

"Well, yes," said Meg, "maybe you are. And that might not

be such a bad thing. You know, I want more for you than this too. I do. You're better than this. I'll call you back. Five minutes. Okay?"

She took Molly to the pool and chased her up and down a few times, made her giggle, made her smile and then headed back to the sun lounger, without a towel, dripping water all over Bill's paperback.

She picked up Bill's phone and switched it on. She found Beth's number in his phone book and pressed Call. But instead of dialing Beth's number, it brought up a call history. Meg squinted at it. *Odd*, she thought. *How odd*. Lots of calls, both to and from Beth's phone.

She stared at the screen for several minutes. The calls between the two numbers went back almost to the day Bill had bought his new phone, three months earlier. There were long gaps between the calls, but when they came, they were three or four a day. She tried to apply sensible theories to the matter of the call history. Another Beth? Unable to get through to Meg? *An affair?* She laughed at the thought. And then she smiled.

Of course.

It was obvious.

It was Meg's thirtieth birthday next month.

They were planning a surprise party for her. Discussing gifts.

She redialed Beth's number but Beth didn't reply.

❧

Beth stared at the phone on her bed.

BILL it flashed, BILL.

Taunting her.

She could not believe that she had called him. During his

holiday. An idiotic thing to do. But still. Two whole weeks. How on earth could he expect her to go two whole weeks without hearing his voice?

The phone call had been agonizing. All she could hear were the sounds of the life she wanted. Children keening with joy. The splash of a pool. The sound of distant waves caressing distant sand. The sound of foreign. Of other lives being lived by other people.

Rory in Spain.

Meg and Bill in Greece.

And Beth still here; unpaid nanny, aging secretary, companion to two eccentric middle-aged women, last vestige of family to a lonely old father, festering and bitter.

She picked up the phone and put it under her pillow.

She'd handled the call quite well, she thought. And it was true, Bill had said to use his phone if she needed to call while they were away. So she hadn't even really been lying.

Lying to her sister.

She disgusted herself sometimes, she really did. But Bill— he was all that lay between her and weirdness. Without Bill, without his approval (and she really did have to assume that he approved of her to take the risk with his future happiness that he did every time he spent time with her), she could not stomach herself. She would take an overdose. Or slit her wrists. Or—God rest his beautiful little soul—hang herself from the beams in Rhys's room. Because as long as Bill wanted her, then there was a chance, a tiny, infinitesimal chance, that maybe she was normal.

From below, up the stairs, around the dogleg and through her bedroom door, came the smell of lamb and rosemary. She heard someone pull a cork out of a bottle of wine. She sighed. *Here we go again.*

And then she thought to herself, *This time next year I will either be dead or I will be somewhere else.*

∽

Rory mopped the sweat from his hairline and pushed open the door of the bar. He greeted Ramon the bartender in Spanish and headed for the phone at the back of the room.

"No está funcionando," said Ramon.

"What?" said Rory. "You're kidding me." He kicked the base of the counter with his right foot. He'd promised his mum he'd call her today. She said she'd be waiting for his call. It was a long walk from the farm to Ramon's bar and at just after midday in nearly thirty degrees, he hadn't enjoyed one moment of it.

"¿Una cerveza?"

Rory shrugged and nodded and Ramon poured him a small beer.

Rory downed it in one. In this heat, beer sometimes felt like a vital nutrient. *"Gracias,"* he said wearily.

"De nada. Feliz Pascua."

"Yeah," said Rory. *"Feliz Pascua."*

He passed his empty beer glass to the bartender. And then he walked all the way back to the farm again.

∽

Kayleigh was sitting on the front step of their lodge. The baby was on her breast, half-covered with a sheet of muslin.

"Shhh." Kayleigh put her finger to her mouth and frowned. Then she mouthed the word, *"Sleeping."*

Rory smiled. *Good*, he thought.

He pointed to the left and mouthed, *"Owen."* And then he mimed smoking a big spliff and Kayleigh tutted and rolled her eyes at him.

162

Owen had arrived on the farm three weeks ago. He was a builder and scaffolder from Essex. Until a month ago, he'd been married to a model, lived in a big shiny house with two cars and a selection of pedigree dogs; then he'd woken up one morning and decided that he didn't want any of it. Left the house, the cars and the dogs to the model, and turned up here with a rucksack and Ken's address on a piece of paper. Ken had given him the camper van to sleep in. In return, he was doing the place up—building walls, fixing leaks, all the stuff that Rory associated with real men.

He tapped on the door of the camper van and took a step back.

Owen appeared at the door a moment later, six foot one, topless, tanned to mahogany, his body as solid as a plank, chiseled and intimidating. He scratched his shaved head; yawned widely, revealing huge teeth full of fillings; and said, "All right?"

"Yeah," said Rory, putting on the weird mockney accent he was painfully aware of using whenever he was with Owen, but seemingly incapable of stopping. "You just woken up?"

Owen yawned again. "Yeah, what time is it?"

"About one."

"Fuck," said Owen. "Christ." He scratched his head again and said, "Fancy a smoke?"

Rory nodded and climbed into the van.

The van was a shithole. It smelled of dusty upholstery and rotting foam, old smokes and Owen's trainers.

He and Kayleigh had spent their first couple of weeks on Ken's farm in the van. Then they'd moved to the caravan. Since the baby, they'd been upgraded to the lodge, which was the next best after Ken's house. And the only real benefit, as far as Rory was concerned, to having had a baby.

"Bad night?" asked Owen, eyeing Rory as he licked two Rizlas together.

"Nightmare," replied Rory. "Baby was awake every two hours."

Owen slanted his eyes and whistled.

The baby's name was Tia. Rory had had no say in naming it. Very much in the same way as he'd had no say in whether or not they were going to have a baby. This time last year they'd been in the UK, ostensibly to see his family, but in reality to have an abortion. Until Kayleigh had decided at the very last minute, literally, twenty-four hours before their return flight, that she did not want an abortion. And they had to fly all the way back again. With the baby growing ever more viable within her body.

Rory was twenty-four when the baby was born. He'd felt as if he was going mad. How the hell had he ended up with a baby at twenty-four?

The baby had some problems. Reflux. Colic. And glue ear. Small problems in the scheme of things but problems that made her cry. A lot. Problems that took them to the doctor in town more than was desirable. Problems that required the administering of antibiotics and medicines. Problems that made it even harder than it might have been for Rory to feel as though this baby was something he wanted in his life.

He could tell that the others resented it too. They resented the piercing screams emanating from the lodge, seven, eight times a night; they resented the constant background noise of griping and wailing. And the stress that went with it. Ken's farm was a place people came to live quietly, gently, selfishly. Rory and Kayleigh no longer really fulfilled the brief. They snapped and they snarled, they threw barbed comments at each other and created atmospheres. And their baby screamed and screamed, her desperate cries blocking out the preferred soundtrack of humming cicadas, the amateur guitar strumming, the earnest chats about life and its many meanings. They were the ultimate party poopers, pissing on the whole beautiful, blissed-out, hedonistic parade.

"Here," said Owen, pulling open a small fridge and passing Rory a freezing can of San Miguel.

"Cheers."

Rory stared at the small can in his hand. He rolled it back and forth a couple of times between his fingers, enjoying the surprise and then the numbness of it.

"It's Easter day," he said.

"Oh, yeah," said Owen. "Are you into that kind of thing, then?"

Rory shook his head. "No. Not really. Wasn't brought up into any kind of religion. But we always celebrated Easter. It was my mum's favorite day."

"Was?" said Owen. "Is she dead, then?"

Rory laughed. "No. She's definitely not dead. Just . . ." He pulled the tab off the beer and sucked up the froth that burst out of the opening. "I had a twin brother. He killed himself. On Easter day."

Owen winced. "Shit. How old was he?"

"Sixteen. Just turned. He hung himself. Yeah." Rory wasn't angry anymore. He'd stopped being angry at some indefinable point during the last few years, since he'd been in Spain. He was just sad now, sad that he'd never know what Rhys was doing or where Rhys was living or who Rhys was going out with or why Rhys had killed himself. Sad that Rhys would never meet his baby or his girlfriend. Sad that he didn't have a brother. Sad that he'd been angry instead of being sad. Sad that he couldn't say he was sorry for being such a crap brother.

"Shit," said Owen again, "what did he do that for?"

Rory shrugged. "No idea," he said. "Didn't leave a note. Never said anything to anyone." He let his shoulders drop. "So that's just, you know, Easter fucked, really."

"Yeah," said Owen, "I can see that. That's tough, really tough. How's your mum about it?"

Rory smiled. "My mum . . . ," he began, unsure where he was going to take this. "Aah," he said, "my mum is unusual. She has her own way of dealing with things, you know. She's not like other people. So, basically, she dealt with it by dumping my dad for the next-door neighbor."

Owen raised an eyebrow at him and poked the roach into the end of the spliff.

"Who is a woman."

"No way!"

"Yeah. 'Late-flowering lesbians'—that's what she says they are. *'We're late-flowering lesbians.'* Like they're trees or something."

"What, and they live together?"

"Yes. In my family home. With the woman's children. And my sister. My dad lives next door."

"What, where the woman used to live?"

Rory laughed. "No, they sold that. Our house used to be two separate cottages so they just put a wall back in and opened up the front door and moved all his stuff across. And now *he's* the next-door neighbor."

Owen chuckled. "I love other people's families," he said. "They always make me feel better about my own." He lit the spliff and inhaled. "So what about your sister, how old is she?"

Rory squinted. "What, Beth? She's nearly three years older than me. And I've got another sister too. Meg. She's nearly five years older than me. She lives in London and has about a hundred kids."

"And you used to have a brother?"

"Yeah." He smiled sadly. "I used to have a brother."

"Tragic."

"Yeah."

Owen passed him the spliff.

"Cheers."

They sat in genial silence for a moment or two. Rory took in the details of Owen's van: the *FHM* calendar, the pristine polo shirts hanging neatly, the bottle of Kouros aftershave, the designer trainers in a row, the gold bracelet left pooled on the table, and he said, "What about you? What are you doing here?"

"Just woke up one morning and had had enough of the whole lot of it. Got talking to a bloke in the pub who was going to a festival in a field somewhere, thought I liked the sound of it, got talking to this other bloke, a singer in a band, said his dad lived out in a commune in Spain. That was that."

Rory shook his head. He already knew all of that. "But really. Why are you really here? What do you want?"

Owen laughed. "Haven't got a fucking clue," he said.

Rory laughed too. And then he stopped when he heard the familiar sound of Tia screaming across the courtyard.

"Poor mite," said Owen.

Rory nodded. It was hard to feel sympathy sometimes.

"What about you?" said Owen. "What do you want?"

Rory smiled. And then he dropped his chin into his chest. He looked up at Owen and he sighed. "I think," he said, voicing a deeply buried thought for the first time, "I think I want the next thing. I think"—he paused—"I want to move on."

Owen nodded sagely, and took the spliff back from Rory.

Outside the caravan, his baby screamed.

7

Saturday 1st January 2011

Dear Jim,

HAPPY NEW YEAR!!!

And what a joy it is to have someone special to send that message out to! Oh, yes, I know I have three children, but (and I am struggling to find a way to put this that will not make me sound like an utter weirdo)—we are, to all intents and purposes, estranged. Urgh, I am shuddering at having written the word. And it is a testament to how close I already feel to you that I am able to do so. Yes, I have not seen one of my three children since the day of my partner's funeral. And that was over four years ago. I speak to my eldest girl on the phone, although we do just tend to come to loggerheads every time, which is rather tiresome so it's best we try not to. I e-mail my boy when I can, although his life is rather chaotic, and that is putting it mildly. I will regale you with some Terrible Tales of Rory when/if I feel able. It's all very lurid and probably does not reflect very well on me as a mother. Beth, my middle girl, well, for reasons I can't quite stomach going into here, we no longer have any contact. I don't even know where she lives. Isn't that awful? My baby. I made her in my body, fed her from my body, lived with her until she was, well, far too old to be living with her mummy, let's put it that way. We were so close, and now I don't even know if she's dead or alive. Oh, Jim, it's all just tragedy upon tragedy! I really am a walking tabloid! And writing these e-mails to you, it's making me think about things in a way I haven't thought about things for a long time. About my life. About ME. About my role in the way things have turned out. (With Rhys, gosh, yes, especially with Rhys. There's a metaphorical can of metaphorical worms just sitting there waiting to be pried open and gawped at. Not yet though, no, not yet.) Megan, my eldest, she keeps telling me I should see a therapist, keeps telling me I've repressed a lot of things and that's why I am the way I am. And I just say PAH! Because that's what I always say to Megan. She's such an old bossy-boots! But here I am, pouring it out to you, a virtual stranger. I hope you don't mind. Tell me to shut up if you do!!

Anyway, I am thrilled to hear that Josie's leg has healed; you must be so relieved! Thank God for pet insurance, eh?! I hope you had fun last night at the pub and your head's not too sore this morning. I went to bed at just past midnight, heard the bells ringing, heard the "auld lang synes," thought of you, thought of my children, thought of lost ones and had a little cry. Only a little one. Nothing to worry about! (Do you worry about me? I hope not!)

Bonne année, my dearest Jim,
All love,
L
xxxxxx

APRIL 2011

Molly dashed out of the hotel's en suite bathroom clutching a bottle of scent. "Look," she squealed. "Actual perfume. Jo Malone! Can I have it? Please, Mum?" She clutched it to her chest and smiled winningly at Meg.

Meg glanced at the room menu and said, "It's thirty-nine pounds. No way. You don't even wear perfume."

"Yes, well, I would if it was Jo Malone."

"It's thirty-nine pounds and you're fifteen. Put it back."

Molly let her shoulders slump melodramatically and shuffled back into the bathroom. "You're mean," she said over her shoulder. But it was meant affectionately. A year ago the Jo Malone exchange would have escalated into a bloody battle with swear words and pronouncements of maternal hatred, and, more than likely, the scent bottle being hurled against a wall and a door being slammed hard enough to dismember a hand. This time it ended with the soft chink of the bottle being gently replaced on the marble-topped counter in the bathroom and Molly padding barefoot back into the bedroom.

"Look," said Meg, waving a small card at Molly. "A pillow menu."

Molly took it from her hand and smiled at it.

"Like the towel menus you invented when you were small."

"Yeah," said Molly dreamily, stretching out backwards onto her bed and holding the card above her face. "*Way* ahead of my time, clearly."

"But no live palm trees."

"I'll make a note of that on the comments form before we leave."

Meg smiled and lay back on her own bed. Quality time with

her daughter. She'd never thought it would happen. She'd given up hope of ever having a nice time with her daughter again. And it had taken the death of her own mother to bring it about.

Her phone rang and she sighed. "Hello?"

"Good afternoon, is this Meg Liddington?"

Not Beth. Meg breathed a sigh of relief. "Speaking."

"Hello, this is Stella Richards, from the coroner's office."

"Oh, hello, yes, hi."

"We've had the final results through, the cause of death for your mother, Lorelei Bird. Would you be able to come to our office? Possibly this afternoon, so that we can talk you through them?"

Meg glanced at the time on the TV display in front of her. Two thirty-five. "We're in Mickleton. How far is that from you?"

"Oh, not far, about forty minutes on the fast roads."

"Fine then, yes, fine. But I'll, er, have my teenage daughter with me. I mean, will it be okay, is it . . . you know . . . suitable, I mean?"

The woman on the other end of the line paused for a moment. "Yes," she said eventually. "Yes, I'm sure it'll be fine. So we'll see you in . . . ?"

"In an hour," said Meg, smiling reassuringly at Molly. "We'll see you in an hour."

APRIL 2003

"Vick! Oh, Jesus, Vick!"

Vicky dropped the pile of post she'd just picked up from the front doormat and turned towards the stairs.

"What, love?"

"Come quick! Come!"

Vicky took the stairs a pair at a time, quite an effort given her frankly dire levels of fitness. "What is it, love? What?"

She followed the sound of Lorrie's plaintive moaning into Meg's old room, the so-called "office."

Lorrie stood on the small patch of carpet still uncluttered by shopping bags and piles of newspapers. She was crying. "Someone's been in here!" she said. "Someone's been moving my things around."

Vicky breathed in hard against a swell of irritation. "Oh, darling," she said, "have they?"

"Yes! I had a new book, I only got it last week, it was almost as good as new, I don't think it had even been read. And I came in here to find it and the whole pile's gone, Vick. All of it!" Her hands were threaded through her hair, pulling at it by the roots.

"What book, love?"

"I don't know. I don't know what it was called. It had a lovely cover, all purple and blue, with a rose. But there were more. Books I haven't read. And they've all gone!"

"Oh, darling, I'm sure they haven't, they're probably just not where you thought they were."

"No," Lorelei snapped. "I know where everything is. Everything. And I know I put it here—" She pointed at an area of grubby, unvacuumed carpet. "Right here. And someone has *moved* it."

Vicky put her hand upon Lorelei's shoulder and squeezed it. "Darling, take a deep breath, calm down."

"I *cannot* calm down, Vick. How can I? That book was precious. You know. Precious."

Vicky repressed the urge to shake Lorelei very hard and

scream, *"No, it was not precious—it was some shitty old paperback that you can't even remember the name of!"*

"We'll need to talk to the girls about this," said Lorelei, pulling her hands from her hair and punching them together rather aggressively. Vicky did not appreciate the flavor of the gesture; it looked unseemly in the context of a twelve-year-old and a nine-year-old.

"Why do we need to talk to the girls?"

"Because it must be them. Mucking about in here. They're always mucking about. With my things."

Vicky breathed in hard again. "Darling," she began, "I do understand your feelings—I appreciate how stressful you find it when your things get touched—but you have to bear in mind that there is very little space in this house for the girls to use. That it is almost, darling, inevitable that they will come into contact with your things. When there are so very *many* of your things for them to come into contact with."

Lorelei let her shoulders slump and tutted. "It's just," she began melodramatically, "a matter of respect. Of respect for other people's things. It's one thing to touch, but where are they, Vick? Where are my books?"

"Well, if you must know, it was me." She felt her heart quicken with nerves.

Lorelei looked at her, aghast.

"There was a secondhand book sale at Soph's school, at the Easter Fayre. A fund-raiser, darling. For their school. And you know how underfunded that lovely little school is. And I just thought, *My God, Lorrie has a lot of books she's never read and never will and it's for such a good cause.*"

"Without asking?" Lorelei's voice was brimming with hurt feelings.

Vicky sighed. "Had I asked, Lorrie, what would you have said?"

Lorrie tutted again and folded her arms. "That's not the point."

"Well, then, love, what is, exactly?"

"It's about respect. It's about privacy. It's about . . ." Her face grew dark and tragic. "I don't know what it's about. But you and your girls, you need to . . ."

"What, darling?"

"You need to butt out. Just *butt out*. Okay?"

"Oh, Lorrie, really and truly, I wouldn't say things like that."

"Why not?"

"Because one day you might just get what you want and I truly believe you wouldn't really want it."

She smiled sadly at her love and walked away.

⌁

"Mummy?" Maddy threw her mother a sideways look.

"Yes, darling." Vicky brushed Maddy's hair off her face and Maddy pushed her hand away as she always did. It did not stop Vicky from brushing Maddy's hair from her face. She was still allowed to do that, she was sure she was.

"I need to tell you something. Something really important."

Vicky nodded.

"No, but I mean, like, *really* important." She sighed and stared dramatically through the car window.

She had the loveliest profile, her older girl. So delicate and elfin. "Go on," she said encouragingly, waiting for some tame prepubescent revelation about a boy or a failed test.

Maddy turned to her abruptly and said, "I want to move out. I want to go and live with Daddy."

Vicky felt her stomach propel itself up towards her heart and she hit the left indicator and the brakes, taking the car off the road and into a lay-by.

She turned off the engine, and the silence as the radio stopped talking at them was sudden and overwhelming. Vicky turned ninety degrees in her seat and looked at Maddy.

"But, baby girl," she said, "you can't move out. You're only twelve."

"It doesn't matter how old I am. I'm not happy and I want to move out and I've told Daddy and he says I can live with him. If you say it's okay."

"But, darling, I don't understand. I mean, what exactly . . . ?"

"It's Lorrie." Maddy's mouth was set hard. "I hate her and I don't want to live with her anymore."

Vicky reeled slightly at these words. She felt as if she'd been kicked in the chest. "What?"

"I used to really like her and she used to be really fun but now all she does is moan about everything I do, and she tuts all the time and she won't let me touch anything or go anywhere and she keeps buying all this rubbishy old stuff and some of it smells and I don't want to share a bedroom with Sophie anymore and I asked her if I could have Rhys's old room and she swore at me."

Maddy swallowed these last few words whole, gobbled them up so fast that Vicky was not entirely sure she'd heard right.

"She did what?"

"She swore at me. She called me a little shit."

"Jesus Christ." Vicky breathed in hard. "When was this, darling?"

"Last week. When you were collecting Sophie from Emma's house."

"But . . . but I don't understand. What happened? Tell me exactly what happened."

Maddy sighed, as if she'd had to tell this story a hundred times over. "Well, she was just coming out of her room and I was just coming out of my room and she said something about how lovely that me and Sophie shared a room, how she'd shared a room with *her* sister when she was my age and how lovely it had been, blah, blah, blah, and then I said, 'Well, I'm getting quite bored of sharing with her now,' and, it was like, you know, I've been *thinking* about saying something about Rhys's room for ages now and I'd been going to say something to you, but then, like, she was just *there* and so I said it and she went all weird and said I was a thoughtless little shit." She shrugged.

"Oh, my God." Vicky clutched her mouth with her hand. "But why are you only telling me this now? Why didn't you tell me before?"

"I don't know. I suppose I've just been thinking about it. I mean, no one's ever sworn at me before. I wasn't sure how I felt about it. And then we were at Dad's this weekend and I found myself telling him and when I was telling him about it, it all kind of started coming out. The way I feel. About Lorrie. And I realized that I don't like her. I don't like living with her. I don't like all her mess and her stupid precious *things* and the way she looks at me as if I'm part of some weird dream she's having and she isn't sure what to make of me. And how I can never invite friends back to my house because it's, like, so embarrassing and everyone's starting to think I'm weird. It just all . . . *came out*. And Dad said I could go and live with him. Now that I'm old enough to walk home from school. I could. I could do it. And then do every other weekend with you and Soph."

"Oh, Maddy." Vicky fought back a sob. "I don't know what to say. I really don't know."

"Just say yes."

"But . . . *I love you*. You're my baby. I couldn't bear it if I didn't see you every day."

Maddy shrugged again.

"I'd be lost, Maddy, utterly lost without you."

"No, you wouldn't. You'd be fine. You've still got Sophie. And Lorrie."

"But they wouldn't make me as happy as they do if you weren't there too."

"Well, then . . ."

"Well, then, what?"

"Move out."

"What?"

"Move out. Find a nice flat for us to live in. Just you, me and Sophie."

"But I can't!"

"Why not? You moved us out of our old house. We could just move again. You could still be friends with Lorrie and still see her all the time. But we just wouldn't have to live with her."

Vicky bit at her bottom lip. "You know, Lorrie, she's a very complicated person, and I'm so sorry she was so awful to you, but it's just been the anniversary of Rhys's death and she was probably feeling a bit oversensitive and that's *no excuse*, obviously, and I shall have a very strong word with her, but, darling, she's such a sweet soul and she loves you so very much . . ."

Maddy, her baby, her little woman-in-the-making, so composed, so sure of her own feelings, put up a restraining hand, as if to say, *"Stop. This far and no further."* "Seriously," she began, "I know you love her and everything. But I don't. I didn't choose her, *you did*. And I don't want to live with her anymore. And if you want to carry on living with her, that's fine, but I don't want to. And I need you"—she paused and stared at her fingers, before bringing her gaze back to Vicky's—"to let me go."

Vicky straightened herself and said, "No. No. I can't do that."

"Then let's move out."

"I can't do that either."

"Well, then," said Maddy.

❧

Beth wriggled her dress down towards her knees and touched her hair. Through the leaded windows of the country pub she could see the sky growing dark and bruised. On the table in front of her was a half-drunk glass of orange juice and 7Up. At the bar was a man called Jason who was ordering himself another pint of something local and a glass of wine for her.

"Are you sure I can't get you a real drink?" he'd said, half-raised from his seat.

And she'd shaken her head and said, "No, honestly, I'm fine." And then she'd watched him heading for the bar, looked at his strong, wide back and his good hair, his well-chosen clothes and pleasant feet in nice open sandals and thought, *This could be it, this could be my chance to be normal.* And as she'd thought that she'd called after him, "Actually, Jason, yes, a small glass of white wine. Please." And he'd smiled and looked like he'd scored a small victory. Another small victory. He'd been chasing her for months, ever since he'd started at her company in January. He was Australian. He was only twenty-five. It had taken her very much by surprise. After all these years and years working at the same place, sitting next to the same people, putting money in the same envelopes for the wedding gifts and birthday presents of the same colleagues, having the same conversations about the same things, eating the same sandwiches at the same desk, suddenly everything began to change. Suddenly the succession of predictable moments that constituted every day at work was punctured by new and unexpected ones. Unnecessary visits to her desk to ask for things that could easily have been requested via e-mail or an instant message. Suggestions for lunchtime drinks. Compliments. Endless compliments. About her hair, her clothes, her smell, her handwriting, her shoes, her parallel parking, her taste in cookies. A walk along a corridor now bore with it the frequent possibility of being stopped for a chat. Questions usually that would begin along the lines of, *"So, you're a local, where would you recommend for good-quality meat?"* Or, *"Is it possible to get a decent curry round here or do I have to go to Birmingham?"*

She had been doggedly ignoring his advances for months. The whole thing was ridiculous. She was thirty, for God's sake. Thirty and still conducting an insanely dangerous affair with her sister's partner. Thirty and still living at home. Thirty and nowhere near as pretty as she'd been in her youth. Past her prime. And she wasn't being disingenuous to think such a thing. Even Bill had stopped telling her she was pretty.

She'd agreed to a date with Jason because Bill had phoned to tell her that they were going on a last-minute Easter break. All five of them. Off to Mallorca to stay in some fancy villa with two swimming pools: one for the adults, one for the children. They were going with "some friends." Beth had shuddered and brought the conversation to a close. Too much there to digest in one sitting. Family. Holiday. Friends. *Last minute.* Beth had not done anything last minute in her life.

And then Jason had appeared at her desk the next day, all fresh skin and thick hair and wide eyes and tangible lust, and he'd asked her what she was up to on the weekend and she'd said, *"Nothing much,"* and he'd said, *"Fancy a drink?"* And she'd said, *"Sure."*

She'd arrived prepared to have a horrible evening. Vicky had asked her where she was off to and she'd said, *"The Black-Faced Lamb."* And Vicky had said, *"Oh, really, who are you going with, friends from work?"* And she'd said, *"Sort of."* And then Vicky had smiled and said, *"Is it a date?"* And Beth had grimaced and said, *"Sort of."* She had put on a dress, though. One of Bill's favorites: pale pink with wide shoulder straps and a full skirt and white trim around the hem. She'd pulled her dark hair back into a ponytail and was wearing her black Converse and a denim jacket.

"You look *adorable,*" Jason had said when she'd walked into the pub half an hour ago. "Totally."

She'd squirmed and said thank you and he'd said, *"What is it with you?"* And she'd said, *"What?"* And he'd smiled and said, *"Oh, nothing."*

He returned with their drinks and placed them on the table.

"I got you a Chardonnay? Hope that's okay?"

She shrugged and smiled and said, "I'm not exactly an expert."

His phone fizzed against the tabletop and he picked it up and turned it off without looking at it.

"Don't you want to know who that was?" she asked.

He looked at her curiously. "Not really. If it's important they'll call back. If it's not important, why would I answer when I'm sitting here with you?"

She thought of Bill, who treated his phone like a special-needs child, fussing over it and caring for it, meeting its every need and demand. She smiled and said, "Oh. Right."

"So, Beth? Bethan? What do you prefer to be called?"

"Beth," she said, "just call me Beth."

He smiled as though there was some inherent joy in her being known as Beth. "Great," he said, picking up his pint. "Thank you for coming out tonight. I really thought you'd say no."

She couldn't respond with any surprise to this declaration given that she had thought she would say no, too, until the precise moment she'd said yes. "That's okay," she murmured. "It's nice to be out."

"Yeah," he said, gazing at her knowingly, "I get the impression—and don't take this the wrong way—that you're quite a homebody."

"A what?"

"A homebody. A person who likes being at home. Staying in. Not going out."

She shrugged. "Yes," she said. "I suppose I am. It's just . . ." She closed her mouth against the distinct possibility of saying something mad. "Yes. I like being at home."

"And you live with your mum?"

"Yeah. I know. Terrible, isn't it? So embarrassing but, you know, I've never really earned enough money to get my own place . . ."

"South Gloucestershire PA of the Year, three times in a decade? And you're not earning enough money to rent a room?"

She flushed at his words. Of course she could afford to rent a room. She could probably afford to rent an entire flat, a small one, at least, somewhere unfashionable. "Yes, well. It's more"—she inhaled—"just family problems. Just family . . . *stuff*." She felt panicky. She wasn't used to talking about this kind of thing with anyone who didn't already know about it. "I'll get around to it, one day. And what about you? Where do you . . . I mean, I know where you live, but who do you . . . ?"

He laughed at her, gently. She didn't blame him. "I've got my own place, near the station in Cirencester," he said. "Overlooks the tracks, bit noisy, but I quite like the noise. I'd rather that than the noise of flatmates."

She nodded emphatically, as though she, too, had known the hell of noisy flatmates. "And why did you come to the Cotswolds?" She was using questions like tennis balls, hurling them at him too fast for him to get one back to her.

"Well, I was in London, *of course*"—he smiled—"and someone invited me to a house party out this way. Thought it was the prettiest place I'd ever been in my life, so I got straight onto the Internet and applied for every IT job I could find in the area."

Beth was barely listening—she was too busy thinking of what to ask him next. "And where did you live, in London?"

"Oh, well, you know, *everywhere*. North, south, west, not east. But pretty much all over."

"And whereabouts in Australia are you from?"

"Tasmania. Hobart. You know."

She did not know. She thought there might have been some connection with yachts. She smiled and said, "Oh, right. And how long do you think you'll be staying here?"

Jason puffed out his cheeks and then exhaled. "Good question," he said. "A few months, at least. My sister's getting married in December—I'll head home for that and then take a view on whether or not to come back. I'll be taking stock of what I've achieved here, what I've invested in, balance it up with family, home, you know, that kind of thing, make a call." He glanced meaningfully at her.

She flushed and looked into her wineglass. "How old's your sister?" she asked urgently. She picked up her glass and drank too much, too quickly. *This was a mistake.* She imagined

Meg and Bill sitting by an unlit rippling pool, abandoned inflatable toys floating darkly across its surface, drinking local wine from blue wineglasses, laughing together with their "friends" about lovely, normal middle-class things. She felt awash with hate and sadness. She drank the rest of her wine without tasting it and realized that Jason had just answered her banal question about his sister and that she had not heard his reply.

"You're very different," he said thoughtfully, "when you're not at work."

"Am I?"

"Yeah. You seem less . . . a bit more . . . just kind of different."

She smiled, rather defeatedly.

"Can I get you another one?" he asked, eyeing her empty glass.

She eyed it too, staring into its depths, analyzing her options. She could leave. They had had two drinks. It was nearly nine o'clock. She could claim tiredness and leave. Or she could stay. She could have another glass of this average wine and try to squeeze some more conversation out of the evening and go to bed tonight knowing that she had been on a date. That she had been "normal." Or she could stay and drink more than another glass and wring something even more eventful from the night: a moonlit walk, a drunken fumble, held hands, maybe even sex. She looked from her empty wineglass into Jason's inquiring gaze and he smiled.

"What?" she asked.

"Nothing," he replied.

She narrowed her eyes at him, accusing.

"Nothing!" he said again. "Nothing. Just thinking how pretty you are. That's all." She saw a pink blush stain his cheeks. It came and went in a moment. She felt her stomach roll gently at his words and at his embarrassment. "That's sweet," she said, picturing Meg, so solid, so matronly. "Thank you. And yes. I would like another one. Please."

He got to his feet. "Small? Big?"

"Medium," she said. "Thank you."

She watched him again, heading for the bar, his body language showing another small victory. She tugged her skirt a little up her legs, showing her shiny kneecaps. She arranged herself into a nice shape.

She tried not to cry.

◇

"So, how did your date go?" asked Vicky, mixing muesli from two separate jars into a large bowl and tipping a handful of raisins on top. "I didn't hear you come in. I thought maybe you'd spent the night out?" She accompanied her words with a big wide smile of vicarious delight.

"No," said Beth, flopping down heavily onto the bench and putting her elbows on the tabletop. She pulled the sleeves of her cardigan up her arms and yawned. "I slept here."

"And?"

Beth sighed. "And nothing. We had a drink. We had another drink. We had another drink. We went for a walk."

"To?"

"To his flat."

"Oh, where's that then?"

"By the station."

"Go on."

"We listened to music. We talked. I ordered myself a taxi. I came home." She shrugged and yawned again.

Vicky looked at her curiously. "So, a success?"

Lorelei wafted into the kitchen then, in her antique silk

kimono, her gray hair piled on top of her head, kohl smudged beneath her eyes. "Morning, all," she said.

Beth stared at her as she stood in the doorway, making her entrance, waiting for Vicky to jump up and serve her. But Vicky did not jump up and serve her. Instead she said, "Morning, my love," took her own bowl of muesli and her mug of black tea and sat down next to Beth. "Beth's just been telling me all about her date last night."

"It *wasn't* a date," Beth protested.

"Well, whatever. Your drinks, with a gentleman." She brought her arm around Beth's shoulders and clasped her to her for a moment. Beth pulled away slightly.

Lorelei stood in the doorway looking a bit lost.

"The kettle's just boiled, darling," said Vicky, and Beth could have sworn there was a hint of antagonism in her voice. Lorelei muttered inaudibly under her breath and shuffled across the flagstones in her lambskin slippers. "Where's the green tea?" she asked distractedly.

"Where it always is, darling, in the blue jar, next to the normal tea. So." She turned back to Bethan. "Do you think you'll be seeing him again?"

"No," said Beth bluntly.

"Oh. Really?"

"Yes. Really." She watched her mother, flapping about hopelessly, the sleeves of her kimono dressing gown dragging through the sugar bowl, tutting under her breath.

"That's a pity. Why not?"

Beth sighed. "Because," she began, "he's way too young. And he's going back to Australia in December, so there's absolutely no point in me getting close to him."

"Oh, sweetness, I'm sure you could persuade him to stay, using your feminine wiles."

"I'm no good at persuading people to do things." After four years in love with someone else's man, this she was very certain of.

"Oh, Beth." Vicky ran her hand around the back of her neck and smiled sadly. "What are we going to do with you?"

Lorelei brought her mug of tea to the table and sat down with a ponderous sigh. "Where are the girls?" she asked.

"They're with Tim."

"But it's not his weekend, is it?"

"No, but I thought it might be nice for us to have a quiet weekend together. Just the two of us."

Lorelei shrugged and sipped her tea.

Beth wriggled slightly. There was a strange atmosphere in here. And she was completely in the way. She imagined that Vicky must have been quite disappointed when she'd heard Beth walk into the kitchen this morning, hoping that she'd be in a strange man's bed instead. She mentally planned a long run and an afternoon movie next door with her dad.

She'd get breakfast in the village, she decided. During her run. They did a good granola. Well, actually, it was a very average granola, but it was a good excuse to get her running gear on and get out of here.

She let her thoughts skirt around the details of the previous night as she jogged along the lane into the village center. She did not want to dwell for too long on her own bizarre behavior, the way she had suddenly, after her second glass of wine, started to flirt outrageously with Jason, she who had never flirted with a man before in her life. And, she could see quite clearly this morning, it would have been fairly obvious to Jason that that was the case. She saw herself in the corners of her consciousness, her elbows on the table, her hands cupping her face, her eyelashes going up and down like defective blinds, licking her lips, and then, oh, yes, after her third, or was it her fourth glass of wine, running her toes along his shins. She pounded her feet harder against the tarmac, wanting to shake the memories out onto the ground, like gravel from her shoes.

She reached the café, *"the best thing ever to happen to the village,"* according to Vicky, who loved everything about the place, from its piles of fresh newspapers and artfully arranged mountains of banana and oatmeal muffins to the handmade oven gloves for sale by the till and the trendy, apron-clad proprietor from Islington called Morgan, after whom the café was named.

She ordered her granola and berries and hid in a corner with the magazine from the *Guardian*. She tried to concentrate on the letters page but her thoughts kept tugging her back to her mouth at Jason's ear, telling him what she was going to do to him once she'd got him back to his place. She imagined her sour-wine breath all over his fresh young skin. She cringed at the thought of her choice of language. She could not, of course, know what he'd thought. He'd said, *"Let's get you a strong coffee."* Which is what you say to someone who's unpleasantly drunk. Nobody wants to sober up a fun drunk, do they? She remembered, *my God*, trying to give him a blow job in the pub car park, tugging at the fly on his jeans.

The waitress—another Australian—brought her breakfast with a cheery smile and a tiny piece of apricot and vanilla tart they were "testing out." "Tell us what you think," she solicited. "Chef's keen for feedback." Beth smiled tightly and said thank you.

And Jason laughing and saying, *"Hey, hey, hey,"* and pulling her up from her knees and tugging his fly back up and saying, *"Will you be okay to walk, or shall I call a taxi?"*

She couldn't remember a taxi, not at that point in the evening. They must have walked. All through those dark country lanes. She spooned thick yogurt onto her granola. It came back to her. She'd felt herself young and girlish. She'd thought herself Bridget fucking Jones. She remembered twirling round and round, letting her skirt fill up, fancying herself a prom princess. She remembered his pulling her back to the curb, laughing again, saying, *"You're going to get yourself killed!"* And there it was, proof, if it were needed, that there was nothing funny about Bridget Jones.

And then, a lift. Someone had given them a lift. Someone yeasty and woolly with a Gloucester bur. She remembered making off-color jokes about Fred West. She remembered Jason apologizing on her behalf. She could not remember what the driver of the car had looked like. In these awful half memories, she saw him just as Fred West, even down to the brown sweater.

And then they were in Jason's flat and she was trying to open his trousers again, trying to pull him onto the bed. *Urgh. God.* She tipped the berries onto her granola and angled a spoon towards it all, as though she had any intention of eating it, as though she would ever be able to contemplate eating again. And then she remembered biting his earlobe and his yelping. And all the while she remembered thinking of Bill. Thinking of him in his holiday bed. With his fat wife. And she imagined all the while that he was watching them, that this was all a show, for Bill. That she was a porn star and Jason was her costar and that they were making porn. For Bill.

She'd done all that stuff.

Squeezed her breasts together. Made ludicrous noises. Asked to be fucked.

Christ.

But Jason had not gone along with her plans. He had peeled her away from him and held her by her wrists and said, *"Stop. You're drunk. You don't know what you're doing."* And she'd said, *"Oh, but I do. I know exactly what I'm doing."* And he'd said, *"Beth. Seriously. Stop it. I'm getting you a coffee."*

The coffee had done the trick. Two thick shots of espresso from a little silver machine. Like a shot of adrenaline to the heart. He'd offered to let her sleep in his bed; he'd sleep on the sofa. But she'd been adamant that she needed to go home. Sleep in her own bed. Be away from all this. So she'd sat sheepishly on Jason's sofa, waiting for a taxi that never seemed to come. She could not now remember much about Jason's flat. She never wanted to see Jason's flat ever again. She never wanted to see Jason ever again. Her stomach lurched at the hitherto unacknowledged fact that she would be seeing Jason in less than forty-eight hours. That she would walk into her office on Monday morning, South Gloucestershire PA of the Year, and he would be there. In all his Antipodean, twenty-five-year-old glory. And he would know what she was really like. South Gloucestershire Weirdo of the Year. And she would know what he was really like. A totally decent man.

She would have to leave.

She would have to find a new job and a new place to live.

And it was all Bill's fault.

She pushed away her uneaten granola and untested apricot tart and unread *Guardian* magazine and she left some money on the table and she plugged her earphones back into her ears and she smiled as normally as she could at the nice Australian waitress and she left the café and she ran. She ran all the way to the cemetery and all the way to her brother's grave. It was a bright Saturday morning, busy and safe, not that she cared if she got raped. Not this morning. Bring it on. She was numb.

His grave was dusty and neglected. She ran her fingers over the engraved words:

RHYS ARTHUR BIRD
1ST MARCH 1975—31ST MARCH 1991
SWEET SIXTEEN FOREVER

Today was 12 April. More than twelve years ago. He'd be twenty-eight now. Older than Jason. How peculiar.

She tried not to think about that day. She'd spent twelve years trying not to think about that day. Maybe that's why she was so weird. Everyone else had dealt with it. Meg had been so strong. Rory had been so angry. Vicky had been so practical. Dad had been so normalizing. And Mum had just . . . well, Mum didn't count. And no one—and she didn't mean to feel sorry for herself—but no one had needed Beth. No one had even really noticed Beth. No, that wasn't fair—Meg had noticed Beth. Meg had noticed that Beth had stopped eating, and said, in that patronizing way of hers, *"I was the one who found him and I'm still eating. We've all got to stay strong, even you, Beth . . . even you."*

Even her.

As though she was a special case.

She felt a surge of anger. She thought again of fat Megan sitting on a sun lounger in a sensible swimsuit shouting at her children. Then she thought again of her own fingers at Jason's fly last night and his howl of agony as she bit his earlobe too hard. Then she thought of her room at the house, the room she'd never left, and the sour atmosphere between Vicky and her mother, and it was Easter next weekend and she'd vowed, hadn't she, vowed to herself that she would not be here for it and it looked as though she would be; she'd discussed it with her mother, she vaguely remembered, the possibility of making a simnel cake.

She brought her lips to the warm stone of Rhys's grave and kissed it long and hard. And then she ran on.

෴

She'd bought three rolls of extra-strong refuse sacks and two pairs of plastic gloves, and cleared out the boot of her car. She'd got a quote for a skip which could be dropped off on Monday if she could persuade Lorrie into going through with it.

Vicky heard Colin tapping at the kitchen window and jumped to her feet.

"Hello, lovely man," she said, greeting him with a kiss to his unshaven cheek. "Thank you so much. You have no idea how much I appreciate this. You're an absolute star."

Colin shrugged and said, "We've got a long way to go yet." Ever the realist, dear Colin. That's why he hadn't been able to hack living with Lorrie. You had to have a core of pink fluff and fairy dust to hack living with Lorrie. "Where's Beth?"

"She went for a run," she replied. "And some breakfast in the village. Said she'd be back later on. She went on a date last night."

Colin raised an eyebrow above the frame of his spectacles. "Really," he said.

"Yes. A man from work. Didn't tell me much, you know what she's like, but really, her first date since she split with Simon. I think she might be finally moving on."

The ancient water pipes that ran throughout the house inside dusty wooden cladding squealed, juddered and creaked, signifying the end of Lorrie's morning shower. Vicky and Colin smiled nervously at each other.

"Have you said anything?" he began. "Anything at all?"

"No," said Vicky, "just been a bit frosty with her. I mean, honestly, Colin, I have managed to steer my way through twelve years of parenting without ever having to swear at one of my children. As much as I may have wanted to, on occasion. But it's more than that, Colin. I could forgive that, just about. It's the fact that my daughter is too embarrassed to bring friends home. I always thought maybe she was just not that interested in having friends home to play, but . . ." She sighed, and held back encroaching tears. "Anyway"—she brought herself back to common sense—"it has to stop. And she'll have to accept that. Otherwise . . ." She broke off as she heard Lorelei's birdlike footsteps crossing the landing upstairs, from bathroom to bedroom. "Otherwise"—she lowered her voice—"I'm not sure I can justify living here anymore."

Colin flicked on the kettle and nodded. "Absolutely not," he said. "It was fine when our lot were small. Just a bit of clutter then, a bit of eccentricity. But this"—he spread his arms out—"this is not tenable. And as you say, not fair at all on your girls."

They both fell silent at the sound of Lorelei overhead. Voices carried in this house. Colin made his coffee in silence and then joined Vicky at the table. When Lorelei walked in a few minutes later she balked at the sight of them. "Good grief," she said, "you two look terrifying. What are you both doing sitting there staring at me like that?"

Vicky smiled at her love. "Sit," she said, "we need to talk."

Lorelei narrowed her eyes. "Where's Beth?"

"She went for a run. Sit."

She tutted and sat. Vicky smiled at her again and held her hands in hers. Lorelei's hands were so thin now, the skin so silky and fragile, like those little sheets of powdered blotting paper ladies used to carry in their handbags. Big blue veins bulged up under the thin skin and her nails were far too long. But still, they were her hands, Lorrie's hands. Vicky swallowed down the sadness of knowing that she was still madly in love with this woman. This woman who had called her precious child a shit.

"Now listen, sweet girl, you know I love you, so much."

Lorelei moved her fingers to her sinewy throat and tutted again.

"Heaven knows why," Vicky continued. "But I do. But we have a problem here. Maddy says you called her a nasty name."

"I did not!"

Vicky sighed away her frustration. She'd known Lorelei would deny it. Like a child. "Regardless," she said, "let us just say that relations between you and Maddy are not good, darling. Are they?"

Lorelei shrugged and tutted. "It's not that," she said wearily, "it's just, my things, Vick, all my things . . ."

"Well, yes, precisely. I do think, Lorrie, that if we could just get to the bottom of the problem of all the *things*, then we might be able to sort out all our other little problems too."

"Yes," agreed Lorelei, sighing wanly as if *finally* someone was trying to help her. "Exactly."

"So, darling, what I thought we could do this weekend, while the girls are away, before the big Easter weekend, you know, and while we've got an extra pair of hands"—she patted Colin's hands affectionately—"is to maybe make a start on dealing with your things. Start to, you know, get some kind of order to it. I think"—she smiled encouragingly—"if we put our backs into it, not to mention our souls, we could make a real difference. I truly think we could relocate a substantial amount. Maybe even half of it."

"Relocate?" Lorelei's lips pursed.

"Yes. I think we could probably do quite a lot of good work for the local charity shops, don't you think, Colin, hmm?" She turned and smiled at him, winked at him conspiratorially. My God, they both needed to handle this right. Use absolutely the right language. No talk of junk or rubbish or getting rid or throwing away. Only positive words. Otherwise Lorrie would lose the plot, throw her toys out of her pram, and nothing would ever change.

"Plus I've been talking to a nice man called Paul who said he can help us. Relocate some of your things. If we get them all ready for him, on Monday morning he'll bring along a big pink skip—isn't that marvelous! A pink skip!—and haul it all away for us." She flinched and bit her lip. *Haul it all away.* Uh-oh. That had blown it. "I mean, you know, rehome it."

"No, you don't," snapped Lorrie. "You mean *get rid* of it." She sighed sadly. "Yes," she said. "You're right. Fine. Let's do it." Vicky gulped as she saw a sheen of tears glaze over Lorrie's sea-green eyes.

"Darling—" she began.

"But," Lorrie interrupted, "not one thing goes without my approval. Do you understand? Particularly *you*, Colin." She narrowed her eyes menacingly at him. "Don't think I won't know, because I will." She laughed then, a delicate shred of a laugh, but a laugh nonetheless. Lorrie had always had the most glorious laugh. Vicky still remembered that first night, with the Beaujolais, before that great fissure of tragedy had rent the whole dream in two. She still remembered Lorrie's lovely laugh, in front of the fire, her long fingers around the stem of her glass.

Colin laughed too, under his breath, and cracked a smile. The atmosphere lightened momentarily.

"Right," said Vicky, capitalizing on the sudden, unexpected

mood of positivity. "We need a plan. And I think the first priority should be the hallway and the staircase."

Lorrie sighed. Vicky squeezed her hands again. "Good girl, darling," she said. "You're such a good girl. Right, let's get to it!"

❧

When Beth returned from her morning run and her visit to Rhys's grave, she could tell immediately that something was afoot. Vicky's car was parked up on the curb with its hatchback gawping open and the curtains on the street side of the house had been drawn open for the first time in years. She brought her face down to the low windows and peered inside, her hands cupped to the filthy glass. Inside she could see the shadowy figures of Mum, Dad and Vicky, in a three-headed huddle on the floor at the foot of the stairs. It looked as though they were fighting. She watched, mesmerized, for a moment. Vicky had hold of one end of an old bath towel and Mum had hold of the other and Dad was trying to stop Mum hitting Vicky and Vicky was looking exasperated and Mum was crying and looking like a crazy old witch and all around them were bin bags and old clothes and, my God, was that . . . ? Yes, it was Beth's old pink polka-dot raincoat and there was Meg's old school duffle coat, the gray one with the fur-lined hood, and there—she squinted hard to see—there was her old duvet cover, the one with the blue and pink squares on it, the one she'd thrown away when all the popping fasteners at the bottom had finally fallen off. What on earth was that doing here? She remembered, distinctly, taking it to be recycled at the charity shop in the village. How on earth had it found its way back into the house? She let herself quietly in through the back door and then tiptoed through the kitchen and towards the hallway.

"You utter fucking *bastards!*" she heard her mother wail. "Rhys used that towel, you know. It was his *favorite!* It still smells of him, for God's sake—smell it, you bastard, smell it!"

Her father sighed and said, "No. I don't want to smell it, because it smells of mildew. Like everything else in this bag. Okay? It is moldy and it smells of mildew and as long as there are bags full of old towels smelling of mildew cluttering up the house, Vicky and her girls are going to find it very hard to live here. Do you see?"

"Stop threatening me!"

"Colin's not threatening you, darling," soothed Vicky. "He's just being absolutely honest with you. And it is true. If we can't sort out this mess, or at least go some substantial way towards sorting it out, then really, well . . ." She trailed off. "Well, it doesn't bear thinking about. So that's why this is so important. So incredibly important. And we have been doing this for"— she consulted her wristwatch—"nearly two hours, darling, and all we have is one tiny little bag of things to leave the house. We have to do better, Lorrie. We have to do much, much better."

Lorelei sank backwards against the wall and put the heels of her hands into her eye sockets. "Take the fucking towel," she said softly. "Just take it. And take my fucking heart out of my fucking chest cavity while you're about it."

Beth inhaled quietly and waited to see what would happen.

"Good girl," said Vicky, making her way towards Lorrie on her knees. She encircled her inside her arms. "Good girl." She pulled away from Lorrie, gently folded the towel into a cube and placed it in an open bin bag. "Right then, what about this old kettle?"

Beth remembered it vaguely from the long-distant land-scape of her childhood. It had started smoking one morning, she recalled, smoking and making ominous buzzing sounds.

Dad had turned the electricity off at the mains, unplugged the thing, and as far as she could recall, had thrown it in the bin. Yet here it was again, like her duvet cover, risen from the ashes of her childhood, still living and breathing.

Lorrie looked up at Colin with sad eyes and then glanced wanly at the blackened kettle. "Oh, but, darling," she said, in her soft voice, the one she'd used when they were all children, "don't you remember that day? The day it exploded? Don't you? It was the morning of the twins' first nativity. It snowed. And they were so adorable, the two of them, with their little matching silver wings and their tinsel halos. Do you remember? And everyone said *aaah* when they came on the stage together, because they were so blond then, the pair of them, remember? So precious. I mean, they actually looked like *real angels*. They really, really did."

Lorelei started to cry and Vicky wrapped her back up in her arms and Colin said, "They did, darling, it's true. And I have photos of them. Lovely big color photographs that we can look at every day, if we want. We can stick them up on the walls and the ceilings and look at them all the time. We don't need old exploded kettles to remind us of that day."

Lorelei sniffed and lifted her head from Vicky's embrace. "Photographs are lies, darling. You know that. They're one-dimensional. They only tell you about one precise moment in a whole infinite string of moments, they don't tell you about the kettle exploding or the snow on the ground. I need *more* than photographs. Much much more. Don't you see?" She looked up at them through her red tear-streaked eyes. And then she saw Beth standing in the doorway and she spread out her arms and she said, "Look, darling, look what they're doing to me. These people who say they love me. They're killing me, Bethy, they're just killing me. Can't you make them stop?"

Beth stiffened at her words. It was happening. It was finally happening. The acknowledgment of the cancer at the core of this house. Here it was, the dressings being removed, the scars being revealed. She flinched. She didn't want to see it. She didn't want to be a part of it. It needed to happen, that much she knew. But she did not want to be a witness to it. She forced a smile and shrugged her shoulders and said, "I was just popping home, just to get a jacket, I'm er . . ." And then she turned, before she could say anything that might drag her into this open wound.

She ran through the house in her socks, seeing it suddenly through fresh eyes. Things loomed ominously over her and at her. How had she not noticed before how dirty everything had got? The layers of children's drawings on the kitchen walls, splattered with cooking grease and dirt, held up with grubby yellow slivers of old Sellotape. The mountains of bin bags covered in dust, the piles of old rags, some stiff with whatever historical fluid they had last been used to absorb. She picked her way up the staircase, past piles of dirty trainers, who knows whose, past mugs and plates with unidentifiable colonies growing on them, heaps of paperwork and tatty magazines. And the books. Teetering towers of them; she stared at one, here by her feet, something from the seventies called *The Best of Clifford D. Simak* with a fantasy illustration of a spaceship on the cover. Who was Clifford D. Simak? And which member of this household had ever had an interest in science fiction? Not one. So why was it here? Where had it come from? And how had her old duvet cover found its way back into the house?

She dropped the tatty paperback and ran for her room. She noticed, properly, for maybe the first time, that in order to get to her room, she needed at two separate points to turn sideways-on in order to navigate her way through piles of bags and boxes that had formed the beginnings of a corridor. When had that happened? She was sure that was a recent development. And then she pulled open her bedroom door—the movement of which was impeded at ninety degrees by yet another pile of her mother's possessions, a cash-and-carry box of pink lightbulbs—and slammed it hard behind her. She waited for a sense of relief to flood through her, a sense of disconnection from her mother's madness, but as she glanced around her room she saw the truth for herself. Clothes left piled up and unhung. Thirty different mascaras on her dressing table. Shoes jumbled up in mismatching chaos inside an old cardboard box. There was nothing nice in here. Nothing pretty. No order. No control. It was a dumping ground.

She thought of her desk at work, of the neat rows of filing boxes, the tiger-stripe orchid in a shiny black pot, the sun streaming through the clean windows onto her light ash furniture, her manicured fingernails set above her newly vacuumed keyboard, her hair neatly folded up on the back of her head, and the lines of people who came in and out of her office all day at whom she flashed a sparkling smile of efficiency and self-assurance. What would they think if they could see her now? Who would they think she was?

From downstairs she could hear the sound of her mother wailing about a broken plant pot. She lay down upon her bed—she had not changed her sheets, she now realized, for nearly two months—and she stared up at the ceiling. She sighed at the strings of cobwebs hanging from the cornices and she thought of the cupboard full of unused dusters and brooms and sweepers and mops downstairs that exploded open every time you touched the door, and she thought about Bill and Meg in their Mediterranean idyll and this time she took not an iota of pleasure from the image of Meg oozing out of her sensible, size-sixteen swimsuit.

She saw herself, possibly for the first time in her life, objectively. She was a prisoner. But not, as she'd always told herself, because her mother needed her. Her mother didn't need her. Her mother had Vicky, her mother had her house and her stuff. No, Beth was a prisoner entirely of her own making. And it was time to go. The only thing keeping her here, apart from her own guilt, was Bill. Her sister's partner. Who barely even looked at her when he picked her up from the station these days. Who didn't call for weeks on end. Who hadn't taken her bra off during sex for over a year. *That had to end too.* It all had to end. *Right now.*

And at the very same moment that she felt her lungs about to fill up with self-hatred and drown her, she heard her phone buzzing from within her backpack. She pulled the bag towards her and located her phone and there it was: a life raft.

Hi there, hope you're okay today. Feeling really guilty about pressurizing you into drinking so much last night. Totally my fault. How do you feel about a rerun tonight, strictly orange juice? I'd really like another chance to get to know you. Take care, Jase.

∽

Six months later, on a particularly dark and long-shadowed October afternoon, Vicky, Maddy and Sophie hired a white van and moved all their things into a little flat around the corner.

When they shut their new front door behind themselves a few hours later, Maddy came to Vicky and encircled her mother inside her arms.

"Thank you, Mummy," she breathed into Vicky's soft sweater, "thank you."

Vicky kissed the top of her daughter's head and wiped away a warm tear from the side of her nose. "Darling," she said, holding Maddy's face in her hands, "I did everything I could, I really did, but silly Lorrie did not want to be helped. No. So. Here we are, the three of us."

"Will you go back, if she tidies the house?"

Vicky sighed and pulled Maddy back towards her. "She's not going to tidy her house, Mads. I know that now." Another tear spilled from her other eye. It was not in Vicky's nature to give up on anything, least of all love. "Poor old Lorrie," she said. "Poor beautiful soul." The timing had been dreadful. Here they were, moving away, and in two months Beth would be gone too, to Australia to try to make it work with that nice boy, Jason. Lorrie would then be completely alone for the first time in her life. The worry was overwhelming. But there you go. It had to be done.

Maddy pulled away from her then and smiled. "Can I invite Jade? To come over?"

Vicky blinked. There it was, the thing she hadn't noticed for all those months and years. That most mundane of childhood requests, which had been absent. She smiled and then she said, "Yes, gosh, absolutely, definitely. Tell her to come over now."

8

Monday 3rd January 2011

Hello, lovely Jim!

I missed your e-mails these last couple of days. Sorry to hear you've been under the weather, and delighted to hear you're all better now. Maybe it was something you had to eat on New Year's Eve? One thing after another, isn't it?!

I'm glad you liked the pics. Thank you for your sweet comments. I was quite a looker in my day, but not vain with it, if you see my meaning. Rather a tomboy, always running around barefoot, forgetting to comb my hair.

Anyway, you asked what I meant by Meg thinking I should see a therapist. Clearly I have alarmed you horribly! (I jest, Jim. From what little I know about you from our e-mails these past few weeks, I have very much taken the impression that you are an open-minded man, unshakable, to an extent—am I right?!) Well, here it is, the truth about me, or should that be: THE TRUTH ABOUT ME . . . ? ! You have been very honest with me about your problems with drink and marijuana, you have used the language of a man who accepts what he is and can put a name to it. So I suppose it is only fair for me to do the same.

I am a hoarder, Jim. I only use this word as using any other word might be misleading. I could say that I am a COLLECTOR, maybe. Or a MAGPIE. I could, perhaps, describe myself as a person who does not like to throw things away. But none of these would be at all sufficient. Because I can only assume that once a social worker has been to your home to assess it in terms of health-and-safety considerations (not for me, you understand, but for my next-door neighbors, the shame, the shame!!) and referred to you over and over again as being a person having a Hoarding Disorder, then really, you just have to hold up your hands, sigh, and say, well, okay. You got me. So. Yes. I am. But remember, Jim, that just as alcoholism carries myriad implications, so the Hoarding Disorder covers a trillion different variations on a theme. I am not dirty. And nor is my house. I just have too many things. Almost to the extent that there is no room for dirt. Ha, ha!

I have heard about people who hoard rubbish. Their own actual litter and filth. That disgusts me. And people who hoard animals. Now that is particularly awful as obviously there is suffering involved. Those poor animals. Me, I just buy too many things. I also like to keep what I call souvenirs, of moments from my life, objects that I can pick up and look at and remember something that may have been forgotten to me otherwise. The human memory is such a cruel, frustrating thing, the way it just discards things without asking permission, precious things. At least here, in my house, I have control over my memories.

Of course, nobody understands. When I say that Meg and I argue, this is what we nearly always argue about. She thinks it is a matter of TIDYING UP. Of having a CLEAR-OUT. She has absolutely no idea . . . and she, I fear, has gone too far the other way. I would call her a neat freak. She is mad about cleanliness and order and minimalism. And she has four children! It confounds me! So I have asked her not to come to my house anymore. In fact, since we're being so frank, you may as well know that no one has been to my house. Not since the funeral. Something happened at that funeral. It was the most appalling day. I'll tell you about it another time. Let's keep this bite-sized for now!! But I made a decision that day that I needed to batten down the hatches and be on my own. Don't misinterpret that though, Jim. I am still quite social. In the shops I visit I am a loyal, beloved customer. I wave and say hello to friends and neighbors. I take phone calls and send e-mails and accept invitations (within reason!!). But here, in my home, I am best left alone. I am happy. ☺

Well, this has been a long one. But I suppose it was quite a BIG one.

Much love to you, lovely Jim, please write soon. I am finding your e-mails to be absolutely the brightest stars in my day.

L xxxxx

APRIL 2011

Molly and Meg sat in silence in the fridgelike cool of the people carrier, absorbing the facts that had just been gently ladled over them by a lady called Stella Richards with a sweet-toned voice in a wood-paneled room in the county offices in St. Georges Road.

Lorelei had died of undiagnosed and untreated tuberculosis, brought about by severe malnutrition. She had weighed six stone eight pounds at the time of her death, had lost all but five of her teeth and had been brought in mainly bald. The contents of her stomach had been hard to identify as they had been more than a week old. But it appeared that her last "meal" had been a rice cake and a mouthful or two of orange juice. They had also found a small cancerous tumor inside her lung cavity, but this was not being recorded as related to her cause of death.

There was more, but Meg had stopped listening at the realization that her mother had starved herself and then died a terrible, painful, protracted death, in her car, on the lay-by of an A-road twenty minutes from the village, all alone. While Meg sat in her comfortable home, surrounded by her hearty (and in one particular case, worryingly overweight) children, watching *The Great British Bake Off* and drinking nice wine.

"Shit," said Molly.

"Mmm," said Meg. She wanted a shower now. A really long one, with scalding water, one that left her pink and raw.

"That was totally the saddest, worst thing I've ever heard."

Meg glanced at her daughter, covered her hand with hers. "I'm really sorry," she said. "Really sorry. Christ, if that doesn't constitute 'inappropriate for a teenage girl,' then it doesn't bear thinking about what else they're dealing with in that place."

"It's fine," said Molly. "I'm glad . . ." She paused, then squeezed Meg's hand. "I'm glad you didn't have to listen to all that by yourself."

"Bloody woman!" said Meg, suddenly filled with the old sense of exasperation and impotent fury she'd been filled with for most of her life. She bashed the steering wheel with the heel of her hand. "Bloody ridiculous, stupid, awful woman! *A rice cake.* A fucking *rice cake*! Like an anorexic teenager, for Christ's sake. Aagh!" She took her hand from Molly's and slammed them both down hard against the steering wheel. She shouted out again and then exhaled, calmed herself. "Sorry, darling," she said. "I'm sorry. I'm just so cross about all this. So cross. She never had a clue, never had any idea how to care for people. Including herself. She knew how to love them, but never to care for them. And if she'd had a shred of normal, decent—God, I don't know—humanity, she would not have left me with all this. All her disgusting filth and shit and mess! It's all just so, so, *lurid*. My whole revolting family. Just one disgusting lurid thing after another." She brought herself to a sudden halt. Too much. Way too much.

Molly looked at her. "You okay, Mum?" she said.

Meg exhaled again, forced a smile. "Yes," she said, running her hand down the side of Molly's cheek. "Yes. I'm just . . ." She sighed. "I'm just dealing with a toxic family. I've managed to keep them away for all these years, and now they're all drifting back and I know it has to happen but, still, it's a lot to take on board."

And as she said these words her phone rang. Once again, the number was unknown. She took the call on her hands-free.

"Yes?" she replied cautiously.

"Meggy?"

She sighed. "Dad?"

"Hello, my darling. I'm just calling to say that I'm on my way. From the airport. I'll be there in an hour. Shall I meet you at the house?"

Meg breathed in deeply. "Are you alone?" she said.

"Yes, yes, of course."

"Good," said Meg, her mouth set hard. "Come to our hotel. I'll meet you in reception."

"Good. Excellent. And, darling, how are—?"

But Meg hung up, before her father could finish his question.

APRIL 2004

He had not been to the airport for months. He had not left his neighborhood for months. It was strange to be back among the hubbub of normal people. Odd to see children and families and teenage groups, people who had not set foot inside a brothel or a girlie bar, people who were not in Thailand to get high or to have sex with anyone. They looked so fresh, these other people, bizarrely, unnaturally so. Rory glanced down at his own self: sweaty polo shirt, baggy shorts, sun-bleached flip-flops, gold link bracelet, skin tanned to the color of roast beef, more tattoos now—new ones on his shins and his calves, around his wrists and his throat. He ran his fingers through his hair: collar-length, burned blond, not related in any recognizable way to fashion. There was no fashion where Rory lived. He just wore what Owen wore. He'd subconsciously started to dress the same as Owen over the years: polo shirt with the collar up, gold jewelry, shades on top of his head, beads around his neck, trainers, flip-flops, combat shorts. He could have been anyone from anywhere; he could have been American, Australian, South African. It was just easier.

He scanned the crowds filing through the arrivals gate. After a five-minute procession of dairy-skinned Scandinavians, the next influx looked English: pasty and pale-faced after a long winter. He pulled himself up straighter, pushed his hair down over his ears. And then there he was and it took Rory totally by surprise, the flood of emotion, the tears.

His dad.

Colin's face broke apart at the sight of him and they hurtled towards each other like victorious teammates, bundled up against each other, lost their faces into each other's shoulders and squeezed hard. Then they pulled apart and regarded each other. It had been four years, almost to the day.

His dad had a rucksack slung over one shoulder and was wearing classic middle-aged-man gear: sensible jeans, a T-shirt with a logo on it, a North Face jacket, cheap trainers. He looked so old. Or actually, no, not old, he looked like a young person with an aging disease.

"Oh, my goodness," said Colin, his eyes twinkling with pleasure, "look at you. Just look at you! So brown! So . . ." He searched for a word. "So laid-back. Wow!"

It was the first time that Rory and his dad had been alone together since that afternoon in the pub, when Colin had given him his birth certificate and set him free. Rory had missed him the most, more than his mum, more than his sisters, more than his niece and nephews (he'd only actually met one of Meg's boys and he couldn't even remember his name).

"Here—" He took his dad's rucksack from his shoulder and slung it over his own. He was glad in a way that he'd never grown taller than his dad. It was nice to be able to look up at him, even if it was only a couple of inches. He'd warned his dad about his circumstances, about the bare-wood room behind a shop on the strip, about the people coming and going, the pounding music and shrieks of delight late into the night. He'd told him about the ineffectual ceiling fan and the cockroaches and the mattress on the floor. But he hadn't told him everything. Not yet.

Rory drove them back in his new car. Well, new to him. It was an old Fiat Panda that he'd bought off someone for a few hundred Thai baht. It smelled of spliff and dog shit but it had air-con and Colin smiled into the chilled blast as they cruised down the freeway.

"Aah," he said, "that's nice." He still had his North Face

jacket on and his gray hair was stuck to his head like wet strips of papier-mâché. "This heat," he said, "it's like a furnace. How do you cope?"

"I have acclimatized." He turned and smiled at his dad. He had not seen a human being he was related to since the day he'd left his baby daughter in Spain four years ago. It was a good feeling. "You must be really tired," he said.

"No. Not at all. Doing nothing makes me tired. All this"—Colin gestured through the windows at the passing scenery—"this makes me feel *alive*."

His father's life over the last few years was as much of a mystery to Rory as he imagined his own life was to his father. He had no idea how Colin spent his days, who he saw, where he went, what he did. He knew there'd been a memoir of some description undertaken, but he didn't imagine that that had ever come to much. He knew that there'd been a girl-friend for a while, someone much younger than him called April or May or something. But as far as he was aware that had not come to much either. And now his dad was fifty-nine, retired from the college he'd taught at for all those years, living alone and traveling for the first time in his life to another continent.

Rory parked the Panda behind his building and pulled Colin's rucksack from the backseat. "Welcome to my very, very humble abode."

His room was behind a curtain made of shredded multicolored plastic. One of the girls from the bar was sitting on his back step, breast-feeding her baby.

"Dad, this is Rochana. Rochana, this is my dad, Colin."

Rochana's face lit up and she pulled the baby's mouth off her breast and got to her feet, barely five feet in cutoff shorts and a halter-neck top. "Aah, your *father*! So nice! So nice!"

She shook his hand and Colin beamed at her and stroked her baby's hair and said, "What a lovely baby. How old is she?"

"She is nine months. She is my angel!"

Colin smiled again and Rory remembered how much his father had always liked babies.

"She's beautiful. What's her name?"

"I call her Star. Because when she is big she will be a *super-star!*"

Rory realized that he had never asked Rochana what her baby's name was. Because he was not interested in her baby, just in when she'd be able to go back to work full-time.

He held the plastic curtain back for his father and ushered him through. "This is it," he said apologetically.

"Oh," said his father, smiling stoically. "It's fine. It's perfectly nice."

"No," Rory laughed, "it's a shit hole. But it's just temporary, while I'm saving."

You could hear the lunchtime show through the back wall, the bang-bang of Evanescence, the tinny drone of the MC announcing the names of the girls.

"Wow," said his dad, "I see what you mean about the noise. What a racket."

"Yeah," said Rory, "all day, half the night. You get used to it, I promise."

"It's fine," said Colin. "I didn't come here to sleep."

Rory smiled and didn't ask the question that threatened to spill from his lips: *Why did you come here?*

He pulled a beer from his fridge and handed it to Colin. Then he opened one for himself and raised a toast. "To you, being here. I really appreciate it."

"Nonsense," said Colin, slurping back the cold beer. "Thank you. For letting me come. And I promise you I won't cramp your style. Whatever you need to do, just let me know and I'll make myself scarce. I've wanted to come to Thailand since I was a student. There's plenty I can be getting on with."

From the strip beyond the bar came the sounds of traffic: horns blaring, mopeds humming, people shouting. "Well," said Rory, "I'm not working until tonight, so we can just hang for a while. What do you fancy doing?"

"How about some lunch? Some street food. Somewhere that does a good pad Thai?"

Rory smiled. If there was one thing he knew about his neighborhood, it was where to get the best noodles. "Come on," he said, "get that jacket off, put some shorts on, I'll take you out for lunch."

～◇～

It was strange seeing his neighborhood through somebody else's eyes. So much of what Rory saw was under cover of night, standing on the street, in the phosphorescent glow of streetlights and neon, sunburned tourists who'd been drinking since noon, stag parties and sad fucks, perverts and freaks. He slept most of the day, while the families and the normal folk were gallivanting on the strip and on the beach. By the time he woke up they were moving on, packing up their bags, heading to hotels and guesthouses for showers and early suppers. Even when he was awake during the day, he only really absorbed the elements of the world he knew; he saw the girls from the bars looking wan and out of sorts; he saw the punters, the dealers, the ravers, all rendered strangely distorted by being out of their nighttime context.

But now, here, in this clean midday, with his sweet father by his side, he saw that he lived in a bustling seaside town, a town where you could buy souvenirs and sun cream, *Now* magazine and the *Daily Mail*. If you hadn't witnessed the underbelly, you might not even notice it was there.

They sat on pavement-mounted stools by a small noodle stall. The guy who ran the stall was the son of the woman who ran the girls at the club. He was married to one of them. Even lunch was interwoven with sex.

"Hello, hello!" said the noodle guy.

"Hi, Rak. This is Colin, my dad." He didn't bother introducing him to his father.

"Ah, good," said the man, "very good. You want pad Thai?"

Colin rubbed his hands together. "Yes, please!"

"Chicken, pork?"

"Chicken, thank you."

Rory walked away from the stall, leaving his father there watching intently as Rak threw things around in a wok. He would have to tell him eventually. He was going to be here for four days. He would have to tell him that he worked for Owen as a door manager at Owen's girlie bar and as a runner for Owen's small but ever-growing cocaine dealership. He would have to tell him that he was a criminal.

He'd tried to put him off coming—he'd told him his room was too small, he worked too many hours—but his dad had just said, *"I don't mind."* He'd batted away every attempt to make him change his mind and eventually Rory had capitulated. Because, in fact, the benefits of seeing his father after all this time had far outweighed his discomfort at having to come clean about the life he was living out here. He just had to hope that his father would not judge him too harshly.

"Oh, good God," he heard Colin saying behind him, "oh, my God." He was halfway through a mouthful of noodles and his eyes were rolling back in his head with pleasure. "This is the most incredible pad Thai I have ever tasted in my life. Oh . . ." He lifted another forkful to his mouth. "How do you say 'thank you' in Thai, Rory?"

Rak passed Rory his noodles and then Rory and Colin sat up at the bar and ate them together, facing a wall.

"So," said Rory, "how is everyone? Dare I ask?"

Colin groaned and wiped some grease from his chin. "You mean Mum?"

"Well, yeah, mainly, I suppose."

"She's okay," said Colin. "She's still not got over Beth moving away. I mean, she was thirty-one years old, for God's sake, I don't know what your mother was expecting, that she would stay at home forever?"

"I think she thought we'd *all* stay at home forever. I think she thought that none of us would ever want to be anywhere else."

Colin sighed. "I know, I know. Poor Mum."

"And how's she doing without Vicky?"

"Not good. I mean, Vicky still comes to stay every other weekend, when the girls are with Tim, and Meg comes up with the little ones as often as she can. And obviously I'm just next door. But basically she's on her own, for the first time in her life."

"And the house?"

"Appalling. Health-and-safety hazard. She completely filled Vicky's girls' room—your old one—the minute they moved out, and then about thirty seconds after Beth went to Australia she started dumping stuff in there. And there's been a worrying development—she's started hoarding newspapers . . ."

"Oh, shit."

"Yes. I know. I've written to that TV show."

"Which TV show?"

"*Life Laundry*. You know, on the BBC. They clear out people's houses for them."

"Cool," said Rory. "Have you told her?"

Colin rolled his eyes at him. "What do you think? Anyway, I doubt it will come to anything—I don't even know if they're going to make another series. But it seemed worth a try. I mean, I just really don't know where to turn. We all keep trying, me, Vicky, Meg. We're always trying to persuade her, thinking up new and ingenious ways of convincing her to part with things. But if anything it makes her worse. So . . ." He shrugged and blew out his cheeks. "Well, you know, you just kind of give up eventually, don't you? When someone doesn't want to help themselves. There's only so much you can do and . . ." He smiled sadly. "I'm not sure I can help her anymore."

Rory scraped the last noodles from the sides of the container and licked them from his plastic fork. He wiped his mouth with a paper towel and considered the issue of his mother. He was so distant from it over here, he barely thought about it. The concept of a troubled, lonely, middle-class, gay fifty-eight-year-old living alone in dusty squalor in a chocolate-box cottage in the heart of the Cotswolds was a hard one to grasp in the context of his sweaty, noisy, hectic, foreign, red-light existence.

"I can't say I blame you," he said. "You shouldn't beat yourself up about it."

Colin smiled and dropped a screwed-up paper napkin into his empty noodle container. "I'll try not to," he said. And then his face became serious. "And what about you, my boy? What's the story with you and Kayleigh and the little one?"

Rory groaned. He dropped his head into his hands and growled. Just the merest thought of Kayleigh and Tia always felt like a knife in his chest. "There's nothing to say. No story. I haven't heard from her. But then, she doesn't know where I am, so I wasn't expecting to, really." He braced his body for his father's response to his next question. "Have you . . . has she been in touch with you lately?"

"Yes," Colin replied simply. "Yes. We e-mail each other a lot. At least once a week. And as you know, she comes over every Christmas, just for a night, on her way back to Ireland. She and Tia. She's a lovely little thing, you know . . . really quite spectacular."

Rory shrugged. He'd already had a full report on these Christmas visits; his father sent him long e-mails about them, attaching photographs which Rory did not open. He'd made that mistake once before, when his father had gone to Spain to visit Kayleigh and the baby a few months after Rory had left. He'd clicked on the attachment unthinkingly and then nearly fallen against the wall with the shock of it. His baby. Who had still been a colic-ridden screaming blob of nothing much when he'd said good-bye to her at eight months old. And there she was suddenly, magically, at fourteen months, with a ribbon in her hair, smiling and long-lashed, standing upright in jeans and sandals. A proper little girl. He'd looked at the photo for long enough to gauge that Tia looked just like him and then he'd pressed Delete. He'd made his decision, he had to live with it.

"Good," he said.

"She's got a new partner, you know, Kayleigh?"

"Oh, yeah?"

"Yes. He's an artist, I think, a fair bit older than her, has a daughter of his own. I think she's very happy."

Rory nodded, just once. He wanted to scream at his dad to *shut up*. To *stop talking*. He wanted to yell at him that he had moved on. That he had drawn a line. That that was then and this was now and he had made a deliberate decision not to lug his baggage around with him. But Kayleigh had other ideas. She had completely inveigled her way into Colin's affections, her and the girl. And Rory could not, in all reasonableness, expect his dad not to bring it up when it was such an important part of his life. But it was *not* an important part of *his* life. Kayleigh was supposed to have left him *breathless in her wake*. Instead she'd tied him up with string and wire, to live out the rest of his life putting food on the table and having to beg for sex. She had broken the terms of their unwritten agreement. She had taken him to the wrong place. He had learned not to feel guilty about what he'd done on that shocking June afternoon nearly four years ago. He had dealt with it.

But here was his lovely dad who did not understand what Rory had done and thought that he still had the power to change things. He did not.

"Good," he said again. "I'm really glad for her."

His father paused, looked at him thoughtfully and then said, "She calls him Dad."

The statement did not register at first.

"Tia," Colin continued. "She calls the new boyfriend Dad."

"Oh," he said. He nodded. "Right."

"Yes, I wondered if you, er . . . how you might feel about that? I mean, I felt you should *know*."

Rory nodded again and said, "Yeah, thank you. That's good then, I suppose."

He looked at his dad and saw raw disappointment in his pale eyes. Colin sighed and said, "I suppose. It depends, really, on what you want. On what your plans are?"

"Well, yeah, I mean, my plans are pretty much just staying here, working hard, seeing what happens. I still feel too young to be a dad. I still feel like I'm sixteen." He looked into his father's eyes, beseechingly, feeling suddenly that he wanted to go home, that he wanted Colin to tuck him in his rucksack and take him home, that he wanted it to be Easter Sunday and for them all to be there, him and his sisters and his brother, *saving the foils*, holding back on the roast potatoes, being a tribe. Because it was true, he did still feel sixteen, but it wasn't true that he had a plan; he had no idea what he was doing here or where he was heading. He was lost. Totally lost. Without Owen here to tell him what to do next, he'd have been clueless.

He smiled at his dad and he said, "I'm really glad you're here, though, really, really glad."

His father's eyes filled with tears suddenly and he grasped Rory's hands in his and squeezed them, way too hard. "Me too, son," he said, "me too."

❧

There was only one way to handle that first night with his dad, only one way to tell his father the truth about himself. And that was to take him to work with him.

He showered himself and dressed himself in his work gear: crisp white shirt, black trousers, sunglasses, sensible shoes in case he had to chase anyone. His dad said, "Wow, look at you. Don't you scrub up well," and put on a scruffy T-shirt and shorts with his heinous Velcro-strapped sandals.

"So, what is it you do here, exactly?" his dad said as they turned the corner towards the front of the club.

"I'm a doorman."

Colin laughed. "Ha!" he said. "A bouncer! Of all things . . ." They walked into the club, past the curious gaze of the cashier at the front desk, past the spangled walls and into the dark womb of the club. It was early, the doors not yet open to the public. Without the girls there, it could have been any old bar, any old nightclub. A guy called Ben washed glasses behind the bar and nodded a hello to Rory and his dad. A girl still in her own clothes but already fully made up passed them on her way to the bar. She hugged Rory to her and called him "sweetie." Colin looked at him curiously and Rory shrugged. His father would put the pieces of the jigsaw together eventually. He knocked on the door of Owen's office. "It's me."

"Come in."

Owen sat behind his desk, all muscles and money and too much aftershave. But still, he found a sweet smile for Rory's dad, and a big warm handshake, and Rory could tell that his dad was impressed. Everyone who met Owen was impressed. "An honor to meet you, sir," he said. Rory saw Colin's look of surprise at being referred to as "sir" by an Englishman.

"Likewise," he said.

"How long are you staying for?"

"Four nights."

Owen sat back down in his big leather chair and said, "Not long then, a flying visit?"

"Yes, sadly so. I was hoping Rory might be able to take some time off, that we might be able to travel around a bit together. But he says he's too busy."

Owen laughed and smiled apologetically. "Yeah, that'll be my fault. Sorry, Mr. Bird."

"Call me Colin."

"Colin. Yeah. I run a very tight ship and I don't really trust anyone. So if Rory's not here there's no one else to put on the door, and if there's no one on the door, the club can't open." He shrugged and smiled again.

Colin nodded and said, "Yes. Sure. Sure."

"But still," Owen continued. "You've got the days free. Plenty to see. Plenty to do." He suggested the ocean beyond the doors of the club with his big tanned arms and then leaned back into his chair.

It was odd to Rory, observing his friend, his boss, this man he'd seen every day of his life for the past four years, seeing him suddenly through someone else's eyes. It was discomfiting and strangely sad.

Outside the office door, the music had been turned up louder. Rory could hear the girls starting to filter through into the club. Owen smiled at him. "Looks like you're up," he said. Then he got to his feet, all six foot odd of him, shook Colin again by the hand, smiled that dimpled smile, wished him well, told him drinks were on the house. Rory led his dad out of the office and towards the front door. The girls were everywhere now, in their work clothes: rhinestone bikinis, hot pants, sequined bras. They oozed and they wriggled and they clucked and they touched Rory's blond hair with overextended fingernails. He turned to his father as they came out onto the pavement and his father looked at him and said, "You left Kayleigh, and the baby, for him?"

Rory did not reply.

"Jesus, Rory. The man's a buffoon! I mean, look at him. *'I don't trust anyone'*"—he rolled his shoulders, mimicked Owen's Essex growl. "Who does he think he is, Tony bloody Soprano?" Colin laughed.

"He's my friend," Rory replied quietly, unclipping the velvet rope from the club entrance, waving through two young men in rugby shirts.

"You think?" said Colin. "He doesn't look like the kind of guy who has friends."

Rory shrugged. "He doesn't have friends. But he has me. We're like brothers . . ."

Colin threw him a look.

"We are. We're soul mates. It's weird. I can't explain it."

Colin continued to stare at him inscrutably. "And this place, it's a titty bar, right?"

"Well, yeah. Pretty much."

Colin laughed again and rocked back on his heels, his gaze reaching into the darkening sky as though there might be something more edifying up there. "Pretty much," he repeated. "Right." He sighed, dropped his gaze to the ground. "Oh, son."

"What?"

"This!" Colin exclaimed. "And what you left behind. Tia. Kayleigh. It's . . . it's . . . Christ. Rory. What the hell is it you're looking for, exactly?"

Rory waved a relatively sober stag party through and scuffed his shoes against the pavement. "I'm not looking for anything."

Colin nodded. He looked for a moment as though he were about to say something. But then he stopped, exhaled. "Just as well," he said, "because I can tell you this. You won't find anything here." He gestured at the bar, at the line of young men waiting to gain entry. "You won't find anything at all."

～

"Oh, my *God*." Meg dropped her weekend case on the doormat and stared at the scene before her. Behind her the three children tried to see what she was looking at.

"What?" said Molly. "Is it really bad?"

"Oh, my *God*," she repeated.

Molly squeezed past her. "Let me see," she urged. She came to a standstill in front of Meg and said, "Oh, my *God*." Then she turned to Meg and she said, "I don't want to go in, Mummy. I really don't. Can you let me into Grandpa's house? *Please*."

"No," said Meg. "Not until we've said hello to Grandma.

Come on. *Boys!*" she called out behind her to the two young-est, who were now grabbing handfuls of the gravel on the footpath. They all trooped in and for a brief moment they were silent.

It was Meg's first visit home since Christmas, six months since Vicky and the girls had finally jumped ship and four months since Beth had moved away, and in those four months Lorelei appeared to have put her kitchen completely out of commission. Dad had warned her. But still, nothing could have prepared her for the devastation that her mother had wrought upon the heart of her home.

The detail that struck her first was that the Aga was no longer visible. The precious orange Aga that had cooked their meat for them, warmed their winter gloves, dried out wet socks and heated pans of bedtime milk was gone, cloaked en-tirely under piles of laundry and cardboard boxes. The surface of the kitchen table was also invisible, loaded up with piles of newspapers and plastic carrier bags tied up by their handles into knots, empty pizza boxes, empty drink cans and a colony of empty wine bottles. The butler's sink was packed up with jam jars and old cellophane in various colors and the kitchen blind had come off its fittings and was slung diagonally across the window. Meg lifted her foot experimentally from the flag-stones and was unsurprised when it came away with a gluey slurp.

"Come on, you lot," she called to her children, "let's go and find Grandma. *Mum!*" she called out, walking blindly through the wreckage of her childhood kitchen. *"Mum! We're here!"*

She had not wanted to come. She and Bill had been busy searching the Internet for a last-minute deal to somewhere sunny when Dad had called to say he was going away, to see Rory and Beth, that Vicky and the girls were going to be at her parents' in Surrey and that Lorelei was going to be on her own at Easter for the first time in her life. She'd ummed and aahed and mentally measured out the constituent ingredients of guilt, duty, resentment and selfishness until she'd finally come up with a recipe for Doing the Right Thing. Bill had stayed at home and she did not blame him in the least.

She traipsed through the kitchen into the front hall, the three children following behind her, silent in awe and wonder. The square space was filled to almost the height of Stanley's head with cardboard boxes from the cash-and-carry. She idly lifted flaps as she passed through the narrow space between the boxes, her breath held against the prospect of what she might find within.

Two hundred citronella tea lights.

A hundred multicolored disposable tablecloths.

Twenty packets of mixed gold and silver Christmas decorations.

Twenty-four packets of Betty Crocker Halloween cupcake mix.

Forty pink polka-dot washing-up brushes.

Fifty one-liter cartons of Aptamil follow-on milk.

She let the flap of this last box drop in horror. Aptamil follow-on milk? When there were no babies in the family? She checked the side of the box and saw that its contents had a consume-by date of August 2001. She sighed.

"*Mum*. We're here!"

They picked their way through the two opposing walls of things that snaked their way up the staircase, leaving a two-foot gap in the middle.

"Mummy," hissed Alfie urgently, as though something important had just this minute occurred to him. "Why has Grandma got all these things on the stairs?"

"Shh," cautioned Meg.

They followed her through the continuing wall of objects and into Lorelei's bedroom.

Meg couldn't see her at first and was about to turn and leave when she spied her, curled up inside her floral armchair, with a huge pair of headphones on, listening to—she presumed—the radio and painting her toenails. She was buried, virtually, within more piles of unidentifiable things, an amorphous mass of bags and boxes and paper and clothes with occasional unexpected outshoots of lamps and broken furniture, hair dryers and ironing boards.

And her mother, like a frog on a lily pad, in the very center of it all.

"Oh," she said, pulling away her gigantic headphones and peering up at Meg suspiciously. "Hello, darling. I didn't hear you come in."

"Well, no," said Meg, "you wouldn't really, would you, with those big things over your ears? I did tell you we'd be here at three. And it's now exactly five past."

"Oh, yes, of course it is. I was just listening to the three o'clock news. D'oh! Silly me. I completely forgot! Hello, you three!" she cried out to the children clustered nervously behind Megan's back. "I'd say come in, but as you can see . . ." She spread her arms apologetically and laughed.

"Jesus Christ, Mum. I mean . . . just . . . *Jesus.*" Meg was having trouble breathing properly. There was a tightness around her stomach and her chest and a kind of putrid green mist clouding her thought processes. She could think of no vocabulary to properly express herself. She could think of nothing beyond her overwhelming need to turn and leave. This instant. Pack everything and everyone back into her fragrant, newly valeted (you had to have it done at least once a month when

223

you had three small children, otherwise things started to take root on the upholstery) people carrier and set off back to London at a significant rate of knots.

She thought of her house in a neat terrace off Kentish Town Road. She thought of her two-thousand-odd square feet of shiny wood-laminate floors and immaculate cream carpets, the rows of storage boxes stacked neatly inside cupboards and the sparkling granite surfaces in her kitchen. She thought of her gleaming windows, washed once a season on a contract, and her louvered shutters, which she cleaned with a toothbrush to remove the film of dust from between the slats. She thought of her monthly clear-outs, the ones that made the children gripe and groan and Bill look at her as if she had a screw loose, as if she should *get a life*.

And then she looked at her will-o'-the-wisp of a mother buried under a mountain of her own seething shit and she felt herself breathe easier. She was not the mad one in this family. Whatever her family might say. This here, this was madness. Right here. She pulled back her shoulders and she said, "What the hell have you done to your house?"

Lorelei shrugged, as if she couldn't have cared less. Then she sighed and said, "I know. I know. It's, well, let's call it a work in progress."

"Mum! This is not a work in progress! Do not dignify it with such a ridiculous description. This is a disaster. Plain and simple. I'm calling the council!"

Her dad had warned her to go easy, but "going easy" was not in Meg's repertoire. And she saw exactly how too far she had gone as the color slowly left Lorelei's face and her features pinched together and her hands turned into fists. "Don't you bloody *dare*!" she growled. "Don't you bloody bloody bloody *dare*!"

Meg felt a pair of small arms grip her tightly around the legs and she hustled the children back onto the landing and said, "Wait there. One minute. I'll be one minute and then we'll all go out in the garden. Okay?"

She stepped back into the entrance to her mother's room and said, "Please don't swear in front of the children, Mum."

Lorelei tutted and folded her arms.

"I'm going to take them out in the garden, to play. Will you join us?"

She tutted again.

"Well, let's put it this way—I can't spend another second up here. I'm feeling half-mad already with all this"—she whispered it—"*shit.* We've driven halfway across the country to come and see you, so please, come outside. Okay?"

Lorelei nodded and sighed. "Yes," she said. "But I'll have to wait for my nails to dry first." Her mood brightened at the mention of her toenails; she pulled up one long leg so that her toes appeared over the mountain of things and she curled them down so that they faced Megan, and then she smiled her yellowing snaggle-toothed smile and said, "Look! Periwinkle! Isn't that the most divine color you've ever seen?"

⌒

Meg flinched when she saw her mother appear in the garden ten minutes later. She shuffled nervously through the garden door, as though there might be wolves or bears. She was wrapped up in a huge rainbow-striped angora cardigan, one she'd owned for most of her life, under which she wore pink floral leggings that hung loose from her spindly legs. On her feet were leopard-print slippers with fur trim, and her long gray hair was piled on top of her head except a long shank that fell down her back like a piece of dirty rope.

She forced a smile and took another tentative step out onto the flagstones. "Chilly out here, isn't it, darling?" she muttered.

"Yes," Meg replied. "But at least the children aren't in danger of being buried alive under an avalanche of your total and utter shit."

"Oh, Meggy."

"No, Mum. Sorry. This is not about me, okay. This is not me being horrible Meg, you know, always the villain of the piece. This is about you. About what you're doing to yourself, to your home. I mean, look at it." She flapped her arms angrily towards the back of the house. "Look at this beautiful place. There are people in this world who would kill to live in this house, in this village, to have what you've got. And you're trashing it, Mum. I mean, what are you thinking? What on earth are you thinking?"

Lorelei put a hand against the flint wall of the house. She caressed the stone gently and sighed. "I love this house," she said. "You know I do. It's the only thing that's never let me down."

"Then why are you treating it so badly?"

She looked up at Meg, her green eyes full of hurt and devoid of understanding. "This house looks after me," she said. "That's more than anyone else in this family does."

Meg breathed in hard. *Go easy*, she thought to herself, *go easy*.

"What have you been eating?" she asked.

Lorelei shrugged. "I eat," she said.

"Yes, but what?"

"Cottage cheese."

"Cottage cheese?"

"Yes. I buy it in those big family-sized tubs from the supermarket, in all the different flavors—you know, they do one

226

with paprika now. Cottage cheese with smoky paprika. A kind of terra-cotta color, that one. It's absolutely delicious. And the pink one with the prawns, that's my favorite. And I have lots of rice cakes, they all come in delicious flavors too. So I kind of mix and match them together, infinite combinations." Her face had lit up with all this talk of cottage cheese and rice cakes and she was kneading the hem of her cardigan maniacally with her fists.

"What else?" said Megan. "Apart from cottage cheese."

"Cookies," she said, "bread. Sweeties. Ooh, and those doughnut things"—she let her cardigan fall and clicked her fingers while she searched for the word—"what are they called? They're so pretty, they come in a big box and they've all different toppings in different colors, from America, you know . . ."

"Krispy Kremes?"

"Yes! Those! I treat myself every week. In fact, I think there's a couple left. Shall I get them out, for the children?"

Megan shook her head vehemently. "No!" she snapped. "God. No, thank you."

"Oh, yes," sighed Lorelei, "I forgot. You're all super-healthy, aren't you? Those poor children."

Megan breathed in again. This was not about her, she reminded herself, not about her. "So you're not actually eating anything hot, then? Nothing cooked?"

"Well, the doughnuts are cooked, I assume, at some point."

"No, Mum, you *know* what I mean. You've no kitchen appliances to cook with, they're all buried. So you're not eating anything hot?"

"No, darling, that is not actually true. I go to Vicky's at least twice a week and she cooks for me."

Megan rolled her eyes. Bloody Vicky, absolving her mother yet again of her basic responsibilities to herself.

"And Daddy often pops something over, when he's at home. Which isn't very often these days."

"So what exactly do you *do* all day?"

"I listen to the radio. I go to the shops. I see Vicky and the girls. I surf the Internet. I'm a silver surfer, apparently, I heard that on the radio the other day." She giggled. "And I still volunteer at the library once a week. So, you know, it's not as if I'm just *hanging around*. Doing nothing."

"Well, no, *clearly* you have been doing something. Nobody accumulates that magnitude of *crap* without doing something proactive. I see you're hoarding newspapers now, as well as bulk-buying baby milk and J-cloths. You know that means you've reached the final stages of your affliction."

"Affliction," muttered Lorelei, and then she tutted.

"What are they for, Mother, the newspapers?"

"I haven't read them yet."

"Right, and you're going to start reading them when, exactly?"

She tutted again. "When I need to remember something."

"Like what?"

"Oh, God, Meggy. You just don't understand, do you? You never have understood. Everything that I possess is part of the context."

"The context?"

"Yes! The big picture!" She made a frame with her hands and then finally joined Meg at the garden table. "For example, today, the tenth of April 2004. Easter Saturday. The day that Meg and the children came to stay. The day that I wore my favorite rainbow cardigan and painted my toenails periwinkle. The day that was cloudy and cool with the threat of localized showers later. The day that I got an e-mail from Daddy in Thailand telling me that he'd landed safely and was on his way out for dinner with Rory. The day that I had yet another argument with you, darling." She smiled sadly and looked tearful. Then she brought her shoulders up and said, "So the newspaper fills in some of the gaps. Of the context. Of the big picture. So does the bottle of nail polish. Once it's empty I can't throw it away. Because it's like throwing away something that happened. It's like throwing away the e-mail from Daddy and the visit from you. It's like throwing away the clouds in the sky and the chill in the air and the very moment we're living in. Do you see, darling, *do you see?*"

Meg shrugged and smiled tightly.

"No," she said softly, "I really don't."

"Oh, well," said Lorelei. "I didn't really expect you to. We've never seen eye to eye, you and I. You've never understood me." She sighed. "It's fine. Other people get me. You don't have to." She reached across the damp wood of the table and squeezed Megan's hand. It wasn't a gesture of affection, it was a gesture of reassurance. It was saying, *"Never mind, darling, we can't all be perfect children."*

Megan could hear the children playing in the lower garden. She was heartened to see that her mother hadn't destroyed the garden too. Between her father and Vicky, it was still a picture-postcard idyll of roses and meandering pathways, bowers and lovingly striped lawns. She stared overhead at the threatening sky, hoping that it would not deliver the forecast showers, that she would be able to spend the rest of the day out here and not have to venture back into that hellhole. Then she pulled her hand away from her mother's and said, "But what about the rest of it? All the cash-and-carry stuff? Why, for example, is there a box of follow-on milk in the hallway that expired three years ago?"

"Oh"—her mother took back her hands and rubbed at her

pointy elbows—"well, obviously I bought that when there were babies around. You know. Thought it would be nice for you not to have to cart a load of formula down every time you came to visit."

"And then?"

She shrugged. "I forgot I'd bought it. And suddenly the babies weren't babies anymore."

"And you have kept it because . . . ?"

"Because buying it brought me pleasure. Because I stood in a shop and saw it and thought of my babies and your babies and your visits and imagined myself with a little Stan or a little Alf on my lap, drinking the milk that I bought them, and I imagined you smiling and saying, '*Thank you, Mummy, what a brilliant idea.*' And all the things I thought when I looked at the milk and bought the milk were good things. And if I throw the milk away then I'm throwing away all those good things I thought and felt when I bought it."

Megan sighed. Her mother's view of the world was an impenetrable wall. "Empty food packaging?"

"Ah, yes"—her mother smiled mischievously—"there you have a point, darling. I really do need to get on top of that. It's just, I'm trying to be good about my recycling, and so often a whole day goes by without me leaving the house and the recycling box fills up so quickly and sometimes I just sort of *leave things* and I intend to do something about them but then once they've been sitting there for a few days I kind of stop noticing them. And then before I know it . . ."

". . . you're living in utter squalor."

"Well, I wouldn't call it squalor."

"*I* would."

"I know you would, Meg. You've always been very critical of the way I live my life. You've always been very critical of *me*."

Megan sighed and reminded herself yet again that she was not here to fiddle around with the knobs and switches of her unsatisfactory relationship with her mother. "So," she said, steering things back to the relevant. "You wouldn't mind, in that case, if I threw away the empty food packaging. *Just* the empty food packaging?"

Lorelei smiled. "Of course not! I'd love it! Vicky always has a little go when she comes to visit. And your father, of course. But it all builds up so quickly, doesn't it?"

"If you say so."

Lorelei laughed nervously. And then she sighed. "I'm quite lonely, you know."

"I know you are."

"I never expected to be on my own. I know it sounds silly, because everyone ends up on their own eventually, don't they? But I never really thought it would happen to me."

"Well, you're not strictly on your own, are you? You've got Dad right next door and Vicky up the road, and you know, don't you, that if you could get on top of things, if you could, you know, *acknowledge* your affliction—"

"That word again."

"—then Vicky and the girls might be able to think about moving back in and you wouldn't have to be on your own. You do know that, right?"

"Of course I do. Of course. I still don't really understand what that was all about. One minute we were all here together having a lovely time, the next . . ." She blew out her cheeks.

"The next, Mum, you were calling her precious girl a little shit and filling their home up with so much stuff that they were embarrassed to bring friends home to play."

Lorelei tutted, into the sky. "I don't even remember it," she said.

"Yes, you do. Of course you do."

Lorelei tutted again.

"Right, so—" Meg got to her feet. "I'll get some things from the car and make a start on your kitchen."

Lorelei jumped up from her chair and said, "I shall want to watch, you know?"

"Yes," said Megan, "of course you will. Come on then, Mother dearest, let's go and have a big old screaming row about egg cartons."

"Oh, no," said Lorelei, "I never throw away egg cartons, darling, they're useful."

"No," said Megan, "they are not useful. And I will be throwing them away. Are you coming?"

Lorelei let her shoulders slump just a degree and then she looked at Megan and she smiled. "Yes," she said, "I'm coming."

◦◦◦

It was, strangely enough, after all Megan's misgivings and resentment about missing out on her last-minute sunshine getaway, a very nice Easter weekend. Vicky came over in the late afternoon and kept the children entertained next door with Sophie (but no Maddy) while Lorelei graciously allowed Megan to empty her kitchen. She did not, of course, allow her to throw away anything apart from food packaging (even that had its fraught moments, a small tussle over a sheet of blue bubble wrap, for example—"*But, darling, it's* blue. *I've never seen blue bubble wrap before!*"—which ended in Lorelei's favor) and was very controlling about exactly where Meg could relocate the objects elsewhere in the house, but all in all, she was quite good-natured about the process and actually burst into tears as they stood a few hours later and admired the newly unentombed kitchen surfaces.

"Oh, look, look. It's my kitchen again! Look at my lovely kitchen! My Aga! My sink!"

Vicky had come in with the little ones and they all stood and smiled at each other and Vicky said, "You've clearly got more sway over her than me. Never in a million years would she have let me do this. And believe me, I've tried."

Meg had smiled sardonically and said, "It's because she's scared of me."

And Vicky had sighed and said, "Ah, yes, indeed. That's where I always went wrong with her. I just always wanted her to like me, more than anything."

Vicky and the girls left and then they all drove up to the supermarket by the roundabout and had what could only be described as a fun time shopping for Easter lunch. Finally uncoupled from her long-standing embarrassment of her mother's "little ways" and distracted anyway by her marauding tribe of children, she saw, for possibly the first time since her very early childhood, some of Lorelei's charm.

Viewing her objectively, she was still very beautiful. She had tied back her unruly hair inside a willow-print head scarf and was wearing what looked like one of Beth's dresses, left behind when she went to Australia—a pink cotton thing with white trim round the hem—with a battered denim jacket over the top. She looked bohemian and youthful, only her haggard hands and slightly drooping jowls giving away the real extent of her age. But it was her manner, her movements, which made her truly a sight to behold. So tall and lean and graceful, so light on her feet, so different from her own rather lumpen eldest child, who had inherited the body of some distant relative from a very different, rather stolid branch of the family tree. She swooped about the supermarket like a swift, touching things and exclaiming over their beauty.

"Look, Meggy, look at these tiny little aubergines, aren't they precious? Do you have any idea how to cook them?"

"Rhubarb-and-custard-flavored yogurt, look, darling! Do you think the little ones would like them?"

"Did you see, Meggy, they're selling these lovely speckled eggs now? Look, all those lovely different shades of blue and green, aren't they exquisite?"

And then of course they came to the Easter egg display and Lorelei stood and for a moment just stared in silence. "Every year it gets more beautiful," she said. "Look at them all. And look! Look at these. Three for five pounds. What a bargain. Kiddos!" she called out to Meg's three. "Look, see these little eggs here—choose one each. A treat from me."

All three stared up questioningly at Meg. She nodded. How could she not? It was Easter, after all. Then Lorelei located the packets of pastel-foil-covered eggs she chose every year and bought three of them because they too were on special offer. They bought an egg for Vicky, and two more for her daughters. "I already have eggs for you and the kiddos," she said. "I bought them days ago. Even before I knew you were coming."

Then they got home and drank wine and prepared the lamb and suddenly it was nine o'clock and time to take the children next door to bed. Lorelei came too and eyed Colin's home suspiciously from the front door. "Your father," she began, her wineglass still held in her hand, "has no eye for a room. No aesthetic sensibilities whatsoever. Look at this place," she tutted. "It looks like a caravan."

It wasn't a pretty house, it was true. He'd painted the walls magnolia and hung them with dreary, framed watercolors. His furniture had been a job lot from the DFS sale, and not from the funkier end of their offerings either. Cold-looking leather in washed-out colors, pale ash veneers and glossy white Formica. Colin had done exactly what Meg had done at the very first opportunity after leaving the Bird House and put order and minimalism above any other kind of aesthetic consideration. Colin's house was neat and clean and soulless. And yes, Megan did have to agree with her mother, more than reminiscent of a caravan. But she could breathe in here. The children could sleep in clean beds with a clear path to the bathroom in the middle of the night and an unimpeded transit down an empty staircase in the morning.

"It's fine," she said, pulling clothes over heads and folding them into neat squares even though she'd be throwing them straight in the washing machine when she got home tomorrow night. "It's perfectly pleasant."

"It's not perfectly pleasant and you know it." Lorelei sat on the arm of Colin's ugly leather sofa and sighed. "It's all such a shame, isn't it?"

"What?" Megan folded up a pair of small boy's pants and reached over for the pajamas that were folded up inside her weekend bag.

"This," said Lorelei, gesturing around the room. "Me and your father. Me and Vicky. I mean, I'd never have got together with Vicky if your father had fought for me. Did you know that?"

"No," said Megan, stopping for a moment. "No. I didn't know that."

"Yes. It was all just . . ." She sighed again. "Oh, I don't know. I think your father had fallen out of love with me a long time before. And I must say, it's pretty awful living with someone who's not in love with you. It doesn't exactly—"

"I'm hungry," interrupted Stanley.

"Don't be ridiculous," snapped Meg. "You've had a huge supper and a whole Easter egg and anyway, under normal circumstances you'd be asleep by now and wouldn't even know you *were* hungry."

"But I am, Mum. I'm *starving*."

"Shall I make them some hot chocolate?" asked Lorelei.

"No!" snapped Meg. "I'm trying to get them into bed, for God's sake!"

"Yes," said Stanley, "hot chocolate!"

"Yes," agreed Molly, "please, Mummy, please can we?"

All three nodded and clenched their fists in excitement and there it was again, thought Megan, there it was. Lorelei's magic, peeled away from its unsavory backing of hoarding and self-centeredness, bright and mesmerizing. Hot chocolate at bedtime. They'd often been allowed hot chocolate at bedtime. It hadn't needed much of an excuse. A late return home. A wet day. A triumph. A disaster. A birthday. An illness. Her mother would make it for them in her peacock-print silk dressing gown, her heavily ringed fingers fluttering around the kitchen at what felt like the middle of the night, collecting mugs and spoons and once even some tiny multicolored marshmallows that Pandora had brought back from America, while her brood sat in a row on the bench at the table, watching and waiting. It would be poured from a battered old saucepan, the same one she'd heated their milk in as babies, the same pan that still hung overhead in the kitchen, replete with the brown rings of old burned milk. And then they would go to bed, contented, not feeling that there was one more thing that could be wrung from the day to expand their sense of gratification.

Megan rolled her eyes and said, "Okay then, but you all have to be in your pajamas, hair brushed and faces washed. Okay?"

They cheered and her mother jumped to her feet to see what she could find in Colin's "sad little kitchen." And they never did get to the bottom of what had happened to bounce Lorelei from Colin's bed and into Vicky's.

As Meg put her children to bed that night, Molly whispered out into the dark, "Mummy!"

"Yes, darling," Megan whispered back.

"I had a really nice time today."

"Good."

"Grandma's really nice. I prefer her when she's not got anyone living with her."

"Oh," said Megan, slightly surprised. It hadn't actually occurred to her before, but her daughter was absolutely right. For all her talk of loneliness, her mother seemed happier than she had been in a long time. She'd put it down to their visit. Their presence. But now that she thought about it she could see that Molly was right. Her mother was happy because she finally had the house to herself. She was in control. The master of her peculiar castle. No one to touch anything, move anything or complain about anything. Just Lorelei and her house. At last.

⌁

Beth's eyes searched for him in the arrivals line at Sydney airport and when she saw him she barely recognized him. He was tanned and rangy, his graying hair bleached to the color of old newspapers. His arms were brown and bare, and there—Beth could barely believe it—was a tattoo. A black inscription in Thai lettering encircling his upper arm.

"Daddy!" she exclaimed before she'd even said hello. "You've got a tattoo!"

Colin held his arm away from his body, eyed his tattoo and smiled happily. "I know," he said. "It's marvelous, isn't it? It says, *'My children are the stars that light the sky.'* I think.

Something like that anyway. And look at you, Bethy. Look. So brown. So happy." He opened his arms out to her and embraced her. He smelled foreign. He smelled hot. He smelled a tiny bit in need of a hot shower and some soap.

They walked to Beth's car in the short-stay car park. Overhead the sun was fierce and white.

"Wow," said Colin as they walked, "culture shock all over again. Amazing what a difference a few hours on a plane can make, isn't it?"

Beth drove her father back to her cute little apartment in a converted town house in Sydney's Spanish Quarter. He talked fast and furious about his four days in Thailand with Rory—he seemed almost high on it. Beth turned and smiled as she pulled up the hand brake and said, "I don't think I've ever seen you so animated before, Dad."

Colin shrugged. "Well," he said, "maybe I'm finally finding myself at the ripe old age of fifty-nine." He chuckled and ran his hand subconsciously up and down his new tattoo. "I always wanted to travel, you know. And I never could. Because of, well, your mother, obviously. I should have started years ago."

Beth smiled at him again and squeezed his arm. "You've still got plenty of time," she said. "Another forty years, potentially."

He laughed. "I think that's pushing it a bit, Beth. But hopefully another twenty. That would be nice."

She showed him into her home. "It's small," she said, "but cozy."

"After where I've just been staying with your brother, this looks like a veritable mansion, I can assure you."

Her first home, at the age of thirty-one, was a one-bedroom attic with a terrace from which, if you stood against the wall and stretched, you could see a slice of ocean. It was furnished entirely from local junk shops and flea markets as she'd brought virtually nothing with her from home. Barely a weekend case. She'd started to pack and then realized that everything she touched had a smell about it, a damp, moldering smell of neglect. She might have been imagining it, it might have been entirely in her head, but she'd left it there, all of it, and taken just a change of clothes and some toiletries. So this now, this place that she called home, was the physical manifestation of her own reinvention. It looked as though she'd been here for years, it looked as though she was surrounded by family heirlooms and mementos, but in reality it was a stage set, bought in a flat-spin retail frenzy over the course of her first few weeks in Sydney.

She was still rather surprised to find herself here. Things had changed so quickly. She could clearly remember sitting on her bed in the Bird House, listening to her mother screaming about broken plant pots, staring at the cobwebs in the coving, hearing the ping of her phone with that message from Jason—everything that had happened after that felt like a blur. She'd called Bill that very night and told him she had a new boyfriend. That it was over. And what was it he'd said? Oh, yes, he'd breathed an audible sigh of relief. Then he'd chuckled and said, *"Thank fuck for that, now you and I can get on with being nice people again."*

A month later she'd said yes to Jason's invitation to be his plus-one at his sister's wedding, and everything had begun to spiral dizzyingly, sucking her up in a vortex and depositing her in Hobart, just over six months later, with only the clothes on her back.

"Oh, darling," said Colin, "this is just lovely. Seriously. What a lovely place you've made for yourself."

Beth smiled and hooked her bag over a vintage coat hook. "Thank you. And about time too, eh?"

"Well, yes, you have been a bit of a late starter. But then so have I."

Beth nodded and laughed. "All Mum's fault."

"Er, yes, and no. I think we both played our own parts in our pitiful existences."

Beth laughed again. She could not argue with that. Long gone now, Jason. It hadn't lasted more than a few weeks once she'd established herself in his hemisphere and discovered exactly how many beautiful, beach-burnished girls had been patiently waiting for his return and exactly how delighted he was to see them again. He'd stayed in Hobart; she'd moved to Sydney. And Beth had a new boyfriend now. Just like that. About a week after she arrived in Sydney. A guy at work. A nice English guy. Richard. Thirty-three. Not tall, but very dark and very handsome. No baggage. No wife. No big age gap. No bullshit. She could barely believe it. After all those years with Bill, followed about by the stale stench of their dead attraction, their affair dragged out beyond the point of human decency, the weight of guilt and disgust always heavy on her psyche, she was finally able to sit across a table from a normal man and feel nothing stronger than liking.

She was still not entirely sure that she herself was normal. When she looked in the mirror she was occasionally thrown by the person she saw there—who was she? What was she doing? Why was she looking at her like that?—but her life was normal. Wholesome. *Clean.* She would work out the rest of it as she went along.

She poured her father a glass of cold water and handed it to him. "So," she said playfully. "What's with the tattoo?"

He shrugged and stroked it again. "Your brother's covered

in the things now, you know, head to toe almost. I felt practically naked in comparison. And this guy"—he pointed at the tattoo—"he's done all of Rory's. I was having the time of my life, I just wanted to kind of *mark it*. Somehow." He shrugged. "Seemed like a good idea at the time. Does it look ridiculous?"

Beth looked at the tattoo and then at her father and thought, no, in the context of her father here and now, tanned and shaggy, loose-limbed and free, no, it did not look ridiculous. "No," she said, "it's a nice tattoo. It looks good. But you'll have to keep up the attitude to go with it, once you're back home."

"Ah, yes," he said, glancing from his tattooed arm to the gnarled wooden floorboards between his feet. "Once I'm home. Hmm." He pulled his hands down his face and grimaced. "You know, darling, I won't be going home. I don't think."

His eyes darted about as he said this. He looked both nervous and guilty.

"You mean, not back to the cottage? Or not back to England?"

"I mean, not back to England."

"Oh, my God." She clasped her hand to her breastbone. "Why not?"

He shrugged and caressed the sides of his water glass with his fingertips. "It's not home," he said. "That cottage, that place. I didn't choose it. You know. I kind of ended up with it, like the burned edge of a slice of cake. What your mother let me have. And I took it because I wanted to be close to you all and now of course none of you are bloody well there!" He laughed hoarsely. "And your mother, she has Vicky. And frankly, she's better living on her own. The more people she has flapping about the place the harder she is to manage. And . . ."

He stopped completely then. His eyes started to dart about again. Beth drew her breath in. She could feel something bad coming her way, like a rush of dirty water through a tunnel.

"I've, kind of, well, I'm with someone. Well, not exactly *with* someone. But potentially with someone. Someone . . . urgh, *God*." He pushed his hands into his hair. "I'm going to live on the commune. In Spain."

Beth nodded numbly, waiting for the bullet.

"With Kayleigh."

Beth felt her hand squeeze itself too hard around the waist of her glass and she put it down. "What?"

Colin took off his spectacles and rubbed his sweaty nose. "I don't really know." He sighed. "It's all crazy. The whole thing. She came to stay, at Christmas. With Tia. Like she always does. But this time something happened between us. Something . . ."

Beth felt warm water rising through her gullet. She felt her temperature drop and then rise again just as quickly. She swallowed hard.

"It's so wrong. And I promise you, darling, that I did not instigate it. Truly. It was the furthest thing from my mind. I mean, we've always got on well, Kayleigh and me. But I promise, I'd never thought of her in that way. And then . . ."

"No," said Beth. She put her hand between herself and her father's words. "No."

"Oh, Beth. I'm so sorry. And truly, I don't even know what it is yet, what this thing is. She still has her boyfriend. Tia calls him Dad. But it sounds like she's tiring of him. And he'll be there. This man. And I'll be there. And I suppose something or other will transpire . . ."

"Fucking hell, *Dad! Jesus*. That's your *granddaughter*. How can you even . . . ? I mean . . ." She made a guttural sound in the base of her throat formed out of all the thoughts she could not stomach and all the words she could not immediately find to express her horror and disgust. "I mean, that's practically *incest*!"

"Well, no, it's not quite that, is it, darling?"

"Yes! It is. It is. Oh, God, Dad, you were the only one in this family I could feel normal about! Please don't do this to me. Please."

Her father sighed heavily, any hope he might have been harboring that this exchange would go smoothly dying in his eyes. "I might still change my mind. I mean, that was partly what this trip was about. I wanted to see Rory, see him eye to eye, really try and understand why he left her, what his feelings are, what he thinks about his daughter and her mother. And honestly, darling, he feels nothing. It's terrifying. He just walked away from that little family he made and felt nothing at all." He shook his head sadly and Beth looked furiously at him.

"And that makes it all right, does it? That makes it okay to shack up with her. I mean, Dad, she's half your age!"

"I know. I know. But she doesn't feel it. It doesn't seem like that when we're together. She's lived a lot of life for a young woman. She's more mature than me in some ways."

"Oh, *God*! I just *knew* you'd say that! That's what dirty old men *always* say. Of course she's not more mature than you. She's younger than me, for fuck's sake, Dad."

"Yes, but, Beth, without wishing to cause you any offense, you are a very young thirty-one."

"So?" she demanded. "What did he say? Rory?"

"I didn't tell him."

"Why not?"

Colin shook his head. "I couldn't quite find the words. Or the moment. And anyway, as I say, nothing's actually happened yet. Nothing concrete."

Beth shook her head slowly in disbelief. "I can't believe this is happening," she said. "You were the only one, Dad, the only one who I could feel normal about." Dark shadows skittered around her head, shadows of moments from the past that she couldn't quite form into memories. Feelings of wrongness and discomfort. She thought of Rhys half-naked in their parents' bed, of the footsteps outside the bathroom door, of Vicky kissing Lorelei in the kitchen one morning when they didn't think anyone was looking, the slick of saliva still shining on her mother's chin when she turned to smile at her a moment later. From nowhere another memory hit her: her mother coming out of Rhys's bedroom the evening before he hanged himself, a look of sheer black horror on her face, her eyes bright with shock. She shook the memory away, not even sure what it was, not even convinced it was real. And then, as a final gift from her subconscious, she saw herself in a cheap hotel room, being roughly and insensitively serviced by her sister's partner.

The dark waters pounding through Beth's head quieted and parted then just long enough for another thought to occur to her.

"Does Meg know?"

Colin looked up at her, aghast. "Oh, God, no."

She gulped. For all these years, Kayleigh and her *little secret,* overheard in the garden of the Bird House that balmy spring night on the last Easter weekend of the old millennium— when Beth's affair with Bill was still new and sweet and not the rancid old hash of bad habits and careless romance that it had eventually decayed into—had been safely at arm's length in an incommunicado hippy commune in the middle of nowhere. Now Kayleigh had slept with her dad and would be bringing her secrets to their shared pillow.

"Are you going to tell her?" she asked in a quiet voice.

"Hmm. I think, perhaps, I was hoping that if it does happen, which it may well *not*, that she would find out via some form of osmosis. I'm not sure I could find the words."

"No," she snapped, "and I'm not surprised. You know you can't do this, don't you, Dad?"

He shrugged. It made him look about ten. "Well, actually, I sort of can. The question really is whether or not I will."

"It'll cause mayhem, you know that, don't you?"

Colin nodded. But then he said, "It might not. Your mother dumped me for the woman next door, split up two families, made us all the gossip of the decade. We survived that."

She grimaced at him. "We're not indestructible, Dad."

He nodded again. "No," he said, "no family is indestructible. But we're pretty resilient. And this might all turn out to be a storm in a teacup anyway. And I'm not asking for your blessing. I'm just telling you. Because you and I, we've always been the quiet ones, haven't we? We've always been the doormats, and now, look at you, finally spread your wings and escaped the evil clutches. Now it's my turn. That's all."

He folded his arms and leaned back into his chair. And then he smiled at her and Beth honestly felt as though she didn't know the man sitting across from her. There was something burning in his eyes she'd never seen there before and it was awful.

She sighed and she tutted and she said, "You're making a mistake."

And he continued to smile and said, "Good."

9

———— ❧ ————

Monday 10th January 2011

Darling Jim!

Thank you for the virtual flowers! How did you know that
delphiniums were my favorites?! It does so often feel like we've
known each other for much longer than a few weeks, don't you
agree? I am searching the Internet for something to send you in
return, so watch this space. And thank you for the new photo!
You are a handsome beast! I must say that even at my age I do
still have an eye for the men, I'm always subconsciously "eyeing
up the talent" wherever I go and I must tell you that were I to
pass you on the street I would give you a very prolonged double
take! I didn't see how much hair you had in your original photo,
all those lovely silver locks, gorgeous!

So, now I think I have a crush on you. Argh! Is that okay? Do
you mind?!

So, you asked about my partner. Well, "he" was actually
a "she." Vicky was her name. And no, before you ask, I would
not describe myself as a lesbian. I would not, I think, like to
describe myself as anything, other than a Lorelei. ☺

But certainly, for the years I was with Vicky, I did not really
think about men in that way. It was all-consuming and lovely.
She was my next-door neighbor and she happened to be here

246

when we found Rhys, the night he killed himself. We got very close very quickly and then one day she kissed me and that was that really. I adored her. Unconditionally. Like everyone else who loves me, she couldn't hack living with me. She moved out after a few years, we stopped sleeping together but we remained best of friends. Passionately good friends. She really was absolutely the best sort of person. I wish she was still here.

So, there you go, another e-mail, another revelation! I haven't looked at another woman since Vicky. Which is why I can't call myself a lesbian. It was, I suspect, a wonderful, beautiful one-off.

All of which means that yes, the father of my children is still alive! Dear Colin! A wonderful man! NOT. Oh, dear. Well, he used to be, and gosh, probably still is in many respects. He was a wonderful father to our children but he fell out of love with me and I never really forgave him. I'm afraid I'm quite high-maintenance in that way. If I'm with someone then it really does have to be all or nothing. I'm a terrible romantic. So he kind of left the door ajar for what happened between me and Vicky. And now . . . oh, dear, how much more can you take?! . . . he lives with my son's ex-girlfriend and her child. Who is—are you ready for this???—his granddaughter. He is sixty-six years old! She is thirty-eight! Oh, dear, it's quite disgusting. Really. I haven't spoken to him in years. Not since I found out. I mean, I should know better than most that love can often be found in the most unexpected places. But not there. No. Absolutely not there. And worse than that is HER! Kayleigh! At least Vicky was a wonderful person. Kayleigh is just an utter bitch. Honestly. A spiteful, terrible person. It was her, in the end, who really rent my family apart. It was her who ruined everything.

Argh!

Another tale of woe for another day, I think.

Until then, lovely man, I send you a passionate kiss, virtual, but heartfelt.

Yours, with love,
L
xxxxxxxxxxx

APRIL 2011

"Hello, Dad." Meg had sat down in the chair next to him before he'd spotted her walking across the plush reception hall of the boutique hotel in Mickleton.

"Oh. Darling." He got to his feet, still bouncy and nimble at sixty-six. "Meg." He leaned in towards her and tried to embrace her but Meg's body would not allow it and the gesture turned into a kind of teenage fumble.

"You look wonderful, Meg, really amazing. You've lost a lot of weight."

"Well, yes," she muttered. "Funnily enough it all fell off me after the last time I saw you."

"Vicky's funeral," he murmured, as though Meg had not just spoken. "Has it really been that long?"

"It most certainly has."

Colin sat back down in the plush armchair and looked around. "This place is nice," he said. "Used to be a shoe shop, I think, once upon a time. *Wide Fittings* if I recall." He winked and laughed and Meg stared at him blankly. "Where's Molly?"

"She's in our room," said Meg, "watching endless reruns of *Come Dine with Me* and texting her friends." Her voice was dry as dust.

Colin nodded and smiled. "So," he said, "how are you feeling?"

"About what?"

Colin let his jolly demeanor deflate a little. "Your mother, of course," he said. "How are you feeling about your mother?"

"Well," said Meg, "you know. Pretty much exactly how any daughter would feel upon losing her mother. Who has starved herself to death inside a house so full of filthy shit that it is going to take her daughter two weeks to clear it out and even then there will probably be another two weeks' worth of crap still left in there. That's how I'm feeling. Thank you."

Meg flopped crossly into the back of the armchair and folded her arms across her chest.

Colin stared at her and then leaned towards her and touched her arm. Meg pulled her arm away from him and said, "No, thank you. I don't want sympathy. Or affection, okay? I just want help."

"Good," said Colin, removing his hand from her arm. "Yes. Good. Absolutely. That's what I'm here for. To help. How bad is it?"

Meg sighed and let her shoulders soften. "It's even worse than the worst nightmares I'd been having about it. I mean, seriously, it's . . . it's . . ." She noticed with some surprise that she had begun to cry. Colin touched her arm again and once more she shook it off. She was not sure she would ever accept her father's touch again. She pulled in her tears and continued. "It's absolutely shocking. Particularly downstairs. I mean, there's literally no daylight down there. It's all piled to the ceiling. There's like, like, this *corridor*. You know. Through the piles. Like *walls*. And it smells"—she put her hand over her mouth— "it smells disgusting. And then there's her place, her armchair, in the middle of all of this and it's all stained and shabby and that was where she lived." She widened her eyes at her father, finally feeling able to make eye contact with him. "She lived on that chair. Slept on that chair. Ate on that chair." She shuddered and lowered her gaze to the floor. "It's all so fucking tragic."

Colin sighed and put his fingers against his mouth. "I feel awful," he said. "I feel—"

"Don't make this all about you, Dad. This is nothing to do with you. It's all of us. It's everything. It's, Christ, I was telling you she was sick decades ago. She's always been sick. This . . ." She paused. "This was always going to happen."

Colin shook his head. "Do you really, really believe that?"

Meg nodded.

"No," he said, "I don't agree with you. I think there was a moment. A moment when all this could have ended differently. When Mum might have found a less screwed-up way through life."

"And when was that, exactly?"

Colin shrugged. "Rhys," he said in a small voice. "I suppose it must have been Rhys."

Meg nodded. "But how could we have stopped that happening? How could any of us have done anything differently? I mean, there was no buildup to it, no signs, no warning. And then afterwards—there was no note, no explanation. It was just like this utterly unconnected *thing*."

"I think we could have done more. To help Mum. Afterwards."

"But Mum didn't want help!" snapped Meg. "That was the whole crazy thing about it. She was *fine*!" She imitated Lorelei's birdlike trill. "Absolutely *fine*! My son's dead! La-la-la! No." She shook her head. "I honestly don't think there's anything we could have done. How can you help someone who thinks, who *believes*, that they're perfectly fine?"

Colin nodded and smiled sadly. "I still, more than any other regret, wish I could have understood. Why he did it. What he was thinking. Maybe that's it. You know. Maybe if there'd been an explanation we could all have moved on. Found closure. But there wasn't and we didn't and we've all gone off at tangents—"

"*I* haven't," Meg interjected brusquely.

"Well, no, *you* haven't. Although that's not to say you haven't had your own demons. But the rest of us and, my God, your poor blessed mother more than anyone. It's almost like . . ." He paused. "As though we all blamed each other. Because we didn't know who else to blame. And then we just carried on blaming each other for everything." He sighed and a silence fell between them.

"Well," said Meg eventually. "You must be hungry. Shall we go up to the room? Maybe we could have tea?"

Colin's face lit up. "Yes," he said. "That would be lovely. Thank you."

MARCH 2005

"You're such an angel, Lorrie, I don't know what I'd do without you."

Vicky turned round in her wheelchair and squeezed Lorrie's scrawny hand where it sat upon the handles.

"Don't be silly, love," Lorelei replied. "It's nothing."

"No," said Vicky, "it's not nothing. I know how much of an ordeal this is for you. I know you'd rather be at home and not ferrying me about all over the place."

"Well, darling, my car is an extension of my home, so it

doesn't feel like an ordeal. And anything to get you better, Vick, that's all that matters now. Getting you better. For the girls. And for me."

Lorelei squeezed her shoulder and carried on pushing her up the corridor. Out in the car park it was a bright and breezy day; lacy clouds danced across the sky and the trees shimmered and whispered. Such a stark contrast to what had come before. Three hours of chemo in a dark hospital ward, flicking mindlessly through the old copies of Sunday supplements that Lorelei had brought for her, delighted to finally have some use for her hoard beyond the inexplicable sense of calm it brought to her existence, drinking room-temperature juice out of plastic cups, the time passing so slowly, even with Lorelei's running commentary and soothing touch.

Two more days of this and then she was done. Well, for now at least. Until the next time. Which was more or less inevitable given the way the wretched cancer was rampaging around her body as if it was on a whistle-stop sightseeing tour. From a pea-sized lump in her right breast to telltale aches and pains in her chest as it passed into her lymph nodes (they'd whipped the lot out like a tangle of seaweed, and taken off the tit too). And then it had shown up like a bad smell in her other boob. They did keep managing to get it and nipping the bugger in the bud. But Christ, it was insistent. It had no respect for these men and women of medicine and their superlative ways with a chemo needle and a radiography machine. But still, as everyone kept telling her, she was as strong as an ox (she wasn't sure she appreciated the analogy, but she could kind of see where they were coming from) and she was a fighter. And yes, that much was true. She always had been, all her life. Never a person just to fold up and roll over. But still, this really was pushing it now. Three lots of cancer, three bouts of treatment, the tits gone, the hair gone, the body gone (no, she did not, as she'd always assumed, have the figure of Pamela Anderson hiding beneath her excess weight, just a slightly deflated old bag of bones, as it turned out). She was tired now, and done with it all. Her fighting spirit, she feared, was ebbing away.

But still, on the up, her being ill really had done a world of good for Lorelei. She had risen to the challenge quite magnificently. She'd taken Vicky to all her appointments, passed her tissues, held her hand, bought her chocolate bars when she wasn't feeling sick and ginger tea when she was. She'd even taken on the role of receptacle of doctors' words. Vicky always felt she was on show during these meetings with consultants, as though she was supposed to smile at just the right moment and nod at the appropriate juncture, like someone being judged by Simon Cowell on *The X Factor*. Or make that *The C Factor*. Anyway, she could never remember a bloody thing they said to her and thank God for Lorelei, taking it all in, even making notes in a little notepad with her jumbo multicolored biro.

Vicky wasn't daft. She knew why Lorrie was being so strong. She knew now that she was all Lorrie had left. Megan, pregnant again down in London, pretty much pegged to the ground she stood on by the sheer weight of all her bloody children. Beth busy being remote and unattainable in Australia. Rory pimping his soul away in Thailand and Colin, urgh, God, *Colin*. She could barely bring herself to think about that utterly revolting can of worms.

So really, Vicky was it. The tattered remnants of Lorelei's once-dazzling family. And she needed Vicky more than life itself. So of course she would pull herself out of her comfort zone to do the right thing. She was so often her own worst enemy. But not now.

Even sweet Lorelei wasn't that bloody stupid.

❧

Lorelei, sensing that this was not, for once, *her* Easter, spent the day with Vicky and her girls in their little flat around the corner.

She arrived at midday, buried under a deadweight of Easter eggs and daffodils. Vicky and Maddy had made a lamb tagine with couscous and roasted vegetables and thick yogurt sauce sprinkled with pumpkin seeds, and they gave each other knowing looks across the table as they watched Lorelei picking at it uncertainly, trying her hardest to accept the untraditional Easter fare, trying her hardest not to say something snippy like *"This is all very nice, but I really don't see how you can improve upon a simple leg of lamb."*

"Yummy!" she said, instead. "Really, you two should have your own cookery show or something. You're both so incredibly clever in the kitchen."

"Not me," said Vicky. "It's all down to Maddy. She's the gastronomic genius in this house."

She smiled warmly at Maddy, who returned her smile with just a hint of long-suffering. Since Vicky had sided with Maddy 100 percent over what they all referred to in private as the "little shit incident" and taken them out of the Bird House and into this cute little flat around the corner, her relationship with her eldest daughter had flourished. And it was such a tiresome cliché to say that your daughter was like your best friend, but really, with her and Maddy it was true. It was almost as if the aftermath of the "little shit incident" had somehow taken them on a different route through these potentially tricky teenage years, a bypass around the hell that Vicky had been expecting ever since she'd first been presented with a baby daughter fourteen years previously. Never a cross word, never a dramatic sigh, never a slammed door. Just companionship. Vicky felt truly blessed. And in this last year, since her initial diagnosis, that bond had grown even deeper. She mouthed the words *"I love you"* across the table at her daughter, who rolled her eyes and smiled.

"How amazing," said Lorelei, oblivious, as ever, to undercurrents. "None of mine can cook. Well, not that I'm aware of, at least." She let out a brittle laugh and pushed some grains of couscous around her plate.

"Meg makes a nice stir-fry," said Vicky, trying to leverage some positivity into the conversation before it got too bogged down in *poor old me*.

"Anyone can make a nice stir-fry," Lorelei responded.

"Well, no, that's not strictly true. It does take a certain knack."

"I did think that at least one of them might end up with some flair in the kitchen."

Vicky and Maddy exchanged another look, another pair of suctioned-in smiles. Just the way Lorrie's children always used to. Those looks that had so angered Vicky when she was crazy in love with her. But she was no longer crazy in love with her. That illusion had been well and truly shattered.

"Says the woman who subsists on rice cakes and Krispy Kremes," she said affectionately.

"Well, really, there's hardly any point cooking when it's just you. I used to be a good cook. When I was younger. When the kiddos were about. I was always in the kitchen. I just don't see the point anymore." She had joined her knife and fork together in the center of her plate, although she'd eaten barely half. Vicky, too, had eaten only a handful of food, just to be polite, just to keep it all ticking along. Her poor poisoned stomach could not have taken any more. The girls were still eating, in that delicate, birdlike way of young girls, as though there were no pleasure to be had from it at all. And maybe there wasn't, thought Vicky sadly. Maybe there wasn't. This time last year she'd been well, Megan and the kids had been here, they'd been high with the euphoria of clearing out Lorrie's kitchen, nobody knew about Colin and Kayleigh, nobody knew about Rory and his sleazy lifestyle. And surely, yes, the food must have tasted better that day. So much better.

"Lovely lunch," said Lorrie, a film of tears over her eyes. "Really lovely lunch."

"Thank you, darling," said Vicky, squeezing her bony hand across the table. "You are sweet."

～∾～

From: Colin.bird@hotmail.com
To: MeganRoseLiddingtonBird@yahoo.co.uk;
RoryBird2@hotmail.com;
Bethanbabybird@arthouseframing.co.au

27th March 2005

Hello, my dearest darling children,

I'm writing this from a café in Madrid. I've decided to spend a few weeks away from the community, I think all of us needed some space. It's been getting a bit messy. Well, messier than usual, let's put it that way. Adie, that's the guy who Kayleigh lives with, he's having some kind of breakdown, or God, I don't know, a manic thing. I'm not really sure, but there's medication involved and he's refusing to take it and yadda, yadda, yadda, he doesn't seem to be quite so relaxed about our "arrangement" anymore and doesn't really want me around. And to be perfectly frank, it's come at a good time. I had hoped that given time the three of you might have accepted the choice I made a year ago but that clearly isn't the case and I'm half-mad with despair and longing for you all. I feel like we're at opposite sides of some warped mirror, like I can see you all, but when I go to touch you you're not there. I realize I'm going through something, something mad and ridiculous, but then I think all of us, in different ways, have made some not-so-great choices over the years. I think all of us have baggage that we didn't ask for. I wanted you all to understand and to give me the time and the freedom to make my own mistakes, but I cannot blame you for not doing that. You are my children. I am your father. I should be better than that. I understand. If my own lovely dad, God rest his precious soul, had done something along the lines of what I have done, I would have had terrible trouble accepting it.

So now, I have two choices: a) go back to the community, see it through, whatever it is (and I know none of you want to hear this, but God, I love her, I really, really do) and hope that you will all come round to the idea but accept that maybe you never will or b) give her up, go home, pretend none of it ever happened and wait for you all to forgive me.

Talk about Sophie's Choice . . .

In the meantime, here is a recent photo of Tia. She's five and a half now, bright as a button, so clever. She calls me Papa, in case you're wondering, and she is desperate to meet you all one day, her aunties and her cousins. We took her back to Ireland for Christmas, it was a perfect joy to see her with all her cousins over there, but joy tinged with sadness because she's not yet met the ones who really matter to me.

So, I'll be here for a while, until Adie is either better or gone, and hopefully while I'm here I can reach some kind of resolution with everything. And quite apart from me and my own issues and ruminations, remember to speak to your mother over the Easter weekend. She's spending it with Vicky and as you probably all know, it may well be the last for the pair of them. Make sure they feel loved.

I love you all so much. You can't ever imagine the physical pain I feel not being with you all, knowing what my actions have caused. Happy Easter, my beautiful glorious children.

Love, hugs, kisses, from your
Dad
xxx

⌒

Megan looked around the table. It was, as they kept telling each other, a bumper day of celebrations. Alfie's eighth birthday. Easter Sunday. And the return of Molly from her first stay away from home after a week on a PGL camp with the rest of year five. And so, arranged around the table in no particular order were all three of her children; Bill; Bill's brother Frank; his girlfriend Sonia; their son Frank Jr.; Bill's recently widowed dad, Bobby; and Meg's recently divorced best friend Charlotte, who also happened to be the mother of Alfie's best friend at school, James.

Extra chairs had been commandeered from other parts of the house and Charlotte had brought four extra place settings. There'd been oysters and shell-on prawns with garlic mayonnaise for starters and now they were clearing their plates of roasted lamb and vegetables with a red-wine gravy. She'd had to do it all from cookery books; she wasn't a natural-born chef and had been up at seven, apron on, everything arranged on the counter, a preprinted timings sheet Sellotaped to the tiled wall, hair tied back, ready to go. She didn't cut any corners the way she normally did; no expensive, shop-bought gravy or ready-to-cook roast potatoes. All from scratch. This was their first Easter at home in four years and Megan was pregnant with what was categorically going to be her last child and she wanted this day to be perfect. In every single way.

Bill smiled at her across the table. "Good work," he said. And Megan smiled and felt the compliment warm her up from the inside out. They'd had some awful times the last few years; she'd even kicked him out two years ago, told him she couldn't live with a man who had two mobile phones and slept in his office every night, a man who shouted at his children and answered all her questions with a grunt. She knew he'd been sleeping with someone else. Possibly even a whole procession of someone elses. She honestly hadn't cared. She'd lain alone in bed at night, picturing him in boutique hotel rooms, slamming himself into some tiny blonde from behind, with wild eyes and his tongue hanging out, and had not been able to rustle up even an iota of upset. She'd imagined him lying on a blanket on a starry London night with someone small and feminine, caressing her face with his fingertips and staring lovingly into her eyes, and she'd simply shrugged to herself and thought, *Well, you know, at least someone's making him happy.*

But that was the problem: they weren't making him happy. Whoever he was sleeping with or romancing or fucking or falling in love with or *whatever*, was making him miserable. And that was why she'd kicked him out. He'd come back three days later with a tiny gold bird on a chain in a Liberty's box and said, *"Please, can you let me try again?"*

And crazy as it sounds, everything had changed. No more shouting, no more nights away, no more monosyllables. And after a year, once she truly believed that this was it, that they'd broken the cycle and found a better way of being together, she'd suggested a last baby. And he'd smiled and said, *"Well, I was going to suggest a wedding, but if you'd prefer a baby . . ."* And she'd smiled and said, *"Baby first, maybe a wedding later?"* Six months later she was pregnant.

She waited for a lull in the chatter and then she said, "By the way. We had the gender scan on Thursday."

Charlotte and Sonia let out little gasps of excitement. After two virtually identical boys (Alf and Stan were almost impossible to tell apart when they were sitting down) and a six-year gap, there was a tangible and rather irritating bias towards a girl from most quarters. And really, honestly, Megan did not mind. Her mother had managed the neat little two boys/two girls combination and look how that had ended. Just a happy child, that was what she wanted. A happy bonny child with a winning smile and a sunny disposition.

"It's going to be . . ." She dragged out the suspense, almost spitefully, knowing that she would not be giving her guests what they were looking for. "Another boy!"

She heard the disappointment buried in the noises of glee and delight that emanated from her guests. And she smiled. Her fourth child. Her last baby. She could not wait to meet him. She would make sure he was at the center of everything, the axis around which they all spun. She would keep him there, fully integrated, if she had to pull muscles doing it. This boy would never miss an Easter lunch, unnoticed, unremarked upon. She held her hand soft against her stomach and thought, *My special boy, my lovely special boy.*

⌀

She called her mother after lunch, taking her mobile into the quietest corner of the house and shutting the door. She sighed as she waited for Lorelei to pick up the call. It had been nearly two months since her last visit to the Bird House and she was racked with guilt. Here she was, in the bosom of her family, warm and loved, her future unrolling in front of her like a feel-good movie, another baby on the way, surrounded, completely surrounded, while her mother sat a hundred miles away and ate food with her dying lover. She should have been there. She knew that. It was probably Vicky's last Easter. It would have taken everyone's minds off everything, the chaos and clatter of her unruly family. But she'd looked at the day from every angle and seen objectively that she had to be selfish. Alfie wanted his friend here on his birthday and Molly had only just got back from a trip away; she did not want to have to pack up and sit on motorways again, sleep in someone else's bed. Bill's dad couldn't be alone today, his first Easter without his wife. She'd invited Lorelei, but purely to ease her guilt. Which it hadn't. In the least.

"Hello!" she said when Lorelei finally picked up after ten rings.

"Oh, hello, darling. How lovely to hear from you. How's things?"

"Good," she said circumspectly. "It's been a nice day. How about you?"

"Ah, well, you know. It's been perfectly nice."

"Where are you?"

"I'm at Vick's. We're just about to have tea and a cake."

"One of yours?"

Her mother laughed wryly. "Oh, no, darling. Not today. Apparently we've got a lovely shop-bought one from Waitrose."

"You mean you've covered over the Aga again?" She tried to keep her voice soft and kind, but even she could hear the strand of annoyance running through it.

Lorelei sighed and Megan felt awful.

"How's Vicky?" She changed the subject.

"Oh, trooping on. You know. She looks absolutely dreadful. But the girls are being amazing. So supportive. They never leave her side."

Megan said nothing. The comment sounded innocent in Lorelei's singsong tones but was as loaded as a double-barreled gun.

"If it was you, Mummy . . . ," she began patiently.

"Yes, yes. I do know that. Of course I know that. But still."

"Still what?"

"Oh, I don't know. It's all such a terrible shame. All of it. What happened to us. We used to be such a tight-knit little bunch. And now we're like a bunch of raggle-taggle gypsies."

Megan thought briefly of the heinous e-mail from her father this morning, that she had both read and deleted in roughly thirty-five seconds. "Well, you know, that's life, isn't it? Families aren't all the same."

"I wonder . . ."

"What?"

"Oh, gosh, I don't know. I do sometimes wonder how different things would have been for us all, if Rhys hadn't . . . well."

"Hanged himself?" Meg winced. So harsh, but really, her mother was nearly sixty. Rhys had killed himself fourteen years ago. She had to find some words for it. She had to have processed it by now. Surely.

"No!" said Lorelei. "Well, yes. I suppose. But do you think, Meggy, do you think we might all have been a bit closer now? If Rhys was still here?"

Meg absentmindedly rubbed her stomach with her spare hand. She sighed. "That's something we'll never know."

"I do sometimes think it's quite amazing, how I've dealt with it. You know. I do sometimes think . . . well, I honestly . . . I barely grieved. Isn't that remarkable?"

Megan took in a sharp breath, felt it bruise against her ribs.

"I mean, I was terribly sad, obviously. But I never felt . . ."

Megan let the silence play out towards her mother's next words with a terrible sense of dread.

"I never felt devastated. Isn't that strange? And he was my baby. My littlest one. And I didn't feel devastated."

The next silence was weighed down with the sense of Lorelei's own surprise. It was clear to Megan that she'd only just acknowledged this fact, that it had just this very minute presented itself to her and that she did not know quite what to make of it.

"It is strange, Mum. Really strange and it's . . ." She rubbed her bump again, *her* baby, *her* littlest one, and she chose her next words carefully, realizing that this was the first time she had ever had a window into her mother's mind and an opportunity to climb in and change something. "I think it's got a lot to do with your habits. Your . . . collecting of things. I think it's a coping strategy. I think that's why you can't let go of things, because they stop you thinking too much, protect you from your own emotions. I think—"

"Oh, Meggy!" Her mother cut in suddenly, her voice lilting and full of delight. "The girls have just brought in the cake! It's simply beautiful—all covered over in yellow royal icing and baby chicks and pastel-colored eggs. I wish you could see it! It's the most beautiful Easter cake I've ever seen! And look, even a little chocolate nest in the middle. How completely adorable."

Megan sighed and brushed her hair away from her face. Less of a window, then, and more of a pinhole. She wrapped up the phone call and made her way back to her party.

⟨∾⟩

Beth sat on the terrace of her Sydney apartment, a book open and unread upon her lap, staring thoughtlessly into space. She had been sitting this way for nearly three minutes. It was something she did more and more these days, almost like blacking out, like fainting with her eyes open. After another moment she came round and shook the blankness from her head. She looked from side to side, trying to remember what she'd been doing, who she was with. She remembered that it was Sunday afternoon, that she was alone, that she was due at her boyfriend Richard's place in an hour, that she needed to have a shower and get changed. She pulled her hair from her face, closed her book and got to her feet.

She should probably see someone about these blackouts. Supposing it happened while she was driving? It had happened at work the other day, while she was in a meeting. Her boss had said, "*Beth? Beth? Earth calling Beth?*" and everyone had laughed and she'd smiled nervously and said, "*Sorry, sorry, miles away.*" But *miles away* was not accurate. *Nowhere at all* was more like it.

She showered and changed, fixed a clip to her fringe, buckled up her black-and-white cork-soled Mary Janes, glanced at herself in the mirror, smiled wanly and drove to Richard's. He met her at his front door in his customary uniform of short-sleeved shirt and jeans. Not a man of style. He wasn't fussed about clothes. She sometimes thought they looked like an odd couple, her all bedecked in girlie clutter, him all straight-up and mannish. He pulled her to him and smelled her, as he always did, like a mother to a baby.

"Mmm," he said. "Yum."

She wore a scent she'd bought in a local boutique, a brand she'd never heard of before, something new to cover over the aroma of her old persona. She was all about signatures these days: signature scent, signature side parting with a single diamante clip, signature Mary Janes in zingy colors, signature pinky-red lipstick. She was instantly recognizable these days. To everyone but herself. To herself, she was still a stranger.

"Look what I've got for us," said Richard, leading her to his kitchen counter and opening up a drawer. He pulled out a pair of Creme Eggs and handed one to her. "Four dollars a pop. Happy Easter!"

She held the Creme Egg in the palm of her hand and stared at it. They always threw her off kilter, these little chunks of home. Richard loved them, knew all the best places to get hold of Anglo stuff. But Beth found them unsettling. She spoke with an Antipodean twang, she used Australian slang, she was assimilated. One hundred percent. She didn't need "little chunks of home." They were like slightly sinister postcards from old enemies.

"Thank you!" she said, and hugged Richard to her. "And happy Easter to you, too. Sorry, I didn't get you anything . . ."

"That's okay," he said. "Wasn't expecting anything. And I know Easter is a strange time for you, so . . ."

She shrugged and smiled. She'd told him early on about Rhys. She had to. You couldn't really get to know someone without having the inevitable *"So have you got any brothers and sisters?"* conversation. And she could have lied, or at least, *omitted* any mention of Rhys. But she wasn't able to do that. She would never be able to do that.

"Do you do anything," he continued, "at home? To, you know, commemorate the day?"

At home. She shuddered at his words. *This* was home. "No," she said quietly, "not really. I mean, it was fourteen years ago, it all seems so distant now. I think we've all moved on."

He nodded sagely, as if this was somehow a satisfactory response. When it clearly wasn't. He poured her a coffee and they sat together on his sofa. He slung his arm around her shoulders and picked up the remote control. The window was wide open, his light curtains billowing in the early-evening breeze. The sun was still high and she could hear the sound of the ocean from here, the reassuring whisper of the ebb and flow, the calls of children on the beach, the hum of the traffic that flowed in between.

"New shoes?" he said, eyeing up her sandals.

She eyed them too, smiled and said, "No, I've had these awhile."

"They're nice," he said. "Pretty. Although I'd still give a hundred dollars to see you in a pair of flip-flops."

She nudged him with her elbow. It was a standing joke.

She stared at the Creme Egg on the table in front of her. Just the merest glance at it filled her head with a dozen child-hood memories. And as these tiny vignettes danced around her head, she could not help but think of England, of her mother, of poor Vicky, of pregnant Megan. And then she thought of the pathetic e-mail from her father that had been sitting there in her inbox this morning like a big festering boil. She'd skimmed it, barely taken in a word, had let the cursor hover above the link to the photo of Tia for a second or two before changing her mind—too early for that, far too early—and then shut it down, shuddering delicately. But her father had been right about one thing. Her family. She should phone them all. If she was normal, really, truly normal, not this arty-crafty, hand-stitched semblance of normal she'd made out of the warm, sweet, thin air of Sydney, Australia, that is exactly what she would do. She would phone them all and say, *"Happy Easter! How are you? How are the kids? How are you*

doing? What are you eating? I miss you all so much! I love you too."
It would take ten minutes. It would make everyone happy. But
she couldn't do it. And she had no idea why.

Instead she buried her head into the crook of Richard's
shoulder, his strong, unquestioning shoulder that smelled of
right here and now, and thought herself, hard, back into the
moment and away from the past.

⌒

Rory opened the e-mail again and reread it. He didn't know
why he kept doing it; it was as though he was fiddling with the
edges of a plaster that sat over a particularly revolting and in-
fected wound. It almost didn't make sense. The content seemed
so far-fetched. This time last year he and his dad had been bond-
ing in a tattoo studio. Now his dad was living with the mother
of his child on a hippy commune. The e-mail needed to be
reread, just to see if it contained some missed word or phrase
that would stop it sounding so unlikely. But no. There it was.
In black and white. The love triangle from hell. Or, God, even
worse, a love *square* if he included himself in the shape.

He saw them every day, men like his dad, old and tired and
scared of the women at home, terrified of being like their
friends, incapable of allowing themselves to be rejected. They
came here, to the other side of the world, and they found
women who made them feel as though it was okay to be a
loser.

And now his dad was one of them.

Pitiful.

Did he honestly, truly believe that Kayleigh was interested
in him for his mind? For his body? For his sexual prowess?

Rory shivered involuntarily.

Of course she wasn't. She was with him to ensure her

connection with Rory's family. To maintain her connection with Rory.

He read the e-mail one more time, and then he shut it down.

He'd first found out about his dad and Kayleigh a few months ago. Beth had e-mailed him. Sheepishly. She'd known since before it had even happened. But his dad hadn't got in touch with him. He'd not heard from his father until now. And then it was in a joint e-mail, addressed to all three of his children.

Rory shrugged to himself.

Whatever.

He didn't care anymore. He'd come so far unraveled from the few remaining bonds that had tied him to his family that, really, who cared? Who gave a shit? Who gave a shit about Meg and all her bloody children? Who gave a shit about his weird mum and her sick girlfriend? Who gave a shit about vacuous Beth and her boring new boyfriend? Who gave a shit about Kayleigh and her kid and his dad and who gave a shit who called who Dad or Granddad or whatever? Who gave a shit about any of it? Seriously.

Rory left the Internet café and pulled his phone out of his pocket. It was Owen.

"Yeah."

"Mate, where are you?"

"I'm on Moo 2. Just heading back."

"What the fuck are you doing there?"

"Nothing, just sending some e-mails."

"Seriously, you need to get back here, like, right now. Right this fucking minute."

Rory's heart rate picked up and he started walking faster. "What? What's going on?"

"Just get here. And make sure there's nobody following you."

"Oh, what?" Rory spun round as he walked. He didn't know what he was looking for but assumed he'd recognize a threat if he saw one.

"Should I chuck it out, Owen? Should I dump it?"

But Owen had already hung up. Adrenaline blasted through him. He half walked, half ran, looking over his shoulder. It took him twenty minutes to get back to the club. By the time he burst through the doors and into the back room he was soaked with sweat. Owen sat behind his desk. A plug-in fan blew his paperwork about in front of him. He looked cool and collected. On the chairs in front of him sat two Thai men wearing short-sleeved shirts and trousers. As he entered the room they both turned and appraised him. Rory vaguely recognized one of them. Had seen him around.

"This is the man," he heard Owen saying. "This is the man who brings the drugs into my bar. Please arrest him."

Both men nodded and one of them stood up and bent Rory over Owen's desk while the other clipped a pair of handcuffs around his wrists. Hands rifled through his pockets, came out clutching little bags of pills and powder, the currency of his work.

"Owen?" Rory breathed out, looking up at his friend from where his head rested against the warm wood of his desk. "Mate?"

"You're not my mate, mate. You're a drug dealer."

Owen stood up and held the door open for the two policemen. Rory stared beseechingly at his friend over his shoulder, struggling against the pressure of the men's hands against his body. "Seriously, Owen, what is this shit? What the fuck is going on, what are you doing?" He was shouting now through a closed door. His heels were dragging against the floor of the club. Girls and customers were staring at him in horror. "Jesus! For fuck's sake! Someone help me! Owen! Jesus!"

Somehow the two policemen had got him onto the pavement. They were shouting at him urgently in Thai, with occasional words of English. "Stop moving! Just come!" A police van sat outside. Rory hadn't even noticed it before. He was pushed into the back and the doors slammed shut behind him. He was on a hot metal floor. The van smelled of sweat and cigarettes. Then they were moving, slowly through the midday traffic. Rory closed his eyes and saw Owen's face again. That cool, hard expression of professional disappointment. The satisfaction buried beneath it of having swerved a curveball, dealt with a problem, sorted it. *Taken care of business*.

Rory let his face fall onto his chest. He'd almost believed that he was Owen's friend. Voices in his head had told him time and time again, *"Don't trust him. He's only out for his own interests. He doesn't care about you."* But he'd ignored the voices and fooled himself that he was the special one in Owen's tightly controlled, sordid little world. He bashed his elbows together against his ribs with frustration.

"Fuck!" he shouted to himself. He kicked the sides of the van with the soles of his feet. "Fuck! Fuck! Fuck!"

He breathed back the tears that threatened to fall. He kicked the side of the van again. And then he breathed out. *Fine*, he thought, *good. Here it is. The thing*. The thing that had been hanging over him ever since he'd left Kayleigh alone in Spain with an eight-month-old baby. The cartoon anvil above his head. Here it was. It had fallen on him.

Fine, he thought again, *good*.

10

Tuesday 11th January 2011

Oh, Jim,

I knew you'd understand. I honestly feel like I can tell you anything, absolutely anything. And I do hope (believe!) that you feel the same way too. I had suspected that the "radio silence" from you over the New Year was probably the result of a "bender." That's okay. At least you have your drinking more or less under control. (Everyone's allowed to let their hair down from time to time, after all! Even alcoholics!) Which is more than could be said for me and my so-called "hoarding." Oh, Jim, even I can now see it's getting out of control. And it's not even so much the actual STUFF. Honestly. I am fine about all the stuff. I love all the stuff (although I do miss my kitchen. I do miss my bath. I do miss all the things I can't even see anymore. Photos and favorite clothes and whatnot, but anyway . . .). No, the STUFF is not the problem. The LACK OF MONEY is the problem now. Colin, my ex, used to give me an allowance, but then the little BITCH he lives with told him to stop, that he was "not helping me." Oh, God, Jim, I was livid. I was beyond furious. And the tone of voice, so PATRONIZING, as though I were a small girl and he was my darling daddy, being cruel to be kind. I can't tell you. I have not spoken to him since. The bastard. So, now I am living off thin air. But still (God help me) BUYING. Yes. I am spending money I do not have on things I do not need and I have absolutely no control over this. None whatsoever. I find myself at the supermarket with an empty purse, scrabbling for coppers to pay for things, having to put things back on shelves. I am often hungry. Isn't that ridiculous???? Hungry, yet buying things I have no need for??? Because I derive more pleasure from buying a nice little painting or a packet of clothes pegs than I do from eating. And that is the truth, Jim. I'm sure you understand. I KNOW you do.

Anyway, MOVING ON.

Rory. You wanted to hear more about Rory.

Well, poor Rory. He was always the superior twin, you know, there has to be one, doesn't there? It's impossible not to draw all these comparisons when two children are born concurrently. And Rory was simply taller, cleverer, blonder, more popular, happier. He just was. He was also more susceptible to things, to peer pressure, to the crowd. He didn't really have a mind of his own. And after we lost Rhys, after he lost his twin, he had no plan, no direction, just seemed to be waiting for somebody to tell him what to do next. And unfortunately that person was her. Kayleigh. She took him away from here to a place with no phones, no cars, no money, got herself pregnant against his will, turned him against me, against US, made him so miserable that he left her and the baby, and went to work for a drug dealer in Thailand.

Well, cutting to the chase, my son is currently serving a five-year jail term for possessing class-A drugs. In a prison in Krabi.

Can you believe this, Jim? Can you believe it???

Anyway, he'll be released any day now, apparently. I only know this because Megan told me. Megan tried to get a campaign started, to appeal the sentence. But he told her no,

THE HOUSE WE GREW UP IN

he wanted to do the time!! He said it was his "destiny"!! And he didn't reply to any of our letters and told us not to see him. He has completely estranged himself from us, turned himself into a stranger, it's like he's painstakingly extracted the DNA from himself, become someone not related to us. I don't know who he is anymore. I have no idea.

Honestly, Jim, would you believe me if I told you we all used to be close? Like a paper-chain family. Inextricably linked. And now we're just ephemera. Scattered across the globe. Nothing to link us together. Absolutely nothing.

Apart from the past.

Do you ever wish you'd had more children, Jim? I'm sorry if that sounds insensitive in the light of what happened to your lovely boy. But I'm curious. Because I truly thought that the advantage of having so many children was that I'd end up close to at least one of them. That one of them would end up being my friend. But not only have none of them ended up being my friend they've all become strangers to me, Jim. My own children!

Anyway. SORRY! This has been a very depressing e-mail. I promise next time I'll be upbeat and full of fizz!

Tell me more about your life, Jim. Tell me about your flat. What does it look like? What can you see while you're typing to me?

Lots and lots and lots of love,
L xxxxxxxxxxx

APRIL 2011

Molly looked shy when she saw her grandfather standing in the doorway of their hotel room. She'd been lying on her stomach on her bed, the remote control in her hand, pointed at the TV. She quickly brought herself up to a sitting position.

"Hello, Molly."

She nodded and said, "Hi," in a barely audible squeak.

"Wow," said Colin, "you're all grown-up."

Molly smiled tightly and looked beyond embarrassed. Meg had tried over the years not to discuss her father in front of the children, not to let her feelings and her opinions filter through to them, but it was impossible to protect them from everything, stuff got through by osmosis sometimes. And Molly was old enough now to feel the full horror of her grandfather living with his son's ex. "It's like one of those 'True Life' stories in those trashy magazines at the dentist," she'd once said in horror.

Meg pulled out the dressing-table chair for her father and switched on the kettle. "Where are you going to stay?" she asked.

Colin smiled, his gaze still on his oldest grandchild, his eyes full of regret. "Oh, gosh, at the house I would've thought. I mean, I don't suppose this place would fit my budget somehow."

"No," said Meg, "probably not. What are you living off these days?"

"Well, my pension, obviously. And Kayleigh makes a bob or two, running these courses, you know."

"What sort of courses?"

"Oh, God, well, I'm not sure how to describe them, I mean,

I suppose, *relationship* workshops." He smiled apologetically and Meg shuddered. It truly did not bear thinking about.

"Well," she said, changing the subject. "If you want to stay at the house, you'll have to sleep in Rhys's room."

Colin shrugged. "I thought as much. It's fine. I'm cool with that."

I'm cool with that.

Jesus Christ, thought Meg, who was this man?

"And you'll need to eat out. There's no kitchen to speak of. And no bath or shower. But the toilet on the landing is still usable."

Colin nodded. "Good. Good," he said. "I'm pretty used to basic living these days."

The kettle clicked off and Meg poured water into a posh glass teapot filled with fresh leaves. She opened a packet of handmade cookies, tied with black ribbon, and dropped them onto a china plate. She tried not to ponder too long on the contrasts between herself and her father: the five-star boutique hotel with the £4.50 bag of shortbread, and the unfurnished bedroom of a dead son. The five-bedroom house in Tufnell Park with off-street parking and CCTV, and the shed on a dusty commune in southern Spain with a chemical toilet and a goat tethered to the gate (she imagined). Her pristine, laundered and pressed White Company top, and his crumpled, sun-bleached T-shirt.

Her father.

It hardly seemed possible.

She saw Molly eyeing him curiously, watching everything he did as though she would be writing a report later. She took a tiny bottle of organic milk from the minibar and poured it into a milk jug.

"We've been to the coroners," she said. She gave Colin the

breakdown, the dreadful details. "They'll release the body tomorrow morning. So, we need to, you know . . ."

"Plan a funeral."

"Yes." She stopped for a moment. She'd been desperate to get her mother's body back, desperate to start organizing everything. And now she could and she felt herself suddenly, dramatically, losing momentum. "You should do it," she said.

Colin nodded. "Absolutely," he said. "Yes. Of course. I'll arrange everything. Did she leave any . . . ?"

"No," said Meg. "Nothing. Although, of course, I think we could all make a pretty good stab at it. You know. Dancing. Music. Color. All the obvious Mum stuff."

Colin smiled sadly. He turned to Molly. "Do you remember her?" he said. "Your grandma?"

Molly shrugged shyly. "Sort of. I remember her in her chair, in her bedroom. I remember her being kind of . . . *weird*?"

Colin sighed. "That's so sad, isn't it?" He turned to Meg. "Sad that her grandchildren never saw her at her best. You know, when she was bustling and mad and full of energy and rainbows."

Meg nodded. Yes, she thought, it was. But then so was all of it. Sad that Molly only knew her grandfather as a sleazy old man, not the sweet, patient, sexless man who'd played such a big part in the upbringing of all his children. Sad that Molly only knew her uncle as a pathetic drug dealer who'd spent the last few years of his life in a Thai jail, not the beautiful blond child who'd been everyone's best friend and the most popular boy at school. Sad that Molly only knew her aunt as a half-formed shadow on the other side of the world, not the sweet, naive child who'd once been the center of Megan's universe. And sad that Molly had never got the chance to know her other uncle at all, because he'd hanged himself when he was sixteen years old.

"And Beth?" said Colin, breaking her train of thought. "What's going on with her?"

She flashed him a warning look, turned her eyes to Molly. Molly did not know. She had managed to protect her from that much.

"I mean, have you managed to make contact? Is she coming?"

"I've sent her an e-mail. But I haven't taken her calls."

Colin nodded understandingly. "So, she could be on her way? In theory?"

"Yes, I suppose she could be. But then again, she might be having another nervous breakdown." She shrugged dismissively.

"So," said Colin, "just us. For now."

"Yes," said Meg, feeling a chill of dread running through her. "For now."

SEPTEMBER 2006

From: Rainbowbelle@yahoo.co.uk
To: MeganRoseLiddingtonBird@yahoo.co.uk;
RoryBird2@hotmail.com;
Bethanbabybird@arthouseframing.co.au;
Colin.bird@hotmail.com

Dear family of mine,

I am writing to you all, because I cannot bear to form the words with my own mouth, but yesterday morning, at 11:16 a.m., my precious Vicky finally passed away. I was honored enough to see her pass and it was very peaceful and very sweet. Maddy and Sophie were both there, Tim and her mother were there too. It was a good end to a beautiful life. And now she is suffering no more.

But now, I have to ask you all something very important. I've tried my hardest these last few years to accept the beating wings of my baby birds as they flew, not just the nest, but in some cases the continent. I've let you all go. And now I need you all to come back. Please. For the funeral. FOR ME. I cannot stand by that graveside with somebody else's children, with somebody else's ex-husband. I need to stand there with my family, all together, at my side.

It's going to be on Friday, three p.m., at the cemetery in Mickleton. And then a party after, at that nice pub next door. Vicky loved you all so much and she's left some things, just little things, in her will, for all of you. It would make me very happy to be able to hand them over in person.

Beth: if you need some money for your flight, let me know. Meg: Maddy and Sophie say you and the kiddies can have their flat, they'll be at Tim's. Same goes for you, Beth, or, of course, you can always stay here, though it is a bit disorganized. AS EVER! Please write back as soon as you possibly can, girls/Colin, I need some support. I'm not as strong as I thought I was.

All my love, with all my heart, your mummy/Lorelei
xxxx

⌀

Beth pulled her velvet jacket tightly to her throat and tried not to flinch when strangers passed too close to her. London looked warped and distorted. Its streets looked like odd memories. People seemed strangely postapocalyptic in their appearances. Nothing felt as it should. The pavement gleamed with lurking puddles in its dips and cracks. Beth negotiated them, gingerly, with horror, as though they might be land mines. A fat woman with a double buggy suddenly loomed before her and Beth pulled herself tightly away, terrified for some reason that the woman might look at her and see something she didn't like, that she would shout at her.

Meg's road was the next on the left. She wanted to check on her smartphone, but was too scared to take it out of her bag in case someone mugged her.

Ridiculous woman.

She hadn't been to Meg's house before. She hadn't seen Bill since 2003. She hadn't seen her niece and nephews since they were tiny. She hadn't seen the youngest one at all. She was thirty-four years old. Single. Too thin. Just shakily recovering from a breakdown the previous year that had seen her in her bed staring at the ceiling and crying for nearly six months. Tomorrow morning she was going to a funeral that would be painfully, unthinkably sad. She had many more worrying things to fret about than someone taking her mobile phone.

But still.

The last thing she should be doing in this condition of pathetic mental frailty was traveling across the entire planet to be reunited with her family. She'd tried to get out of it. She'd tried to persuade her mother that it would be better if she didn't come. She'd invented logistical hurdles that her mother had batted effortlessly out of the way. And then she'd found an iota of strength from somewhere and persuaded herself that she could do it, that she should do it, that she would do it. Meg had booked her flights and insisted that she come with them. "Plenty of room in the people carrier."

Beth had shuddered at the very concept. But also, upon

reflection, quite liked the simplicity of it. Once she'd made it to Meg's house she wouldn't have to think about anything else until it was time to fly home again. Meg would look after everything.

As for Bill. No. There was no room in her head for thoughts of Bill. Bill was just a man. Her sister's partner. Nothing more.

She turned the next corner and found herself in a street of large semidetached Victorian houses, each with off-street parking and mature trees and nice front doors. It was still fairly early. Her flight had landed at nine a.m. She would not have to face Bill until much later and had already decided that she would claim jet lag and put herself to bed before he came home from work. Meg's house stood before her. A huge step up from the garden flat she'd been living in the last time Beth had been to visit. Three stories high, four windows wide, a gigantic people carrier parked in the driveway and louvered shutters at the windows. It looked as if it had been freshly painted and pointed that very morning. She rang the doorbell, adjusted the collar of her jacket, the thick flick of black hair that sat on her forehead. She glanced down at her yellow Mary Janes and cleared her throat. She fought the urge to turn and leave. And then there she was. Her big sister. In a red Lycra dress with big square-toed boots, her curly hair cut unflatteringly short. And large. So incredibly large. Beth stared at her, openmouthed, for a moment. "Hi," she said eventually.

And then suddenly she was being squeezed between those big arms and squashed against that huge soft stomach and she could feel it underneath, the unyielding shield of a support garment, almost but not quite like flesh. And she thought, through the fug of jet lag and culture shock, that her sister had put it on for her. To look thinner and less lumpy. For Beth.

"You look lovely," she said, once Meg had released her from the embrace.

"No," said Meg. "I don't. I look fat. Horribly fat. But thank you. And you"—she stared into Beth's eyes fondly and Beth wanted to shrink to the size of a dandelion seed and be blown away down the street—"you look amazing! I can't believe you've just got off a long-haul flight. Look at you. I love the velvet jacket." Meg closed the front door behind her, removed Beth's rucksack from her hands, placed it at the bottom of the staircase and led her into the living room. Cream sofas, cream carpet, framed photographs, marble fire surround, glass coffee table, everything just skirting the edges of modern, but not quite getting there. As though Meg was too scared to make any kind of statement in case she got it wrong.

"This is lovely," she said.

"Ah, well, it's home," said Meg, plucking a red-haired baby out of a wheeled device and presenting him to her. "And this is Charlie Bear!"

The baby looked at Beth curiously. He was very fat, with a slightly angry look about him, but he wriggled his legs delightedly at the sight of Beth and delivered a winning smile.

"And this is your auntie Beth," Meg twittered into the baby's ear. "She has come all the way from Australia to meet you. Yes, she has!"

She bounced the boy vigorously in her big arms and he beamed with pleasure.

"He's gorgeous," said Beth. "Looks exactly like his brothers!"

"I know," said Meg, "daft, isn't it. Like I had triplets with eight years between them. Want to hold?"

Beth eyed the proffered baby cautiously. He looked so happy there in his mother's big meaty arms. "Er . . ."

"No problem," said Meg, pulling him back towards herself.

"Some people like holding other people's babies. I'm not one of them. I only like holding my own babies—isn't that right, Charlie Bear?"

Meg peered at Bethan over the top of Charlie's head and smiled. "It's so good to see you. I've missed you so much."

Beth smiled and yawned. "Me too," she said.

"It's crazy. We're sisters. We used to do everything together. And now we never see each other. We don't even talk to each other. Nuts!"

Beth nodded. Her vision was starting to blur. Deep down inside the marrow of her she could feel liquid weakness spreading through her body.

"I mean, I just never in a million years thought you'd suddenly bugger off to the other side of the world. I mean, of all the unexpected things to do!"

Beth could hear blood whooshing through her head, through her ears. She could see two Megs and two Charlies. Her mouth was dry. She tried to stand up, to go somewhere. She didn't know where.

"Bethy? Are you okay? Beth?"

The sides of the room started to close before her, like curtains. And then she blacked out.

＜◇・

When she came round, she was on her back on the cream sofa, her yellow shoes in a neat pair on the floor, her velvet jacket draped over her body like a blanket. Meg sat by her side with a glass of water and an expression of concern. "My God, Beth, you scared the total shit out of me. Are you okay?"

Beth nodded and sat up slowly, feeling the blood starting to pump regularly once more around her body. She took the water from Meg's hand and gulped it. "Sorry about that," she said.

"What's going on, Bethy?"

Beth shook her head. "Nothing," she said, "just jet lag, I suppose. And I should probably eat something."

"Here." Her sister presented her with a cereal bar. "Eat it," she demanded.

Beth peeled it and nibbled at the corner. She hadn't eaten on the flight. Only the crispy snack things that came with her drinks. She wasn't sure why. Something about the smell of it, that vinegary, gravy smell. But that wasn't why she'd passed out. It wasn't hunger, it was panic.

The baby sat on the floor, playing with the buckles of her shoes. Meg snatched them up and said, "No, no, Charlie Bear, dirty shoes. Dirty shoes. Yuck!"

Charlie stared at her curiously. Beth wanted to say something to him, say, *"Yeah, I know, she's nuts, right?"* Instead she shared a complicitous look with him and ate some more cereal bar. And then, just as she was putting herself back together, starting to relax even, she heard footsteps down the stairs and she looked at Meg for some kind of explanation and then there he was. Bill. Standing in the doorway with his phone in his hand and a confused expression on his face. Then he looked at Beth and said, "Well, hello, stranger!"

He looked exactly the same. The thick whorls of guinea-pig hair, the soft features, the expression of wry amusement as though the whole world were just one big silly joke that he was too clever to laugh at.

"Bill," she said, "what are you doing here?"

He pretended to look around the house for something and then laughed, his growling laugh, and said, "I live here!"

She felt annoyed but forced a smile. "I thought you'd be at work."

"Working from home today," he replied, and then he

turned to Meg and said, "Any idea where the charger is for my phone?"

Meg sighed and said, "No, darling man. I have no idea." She raised her eyebrows conspiratorially at Beth. "And aren't you going to say hello properly to Beth? Who you haven't seen for almost a hundred years?"

Bill frowned and then smiled and said, "Sorry, of course, lovely to see you, Beth." He strode towards her, clasped her shoulders and kissed her firmly on both cheeks. "Sorry it has to be under such sad circumstances. But still. Always a treat. You look lovely."

Beth waited for it, the lurch in the pit of her stomach, the longing. She waited and it did not come. She smiled and said, "Thank you, so do you."

She saw him puff up, almost imperceptibly. "I don't. But bless you. And I'd better get on. But I'll see you later. In fact . . ." He paused. "It's my turn to collect the kids from school today. Would you like to come with me? Give you something to focus on to keep your mind off the jet lag?"

Feeling herself, *knowing* herself to be cured, she smiled and said, "Yes! Sure."

⌒

"So," said Bill, his hands on the handles of the buggy, Charlie wrapped inside a gray blanket, his feet poking out of the bottom, fast asleep. "It's been a long time, Beth."

The first of the autumn leaves littered the pavement. Beth kicked at them with the toes of her Mary Janes and smiled. "Yes. Thank God."

Bill laughed. "It wasn't that bad, was it?"

Beth glared at him disbelievingly. "Bill," she said, "she's my sister. You're my brother-in-law. Of course it was that bad."

"That's not what I meant," he said softly.

"No. I know. But still. It's not something I can look at in those terms. It should never have happened. I was sick."

"Charming."

"No, but I was. I wasn't normal. I mean, I'm still not normal. I've got a long way to go before I can contemplate normal. But back then . . . I don't know what I was thinking." She shook her head.

"Oh, come on," said Bill. "You're making out you were a basket case. I can assure you that you weren't. You were charming. You were adorable. You were—"

"Sleeping with my sister's partner." She shook her head again. "No, Bill. I don't know how you've processed the thing, but I can assure you that I have processed it to the point of negation. Do you see? It can't have happened. It mustn't have happened. There can't be fond memories or, or, rose-tinted nostalgia. It *did not happen*."

Bill slowed his pace and looked at her. He looked as if he was going to say something. But then he sighed and turned back.

"I can't be that surgical about it, I'm afraid. It was a terrible mistake. I should be shot for the risk I put our relationship at, for what I could potentially have done to my family. And believe me, I'm glad it's over, too. Really. But it was also amazing. Wasn't it? At the beginning, you know. I mean, do you remember—"

"Stop!" Beth spun round and pushed her hands against Bill's chest. "No."

He smiled, put his own hands up in a gesture of surrender. "Fine," he said. "I'll keep my memories to myself."

"Good. Yes, please."

He sighed theatrically and for a moment they continued in silence.

"So," he said, after a moment, "anyone in your life at the moment?"

She shook her head.

"What happened to the Aussie?"

"Jason?" she asked, slightly surprised to be using his name again after so long. "God, nothing, no, that lasted a nano-second."

"But it got you out of your rut?"

"It did. Yes. Just in the nick of time. And then there was Richard."

"Ah, yes, I think I remember Meg mentioning a Richard . . ."

"Yes, he was British. Lovely, too lovely. Everything was lovely. I had a great job, I got my citizenship, nice flat, and then . . . I had a nervous breakdown."

Bill raised a pale eyebrow.

"I think, if I'm honest, I'd been on the cusp of a nervous breakdown since I was a teenager. Since Rhys died. I think I'd been hanging on to this precipice. Without even realizing it. If I hadn't met Jason, if he hadn't been so bloody insistent, I'd probably never even have left home. Isn't that terrifying? That I could have just let myself stay there, in that disgusting house, forever? So, anyway, the whole 'new me' thing in Sydney, it was all a total facade, none of it was real. And it was like the foundations beneath the dream house were made of sand and the whole thing collapsed. And that was me—six months in bed. Bye-bye, job. Bye-bye, Richard."

"He didn't stick around?"

"I didn't want him to!" she replied crossly. "He was part of the problem. He was a prop. On the stage set. That was my life." She shuddered. "I'm not recovered," she said. "I shouldn't be here. I should have stayed at home."

"Home."

"Yes. Sydney. Home. But Mum insisted."

"Might do you good."

Beth glared at him. He was an idiot. She had no idea, *no idea*, what she'd been thinking for all those years. They were in front of the boys' school. It was a redbrick Victorian block, five stories high. It looked very urban and very imposing. Clusters of parents stood around the playground and the gates. Some of them were smoking. Beth would not send her children here. She would want them to go to a small village school, cozy and cartoonish, like the one she had been to.

"Are you going?" she asked, as Bill negotiated the buggy up the three steps into the playground.

"To the funeral?" he asked, nodding hello to a mother in a head scarf.

"Yes."

He shrugged. "I don't know," he said. "I shouldn't, really. Work is nuts at the moment. But, Vicky, I don't know, I always had such a fond spot for her. We were quite close. In a way . . ."

"Mmm," she said noncommitally.

"I'll decide tomorrow."

"It's going to be horrific," she said. "Those girls."

He nodded. And for just a moment she saw something in his eyes, something that reminded her what she'd loved about him for all that time. They clouded over, for just a second, with a film of tears. He was a human after all. He pulled Charlie out of his buggy and held him tight.

～

"I kicked him out," said Meg later that evening over a large glass of wine. "About three years ago."

Molly was watching TV next door and the boys were in the back garden playing cricket with Bill. The baby was asleep. It was a watery evening, early dusk, the tired tail end of summer. Beth had a can of Coke on the counter in front of her and was idly watching Bill charging about in shorts, socks and trainers through the bifold glass doors, thinking what a fool he looked.

She turned sharply at Meg's words. "What!" she cried. "Bill? How come?"

Meg sighed luxuriously, clearly relishing the prospect of her next announcement. "I just got sick of him," she said. "I mean, I was pretty sure he was having an affair . . ."

Beth nodded and lifted her Coke can to her lips.

"Or a *number* of affairs. And he was just so cross all the time. But worse than that, he was horrible to the children. That I really couldn't bear. I thought we'd be better off without him."

"Oh, my God, when was this?"

"Oh, ages ago. Just after you left for Australia, I suppose."

"And was he?" she asked. "Having an affair?"

Meg shrugged and topped up her enormous wineglass. "I have no idea. And neither do I wish to know. All I know is that kicking him out changed everything." She slammed her hands down on the kitchen table to establish her point. "Everything."

Beth stared deeply at her own hands on the counter. "Well, that's good then," she said. "Right?"

"Yes, from a purely philosophical point of view, yes. Although, honestly, at the time I thought I was in hell. Living with a man who hated me. Who hated my children. When we all loved him so, so much. It was like a nightmare. Seriously. And that's the thing," she said, leaning in towards her sister, "that's what these *stupid, stupid* women don't realize, when they sleep with a married man. They're not just sleeping with him. They're sleeping with his whole *fucking family*. His whole *fucking family!*"

Beth smiled tightly, but her eyes did not meet Meg's.

~

The following day the sky glowed with illuminated clouds; thin drops of rain fell at intervals. But it had promise. *And my God*, thought Meg, *some sunshine would be good on a day like today.*

Bill did not come in the end, and Meg was glad. She wanted her sister to herself. She wanted the funeral to herself.

So he had stayed at home with Molly, who didn't want to miss school. (An unlikely excuse, Meg had suggested. It was more likely that she just couldn't stand the thought of numerous weird family members asking her stupid questions about school and telling her how tall she'd got.) It was just the three boys and Beth, zooming up the middle lane of the M40, dressed in pink (Vicky's last, rather clichéd request) and girding their loins for a testing day ahead.

They talked about Rory.

He'd been in jail for nine months, on remand since the previous Easter. He did not want any help. He did not want any contact. According to their dad he'd been stitched up by that Essex boy he'd run away from Spain with. Apparently Owen had used Rory as a "sacrificial lamb" to get the police off the scent of his underground drug operation. According to Colin, Rory was taking the flak out of some kind of misplaced loyalty.

"I don't think so, though," said Meg. "I honestly don't. I think it's more than that. Deeper than that. I think he wanted to be punished."

"Punished?"

"Yes. For letting Rhys fend for himself at secondary school. For being so angry when he died. For leaving Kayleigh and the baby. For being alive when his twin was dead. I think he thought he was due a whipping." She shrugged and left the theory there, in the air, to be mulled over.

Beth sighed. "Yes," she said, "I'd never really thought about it like that before, but yes, I think you're right." She paused and turned to gaze through the window for a moment. Then she turned back and said, "Do you think that's why Mum lives like she does? Do you think she's punishing herself too?"

Meg shook her head. "No. I think Mum lives like that because she's sick. End of story."

Beth sighed again. "Poor Mum," she said. "She's going to be in pieces today."

Meg changed lanes, peering from wing mirror to rearview mirror and back again, and said, "No. She won't be. She'll be fine. She *is* fine. I promise you. She has once again processed her grief through some bizarre, unknowable channel, and come through the other end just as nuts as ever."

"Who's nuts?" asked Alfie, his voice barely audible from his seat at the very back of the people carrier.

"No one's nuts," called out Meg. "No one. We're all one hundred percent sane!"

She laughed out loud at her own words and smiled at her eldest son in the rearview mirror.

He returned the smile and then popped his earphones back in.

"I know who you're talking about," said Stan, sitting behind Beth. "You're talking about Grandma."

"No, we're not," said Meg, checking the signs for the next junction. "We're absolutely not."

"But Grandma *is* mad," he countered. He began to count

things off on his fingers. "She keeps *absolutely everything*"—
he tapped on his thumb—"she doesn't brush her hair; she's
obsessed with rainbows; she does cartwheels and handstands,
even though she's, like, *really old*; she shouts a lot; and she
called Vicky's daughter a little shit." He leaned back triumphantly. "And that," he added, "is just *some* of it."

Beth and Meg exchanged a look.

And then they both laughed out loud, a spilling over of all
the politeness and strangeness that they had both been bang-
ing up against for the past twenty-four hours.

"What?" said Stanley.

But the two sisters were laughing too hard to reply.

·◌·

The cemetery was a sea of pink. In spite of her misgivings
about the concept of a pink funeral, Meg was strangely moved
by the communal, cross-generational, cross-gender adoption
of a dead woman's wishes. She spotted Sophie and Maddy immediately: two tall, blond almost-women, in short skirts and
ankle boots, with pink flowers in their hair. They looked like
adults from a distance, but with every step closer their youth
became more obvious, until, as she stepped towards them to
embrace them, they were children once more. She breathed
into their soft hair and told them she was sorry, and they were
brave and stoic and they told her they were fine.

Mum was talking to Tim. She was monstrously thin and
looked simultaneously incredible and bizarre, in a fuchsia
cocktail dress with feathers, pink zip-up boots and a pink beret
with a bobble on the top. She beamed her toothy grin and
opened up her arms to her daughters and her grandsons.

"You're too thin," said Megan, who hadn't seen her mother
in about eight weeks.

LISA JEWELL

Lorelei threw her a sad look and said, "Darling, I've just lost the love of my life." And Meg nodded apologetically and felt guilty. Lorelei held Beth in her arms for a count of at least twenty, until Beth was forced to pull herself out of the tangle of her embrace and adjust her clothing. Lorelei turned to Tim and said, somewhat theatrically, "I have not been together with my daughters for almost three years. *Three years.*" Tim nodded sympathetically and left them to it.

Lorelei took the baby from Meg's arms and cooed at him, and Charlie, thankfully, responded well, gifting his grandmother a smile and an expression of enchantment. "What a lovely, lovely boy you are," she trilled. "What a lovely, lovely boy!" They chatted brightly, strangely, to people they vaguely recognized. Lorelei told Meg she needed to get her figure back, Beth looked blank, the boys stood shyly with their hands in their pockets, the baby gurgled and complained when he was strapped into his buggy. And then Lorelei linked her arms into her daughters' and the three of them walked together into the crematorium, followed by Stan and Alfie, who was pushing Charlie in the buggy. A sudden blast of golden autumnal sun shone on them from behind and this could have been a poignant and tender moment, possibly even the beginning of a new dawn, if it had not been for the fact that upon entering the chapel the first thing they all saw was Colin and Kayleigh sitting side by side, with a small girl on their left.

They were the only people in there and they had been whispering to each other, complicitously, before they both turned at the sound of voices. Meg felt Lorelei turn brittle with shock. She and Beth gawped at each other. "Jesus *Christ,*" said Lorelei, not quite as inaudibly as would have been desirable under the circumstances.

Colin's face broke open into an emotional smile and he leapt to his feet. Meg and her mother and sister all froze, instinctively, to the spot.

"Oh, wow! Girls! And boys!" Colin glanced behind at the row of somewhat shell-shocked grandsons. He walked quickly towards them all, looked as though he wanted to take them all in his arms and squeeze them, but pulled himself up short at the sight of their faces, set hard with surprise and displeasure. "Wow," he said again, looking in turn from face to face, "you all look so lovely. You all look so . . ."

Lorelei simply walked off halfway through his declaration. She swanned off, the sound of her pink Cuban-heeled boots echoing across the room, and sat herself down at the front of the chapel, on the pew nearest the front. Beth and Meg looked at each other and then at their father.

"What is she doing here?" Meg whispered.

Colin looked from Kayleigh to Meg and shrugged and said, "She wanted to come. She wanted to say good-bye."

"But she didn't even *know* Vicky!" exclaimed Beth.

"Well, that's not quite true. She met her a few times. Thought her a great person. And besides. It's an Irish thing. An Irish Catholic thing. Paying respects. The need to observe the rituals. You know."

Kayleigh turned, looked at Meg and nodded a judicious greeting. Meg caught her breath, hesitated for a split second and then nodded back. Kayleigh looked different. Softer. Prettier. Older. Her hair, which had been brilliant scarlet the last time she'd seen her, was long, highlighted and held on top of her head in a ponytail. She was wearing a baby-pink jacket, a Chanel rip-off type of thing with braiding and gold buttons, and a high-necked Victorian-style blouse underneath. And her face, which had once been a sharp thing, all angry angles and set-in lines, had loosened and mellowed into something almost beautiful.

And then the girl turned round, to see what her mother was looking at, and Meg gasped. This was Tia. The name in countless e-mails. Countless bitter conversations. The purely conceptual child who had been discussed and abandoned over the years but never before seen in the flesh. And here she was. In, as her children often said, *real life*.

The child was beautiful. Ethereally, classically, remarkably beautiful. She had Rory's white-blond hair, falling down her back in fat ringlets. And she had Rory's fine features: his dark-lashed blue eyes, his full lips, his aquiline nose and high cheekbones. She gazed questioningly at Meg. And then she saw the three boys standing behind her and blushed, turned her head away. But her face stayed on in Meg's consciousness like a sunspot. Her niece. Six years old, only a few months younger than Stanley. The image of her father. The very image of him.

Other people were filing into the crematorium now. Some of them looked curiously at Meg and Beth, at Colin, at Lorelei sitting alone at the front of the chapel. Some of them had no idea of the significance of this arrangement of people and the unfinished conversation that hung among them.

"We'll talk afterwards," said Meg, her voice softer for the shock of seeing her niece's face. She put out an arm, touched her father's sleeve, and then headed to the front, to sit next to her mother. Beth and the boys followed behind.

"Are you okay?" she whispered into Lorelei's ear.

Lorelei nodded and kept her gaze to the front. "Arsehole," she muttered under her breath. "Fucking *arsehole*."

Stanley snorted and Meg glared at him, then said, "Please try not to swear, Mum."

Lorelei tutted loudly and stared resolutely ahead.

"I cannot believe it," whispered Beth. She looked pale and clammy and Meg squeezed her hand and said, "Are you okay? You're not going to faint again, are you?"

Beth shook her head tightly and swallowed hard. "I'm fine," she muttered. "I just, I can't believe she's here . . ."

Meg handed the baby a small toy to occupy him in his buggy and passed Polo mints around. "She's very beautiful, isn't she?" she whispered, after a moment, to Beth and her mother. "The girl? Tia?"

Lorelei tutted and shook her head. Beth nodded and smiled. But neither of them replied. And it hit Megan, then, really quite hard, just exactly how odd this was. That girl was her niece. That girl was Lorelei's granddaughter. She was six years old but none of them had ever met her before. She had not seen her own father since she was a baby. Her grandfather shared a bed with her mother.

"Total and utter fucking *prick*," said her mother.

Megan nudged her hard.

"Well . . ."

"I'm not going to the wake," said Beth quietly.

Meg looked questioningly at her.

"I can't do it. Not with her there."

"Beth! You have to! I can't do it alone!" Meg whispered urgently.

The chapel was starting to fill up now. They shifted up the pew a few feet to allow Tim and his new girlfriend to squeeze in.

They all smiled tightly and politely at one another and the conversation ended and another one began, about motorways and the rather irreverent humanist funeral celebrant who'd been appointed as per Vicky's instructions, and the cardboard coffin and the wild meadow flowers that had come from the garden of the house where Vicky had grown up.

Lorelei had agreed to give a eulogy. Megan had never seen her mother stand in front of a crowd before. She had never heard her speak in public and could not quite imagine how it would be. She was feeling slightly anxious about it. But she needn't have worried. Her mother took to the small stage and adjusted the height of the microphone and she let her eyes range across the room, taking in everyone, stopping at Colin and Kayleigh and redirecting them back to Sophie and Maddy, where they lingered and filled with tears.

Then she smiled, her lips closed over her teeth and she pulled a piece of paper out of the pink handbag slung across her chest, unfolded it, cleared her throat and began to talk.

"I first met Vicky in 1991. She'd moved in next door, taking the place of a rather precious friend who I'd assumed I'd be friends with for the rest of my life. So I was rather cross about this interloper. As it turned out, I never saw the old neighbor again after they moved out and it was Vicky who became that lifelong friend. I invited her over for Easter, her and her nice-looking husband and adorable little baby."

She nodded and smiled at Maddy.

"I thought she'd say no, make her excuses, but she said yes. Just like that! On the spot! So rare in people, that quality. Most people have to check and double-check, keep their options open, you know. Nobody wants to commit to anything on the spur of the moment. And they came and it was lovely, and I thought, what a charming woman. What a vibrant, joyful person."

She paused and surveyed the congregation again.

"Well, as some of you know, but most of you don't, poor Vicky was witness to a terrible, terrible tragedy that Easter day.

Awful, just awful. And I could not have got through it without her. She'd experienced a similar tragedy herself, her first love, a young girl, who'd hung herself simply because she was gay and couldn't deal with it.

"And yes, Vicky was a lesbian. Albeit one who'd made a magnificent marriage with a good man for many years before, made beautiful babies with him and been a kind and wonderful wife. But she was, at heart and fundamentally, gay. I'm not sure I ever was. But that wasn't really the point somehow. The point was, we loved each other. We found each other to be beautiful and desirable and lovable. We were nuts about each other. I needed her. She needed me. And I am going to miss her more than any words could ever express. She simply was the world to me. And without her I am untethered and lost."

She stopped then, her eyes shining with tears. She folded the piece of paper into a small, tight cube and smiled. "Sorry," she said. Then she came down from the podium and slid back next to Megan in the front pew.

Meg squeezed her hand. "Well done, Mum."

Lorelei shrugged. "There," she said. "Now it's done. Now," she whispered sadly, "I really am all alone."

❧

The wake was in a pub a short walk from the crematorium. It was a classic Cotswolds pub, yellow brick, pale-gray paint, Georgian fireplaces and high ceilings. A function room with five tall windows overlooking the countryside had been hired and bedecked with pink balloons and stocked with bottles of pink sparkling wine and pink fairy cakes. There were French doors out onto a small terrace where there was a table with a pink book of remembrance and a number of photo albums. People were bustling about this table, looking thoughtfully for the right words, champagne flutes held between their fingers.

The boys had found themselves a table for two, where they sat and played on their DSes and ate crisps from a pink paper bowl. The baby was asleep in his buggy, tucked away behind a curtain. Beth, quite uncharacteristically, was drinking a pint of lager and Meg was making her only permissible glass of wine last as long as possible.

She'd had to beg and cajole Beth to get her into the pub. They'd seen Colin, Tia and Kayleigh heading in the opposite direction from the pub after the service and Meg had persuaded Beth that they probably wouldn't be coming. And certainly there was no sign of them yet. Megan felt herself fill slowly with relief, but Beth still looked tense and terrified, clutching her pint glass tightly between her blue-white fingers and casting her gaze about anxiously.

The service had been wonderful. Meg first thought this and then repeated it, over and over, each time she encountered a new person. "Oh, yes," she would say, heartfelt, again and again, "yes, it really was wonderful. Vicky would have loved it."

Beth, meanwhile, stood silent and teenagery, shoulders tensed, letting her older sister do all the conversational work. Megan was growing tired of this state of affairs and was about to walk away and leave Beth alone to fend for herself when the door to the function room opened and they walked in.

Now that Kayleigh was standing up, Megan could see that she had paired her demure woolen jacket and buttoned-up blouse with a pair of leather trousers tucked into well-worn spike-heeled boots decorated with silver studs. Tia was wearing a slightly grubby silver-sequined dress with ripped pink tights and pink flamenco shoes. Colin was wearing gray combat trousers, with a white shirt and a pink cravat. His thin silver hair had grown long, covering his face, which was brown and gaunt. He had an earring. He looked strange. The three of them looked strange. She thought of an exhibition that Bill had staged a few months back at his gallery, a series of photographs of families living in homeless shelters in dead-end towns in unfashionable US states. Each family had been requested to put on their best clothes for the shot, and the portraits had been heartbreakingly poignant, the bittersweet fusion of pride and hopelessness visible in their eyes. Particularly the fathers.

This family standing in the doorway, looking around nervously as they pumped themselves with resolve, in their cheap clothes, their out-of-placeness, their delicacy, reminded her of those families.

Meg saw Colin find Kayleigh's hand and squeeze it in his. She saw Kayleigh squeeze his hand back.

She gulped back a swell of emotion and turned away, back to her sister.

But Beth was gone, a lipstick-imprinted pint glass on the table the only sign she'd ever been there.

⌒

"Here," said Lorelei, ferreting through her shoulder bag, an empty champagne glass slung loosely from the crook of her thumb and forefinger, dripping its last drops all over her dress. She smelled of wine and a sweet, cinnamon-noted perfume. She also smelled of damp and mustiness. "For you," she said, pulling a small package from the bag and handing it to Megan. "From Vicky. Where's Beth?" She looked around herself, full circle, then spun back to Meg. Her green eyes were slightly unfocused.

"She's out there somewhere," Meg replied. "Did a runner the minute they arrived." She pointed towards Colin and Kayleigh with her eyes. "I was just on my way out to retrieve her."

Lorelei wrinkled up her nose, in distaste, in the general direction of her ex-husband. "They look horrible," she hissed. "Don't they?"

Meg muttered something neutral under her breath. But couldn't lose the tender spot in the pit of her stomach that had formed when she saw them walking in together, looking so pitiful. "Wait there," she said. "I'm going to get Beth."

She was leaning against Meg's car, staring ahead, looking clammy and tense, an almost-empty champagne glass in her hands. Meg frowned. "You're drinking," she said. "Why are you drinking?"

Beth shrugged, like a teenage girl. "There's no law against it." Her words were slightly slurred. Beth was drunk. Meg had never seen her sister drunk before. She shook her head and let it go. "Come on. Come in," she commanded. "We need to get this over with."

"What, you mean talk to them?"

"Yes," said Meg. "We need to talk to them. That's our niece in there. That's our father. Forget everything else. They came all the way here. They're really poor and they came all the way here."

Beth shuddered. "Christ, you almost sound like you feel sorry for them."

"I do. A bit. I mean, you can't help who you fall in love with, can you?"

Beth shuddered again. "I'm sorry," she said. "You've always been more open-minded about stuff than me, less emotional, and I just can't . . . I can't even bear to look at them."

Meg felt herself tense up with frustration. "Beth," she said, "you are a grown woman! You're not a teenager. This is the real world. We are real people. This is real life. And things sometimes happen that don't fit in with how we think the story should go, but we just have to take a deep breath and get on with it, not sit there in the corner sulking because it's not what we were hoping for. Come on!" she barked. "Stop being a big baby and get in there and talk to your bloody father!"

"I'll talk to him," she said, "as long as *she's* not there."

Megan sighed and paused. "She's his partner," she said. "There's nothing much you can do about that."

"It's disgusting."

"It is what it is. Nobody's breaking the law. Nobody *died*. Come on . . ."

Beth sighed and pulled herself away from the car. "Fuck's sake," she muttered under her breath.

Colin and Kayleigh were talking to Tim when they returned to the function room. Tia was standing between them, her arm held around her mother's waist, her head nestled against her rib cage.

Kayleigh looked at Meg and Beth with carefully concealed surprise as they approached.

"Hello," said Meg. "Lovely to see you." She was spared the discomfort of a physical greeting as she knew that Kayleigh was not the type.

Kayleigh smiled laconically. "It's been a long time," she said.

"It certainly has. It was Easter, wasn't it? The Easter before your daughter was born." She looked down at Tia and Tia looked up at her, curiously. As well she might, thought Meg, as well she might. "Hi," she said to Tia, "my name's Meg. And those boys over there"—she pointed at Alfie and Stan, now engaged with scraping the pink buttercream icing off the fairy cakes and depositing it into the empty crisp bowl—"they're my sons and I think"—she looked inquiringly at her father, who nodded, just once—"they are your cousins."

Tia nodded too and put her hands over Kayleigh's arms, which were now draped loosely around her neck. "I know," she said, "Papa told me."

"Papa?" Meg looked questioningly from Kayleigh to her father.

"Yes, Papa." Tia indicated Colin with her eyes.

"Aah," she said, feeling her sister bristling behind her.

"Which one is which?" she continued. "Papa didn't know."

Meg grimaced at her father. "What, seriously?" she said. "You didn't know?"

Colin looked sheepish. "They look so alike," he said.

It was true. But still incredibly irritating. "Well," she said, turning back to Tia. "The one on the right is Alfie. He's nine and a half. And the one on the left is Stanley, and he's seven—the same age as you, I think?"

Tia nodded. "I'm seven in October."

"Oh!" said Meg. "Well then, happy birthday for next month, Tia!"

"And you two are my aunties. Papa told me that, too."

"Yes!" she exclaimed. "Yes, we are."

"I've got loads of aunties," she continued, "back in Ireland. But they're all Irish. And you're English. So that's kind of . . . *different*."

"Yes," said Meg, charmed by this white-ringleted angel. "It is."

The boys looked over curiously. "Do you want me to introduce you," she said, "to the boys?"

Tia looked round at them, flushed slightly and nodded.

Meg beckoned to the boys and they shuffled over, covered

in cake crumbs, hands in pockets. Meg brushed them down and introduced them and suggested they all three go and explore the garden. She watched as they wandered away together, Tia talking ten to the dozen, the boys looking dazed and confused in their shirts and waistcoats.

"So," said Meg, turning back to Colin and Kayleigh. "She's delightful. What a doll!"

Kayleigh looked at her, spikily. "She's not a doll," she said, her face deathly still. "She's a human being."

Meg felt the blow of Kayleigh's words almost knock her backwards. "No," she said. "No. Of course, I meant . . ."

"I know what you meant," said Colin, jolly and oversweet.

Beth quivered and twitched at her side, a fresh champagne glass held tightly between her hands.

"Where are you staying?" asked Colin.

"We're not," Meg replied. "We're driving back, later on. Soon."

"Oh," he said, "that's a shame. I was hoping we might . . ."

"I didn't even know you were going to be here. You didn't tell Mum."

"No. I thought it was best. Just to. You know. *Arrive.*"

"Under the circumstances, you mean," muttered Beth, her first words since they'd walked back in.

Colin glanced at her, with surprise. "Yes," he said, "I suppose."

"You know," said Beth, "if you'd really wanted to see us, properly, you'd have told us you were coming. You can't just show up here and expect us all to be available."

"I wasn't expecting anything, darling," said Colin softly. "I'd just . . . it was . . . well, the whole thing. It's all so sad and awkward and strange. Isn't it?"

"And whose fault is that?"

Kayleigh gazed at Beth through those tired, cynical eyes. "Can you not be nice?" she said. "Today? For Vicky?"

Megan had been trying, really trying, to make this situation civilized, for the sake of Vicky, for the sake of Vicky's girls, for the sakes of all their children. She took a breath. "I think," she said, "this is a difficult situation for all of us. I think we're all just trying our best. I don't think Beth was not 'being nice.' She was just . . ." She sighed. "We're *all* just trying."

Kayleigh put her empty champagne glass down heavily on the table behind them. Megan could see the sinews in her thin neck straining angrily against things she wanted to say and punches she wanted to throw. She saw a large moth hole in the back of the pink jacket, the pink jacket she vividly imagined as a last-minute purchase from a charity shop in the town.

"Where are you staying?" she asked quickly.

"We're camping," said Colin, "at a site just up the road."

"Oh!" said Megan. "Camping!" She sounded shrill and middle class, horribly patronizing, even to her own ears. "And when are you going back?"

"Well, we'll be going home via Ireland. We'll spend a few days over there, with, er, Kayleigh's family."

Beth growled quietly under her breath and shook her head.

Kayleigh looked at her. "Sorry?"

"I didn't say anything."

"No, but you made an odd sound. Here." She touched her own throat with the side of her hand. "Almost like a kind of moaning thing?"

Beth shrugged.

"I'm thinking that you don't like your father coming to Ireland? To see my family?"

"I don't care what he does."

Meg winced. She could not predict what her sister would

say or do now she'd been drinking. She'd seemed utterly passive these past twenty-four hours, like an empty vessel, pale and on the edge of expiration. But suddenly she looked fiery—cross and full of feelings. It was usually Meg who was the spokesperson in these situations, Meg who would speak up and be heard and not worry unduly about making a scene. But she could feel it here, the gossamer slightness of everything, the potential for a terrible, bloody mess. And so she restrained herself. But the more she restrained herself, the more volatile the situation seemed to be becoming. So she held her breath and smiled tightly, pleadingly, at her sister.

"No," said Kayleigh, the touchpaper at the other end of the time bomb. "No. I don't suppose you do."

"What do you mean by that?" said Beth.

"Oh, just that I don't think any of you care all that much about each other. Not really."

"What!" said Beth. "Of course we do."

Kayleigh just tutted and rolled her eyes. For a moment she looked as though she was not going to comment further but then, suddenly, her head snapped into place and she fixed Beth and Megan with that terrible accusing gaze of hers. "Your brother rotting in jail. Your other brother unvisited in his cold, lonely grave. Your mother living in her own filth. Your niece a stranger. A dirty secret. Your father, cut off, because you don't approve of the woman he loves. You are two heartless bitches, if ever there were . . ."

She rolled her eyes again.

Colin's smile finally faltered and he said, "Kayleigh, now, that's not entirely fair and you know—"

"I know what I know, Colin," she snarled. "I know what I know."

"Why do you hate us so much?" asked Beth.

"Oh," said Kayleigh, "no. I don't hate you. To say I hate you would be to suggest that I had any feelings at all for you. And I don't. I can assure you of that."

"You don't know anything about us," cried Beth, her face pink, her fists in balls. "Nothing! You only met us once! And we were really nice to you!"

Kayleigh nodded. "Yes. You were all perfectly polite. In that way that people like you always are."

"And you," said Beth, looking as though she had just remembered something, "you were rude to Vicky that day! Don't you remember? Dad! Do you remember, she accused Vicky of pretending to be gay to get her feet under our table. That's what you said, Kayleigh! And now you're here at her funeral acting as if you really cared about her."

"I did care about her. Of course I did. She was a good person. But you're right. I had other reasons for coming today."

"Like what?"

"*Her.*" She arched her eyebrows in the direction of the doors to the garden, where Tia, Alfie and Stanley were kicking a pink balloon about on the lawn.

"My daughter. I wanted to show her to you. To show you what you've been missing all these years. And us." She pulled Colin gently towards her and placed her hand in the small of his back. He smiled awkwardly. "I wanted you to see *us*. To see that we are good and we are fine and we are nothing to be ashamed of. Nothing at all."

"I'm not ashamed of you," said Beth.

"Oh, for *Christ's sake*. Of course you are! You think it's disgusting. All of you. Her too." She pointed at Lorelei across the room, who was laughing uproariously but somewhat unconvincingly at something a fat man in a pink waistcoat was saying. "You think we're disgusting. You do! And how do you think that feels? Eh? To be with a good man, a man who loves you, and you love him and you wake up every morning and look at him, and he smiles at you and tells you you're beautiful and he smiles at your child and tells her she's clever and grand, and you look at him and feel safe and happy and good. How do you think it feels to know there's a gaggle of bitter-faced ol' hags across the channel who think that's disgusting."

Kayleigh's voice was low and level. There were no spikes in the intonation of her words. Nothing to draw attention to them. Colin put his hand on her arm and said, "Remember, please, darling, these are my children. I can't really have you . . . it's not right."

Kayleigh shook his hand from her arm and said, "No. Fair play. You're right, Col, I'm sorry. I should not be mouthing off about your own flesh and blood. But listen . . ." She looked from Beth to Megan and back again. "You two. Enough already. This is your daddy. That out there is your niece. We are, whether you like it or not, your family. You're going to have to find a way to accept us. To accept this. For the love of God."

Meg nodded. She felt a trail of unacknowledged guilt run down her spine. A man. A woman. A child. What could be wrong about that? She was about to say something, something soft and therapeutic. But before she could find the words, Beth had spoken.

"I'm sorry," she began, her words raw and slurred, her face red with drink and fury. "I'm really sorry. But no. I can't accept it. I won't. He's my father. I'd have trouble accepting any relationship he was in that wasn't with my mother. Any daughter would. But this," she said, her voice sharp with disgust, "having sex with a woman his own *son* has slept with. The mother of his *granddaughter*! It's not natural. Whatever you say. It just *isn't*."

There was a moment of silence then. Meg would always remember it, as she would always remember that moment of innocence fifteen years ago when she'd sat in the window seat, halfway up the stairs to Rhys's room, with a lamb sandwich and a can of Coke on a tray for him. A moment between two worlds.

The newly acquainted cousins shrieked outside, Lorelei laughed out loud again, Meg observed the purposeful kick of Charlie's socked foot from the buggy, just visible at the edge of the curtain. He had awoken from his nap. And this is what she would always remember about the tiny moment before Kayleigh opened her mouth and said, "Which is just *grand* coming from the woman who fucked her sister's husband behind her back."

Meg felt the room fold itself up around her, fast and tight. She looked at her father questioningly, as if he might be able to rewind time and take back Kayleigh's words. As she glanced at him she saw with a terrible, visceral kick of pain that her father had heard these words before. That Kayleigh had said these words to him. Before. That these words were not new to him and that therefore he could not spool them back into nonexistence.

Then she turned to her sister. Beth was puce; she shook her head from side to side. "You fucking liar," she said to Kayleigh.

Meg looked at her father. He was silent, his gaze resting upon the floor. "You believe her, don't you?" Meg said to him.

"Oh, Meg, Christ, I don't know."

"She's lying," said Beth, "she's just totally lying." And then she brought her hands into two tight fists at her sides and stormed off, half knocking over a chair as she passed it.

Meg watched her leave, the fury of her, the rage and compactness of her. She saw Charlie's socked foot kick again. She looked once more at her father. He merely shrugged. Kayleigh pointed at Beth's retreating back as if to say, *Look, look at her, guilty as charged.*

And then Meg began to remember. She remembered the call history on Bill's phone by the pool in Greece; there never had been a surprise thirtieth birthday party, had there? There hadn't even been an unexpected gift—just a ring, thin, gold, feminine, the sort of ring that Bill liked, that he always chose.

She thought of Beth suddenly turning into a social smoker, sneaking off with Bill for those late-night cigarettes. She thought of Beth disappearing to Australia, out of the blue, of the terse, infrequent phone calls, the lack of interest in the niece and nephews where once there had been adoration. She thought of "Bill's affairs," the terrible faceless women that she'd known without a doubt were having sex with Bill, her certainty that he was being unfaithful to her.

She'd known.

But no. The thought went by in a flash. Of course it wasn't Beth. Beth was her sister.

"She smells nice, your sister."

She heard Bill's voice in her head. He'd said that once. She couldn't remember when or where. But it had lodged itself in there, more than any other careless comments about other women. She'd held on to it, subconsciously, for years.

"She smells nice, your sister."

She saw Charlie's foot shoot right up into the air and she heard him calling out.

She shook her head. "Er, I can't do this," she muttered. "The baby's woken up. I can't do this."

She strode across the room and unbuckled Charlie. He beamed at her.

The baby they'd brought into the world to celebrate the

fact that they'd been to the end of the road together and found a way back.

Their Elastoplast baby.

"Hello, sweet boy," she said, squeezing out a smile and scooping him into her arms. "Hello! Did you have a lovely sleep? *Did you?*" Her voice was sugar but her throat was bitter with bile.

She glanced towards the garden, looking for her sister. The boys and Tia were heading back indoors, their cheeks pink and flushed.

"We're thirsty!" gasped Stanley. "Can we have more Coke?"

She nodded distractedly.

Stanley looked at her wide-eyed. "Really?"

"Yes," she said wearily.

"Mum says yes!" he reported back to his older brother, whose eyebrows shot incredulously up his forehead.

All three headed towards the bar. She glanced from them and back to Kayleigh and her father. Kayleigh raised an eyebrow at her and then headed over.

Meg turned away, hoping to discourage her approach, but she felt a hand on her arm and turned again. "What?"

"I'm really, really sorry, Meg. I so absolutely did not mean to say that. I so absolutely was never going to say that. But your sister, she was so angry, I just . . . I'm really sorry."

Because it's not true, Meg silently willed her to say.

But she didn't. Instead she squeezed Meg's arm, and then moved her touch to Charlie's little hand and she smiled at him and then at Meg and she said, "He's a lovely little fella, isn't he?"

Meg nodded. "He's perfect."

"I'd say." They exchanged a look then, a look between two mothers, soft and understanding. And there it was, just there, for a brief moment, the woman her father loved—a human being.

Meg looked at the spot where Kayleigh's hand touched her baby's hand. Her blood raged through her body, her heart banged like a door in a storm. Her thoughts veered crazily through her head. Her sister. *Her sister.*

"What *was* that?" she asked quietly. "What the hell *was* that?"

Kayleigh let her hand drop from Charlie's hand. "It was the truth, Megan. I heard them. In the garden. At the cottage. I heard them."

"What? You heard them having sex?"

"No, no, no! *Talking* about it. Talking about the likelihood of being caught. About whether or not Vicky had suspicions. That kind of thing."

Meg narrowed her eyes at her. *Not enough*, she thought, *not enough*.

Kayleigh sighed. "I could have been wrong," she said. "I could have misinterpreted it. There's only two people who know the truth. The absolute truth. And I'm not one of them."

Tia arrived at Kayleigh's side then, clutching a glass of Coke and smiling widely.

"Have you been having fun, my sweet, darling girl?"

Tia nodded. Kayleigh stroked her hair. "Good," she said.

Suddenly Meg needed to see Beth. Now. While this was still happening. She offered the baby to Kayleigh. "Could you, would you mind?" Kayleigh plucked Charlie from her arms and nodded.

"Go," she said. "We'll be fine."

Meg ran then, out through the French windows, out onto the long-shadowed lawn, through a path of discarded pink balloons and fallen leaves.

She looked from left to right. The drop in temperature had sent everyone inside. The pub was in the middle of nowhere. All that was here was the cemetery, and beyond that, quickly darkening countryside.

And then she knew. There was only one place Beth would be. She pulled her cardigan tight around herself and headed there quickly, before the dusk swallowed the place whole.

Beth was there, sitting on her haunches in front of Rhys's grave. She rocked back and forth on her heels and jumped at the sound of Megan's footsteps.

She got to her feet and stared at Meg imploringly for a second.

Megan waited for her to say something, for the conversation to begin, the conversation that would end with the two of them laughing and hugging and saying, *"God, what a totally ridiculous misunderstanding."*

But she didn't say anything.

Instead she looked behind her, then back at Megan, then she croaked something that sounded a bit like "sorry" and then she ran. Away from Beth, away from Rhys, away from the wake and into the deep, awful darkness.

Megan did not chase her sister. Instead she sat by Rhys's grave and held her hand against it. Her other hand she let slip into the pocket of her cardigan, to keep it warm. She felt an object there, small and hard, and brought out the gift that her mother had given her. Earlier. *Before.*

She peeled it open and found a pebble, polished to a shine, with a pinkish gleam in the dusky light. The wrapping revealed itself as a note, written out in solid schoolteacherish shapes:

> Remember, Megan, that wherever
> you find yourselves, you are all pebbles

from the same beach. Look after each other.
Your friend,
Vicky

She tucked the pebble and the note into her pocket and headed back to the pub.

11

―――――⚬――――――

Thursday 13th January 2011

Good morning, lovely Jim!

Yes, yes, you're right. I know. I must not go hungry. I'm a
ridiculous woman. This whole thing is, well, ridiculous! I do
sometimes wonder if it was just the other people in the house
with me that were keeping this side of me at bay. If maybe I'd
have been living like this years ago if I hadn't met Colin and had
all the babies. Who knows??! But I've taken your advice and
made sure I went to the supermarket *before* I went to my shops,
stocked up on things I like to eat. It's interesting that I can take
being bossed about by you, Jim, but not by anybody else!

Your flat sounds very sweet. It's strange how I never
imagined a place like Gateshead would have any lovely
Victorian architecture, I imagined it all as high-rises and dreary
old terraces. But I suppose everywhere has its "good parts" and
I'm glad that you live in one of them. And I'm also heartened
to hear that you are surrounded by nice things. My husband,
my *ex-husband*, he lived for a while in the other half of this
house after we split up and it was odd to me to see his notion
of "interiors" once cut loose from me and my ideas. And it was
quite chilling, in fact, to see that for all those years and years
I'd been married to a man who, when left to his own devices,

would go out and buy a buttermilk-colored leather sofa. Absolutely bizarre!

I think things are so important. Pretty things. Mementos. That's part of it all, you see, when I go into one of my shops and see that someone has given away a little china vase, say, something pretty, that someone designed, that someone created, that someone liked enough to buy, and bring into their home, it imbues that object with so much *substance.* So much importance. To my way of thinking, at least. So seeing it there, in a charity shop, given away, given back to the universe, it goes against the grain. It makes me sad. So I have to buy it. To redress the balance.

Oh, really, I am quite, quite mad!!

Anyway, yes, you were asking about the funeral. About what happened there. My God, Jim. It was four years ago and I can still feel every hideous moment of it.

It all came out, at the pub, afterwards, in the quietest, least dramatic way you can possibly imagine, that Beth, my youngest girl, had had a long affair with Megan's husband. I mean, honestly, Jim, I had no idea about any of it until I suddenly saw *her,* the Irish girl, my husband's lover, WHATEVER. I saw her holding Megan's baby and I said, "What on earth is going on here? Where's Megan!!" And she told me she'd gone to find Beth. And I said, "Why?" And she said, "You'll have to ask them that."

Five minutes later Megan returned, looking pale and traumatized. Her lovely pink shoes were covered in mud and for one dreadful moment I thought she'd been attacked. She wouldn't tell me what had happened, but she went straight to her car, said she had to find Beth.

She drove around for half an hour, but never found her. And the next thing was a text message from Beth saying she was at Heathrow, heading home. We never found out how she'd got there, from the deep dark countryside, all the way to London. It really doesn't bear thinking about.

Anyway, that was the last any of us heard of Beth. She changed her phone number and her e-mail address and literally disappeared into thin air. And Megan told me what that Irish girl had said to her. And none of us would have believed a word of it if it hadn't been for Beth's reaction.

As for Megan, she was magnificent. She absolutely dealt with it. Confronted Bill, got the truth out of him, made him suffer almighty pain for quite a long time and then made him marry her.

Does it seem terribly strange to you, Jim, that two of my babies are floating about out there, untethered? That I don't speak to them? That they might, in fact, be dead for all I know? (Although I do have to assume that SOMEONE SOMEWHERE would find me to tell me if they were.) It seems both strange and NOT strange to me. I can't really explain it. It feels, almost, in some utterly foul way, preordained. From the precise moment that I saw poor Rhys hanging there, it was almost as though this were all inevitable. Or actually, no, from before that. From just before Rhys died. From the night before he died. When something happened that was completely irreversible. That would change the way I felt about all of my children forever more.

That sounds dramatic and it is, Jim. Truly. I don't even have the words for it yet.

And as long as I don't find the words for it, then maybe I can keep on pretending that it never happened.

Much love, beautiful Jim. How I wish that I could just step into your arms and let you hold me. I bet you smell lovely.

L
Xxxxxxxxxxxxxxxxxxxxxx

APRIL 2011

Colin greeted Meg and Molly at the back door of the Bird House in a T-shirt and boxer shorts. Meg recoiled slightly at the sight of his numerous tattoos.

"My God, Dad, what the hell have you done to yourself?"

Colin glanced down at his body and laughed. "I have to admit, it's kind of turned into an addiction," he said, adjusting his glasses.

Megan frowned. "Don't get any ideas," she said to Molly, who merely gave her mother her *eugh* face and said nothing.

"I'd invite you in, but . . ." He gestured behind him at the dark piles. "Shall we sit out? It's another lovely morning, I see."

He had Lorelei's laptop under his arm. He laid it on the table in the garden and thanked Megan for the takeaway coffee and croissant she'd brought him from the local café. "I've been trying to work out Mum's password," he said, lifting the lid on the laptop. There was a piece of paper inside, with a long list scribbled on it. "These are all the ones I've tried," he said, passing it to Megan. "Can you have a look at it, see if I've missed anything obvious?"

Meg pushed her sunglasses back into her hair and read the list, Molly peering over her shoulder smelling of boutique hotels. He'd been thorough, that was for sure. He'd tried every conceivable combination of birthdays, children's names, addresses, pet names, maiden names and favorite colors. "Oh, Christ," she said, putting it back on the table. "I mean, this is impossible, surely? We don't even know how many characters it's supposed to have."

"There used to be a guy at our school who could crack passwords," said Molly.

Meg and Colin looked at her and she shrugged. "Don't know what happened to him."

"Well," sighed Meg, "I think that'll be our only real option. We'll have to take it somewhere and get some propeller-headed genius to crack it for us."

Colin shrugged. "I'll keep trying," he said, taking back the paper and folding it in half. "Your mum wasn't exactly Steve Jobs, so I'm sure it'll be something pretty obvious."

"You know she had an 'online lover,' don't you?" Meg asked Colin.

Colin smirked and shook his head.

"Someone called Jim," she said. "From Gateshead. Apparently they were madly in love with each other." She rolled her eyes.

"Well, that's nice, isn't it?" said Colin. "Your mum always did need to have someone madly in love with her. Like a drug."

"We'll be able to read their e-mails if we get her password!" said Molly, her eyes wide with excitement. "Her and Jim's love mails."

Now it was Megan's turn to make a *eugh* face. "Oh, God," she said, "I hope they weren't sexting."

Molly laughed. Colin snapped the laptop shut and glanced at his watch. "What time are the skips coming?"

"Any minute," said Megan. "Well, now, in fact." She looked up at the clanking sound of metal chains outside the house.

Two big yellow skips were lowered onto the road. Megan handed over £100 in cash. An arrangement was made for the skips to be replaced the following morning at the same time. And the morning after that. And the morning after that. "We'll just keep coming every morning till you tell us to stop," said the driver. "Bad, is it?" he asked, eyeing the scruffy house behind him.

"Really bad," said Megan.

"Funny thing," he said. "Funny how people deal with stuff." He looked at the house again, almost tenderly, and he shook his head. "Good luck. We'll see you tomorrow morning."

She stood for a moment on the pavement after the skip truck had left. The morning sun was already hot. She held the delivery note in her hand and stared for a moment across the street. The enormity of the task ahead of her felt heavy on her skull. Not just the physical work of it (Megan liked physical work), but the prospect of unearthing her childhood and finding it riddled with rot.

"Right," she said a moment later, clapping her hands together. "That's it. No excuses. Let's get going."

Friday 28th January 2011

Darling Jim,

I knew it would come to this eventually. I had hoped that you would have read between the lines of my words and seen the truth squirreled away in there. When I close my eyes at night, I dream about being with you. I pretend that you're there with your big strong arms around me, I imagine running my hands through all that glorious silver hair, I fantasize about seeing you across a room, sharing a complicitous smile, walking into a pub, hand in hand, sharing a bottle of, well, water, I suppose. In another, parallel world, you and I are living together. In a parallel world, your lovely things sit side by side with my lovely things, your dog rests its chin on my lap at night as we watch TV together. In a world where I hadn't made such a mess of everything and everything hadn't made such a mess of me, you and I would be together. It's obvious, isn't it, Jim? It has been from the minute we first read each other's words. We are soul mates.

But, darling, in this world, in this actual world, which may or may not be the best of all possible worlds but is bloody well the only one I'm aware of, we won't ever meet each other. Will we? Because I can't leave here. And you can't stay here. There's nowhere for you to sleep, my love. There's nowhere for *me* to sleep. Yes, it's that bad, darling. That bad. I can't bring you here. I can't come to you. And I know we could share a few hours with each other, meet for a coffee, something like that, but really, what would be the point? An hour or two, snatched in the day, barely a chance to get to know you. I'd be desperate to prolong it, to make it more, but I'd be snapped back to the pigging reality of everything, the pull this house has on me, the hold it has on me. I've given up everything for this house.

But please, Jim, don't make me give you up too. Please. Can't we just continue as we are? These lovely e-mails that make my heart sing when I see them in my inbox? Can we do this forever, please?

And yes, Jim, I love you too.

XXXXXX

APRIL 2011

By the end of the first day, they had filled both skips to the absolute limit and yet barely got halfway through the kitchen. The sun had blazed unforgivingly, more like August than April. "Do you remember," Meg had asked her father at one point, "that Easter before, when we were small, when it was hot? Do you remember the Easter eggs melting? And the paddling pool popping?"

Colin had nodded and smiled, sweat rolling down his temples, a dusty box of tea lights in his hand, and said, "Of course I do. It was one of those times. Those golden shiny times. When nothing could possibly go wrong."

They sat now, the three of them, around Lorelei's table in the garden, drinking Coke and letting the sweat dry onto their bodies.

"When do you have to go back?" asked Colin.

"Bill and the boys get back next Monday. Monday week. School goes back on Tuesday. So in theory we could stay for two weeks. But hopefully not."

Megan thought about the boutique hotel, the £180-a-night bedroom. She'd packed fresh bed linen and pillows into the boot of her car. She'd brought soap and flannels and towels and shampoo. She'd thought that within three or four days she'd be checking out of the hotel and moving into the Bird House. She'd thought it was a matter of a bit of sorting and chucking. She'd had no idea. Absolutely no idea.

"Come back to the hotel," she said to her father. "Come and have a proper bath. And we'll have a nice dinner somewhere."

Colin looked at her gratefully. "Thank you, darling," he said. "That would be lovely."

༄

The three of them ate together at a seafood restaurant in the village. It was chi-chi with dove-gray walls and prices written on the menu in fractions. Molly had ordered a tuna steak and was eating it like a man.

"That was the hardest day of my life," she said, pushing her cutlery together and swinging her hair behind her shoulder.

"Plenty more where that came from," said Megan.

"We need more people."

"Well, actually," said Megan, "even if we had more people, there'd be no room for them."

"No, but outside, in the garden, to go through things. That's what's taking the time. Sorting everything out."

"I just wish we could bin the lot," sighed Meg.

"No way," said Molly. "That's, like, her whole life in there. In among all the rubbish. Imagine if we threw away something really important."

"I know," sighed Meg. "I do know that. It's just so infuriating."

"We could still get the council in, you know," suggested Colin.

"No." Megan shook her head. "No. I'm not having anyone we don't know in there. It's our house. It's our life. No way."

Colin nodded. "I do agree with you," he said. "It would feel wrong, somehow."

His phone rang and he pulled it apologetically from his jeans pocket. He began talking sweetly into his phone and Megan assumed it was Tia. "Hello, sweets," he was saying. "Yes, we're all fine. No, not the boys, just Molly. Yes, the big one. She's sixteen." He looked to Meg, who shook her head and mouthed, *"Fifteen."* "Sorry, *fifteen.* Yes. I know. Yes, she's very pretty." He smiled at Molly as he said this. "Erm, yes, please, darling, thank you." He paused for a moment, as Tia apparently passed the phone to someone else, and then he laid his napkin on the tabletop, smiled at Meg and Molly and took his phone call to a quiet corner of the restaurant.

"Why has Grandpa gone over there to talk?"

"Because he's talking to Kayleigh."

Molly nodded knowingly. "I'd like to meet Tia," she said a moment later.

"Yes," said Megan. "I know. And you will. One day."

"Yes, but when? I mean, I'm like, nearly an adult. I'd like to meet her while I'm still a child."

Megan smiled. She sighed and said, "Yes, definitely. You're right. It's crazy. It's just, you know, not talking to Grandpa for so many years. It's all been rather complicated. But definitely. Now we're talking again. Now I know . . ." She paused, sorting her thoughts. "Now I know that he's still just my dad, we'll sort something out. *I'll* sort something out. We'll go over. To Spain. Or something. I promise."

She covered her daughter's hand with hers and thought of Tia. Her beautiful lost niece. And she was just one piece of the puzzle. One tiny piece.

"Maybe she'd like to come to London," said Molly. "Maybe she'd like to come and stay at our house. She could sleep with me. If she liked."

"Yes!" Megan beamed and squeezed Molly's hand. "Wouldn't that be lovely?"

"Sorry about that," said Colin, retaking his seat.

"That's okay," said Meg. And then she took in a deep breath and prepared herself to say something unnatural. "How is she?" she asked. "How's Kayleigh?"

Colin looked at her with some surprise but then smiled and said, "She's grand. She is. She's good. Really good. Yes . . ." He petered off, aware that this was a new and slightly awkward development.

"How's her business?" Meg forced it out. She had to. They were here now. They were a father and a daughter having dinner together. They were part of the same world again.

Colin's face lit up. "It's great!" he said. "She's ever so good at what she does, you know. She really, really is."

"Good," said Megan, "that's good. And does she ever . . . do you ever . . ." Megan held her breath, considered her next question. "Will you have another baby?"

Colin laughed. "Oh, God, no!" he said. "No, no, no! We did talk about it. A long, long time ago and we both realized it was just, well, a step too far."

Megan looked at him questioningly.

"Well, for Tia. I mean—how would that have been for Tia? A brother or sister who was also her aunt or uncle. Or, God, *whatever*. The technicality of it has always slightly eluded me. But no. A huge age gap. A cultural divide. I felt, we *both* felt, that there were quite enough challenges to be going on with. So, yes, Tia is my granddaughter and Kayleigh is my partner and we shall leave it at that. As awful as everyone thinks it to be."

Molly stared at the table and said, "I don't think it's awful."

"Don't you?" said Colin, with a soft laugh.

"No! I think it's just, you know, it's life, isn't it? All these years I've just thought it was kind of gross, and I mean, I, personally, would not want to go out with my child's grandfather. But maybe I'll end up doing something else unconventional. Who knows. And I really hope that if I do, and as long as I'm not hurting anyone or doing anything, like, *illegal*, that everyone would accept it, you know, just carry on loving me anyway."

Meg and Colin exchanged a look. A look that said, *"Dear God, what a bloody mess we've all made of everything."*

Then Megan's phone ding-donged and she switched it on to find a text. It was from Bethan.

I'm here. I'm staying with Sophie. At Vicky's old place.
I want to help. I'll see you at the house tomorrow.

Megan switched off her phone and let her head drop on to her chest. *Fine*, she thought to herself, breathing in deeply, *fine*. "Beth's coming," she said, forcing out the words. "She's coming to the house tomorrow."

"Yes!" said Molly. "Yes!"

Meg smiled grimly at her and in a small, dry voice she said, "Hurrah."

12

Saturday 29th January 2011

Darling Jim,

I knew you'd understand. You always do. And you're right, of course. I'm acting like the future is inflexible and set in stone, like people can't change, like *I* can't change. And of course I can, Jim. Anyone can change. You should see my ex-husband! He went from being a rather mild-mannered college lecturer, a bit of a mouse really (or maybe that was my influence! Argh!), and now he is all cool and groovy, living on a commune with a young girl, working with his hands, covered in tattoos by all accounts! It was as though this other person had been living inside him for all those years, just waiting for a chance to escape. And maybe I have another me, living inside my daft old body, a me who might wake up one morning and say, ENOUGH! A super little Lorelei Bird who's all spick and span and in the mood for throwing stuff away. Who could contemplate a night away from home without breaking out in a rash. And my goodness, Jim, if that super little version of myself ever did find its way to the surface—assuming that it is there to begin with!!—you will be the first to hear about it, I can tell you! I would be on a train to Gateshead IMMEDIATELY. Oh, Jim, what I would give to have a night with you. (I strongly suspect that you are spectacular in bed!) But sadly, it is *this* little version of Lorelei talking, not that other fabulous one. So, yes, Jim, I will not close my mind to the possibility of CHANGE. And who knows, maybe this love affair will change me. Yes! Maybe it will. Maybe I will find that other part of myself through you, you darling, beautiful man.

Until then, SIGH, I will just ache for you. I have not had sex with a man for such a long time. When did you last have sex, Jim? Or actually, don't tell me. I'm not sure I want to know. Supposing you said it was last week! I'd have to die!

I do love you so much,
Yours, forever,
Lorelei

Friday 4th February 2011

Oh, thank God, Jim!

I thought I'd lost you! I can't tell you how relieved I was to find your e-mail in my inbox just now. I thought you'd finally had enough of me! That I'd lost you on the Internet forever. And then I thought, how the HECK does one find a lost person on the Internet?! I wouldn't have a clue! So to find that your silence was nothing to do with me, that it was just your nasty old demons. Such a relief.

What is it like, Jim? If you don't mind me asking. What is it like when you lose control like that? On one of your benders? What do you drink? Do you have a tipple of choice? Or is it anything and everything? Are you happy when you're wasted? Do you feel better? Or do you feel worse? Do you get drunk with other people? Are you a part of a big rousting, jousting gang of boozers, all singing songs together? Or is it just you? Alone in a room? Or on the last bar stool on the left? Do you get into fights, Jim? Do you get into trouble? Are you a messy drunk? Or a quiet drunk?

I feel the need to ask you these questions, purely because I love you and because this is a part of you. I want to understand all of you. When I don't hear from you for a week, I want to be able to imagine what you're doing. I want to know how much to worry about you. How long I should expect you to be out of contact. Because if the super-version of Lorelei that may or may not reside within me fails to materialize, then I am asking you to stick with this version. And if the super-version of Jim, the one who stays on the Twelve Steps, who doesn't drink and doesn't keep vanishing, fails to materialize, then I fully intend to stick with this version. So I need to know it. Good and bad. Do you see?

Anyway, I was absolutely dancing-like-a-loony delighted to hear that you haven't had sex for many years. Sorry if that's selfish of me, but there you go. If I can't have you, then neither can anyone else! And if I ever get my hands on your beautiful body, I want it PURE!!

I have no news to report, lovely man. It's business as usual here. Swimming, shopping, surfing the Net. Oh! I forgot to say. I had an e-mail from Rory! He is out of jail! He didn't have much to say for himself (but then, he never did). Just that he's out and he's considering his next move. Thank God for that! One tiny little sun ray of normality shining down upon this wretched family!

Love love love love love love love love
L xxxxx

APRIL 2011

Beth sat at the table in the garden. It was just before nine o'clock. She already had a faint sheen of sweat upon her brow. She ran her hand up and down the cool sides of a bottle of Evian. Sophie had given it to her from her fridge that morning. Sophie had been so sweet to her, mothering her almost, even at twenty years her junior. *"Make sure you drink tons,"* she'd said, looking at Bethan with concern. *"You mustn't get dehydrated. It's forecast to be thirty degrees today."*

She'd given her a bag of yogurt raisins and a banana and sent her on her way.

On the street outside, Beth heard the clank of heavy chains. She got heavily to her feet and peered out. It was the truck, come to replace the skips. Pulling in behind the huge vehicle was a people carrier, one that Beth recognized from her last visit to London. She pulled herself straight. She adjusted her smock top and wiped a glow of sweat from her upper lip.

Megan slammed her door shut, beeped the car locked and turned to see Bethan standing there.

"Oh, my God!" she said, her eyes locked upon Beth's stomach. "Oh, my God. Beth!"

Beth waited, rooted to the spot. She could not, for some reason, make the small movement that might propel her towards her sister. Instead she nodded and stroked her belly, waiting, as ever, for her sister to do the thing that needed to be done.

Megan walked towards her, her eyes still on her bump. "My God, Beth, how far gone are you?"

"Thirty-two weeks," she said. She was blushing. She didn't know why.

"And they let you fly?"

She nodded. "I had a letter," she said, "from my doctor."

She saw Meg's eyes scan the fingers of her left hand. "Wow," she said, that one syllable full of a hundred questions. "Wow." She brushed the side of her face against the side of Beth's face, vaguely, as though she'd met her only once before.

Beth saw Molly step out from behind Megan, and she smiled. "Hello, Molly!" she said, swallowing a gasp of amazement. Her niece looked like a model. All legs and hair and perfect feline features.

Molly came towards her and embraced her. Then she rested a hand on Beth's tummy and said, "A cousin!"

Beth could see that Megan was surprised by her daughter's actions. So was she. "Yes!" she said. "A girl."

"A girl!" said Molly, turning to face her mother. "Did you hear that? She's having a girl."

"How wonderful," said Meg, and Beth could not tell if her words were genuine or facetious.

They all stood and watched the skips being taken away and replaced, the teetering piles of cardboard boxes, of newspapers, bin bags, broken lamps, ugly vases, stained duvets, odd shoes, splintered chairs and burst Pilates balls. "That was just one day?" asked Beth.

Megan nodded. "One day. And approximately three percent of the hoard."

Hoard.

Beth had never heard her mother's possessions referred to as a hoard before. It had always been her *mess*, her *stuff*, her *crap*. A hoard. It made it sound almost like a single, enormous entity. "Well, hopefully an extra pair of hands will help."

"You won't be able to get in there," said Megan, nodding

at her belly. "I mean, seriously, I can only just about squeeze in there."

"Oh, I'm sure . . . ," she began.

"No," said Megan sternly, "really. You have no idea. You have absolutely no idea."

Beth laughed nervously and nodded. "You look very well," she said, as the three of them turned towards the house. "You've lost a lot of weight."

"Well, yes."

"And you, Molly, wow. I can't get over it. I mean, you were still a child last time I saw you."

Molly turned to smile at her. "I remember," she said. "You fainted."

Beth felt a solid kick against the wall of her stomach and instinctively held her hand to it. "Gosh," she said, "how did you know?"

"Mum told me."

"Oh." She wondered how much else Megan had told Molly. Beth had assumed that Molly would know everything. She'd been expecting a cool reception. But Molly seemed almost excited to have her here.

"What are you going to call her?" asked Molly, as Megan rang the doorbell.

"Oh," she said, staring in awe at her niece's satiny skin, her doll-like cheeks, the sweeping lashes and perfect nose. "Erm, I don't really know. I was thinking of something old-fashioned. Agnes, maybe. Or Maud."

"Oh," said Molly politely.

Beth peered through the grimy glass of the back door. "Is there somebody actually in there?"

"Yes," said Meg. "Dad."

"Dad?!"

"Yes, he's staying here."

Beth blinked. She had not considered this possibility. "On his own?"

"Yes," said Meg. "On his own. It's all fine," she said somewhat tersely. "It's no big deal."

Beth nodded and peered again through the back door into the kitchen beyond. "Are you sure he's there?" she said, as the seconds ticked by.

"Yes," said Meg, in that same slightly impatient tone of voice. "It's just rather a journey, from upstairs to downstairs."

"You'll see," said Molly, "when we get in."

Finally the door opened and Beth saw her father appear, in a scruffy T-shirt and shorts. His lanky old body was covered in tattoos and she swallowed down a bubble of distaste. *Move on,* she reminded herself, *move on now.* So she smiled and let him embrace her.

"Beth," he gasped happily.

"Hello, Dad," she said.

"And who is *this*?!" he asked, cupping her belly.

She smiled down at herself and said, "This is your next grandchild."

"Grand*daughter*," Molly corrected.

"Yes," she said, "grand*daughter*."

Colin looked from Beth to Meg and then back again and then his eyes filled with tears and he began to cry. "My cup runneth over," he said.

Beth thought of the last time the three of them had stood together like this. She thought of all the hurt and spite and anger that had controlled her actions that day. She had been so brittle and furious. Now she felt centered. She felt strong. She and her swollen belly. She and the baby girl who had finally made her normal.

"You daft old fool," Meg said to Colin, and he smiled.

"Come," he said, gesturing theatrically behind himself, "come into my humble abode."

Beth couldn't make sense of it at first. It was definitely the kitchen. But it seemed suddenly to stop about a quarter of the way in. There was a wall of stuff, with a small gap in it. And nothing else. She turned to her sister. "Is that . . . ?"

Meg nodded. "Yes," she said, "that is the only way through to the rest of the house. Yesterday morning it came all the way to back here." She pointed to the doorway. "Do you see, now? Do you see that you won't be able to get in?"

Beth nodded numbly.

"So, I think we'll need to put you on box-sorting duty. We pass stuff out to you. And you sort it."

She nodded again.

"But, Beth, listen," said Meg. "We've only got a few days. You're going to need to be ruthless. Do you understand? Really ruthless. There's no room for sentimentality here. Unless it's important, unless it's documentation, photographs or it's worth actual money, it goes in the skip. Yes?"

Beth nodded. And then she said, "But what about—?"

Meg threw her a terrifying look. She recoiled. "Nothing," she said mock-nervously. "I understand."

"Good."

They shared takeaway coffees and croissants in the garden. They discussed the possibility of animal feces and decided that Beth should wear latex gloves (there had, of course, been a full, unopened box of the things in among the hoard). They talked about the horror of the coroner's findings, and plans for a funeral. They talked about Lorelei, about her laptop and the mysterious Jim. The sun shone. Bees hovered around the Saint-John's-wort bush. A blue butterfly landed momentarily on the sleeve of Molly's hoody and they all cried out in delight. It was a perfect spring morning and hard for Beth to believe she was here. With her sister and her father. She'd thought she'd never see them again. She'd planned never to see them again. And now here they were.

But they had not talked about the things that needed to be talked about. They had not talked about Bill. They had not talked about the father of Beth's child. And all the while, Lorelei's house sat behind them, with its thick layers and crusts and walls of composted newspapers, waiting, patiently, ominously, for them to unclog its arteries and bring forth its buried secrets.

Megan could feel herself physically bristling with questions. They were like tiny crackerjacks going off under cushions. She had barely recognized her sister standing there outside the house. She looked so solid. So substantial. Her black hair, which had been drab and dry last time she'd seen her, was gleaming and multihued. Her skin was plump and soft, like that of a girl half her age. Megan had had to remind herself that Bethan was actually thirty-eight years old. Nearly forty. Not a child. Not the wan, feeble thing who'd fainted on her sofa all those years ago. And that bump! So big, so proud. So full of baby and wonder and awe. But where the hell had it come from? For all the dazzling good looks and the big tits and the shagging of her husband, Beth had always seemed curiously sexless to Meg. Like her dad. The two of them. The dark horses.

She had never before contemplated the possibility of Beth

having a baby. Because Beth had always been a baby. She'd always been the biddable dolly in the pink polka-dot raincoat. Even Bill had said she wasn't sexy. Not in that way.

And now here she was, awesomely, in-your-face fertile. And sexy with it.

Where have you been? she wanted to screech. *Whose baby is it? What made you decide you were ready to be a mother? Why did you leave me alone for so long? What the hell have you been doing all this time? Who are you?*

She saw Bethan eyeing the wedding ring on her left hand. She pulled it away subtly. Bethan clearly had questions of her own, but not now, she thought, not yet. They could wait. Right now they had a hoard to sort.

◌

Colin left the house for an hour and returned with four large storage boxes. "One for each of us," he said. "For things we want to keep, for ourselves."

Megan eyed it suspiciously. The thought of anything from this moldering freak show of a house coming back into her own temple of pristineness made her feel queasy. But as the day went on she did find herself slipping the occasional object into the box: a set of four cereal bowls in lustrous pearlized pastels, an art nouveau soup ladle with roses on the handle, four unopened packets of plain red paper napkins (perfect for dinner parties), a simple turquoise glass vase, an ornate bone-handled cake slicer. Beth found things to keep too: a pair of mosaic vases, a set of fish knives in a velvet-lined box, lace-edged napkins, newborn nappies, unopened packets of pink Babygros, baby muslins and a box of brand-new baby bottles. Molly put aside some trashy jewelry, retro sunglasses, candles, opaque tights, bundles of multicolored elastic hairbands and a framed painting of a kitten which she said was "so bad it's good." They filled the two skips again, mainly with newspapers and broken furniture, out-of-date food, things that smelled and things that had no use.

In between they drank cold water in the garden and lay in the sun. Like any challenge in life, once the mind was focused on the job in question, it became a simple matter of getting on with it, inch by inch, step by step. They tried not to ponder the magnitude of the project, tried not to think about the big picture—just each box, each bag, each drawer, each cupboard. And in this way, it began to feel almost normal, what they were doing here.

As the shadows grew long across the unkempt lawn (Colin was saving the mowing of the lawn back into stripes as a treat to look forward to once the house was cleared), Meg told Molly she'd be back soon, and she took cold Cokes and a bag of Maltesers to the end of the garden, where she'd seen Bethan heading a few minutes earlier. Beth was lying in the green rope hammock, cloaked in gold light, her bare feet crossed at the ankles, her hands resting together on her belly.

"Hammock's still here," said Megan.

Beth nodded and smiled and pulled her feet towards her to make space for Megan. "I know," she said, "hard to believe. And still in good nick."

Meg sat down gingerly, fairly convinced that the thing would rip apart beneath their combined weight, feeling pleasantly surprised by the sense of being the lightest sister on the hammock, the smallest person. "Here." She passed Beth a Coke. "Unless you're doing one of those really uptight, my-body-is-my-baby's-temple kind of pregnancies?"

"No!" She snatched the can from Meg's hand and cracked it open. "No way. Thank you."

She took a sip and then said, "Sorry. I needed a break."

"I didn't come down here to tell you off. I think we're about done for the day anyway. You've done brilliantly. Considering."

Beth smiled and stroked her stomach.

"Are you having a good pregnancy?"

Bethan nodded. "Yes," she said. "So far so good."

There was a brief silence. Hardly surprising, as everything in the universe sat on the other side of it.

Megan pulled open the bag of Maltesers and offered them to Beth. In another world they would be like the girls in the adverts, finding childishly adorable ways to make each other laugh with a packet of sweets. In this world they were about to be very serious indeed.

Megan started, because Megan always did. "So," she said. "Where are you having her? Will you stay here?"

Bethan nodded. "Yes," she said, "it's good timing." She flushed at the realization of her words. "I mean, God, obviously, it's not good at all. But I'd been dithering for weeks about where to give birth. And then I got your e-mail about Mum. And it made my mind up for me."

Megan nodded and then let loose the next big question. "And what about the father?"

Bethan shrugged, plucked at the ring pull on the drink. "Good question."

"I mean, will he join you here for the birth? Is he Australian? Or . . . ?"

"I don't know." Beth stared darkly into her own lap. "I don't know who the father is."

Megan nodded, possible scenarios crowding her head.

Beth sighed and raised her gaze to the back of the house. "It could be . . . I mean . . . I went through a kind of phase. I don't remember much about it now. It was after therapy. I had all this therapy. After . . . you know, Vicky's funeral, and it wasn't just that, what happened that day. It was everything. It was the panic attacks, the blackouts. It was Jason and Richard and you and Rhys and Mum—"

"Me?" Megan cut in.

"Well, yes, I mean, my relationship with you. With *everyone*. Not just you. But you were part of it. And we went over so much stuff, I mean, things I hadn't remembered, thought about for so long. Like, for example, we worked out that the reason I'd always been teetotal was because of the smell, that day, when we found Rhys, and Mum and Vicky, their breath, the red wine. It was so strong on them, so rancid. And Vicky's teeth were stained red and I'd obviously made this association, subconsciously, between alcohol and tragedy." She looked at Meg, then dropped her gaze and shook her head. "And I got better and better and the panic attacks stopped and I was strong and excited and thinking about coming home, thinking about you and Bill and the kids and Mum and . . ." She stopped again. "I went kind of too far the other way. Started drinking."

"Drinking?"

"Yes, I know. And sleeping with lots of men. Lots and lots of men. One-night stands, mainly. I don't know why. I really don't. I mean, I've never been that interested really, in men, in sex. Christ, I know that probably sounds weird to you . . ." She finally looked at Megan then. Her eyes were filled with shame.

"Well, no," said Megan, "no. Bill said you weren't that into the, you know . . ."

"Urgh." Beth shuddered and brought her arms around her knees. "God. Sorry. I mean, *shit*. Sorry! Meg! I can't even . . ."

"It's fine."

"No!" Beth snapped at her. "No! Of course it's not fine.

It's awful. It's evil. It's shocking. It's the worst thing I've ever done in my whole entire stupid life! And I don't understand it! I really, really don't. I mean . . ." Her gaze went once again to Megan. "You're my sister. My *sister!*"

"But honestly, Beth . . ." Meg's voice was soft, soothing. She'd come so far since that day at the funeral. She'd come through the long nights when she could have killed Beth with her bare hands. When she might have thrown Beth and Bill out of an airplane and enjoyed watching them spiral to their deaths. She'd come through fury and humiliation and shock and agony. And now she was here. In this bland place. And she didn't want her sister making it raw again. "Honestly. That was then. We were all different then. I was different, Bill was different. And now we're different again."

"Yes, but that doesn't forgive what I did, does it? Nothing could ever do that. Not you, not the passage of time, nothing. It's here"—she clutched at her heart—"buried in there. All the time. Everywhere I go. And it hurts me."

Meg nodded and touched Bethan's knee. "It hurt me too. It hurt more than anything ever hurt me in my life. But look at us now. You're about to have a baby. Me and Bill are happy."

"Are you?" Beth sniffed and looked up miserably at Megan. "Seriously?"

"Yes. We are."

"But I don't understand how you could be."

"Because we wanted to be," said Megan simply.

Beth flinched. "You're married," she said, after drawing a breath.

Megan glanced at her ring. "Yes. Last year. Finally. Although we got engaged a year to the day after I let him back into the house."

"How long was he out of the house?"

Megan sighed. She didn't want to do this. She'd put this all in a box and had no desire to unpack it again. "A few weeks." She shrugged. "It was bad. He wanted me to understand. I did not want to understand."

"He's always been nuts about you."

Megan frowned. "Yes."

"I was just . . ."

"I know what you were. He told me. He said . . ."

Beth stared at her imploringly. She wanted to hear it. She didn't want to hear it. It would hurt her. It would help her. Meg sighed. "He said that you were the other side of me. The side I wouldn't let him get to."

Beth flinched. "I know," she said after a moment. "I knew. It was obvious. I knew it was never, ever about me. It was always about you. Everything was about you."

"Is that what your therapist told you?" Meg asked with a grim smile.

Beth laughed a small laugh and let her head fall onto her chest. "Kind of, I suppose. He said lots of things. Lots and lots of things. You were definitely part of it. But, shit, I mean, there was so much other stuff. About Mum, and Rhys. I think . . ."

Megan watched her sister searching for words. She was plucking at the loose threads on the hammock, her Coke can nestled in the triangle between her crossed legs.

"I think," Beth tried again, "that something happened, the night before he killed himself. And I think I might have seen it. Or been part of it."

Megan straightened at these unexpected words. "What?"

"I don't know. It's just this feeling, I've always had it. Like it was my fault. Like something happened and it was my fault. And I've kind of blocked it out. I used to have these dreams."

Megan stared at her encouragingly.

"Awful dreams. About all of us. Kind of . . . *sexual*." She shuddered lightly.

"Well, that's fairly normal, isn't it?"

"Well, yes. And no. Because I was never in them. It was the rest of you. I was watching the rest of you." She shuddered again. "And Rhys. Always Rhys. My therapist and I, we never got to the bottom of it. But he thinks it's connected. To that night."

Megan shook her head lightly, trying to rearrange her thoughts into a recognizable pattern. "What did we do that night?" she said. "I can't even remember."

"Neither can I. Not in any detail."

"I remember I had to sleep on a mattress in your room," said Meg. "Because Mum had dumped loads of stuff in mine. I remember us lying there in the dark, talking about you coming to live in London."

Beth smiled sadly at the memory. "It was before that," she said. "Early evening. It was still light." She sighed loudly and stroked her belly. "Everyone was downstairs playing Monopoly or Trivial Pursuit or something. Something noisy, anyway. I came upstairs for some reason or another—I can't remember—and I saw Mum coming out of Rhys's room. And she looked . . . I can't really explain it but she looked freaked. Totally and utterly freaked out. And I stared at her and she stared at me and I said, *'Are you okay?'* And she nodded, but I could tell she wasn't. And I just knew that something awful had happened, and I felt like it was something . . ." She stopped. A significant silence stretched out. She smiled. "Oh, I don't know. I guess I'll never know. And maybe I'm imagining it, anyway. You know, maybe I was so desperate for there to have been a reason for why he did it that I invented one." She shrugged.

Megan smiled at her sister. She patted her kneecap and

said, "The hardest thing to accept is that some things happen for absolutely no reason at all."

"I'm not sure I can ever accept that," she said, and then her face brightened and she sat up. "Ouf," she said. "She's kicking. Wow, really hard!"

"Can I feel?"

Beth nodded and Meg put her hand on the hard, tight bump. And there it was. *Bump* against the palm of her hand. *Bump* again. The small heel or fist of her unborn niece. She looked at Beth, her baby sister, one of the greatest loves of her life, and she said, "I missed you."

Beth took her hand, smiled and said, "I'm back."

"Are you doing this on your own, then?"

Beth nodded. "Just me and her." She looked up at Megan. "And you," she said, in a small voice, "if you'll have me?"

Megan squeezed her hand. "Of course," she said. "Of course."

13

Saturday 5th February 2011

Thank you, Jim, for your honesty.

It was awfully nosy of me to ask but as ever you took me the right way. You are about the only person, Jim, in my whole life, who has really known how to take me. It is a glorious thing! It was fascinating for me to hear in your own words how you feel when you're on a bender. Although it did, of course, also make me feel unutterably sad. It made me want to rush up there on the first train and look into your eyes and hold your hands and tell you that I had the key to make you stop. But I don't, of course. I know as well as you do that only the individual has the key to change themselves. It's buried deep inside each and every one of us and although someone else can help us to find the key, we're the only ones who can use it. And there, of course, is the pathetic irony that in order for me to come to you and help you find your key I'd have to find my own first. It's all just a series of tightly wound threads. It's all just impossible, Jim, truly.

    And thank you, as well, for sharing with me the things that happened to you when you were young. You poor, poor little thing. Is it any wonder, really, that some of us can't cope with being grown-ups when adults treated us the way they did? If an adult cannot do a simple thing like take care of a child . . . well, it's just an endless cycle. I'm sure your mother had her own stories, her own bad experiences and so it goes on. You wanted to know about the blemish on my childhood. I can see what you're trying to do here, Jim, you're trying to fix me, aren't you?! Long-distance analysis so that maybe one day I might be well enough to come and see you. And my goodness I would like to be well enough to come and see you, so I will offer myself up to you for you—analyze away!

My mother was raped. By a family friend. I knew nothing about it at the time, but my sister told me when I was about sixteen. Turns out it was the same family friend who'd tried to stick his tongue down my throat the week before she told me. I'd laughed that off, dirty old man, you know. But then to discover that that same sleazebag had done what he did to my mother. And no, we never discussed it. I always wanted to. I always meant to. Every time I found myself alone with my mother I'd open my mouth to ask about it, but the words wouldn't come, I was terrified I was going to rip open a wound that had healed. And then she died. And then my dad died. And that was that. Her rapist turned up at her funeral. I punched him. Can you believe that? Me! Lorelei Bird! I punched a six-foot man, clean on his jaw, hurt me more than it hurt him, I'd wager. But it made me feel good. I think it changed me forever, that punch.

But yes, there it was, all the way through my childhood, first the stillborn girl, then the rape and all the silence and all the secrecy. The atmosphere, always there like a sinister fog. The resentment (my father clearly believed it had something to do with my mother, that she'd *brought it on herself* in some way. He used to talk to her as if he HATED her) and the focus on the SELF that such a psychological injury can incur. My mother was always gazing at her own navel, to the detriment of her daughters. Awful, awful. So I leapt on the first undamaged man to cross my path and made him fill me up with babies so that I could do it my way. And hey, whaddya know, my way has ended up full of secrets and silence too!! Different silence. Different secrets. But still, it's all there. The Things We Cannot Talk About. And I can see now how it's poisoned everything. It's all such a terrible shame.

But well, hopefully the rot will stop with Megan. She's such a super mother and wife. Really. I know I moan about her and her obsession with cleanliness and order. But really, she is doing an amazing job. She's so grounded and I have no idea how or why. Her children adore her and they adore each other. And as for her husband (if she can forgive him, then so can I), he worships the ground she walks on. So yes, hopefully, there it is. The end of the cycle. For them, at least.

So there you go, gorgeous Jim. Another chunk of ME for you to play about with. Can you fix me? Could you? Please? I dream about your belt buckle, Jim, I dream about unclasping it . . .

xxxxxxxxxxxxxxxxxxxxxxxxxx

Monday 14th February 2011

Happy Valentine's, darling Jim! Not that I'm a fan of Valentine's, really. I always thought that every day should be Valentine's. Well, POTENTIALLY Valentine's at least, if you see what I mean. You know, why wait for a certain day if you want to buy flowers now? Unimaginative really, isn't it, buying overpriced roses on the same day as everybody else. You know, you see a woman walking home with a bouquet of flowers, you think, Wow, someone really loves her! You see the same woman with the same bouquet on Valentine's and you just get the feeling that someone was going through the motions.

But anyway, that's just me. Good luck to the rest of the world! And out of special consideration to my feelings on the subject I declare this e-mail a romance-free zone!

So instead I shall regale you with the fact that I have spent the last twenty-four hours on the toilet. Sorry. Probably TMI, as they say. But there you go. Something I ate probably. Or maybe a bug I picked up from the swimming baths last time I went. Either way, YUCK. Horrible. And it's times like this that I miss living with another human. Do you feel like that, Jim? So many advantages to living solo, until you've got a dire case of the squits. Then you just want someone there so you can say, Poor me, aren't I a poor, poor, thing? And have someone stroke your back and say, Yes, YES, you are a poor, poor thing. And make you drink fluids and give you things to help. Ah well. Choices made. Paths chosen, etc.

No word from Rory since his last e-mail. I've written a few times, but he still doesn't have a proper e-mail account set up. So I suppose I'll just have to be patient. I spoke to Meg on the weekend. They're planning a skiing trip for the Easter holidays, apparently. Skiing. Eugh. Can't imagine anything worse. God gives you a pair of perfectly good feet and then you go and stick some big long bits of metal on them and throw yourself down the side of a mountain. No, thank YOU! And it costs a fortune. I try not to get too cross when I think of all those thousands of pounds spent in a fortnight that would last me all year probably. But Meg won't give me any money. Says she'd like to but she's convinced I'd spend it all on tat. And she's probably right. Oh, God. What an absolute pain in the arse I am!

Well, on that note, I will leave you. I sincerely hope you're

not out on the razz tonight at a table for two with some lovely
young thing clutching a bouquet. Oh, the very thought of it
makes my blood boil and bubble! And, well, rest assured that
I am here (close to a toilet!!), my thoughts with you, my heart
with you, my everything with you, tonight and every night.

My love,
Xxxxxxxx

Tuesday 15th February 2011

Urgh, I am STILL not well, darling Jim. I have been pretty
much glued to the toilet for the last forty-eight hours. I feel
very weak with it. I am making myself eat (although I have no
appetite WHATSOEVER), but it's all just coming clean through
me moments later. I suppose, if it's still like this by this time
tomorrow, I should make an appointment to see my GP. Yuck.
I hate my GP. Big loud woman with meaty fingers. She's very
patronizing, she calls me "dear." As if I was an old lady. For
God's sake! I can't bear her. And the thought of her putting
those big meaty fingers of hers anywhere near my back
passage. Oh, good grief, Jim! I think I'd throw up! So keep your
fingers crossed for me that this all blows over very soon and I
am spared that particular humiliation.
   But I have an announcement to make. Jim, I have decided I
am going to work on getting out of the house. I mean, properly,
so that I can spend the night with you!!! I truly believe that all
this is helping, you know, all this talking, all this analyzing. I
truly believe that. I was speaking to Madeleine yesterday, she's
Vicky's eldest, she's twenty. Delightful girl. We went through a
rough time together when she lived here (my fault, all totally

and utterly my fault), but we've made a kind of friendship now. She lives with her boyfriend just outside Cheltenham and I was telling her about you, about our chats, about your problems and my problems, and she said I should try a night at hers. Soon. You know, she's only three-quarters of an hour away. If it was a total disaster I could always drive home. Obviously I'm making this sound a thousand times more straightforward than it was when actually, had you been there, you'd have seen me shaking uncontrollably in a coffee shop, halfway to a panic attack at the mere thought. I had to go outside for air! Daft COW!

Still, it is a start, it is something to focus on. I hope that makes you happy, Jim. I do so want you to be happy. But in the meantime, we must keep talking, we must keep this open, this incredible, life-changing connection we've made to each other. It's becoming like oxygen to me, Jim, it really is. I need it more and more, every day. You are making me stronger. I love you so much, more than I've ever loved anyone.

Oh, here we go again, the toilet beckons.

More anon, beautiful man of mine xxxx

APRIL 2011

The following morning all four of them strapped themselves into Megan's people carrier and headed to the funeral parlor where Lorelei's body had been sent from the coroner's office. Megan had had a call the previous evening, while they ate in the pub in the next village along (too many curious gazes and awkward reunions in the local). "Your mother is ready," said an earnest young man named Samuel Moss. "We've made her look very nice. I think you'll be pleased."

Megan could not begin to imagine. She had never seen a body laid out for a funeral before. "Thank you very much," she'd said. "We'll see you in the morning."

They'd laid her out on a bed in a tiny room in the back corner of the parlor. She was surrounded by silk flowers and attended by the boy named Samuel Moss, who was dressed in a suit, his thin hair greased down like a pensioner's, and so theatrically respectful he was bordering on a character from *The Fast Show*. "I'll leave you all to treasure your time with Lorelei. If I may call her that?"

Megan and Beth looked at each other and exchanged pained looks, their cheeks sucked in with repressed laughter. "Yes," Megan managed, "you may. Thank you."

The laughter dissipated as Samuel left the room and they moved in closer to their mother's body.

"She's so *thin!*" Bethan cried out in a loud whisper.

"Six stone eight," said Megan.

"God."

"But she looks sweet, doesn't she?"

Bethan put her hand against Lorelei's hand and nodded. "So little."

"Like a child," said Colin, laying his hand against her cheek.

"What the hell is she wearing?" said Bethan.

"Christ knows." Megan turned to check that Samuel wasn't listening at the door. "It's revolting—it looks like something an old lady would wear."

It was a pale-blue dress, devoid of any of Lorelei's precious colors. It sat loose around her hand-span waist and ended just an inch too low below her knees. It had a row of three buttons on a placket down the front and long sleeves.

"We should have brought her something," said Bethan.

Megan sighed. "They asked me to. I tried to find some-

thing, but honestly, as ridiculous as it might sound, I couldn't
find any of her nice clothes. I have no idea where she kept
them. We'll have to buy her something," she said decisively.
"From that boutique. We'll buy her something colorful. Bring
it over later."

"Oh," said Colin, "surely that's a waste of money. She's
only—"

"No," Beth interjected. "Meg's right. We'll buy her something lovely."

Colin nodded and smiled, happy to be outnumbered.

"She looks pretty," said Molly.

Megan smiled and put her arm around her daughter's
waist. "She does, doesn't she?" She didn't want to say that
she thought her mother looked like an awful shrunken-down
witch, her unkempt hair tamed into a long gray plait, her
skin the color of cement. She had to remind herself of what
her mother must have looked like before they'd worked their
magic on her, this woman who'd starved herself to death and
been found dead in her car on the side of the road with her
insides eaten away by disease.

She should be grateful for small mercies.

They spent another half an hour in the room with Lorelei.
Nobody cried. Not even Bethan with her body pumped full
of hormones. But it was sweet and tender, nonetheless. The
three women left Colin to talk about arrangements for the funeral with the director and drove into the village. They parked
outside the funny boutique that had been there for always.
Their mother had brought them here when they were young,
left them to roam about the trailing jungle of clothes rails
while she tried on brightly colored dresses and an ingratiating
woman called Grace said things like, *"Oh, Lorrie, that's the one,
it really sets off your amazing figure. Not many people round here*

could get away with something like that. You're a natural clothes-horse."

The boutique had changed with the times and Grace, with her plume of silver hair and chunky paste jewelry, was nowhere to be seen, just a bored, beautiful young girl who looked as though she was home from boarding school for the holidays, perched on a stool behind the till.

The dress they chose, at £219, was ludicrously expensive. But it had been reduced from £395, owing, Megan assumed, to the fact that it was in such an unfeasibly small size, a tiny size 6 scrap of silk chiffon printed all over with peacock feathers in gemstone colors. On the way back to the funeral parlor they dropped Lorelei's laptop into a repair shop.

"This laptop belonged to our mother," she said to the jolly-looking middle-aged couple behind the counter. "She just passed away."

They expressed their condolences in lush Cotswold burrs.

"We need to access her laptop. We don't have a password. Is there . . . ? Do you . . . ?"

The couple looked doubtful but keen to help. They mentioned a nephew, who lived in the next village. He might know someone. They said to leave it with them and tore off a deposit slip from a small pad underneath their desk. At no point did they suggest or imply that there was anything untoward about this request and Megan smiled as she tried to imagine the equivalent reaction in the laptop repair shop at the top of her road in Tufnell Park. The police would have been involved in moments, she suspected.

They took the dress to the funeral parlor and collected Colin, and then Megan drove them all back to the Bird House. It was around eleven a.m. as they pulled up on the curb outside the house. The skip men had been and gone; two empty containers sat on the road. The sun shone on, the day stretched ahead. They turned the corner onto the garden path, talking loudly about plans for Lorelei's funeral, laughing about Samuel Moss's precocious obsequiousness, joking about how he probably met his friends in the pub after work in a hoody, talking like a South London gangster. And then Megan stopped and stared. Her eyes widened and her jaw dropped and she looked at the wiry, blond-haired, leather-skinned man on the doorstep and whispered, "Rory."

14

Sunday 27th February 2011

I'm coming, Jim. I really am.

I spent the night at Madeleine's! The whole night! Well, to be accurate, I arrived at ten p.m. and left in the pitch-black before she'd woken up, but I did manage a couple of hours' sleep. I'm not saying that it was easy. It was, to be horribly honest, a bit of a nightmare. But God, Jim, it's a start. What is it the psychiatrists say? BABY STEPS. Yes, baby steps. And I shall do it again, I promise you that. Baby steps towards you, Jim, and your body. And all the wonderful things we will do together in the blissful dark of night. Christ, I am yearning for you. For it. I truly am.

Xxxxxxxxxxx

Tuesday 1st March 2011

Darling, thank you, you are so encouraging and strong for me. I honestly feel like I could do anything for you. I am truly starting to believe I might change. Imagine that! I put my car in to be serviced today, Jim. If I'm to drive it all the way to you, the last thing I need is a blown tire or a gasket or whatever all those other bits and pieces of cars are called! Wouldn't that be tragic, to overcome these wretched demons of mine and then be scuppered at the last fence by a flat tire! So I am selling a ring of mine to pay for it and having it done. Luckily the mechanic's is the wrong direction from the shops so hopefully I won't be tempted to go and spend the money before I pay for the repairs! And if I am tempted I will just think of you, Jim, standing tall and handsome in your doorway. I will think of me stepping into your big, strong arms, taking your hand and following you to your bed, and that will be enough for me. That is all I want now.

xxxxxxxxxxxx

Wednesday 2nd March 2011

No, Jim, I do not want a penny of your money! You are a beautiful, wonderful man but you are as financially constrained as I am and there is no reason why you should have to pay towards my old banger. Cook me a lovely meal upon my arrival instead.

Well, I was going to have another "dry run" at Madeleine's house last night but I seem to have caught a nasty cold. I'm very phlegmy and hacky, keep getting terrible coughing fits. Really, it's just one thing after another! I blame the public baths, I really do. I might stop going. They never look quite clean in there, black mold and all that. Horrible. So I will wait until I have shaken this cough and then make another plan with Maddy. Are you bored of waiting for me yet, Jim? Are you fed up with endless words and no action? I am doing all I can. I truly am. I am changing, for you, Jim. Slowly but surely.

xxxxxxxxxxx

APRIL 2011

Rory had no words at first. He'd forgotten how to talk to his family. He'd more or less forgotten how to talk, full stop. He'd spent six weeks at a Buddhist retreat, twenty-three hours a day of silent prayer and contemplation among whitewashed walls and shaved heads. No music. No television. No traffic. Just cicadas and chanting.

He did not want to be in this country. He did not want to be looking at these staring, gawping faces, at the tear-sodden cheeks of his father, at the confusion and curiosity of his sisters. But he'd had a moment of deep understanding halfway through the retreat. He'd come to understand that everything was his fault. Rhys had killed himself because of him, because he was such a bad brother to him. Kayleigh had been forced into the arms of his father by him, by his abandonment of her and their child. That union had brought about the events at Vicky's funeral that Megan had told him about in a badly punctuated e-mail shortly afterwards. And now his mother was dead because he had not come home to look after her once he'd been released from jail. He should have been here. And he wasn't. And now she was gone. All his fault. All of it.

They all looked so old. His father looked ancient. His sisters were no longer girls. They looked meaty and matured. His younger sister was pregnant. He could not remember how old she was. He could barely remember how old he was. They looked fat. They weren't fat, but they looked fat. Compared to himself. Compared to the people he'd eaten rice and broth with three times a day for six weeks, compared to the peasants and farmers who worked the land around them in a hundred degrees.

And this house, his mother's house, the house where he grew up, where he lost his brother and then lost himself. It was everything that the retreat had not been. He had walked the perimeter of the house, again and again, waiting for someone to find him here. He had peered in through the windows, through the glass in the doors, seen the piles and the boxes. All the things. All the stuff. He thought how as a child he'd laughed affectionately at his mother's ways. He remembered the trips to Poundstretcher and the cash-and-carry, the endless amounts of stuff coming into the house, the endless sums of money being spent, the endless, filthy accumulation. How could he have thought it was funny? How could he have thought it was cute? It was obscene. What his mother had done here, as poor people scavenged for food in landfill, as parents watched their children die, as disease wiped out villages and water holes dried up, it subverted everything. It was grotesque. His sisters with their mascaraed lashes and daft shoes. His niece (he assumed she was a niece) with her big nest of blond hair, her neon fingernails and spoiled demeanor. They looked alien to him, as alien as if they had green skin and tentacles.

But he needed to get over that. He needed to shut his mind to its complaints and outrage. Here he was, what remained of him, and he had a job to do.

He smiled, and he got to his feet and said, "All right?"

Colin brought Rory a box, like the one he'd brought for the two girls. But Rory shook his head and said, "No, thanks. I don't want any stuff."

"You might be sorry," said Colin, "if you don't. One day you might wish you'd kept something and it'll be too late."

Rory shook his head again and said, "No. I won't. I don't know much about me, but I know that much. And besides, I'd have nowhere to put it."

"I can keep it for you," said Megan. "Until you're settled."

Rory smiled and shook his head. "No," he said, "honest. I don't want it."

"Where are you going to stay?" asked Megan.

"Here?" he said, looking from Megan to his father and back again. "If there's room?"

His father took him upstairs to show him Rhys's room, with talk of finding a mattress. "I can sleep on the floor," he said. "I've been on the floor for the past six years. I've got kind of used to it."

The three girls turned to each other after Rory and Colin had gone.

"He looks really sad," said Beth.

"He looks terrible," said Megan.

"I think he's kind of cool," said Molly.

Rory's presence galvanized them. By the end of that day they'd come almost to the back of the kitchen. They cleared the hoard all the way to the kitchen windows so that the sunlight finally had a way through and the sudden burst of daylight really spurred them on. Molly and Rory worked together as a team, being the youngest and the thinnest. Megan appraised them from a distance. They looked like father and daughter with their golden hair, their lean bodies and fine features. They talked a lot, and there was a lot of mutual laughter.

In the presence of a grown man who she for some reason saw as being her peer, Molly reverted to some of her old teenagery habits, talking to Meg as if she was slightly subnormal. Megan couldn't catch half of what they were saying but it was clear that Rory felt more comfortable with his niece than he did with his sisters and his father. Molly didn't know him. She wasn't a threat. There was also a sense that he aligned himself more closely with a teenager than with people of his own age, as if he was Peter Pan. And of course, Megan pondered, he hadn't come close to growing up, had he? From home to commune, from commune to drug dealer's lackey, from lackey to prison and from prison to a retreat. All his many experiences had been so one-dimensional, so cosseted. He'd never had to take responsibility for himself.

As they ran out of light, a rainstorm threatened overhead so they packed themselves into the people carrier and headed for the pub. It was one of the few locals that hadn't been turned into a gastropub, that still had patterned carpets and laminated menus.

"I used to come here all the time," said Rory, taking it all in, his hands stuffed into the pockets of one of his dad's fleecy jackets. "This was where me and my mates used to do all our underage drinking. The landlord turned a blind eye." He shrugged.

Colin went to buy them drinks at the bar and they shuffled themselves into a booth by the open back door. Rory was talking about the mates he'd left behind, wondering what happened to so-and-so and what's-his-name, remembering terrible tales of multicolored vomit and setting fire to bins. Molly was staring at him adoringly. The rain was coming down now outside the door in weighty sheets, rumbles of thunder on the far horizon. Colin returned with a metal tray and offloaded the round: red wine for Megan and himself, J20 for Molly, fizzy water for Rory and Beth. And there they sat: Colin, Megan, Bethan, Rory and Molly. In the pub, having a drink together.

Megan sucked it in. She felt an odd nostalgia—odd, because this had never happened before. She had never sat in a pub with her family before. But she liked it. Very much.

"What are your plans?" she asked Rory.

He grimaced. "I want to make amends," he said.

"What?" She'd been expecting a more prosaic response.

"I want to make amends. I want to make up for it all, for all the mess I made. I want to clear out Mum's house and make it beautiful again. I want to grow up."

Everyone nodded, but it was clear that nobody really understood what he was saying.

"How's Tia?" he said to Colin, and the shock of the words sent invisible ripples across the table.

"Oh!" said Colin, flushing slightly. "She's great. Really, really great."

"Would she like to meet me, do you think?"

Megan gulped. My God. Rory had never been one to say what was on his mind. He'd never, as far as she was aware, actually *had* anything on his mind. And now here he was, up front and saying it plain.

"My goodness, well, *yes*," said Colin. "Yes, she would. I know she would. I've only ever said good things about you. Both of us have . . ."

Rory nodded staunchly. "That's good," he said. "Maybe she'll come for the funeral?"

"Yes," said Colin, "I expect she will. Especially if she knows you'll be here."

Rory nodded again. Then he put down his water, looked around and said, "I'm sorry. I'm really sorry. For everything. If it hadn't been for me, everything might have been so different."

Beth and Megan both said, "What?" at the same time.

"I was so self-centered," he said. "When we started big school I just abandoned Rhys. Left him to get on with it. He used to sit outside my bedroom door sometimes, just listening to me. I knew he was there and I never asked him in. I never asked him out with my mates. I never let him into my life. It was like I dumped him, you know? Like he was a girlfriend I'd had enough of." He let his shoulders slump and he sighed. "He killed himself because of me. And it's time to stop running away from that fact and to start dealing with it." He shrugged. "So here I am. Cheers."

He raised his glass of water and everyone else raised their drinks and it was the strangest toast that Megan had ever heard in her life.

"It wasn't your fault," she said, more to normalize the situation than because she knew it to be true.

"Yeah," he said simply, "it was."

Megan and Bethan looked at each other.

"I've had plenty of time to think about this," he continued. "And I know I'm right."

"It's my fault," said Colin, in a tone of voice that suggested the unburdening of a great weight.

"No," said Bethan, her voice catching. "It's mine."

A crack of lightning lit the bruised sky. Another roll of thunder followed suit.

"It was none of us," said Megan, looking at her family. "It was all of us."

15

Saturday 12th March 2011

Oh, Jim, I cannot shake this blasted cough. Honestly. I feel like an old woman, like I've aged a decade in a few weeks. It doesn't help that I'm losing all this weight. It's a vicious cycle—I'm too weak to eat, then I get weaker because I haven't eaten. I have, you'll be thrilled to hear, made an appointment at the GP's. I can just about bear the thought of that woman's hands on my esophagus. JUST ABOUT. In the meantime, Project Go and See Jim has ground to a halt. And to be frank, right now, Jim, sex is about the furthest thing from my mind. And it's not often I can say that!

So, I've been thinking about Rhys again. I've thought more about Rhys in the past few months than I have in the past two decades. It's like he's back, in this house sometimes. You know how you have a memory of something, and it's flat, you know, like a piece of paper. It's just a fact that you can recall. A moment. And then other times that memory extrapolates itself into something three-dimensional with smells and textures and color? And you think to yourself, where was that hiding all this time? Do you ever get that, Jim? Well, as you know, that's why I keep so many things, because of that innate energy that things carry, that shadow of a memory that each thing casts. And the other day I went into Rhys's room (did I tell you that I keep it as he left it? Completely uncluttered? Isn't that odd? Maybe you could find a theory for that. You're so good at theorizing, Jim) and I walked in and it was as though he was THERE! In the room. And I've never felt that before, not once in all these years, and I'm a pretty spiritual person as you know, Jim. So it's odd that I've never felt it. But I realized it wasn't a ghost, it was his SPIRIT, and then I realized that a spirit is just another word for a memory, isn't it? The stronger the memory the stronger the spirit. Because as much as I'd love to believe that the spirit lives on as a thing separate to humanity, I know that's not true. It's in our minds, in our hearts, that a person's spirit lives on. And I felt SO SAD, Jim, that all these years I've denied his spirit because I couldn't bear to think of him. Like I'd stifled his spirit. Let it fester.

And for some reason this day, I was open to it. I let it in. All the memories. All the power. And there he was. My little boy. With all his confusion and oddness and frailty. I could smell his scalpy hair smell, see the way he used to sit with his knees together and his toes pointed in. I could feel the tension around him. It was always there, like a force field. I heard his voice, that flat monotone he used to speak in. And I remembered, VIVIDLY, the day before he died. I was in his room and he was sitting on his bed with his back against the wall, his knees up, picking at some dry skin on the heel of his hand. He had a watch, a big chunky plastic thing that had buttons on it. He had a sweatband on the other wrist, a bit grubby. I was hoovering (ha! Imagine that! Having floor to hoover!) and he just watched me. Through his fringe. With those dull blue eyes. I remember wondering if he would ever find anyone to love him the way I did. If there was anything there for another person to see and to want. Isn't that awful? Never came close to feeling anything like that for the others. I just knew they had qualities that other people would want. But not him. Not Rhys.

Oh, God. It was wonderful (like he was alive!) and dreadful (I hadn't loved him properly!). And then it was gone. Like a popped bubble. And I started to think, seriously, for the first time, about what happened later, what happened that evening. Oh, Jim, I almost threw up, you know? Literally, my food came up my throat. So I stopped the thoughts. But I'm going to go back into his room later, or maybe tomorrow. I'm going to go in and see if I can bring it back, what happened. Properly. Not just the aborted moment I've been playing over and over in my head all these years, like a disembodied bar of music. I need to remember the whole thing, every moment. And if I can do that, Jim, I'm going to tell you all about it. Because I want you to know. And this is it, I suppose. This is the kernel of the thing. The piece of grit that got stuck inside me and turned everything else into what it is. And as you know, Jim, it ain't no pearl. ☺

Thank you, Jim, thank you for being here. For listening. For wanting to know. I don't know what I'd do without you, my love. I truly don't.

xxxxxxxxxxxxxxxxxxxxxxxxxxxxxx

APRIL 2011

Molly and Megan were still in the expensive boutique hotel. Megan was no longer thinking about the tariff. She could not imagine settling it without passing out or laughing maniacally until she fell over. But there was absolutely no imminent possibility of moving into Mum's house. They were on day four. The kitchen was empty. They had celebrated by cooking a meal and sitting together at the table. The kitchen had not exactly sparkled and gleamed; there were dust balls in the drawers, shelves hanging off the walls, stains on the pine table, and the flagstones were almost black with entrenched dirt. But still, there it was. A kitchen. An Aga. A roast chicken and steamed broccoli. Microwaved chocolate pudding. Wine, beer, candlelight.

The uncovering of the yellow walls had been momentous, revealing the children's gallery that had been obscured for so long. Molly had examined it in great detail, endearingly searching out pictures by her mother. "Look, Mum! Look, you drew this when you were five! It's so adorable!" Colin and Megan had photographed the gallery in situ before painstakingly unpeeling each drawing, choosing ones to keep and recycling the rest. The wall of art had preserved the brightness of the paint beneath and it was an atypical and welcome jolt of color in a house that had grown gray with neglect.

And now here they were, Molly and Megan, back in their hotel room, bathed and pink, in fresh pajamas, Molly cross-legged with her hair in a turban, oscillating between texting a friend and watching *I Didn't Know I Was Pregnant*. Megan had just got off the phone with Bill, and was about to open a book when her phone rang. It was Colin.

"Darling," he said, "Rory just found something. In Mum's room. It looks like it might be her computer password. Can you try and collect her laptop tomorrow morning? On your way here?"

"What is it?" she asked.

"Just a scribbled thing. In a notepad. It says"—she envisaged him lowering his reading glasses—"abc123mbrr."

Megan. Bethan. Rory. Rhys.

"Sounds likely," she replied, scribbling it down on the hotel's paper pad. "I'll drive over there first thing."

She hung up a moment later and turned to Molly. "I think we've got the password for Grandma's laptop. We'll try it out tomorrow."

Molly made a circle of her mouth. "Ooh," she said, "wicked!" And then she turned back to the telly and frowned. "Honestly," she said, "what kind of idiot has a baby's head hanging out of their vagina and still thinks they're just having a bad period?"

⟡

Rory lay back against the scorched grass. The moon hung above him, almost full. Stars glittered in constellations. It was the same moon he'd stared at in Thailand. The same stars that had bedecked the same velvety sky. Extraordinary, but starting to feel more likely by the day. He got to his feet and wandered barefoot across the warm grass. He remembered it now. He remembered home. He remembered having sex with Kayleigh down there, by the hammock. He remembered chasing Rhys around the flagstone paths, a loaded water pistol in his hand. He remembered his mother turning cartwheels, without preamble or announcement. He remembered people, members of the cast of his childhood who'd wandered off the set, never to be seen again: aunts and uncles and cousins, dogs, neighbors, friends. He turned back to appraise the house from this distance. It had always been so full of people and so full of life.

Tonight had been good. They'd cleared away enough of the junk in the kitchen to cook a meal. They'd sat there, the five of them, faces over flickering candlelight, eating, drinking, remembering how to be a family. And then, after the girls had left—Megan and Molly back to their posh hotel, Bethan to Vicky's old flat—Rory had gone up to his mother's room. He'd had a sense of needing to find something. He wasn't sure what. He had no particular question in mind, just a series of black holes needing to be filled. He'd sat in her chair, inhaled the scent of her hair on the back of it, dusty and dry, with that hint of stale spice cupboard that he always associated with her. He'd put on her enormous headphones, her *cans*. He'd laughed to himself. *DJ Lorelei in da house*. He'd pulled her duvet up to his chin, smelled the unwashed skin on it, the dampness and the death. She'd let herself die. Was that the same as killing yourself? He didn't know.

Then he'd started rifling through her things, the papers that sat on either side of her. Old newspapers, unopened bills, her horoscopes neatly torn out of magazines and papers. Hairpins, velvet hair scrunchies, bottles of dried-up nail polish, old tea bags and half-eaten packets of cookies and rice cakes. A notepad full of lists. Names of social workers. Phone numbers for the Department of Health. All the people who'd phoned her, trying to help, their numbers duly noted and then forgotten about. Because she didn't want to be helped. He'd found two little parcels, wrapped in pink paper, one with his name on it, the other with Beth's. He'd put them in his pocket. Saved them for tomorrow. And then he'd found a small piece of lilac paper, taken from one of those paper cube towers, housed in red Perspex. On it was written the code: *abc123mbrr*.

There, he'd thought, *there*. A key. A way in. Maybe.

He walked around the garden now, from corner to corner, trying to fill his head with more and more memories. It was as if he was rebuilding his childhood, step by step. The garden had been more important to him, growing up, than the house. This was where it all happened. Balls and dogs and water and mud, slides and swings and wrestling and horseplay. And egg hunts, of course. He remembered each nook and cranny now. The cracks in the stone walls. The flowerpots and crooks of trees. He heard the echo of the noise his wings might have made as he'd flown from home, so suddenly, so starkly, without a moment of nostalgia or regret. And then he ran his finger through the gaps in the wall, praying to the gods of all above, *Just one egg. Just one little egg.* Just to know that it had all been true, that he hadn't imagined it. And there it was, a moment later, held between his thumb and his forefinger, a small pink egg. He held it triumphantly to the moon.

Then he put it in his pocket with the two little parcels he'd found in his mum's drawer and the slip of paper with the password on it, and headed back inside.

Bethan lay on her back in Vicky's old bed, in Vicky's old room, staring at the paper shade over Vicky's old light. She'd gone straight to bed after Megan had driven her back. Sophie had some friends over, young friends, squawking and shouting and talking over each other the way teenagers do. Sophie, eyes glazed and heavy with cider, had said, "Come in! Come in!" There'd been pizza boxes everywhere and all eyes had come to rest on Beth's bump as though it was the last thing anyone had expected to see, as though she'd brought a baby hippo into the room with her. She'd said, "No, thank you, I'm exhausted. But have fun."

"We'll try and be quiet," Sophie had said.

"You don't have to," she'd replied.

She turned heavily onto her side at the sound of her phone receiving a text message, and squashed a cushion under her bump. It was from Megan:

Dad found a password, might be for Mum's laptop. I'll pick you up 9 a.m. and we'll go via the repair shop. Sleep tight, Bethy. Sleep tight, baby bump. Love you both. x

Bethan's eyes widened. Her heart filled with pleasure. Megan's love. She had missed it so much. She kissed the screen of her phone. She typed back:

Love you too. xxx

Then she slept, deep and peaceful, for the rest of the night.

༺

The repair shop had sent Lorelei's laptop to a nephew in Tetbury. The nephew in Tetbury was not answering his phone so Megan, Beth and Molly had to drive all the way there. The nephew opened the door of a tiny cottage in a back lane in just a towel, with a cigarette burning in his hand. He hurriedly stubbed it out when he saw Bethan's bump and went up a tiny staircase in the middle of the house to get changed. A moment later he returned, dressed and combed, with Lorelei's laptop in his hands.

Megan stared greedily at it. On there was the story of Jim. On there, potentially, was the story of why her mother had died in the front seat of her car, half a mile away from her own home.

"I'm really sorry," said the nephew, whose name was Josh, "but I don't think I'm going to be able to crack this for you." He then launched into a very technical, jargon-heavy explanation for his failure which Megan interrupted by waving a piece of paper with the hotel's logo on the top at him and saying, "Yes, yes, thank you, but we think we've found it. The password."

"Oh," said Josh. He plugged the laptop into the wall and opened it up. Then, with large, bitten-down fingers, he typed the password into the login page. The laptop made a pretty noise, and then, there it was. Windows.

Megan smiled and brought her fist to her mouth. "Yes!" she said in a loud whisper. "Yes!"

They whisked the laptop away from him, thanked him for his trouble and then drove, quite fast, back to the Bird House.

16

Wednesday 16th March 2011

Jim. I relived it. The whole thing. From beginning to end. I feel weak now. Weak and horribly sick. But I'll write it down. So it's there. Maybe for you to understand me better. Or maybe for someone to read when I'm gone. I don't mean to sound morbid, Jim, but I'm sixty-five. I'm not well. I'm not going to last forever, am I?

So, back to that day, that same day I hoovered his room, that I wondered if anyone apart from me would ever love him, the day before Easter.

He hadn't come out of his room all day. That was normal. Normal for him, normal for a lot of teenage boys, I suppose. But it was the day before Easter and Megan was back. We were all having so much fun together, down in the kitchen, we were playing a game. Trivial Pursuit, I think. And there was wine and music and teasing and, oh, all that lovely family stuff. So I went up to try and tempt him down. I took him a bowl of sticky toffee pudding. I sat next to him on the bed. He looked so sad, Jim. I said, "What's the matter, my darling boy? Why do you look so sad?" He just shrugged. He always just shrugged.

He was always my favorite, you know. Not in that OH MY GLORIOUS PERFECT CHILD way, just in that he was my baby. He'd been so small. The weight of him in my hands when they passed him to me, like a bag of air. He was my shadow, he followed me about. He was always looking to me, for guidance, for approval, for everything, long after the others had lost interest in me. Always looking at me, watching me with those sad, empty eyes.

I brought his head against my shoulder. I was a bit tipsy. He said, "Get off, you smell of wine." But he was only joking, so I tapped him on the arm and said, "Hold your breath then, I want to hold my baby boy."

He resisted at first. Struggled, in that way that children do when they think they're too old for cuddles but still have this residual need to be held by Mummy. It was obvious to me he wanted the hug, he wanted the attention. I squeezed him hard and I felt him soften, I felt him allow it. And then, he was suddenly there, his face against my face and I thought it was a joke, that he was trying to smell my breath. I was about to say something like, "Okay, okay. I'll get off you." But then his mouth was on top of mine and I realized he was trying to kiss me! My God! My own son! My tiny little baby boy. His thin boy's body pressed sharp up against mine.

Oh, Jim.

I pushed him off and he fell back against the wall. He stared ahead. He wiped his mouth with the back of his hand. I should have said something, Jim. I know I should have. I should have found a way to talk about it. My baby. I shouldn't have just left him there. But I did. I ran from his room, as though running from a monster. I bumped into Beth coming out. I saw her look at me. Then look into Rhys's room. She asked me if I was okay. I think I managed to squeak that I was.

We went downstairs and we finished the game. Nobody asked about Rhys. Nobody wondered why I'd come down without him. Nobody noticed.

I didn't see him the next day, it was Easter day, we had

guests. I wanted to talk it through with Colin, what had happened. I wanted to find the right moment. I wanted it to be right. It had to be right. And then there was Vicky, standing in my hallway with a bottle of Beaujolais, and I just thought, not yet. I can't deal with this JUST YET. So we drank and we laughed and I put it off. I thought, TOMORROW. I'll deal with this tomorrow. When Megan's gone. When the house is quiet. And of course by then it was TOO FUCKING LATE.

So, darling, what do you think? Was it my fault? I'm so confused, Jim. He was my favorite. And I let him down. I let him down so horribly. Drinking wine when I could have been saving his soul. And can you see now, why I might have tried to avoid thinking about this? Talking about this? Because *I* can. I didn't just lose a son, you see, I lost a sense of myself as a mother. And a mother was the only thing I'd ever really known how to be.

Oh, Jim. Write back soon. This is the hardest thing I've ever done. I need you to tell me it was okay. PLEASE.

xxxxxxxxxxxxxxxxxxxxxxxxxxx

Thursday 17th March 2011

Thank you, darling. Thank you. You are so insightful, Jim, so, what is it they say?—*emotionally intelligent*. I can't believe I had never thought before of the parallels running through everything, the threads that connected it all together. Of course that is why I reacted so strongly to Beth's affair with Bill, to Colin getting together with Kayleigh. And yes, even the man who raped my mother touching me the way he did. It's all vaguely incestuous, isn't it? It's all just a shade away from natural. And you know something, Jim, you know something terribly, terribly sad? I never hugged my children properly again after that day. I'd give them a squeeze, you know, or an arm around a shoulder, but I never ever held them properly again. I was always ready to back off. Poor Beth, I think she suffered the most.

Well, my love, I'm too tired to type much more now. (This blasted, blasted chest infection. The antibiotics are making no difference at all and I honestly cannot face another trip to that awful place, surrounded by all those ghastly ill people and that woman's beefy hands all over the place.)

I'll type more later, darling, but for now, you have no idea how much better your thoughtful, loving and intelligent words have made me feel. About everything.

God, I love you.

Xxxxxxxxxxxxxx

Friday 25th March 2011

Oh, God, Jim, don't do this to me now, darling, please. I need you now, so much. I feel so raw, like someone's peeled off all my skin and left me out on the beach. It's been over a week since I heard from you. I can't bear it. You've never gone this long before without writing. Oh, Christ, are you okay? You're not hurt, are you, you're not in trouble? I just can't be on my own right now. I opened Pandora's box, darling, I opened it for you, and I'm glad I did, it had to happen. But I'm not dealing with it very well. And I'm not well. I'm really not well. I can't even think about making it to the doc's. I can barely move.

Please, Jim, write to me. Anything. Even if it's bad. PLEASE.

Xxxxxxxxxxxxxxxxxxxxxxx

Thursday 31st March 2011

So, is that it, then, Jim? Are we done? Did you finally tire of me? Oh, GOD, I don't blame you. How could I? I mean, look at me! I've been wearing the same clothes for over a week. I smell, Jim. I know I do. Of illness and old hair and dehydration. I'm losing the plot, Jim. Where are you???????

Xxxxxxxxxxxxxxxxxxxxxx

Wednesday 6th April 2011

I can't be here anymore, I hate this house now I've let Rhys back into it. I'm tired and I'm cold and I'm dirty and I'm coming to see you. I'll find my way to Gateshead, somehow. Please be there for me. I've lost my way. I'm half-gone. I'll see you in a few hours. Don't try and stop me.

xxxxxxxxxxxxxxxxx

17

APRIL 2011

The heat wave finally broke on Good Friday and as the bank holiday weekend began, more people arrived at the house. Pandora, from Corfu, freshly divorced and terribly brown. Sophie and Maddy, Lorna and her new husband, even Ben. The house was filled with people, the pavement outside parked up with cars; shift systems were devised, to take things to the landfill, to take other things to charity shops. Lorna's husband, an antiques dealer, usefully ferreted out things of worth. Pandora and Megan led the cleaning team of Molly, Maddy, Sophie and Rory. Bethan sat sedately and sorted through the boxes of smaller objects, sifting through for things worth keeping. Ben collapsed boxes and took them to be recycled. They all sat each evening in grubby clothes, eating at the huge kitchen table, uncorking cheap wine, eating bread and fancy cheeses from the fancy cheese shop in the village. Ben played guitar, Molly moved the focus of her attentions from Rory to Ben. They talked, they gossiped, they laughed, they cried. It was one of the best Easter weekends Megan could remember.

And then it was over. Ben, Maddy, Lorna and her husband headed back to work, Sophie went back to college, Pandora had things to do in London. By Monday evening it was just the five of them again.

And by Monday evening, the hallway had been cleared, the staircase had been cleared, the living room had been cleared and the rooms that had once made up Colin's half of the house had been cleared. Carpets had been ripped up, rolled up and taken away, revealing untouched marquetry parquet underneath. All the old lampshades had gone, and been replaced with white paper balloons from the Asda megastore. The curtains had been taken away and burned, windows scrubbed and vinegared, paintwork bleached back to white. The two tatty sofas in the living room were disguised under white throws, two nice pieces of walnut cabinetry polished back to life and everything else taken to the tip.

Megan walked through the house now, Molly following behind. It bore no relationship to the house she'd grown up in. It was so subdued and empty. So calm and elegant. The rooms felt enormous without the ever-present sacks of crap and boxes of clutter, the shelves loaded with ornaments and paperwork, broken clocks and obsolete party invitations, the patterned rugs and bits of ethnic tat. The walls looked so blank and broad without the higgledy-piggledy arrangements of junk-shop art and framed photos and posters torn from magazines, all randomly adhered to the wall with Blu-Tack. The staircase was so wide, the light through the windows so bright. As she walked Megan realized that even before the awful events of Easter 1991, this house had been a depository for all of Lorelei's deepest buried issues and emotional unrest. She had wanted, as she said to Jim in Gateshead, to give her children the childhood she hadn't had. A childhood without secrets. Without resentment. But even before Rhys had subverted the mother/child relationship and turned her world on its head, she had been building up to this. Piece by piece. Minute by minute. If it hadn't been Rhys, it would have been something else. Because the damage had been done long before that day. Long before any of them were even born.

And so, in the end, it had been no one's fault. No one's fault at all. It wasn't Lorelei's parents' fault, or the fault of the man who'd raped her mother, or of God above for taking away their baby daughter before she'd drawn her first breath. It wasn't Rory's fault, it wasn't Bethan's fault, it wasn't Colin's fault. It certainly wasn't Lorelei's fault. (*"Poor, poor Mum, all those years, carrying that burden alone."*) It was life. One of those things. Somewhere along the line a seed had been sown in Rhys's little heart, maybe even in the womb, and that seed had grown into something completely unconnected to any of them.

For years they'd all let the guilt eat away at them, and their family. But now it was gone. Cut out and disposed of, like a tumor in an operating theater. Now they were free to go on, to be healthy, to love. Now they could be a family again.

At this thought Rory appeared at the top of the stairs, his dirty blond hair on end, his skinny-ribbed, tattooed chest bare and hairless.

"Here!" he said, raising his arms out from his sides. "Here am I! Standing at the top of the stairs! And there are you! Standing at the bottom! And look at all this space that lies between us. All this clean, sane, beautiful space. Isn't it amazing?"

Megan blinked at her brother. He looked happy. Happy the way he used to be. As though he was the most popular boy in the school again.

"Yes," she said. "It really, really is."

◦∼◦

From: JimLipton@yahoo.co.uk
To: MeganRoseLiddingtonBird@yahoo.co.uk;
RoryBird2@hotmail.com; Bethanbird@hotmail.co.uk

Saturday 30th April 2011

Dear Megan (and all the many, many, many of you!),

I just wanted to write and say how much I loved meeting you
all yesterday. I was terrified coming down, as you can imagine,
especially so soon after getting out of prison. It was all a bit of
a whirlwind, from release, to home, to getting your e-mail, to
taking on board what had happened to Lorrie, to the funeral,
and I feel as though my feet have barely touched the ground.

The service was beautiful, truly. Your mother would have
loved it. I never met Lorelei, but I felt I knew her so well from
our almost daily e-mails. She was always so honest with me,
she never hid a thing from me. It makes me feel so terribly guilty
that I should have hidden from her the fact that I had that court
appointment. I don't know what stopped me from mentioning
it. I suppose I was scared of losing her. Which is crazy, as she was
always so accepting of me and my many flaws. Anyway, I think
I'd been in denial myself about the court hearing. Lorelei wasn't
in my life when I got the date through and it seemed such a long
time away. And my solicitor had told me I had a very strong case.
We were expecting a fine, possibly some community service. I
thought I'd be home an hour later. I mean, drunk and disorderly!
How bad could it be?! No criminal damage. No assault. No drink
driving. Just being a lairy, awful tosspot in the wrong place, at
the wrong time. Such a harsh sentence. And because of that, I
wasn't here for your blessed mother when she needed me. I will
never forgive either myself or the magistrate. But mainly myself.

And to that end I wanted to say how grateful I was to you and all your family for the warm welcome you all extended to me yesterday. I do not feel I deserved it, not in the least. I know you've read the e-mails between myself and your mother, so you know how she felt about you all, how much she loved you all, how proud she was of all of you and how hard she found it to come to terms with all the damage that had been inflicted over the years. She blamed herself for most of it, but hopefully, I went some way to helping her see that it wasn't her fault.

Thank you, also, for taking me to see your mother's house. I always had such a burning curiosity about it. I used to watch all these shows about hoarding, you know, trying to get a better insight into Lorrie's syndrome. I even read a couple of books. I so wanted to help her. I thought we had all the time in the world. I was taking it slowly. *Baby steps*, as your mother would have said! But we *didn't* have all the time in the world. We had five months in the end. And of course, by the time I saw her house, you'd cleared it, but thank you for showing me the photos. Such a fascinating record of such an extraordinary process.

Anyway, I've blathered on for much longer than I intended. I hope you don't mind if I stay in touch. I won't bombard you with stuff. Just, Lorelei was such a huge part of my life and now she's gone there's this big hole and I know she'd want me to keep a benevolent eye on you all. Well, I think she would. She was halfway to doing it herself, you know, when she got ill. That's the real tragedy. She was halfway to remembering how to be a mummy again.

Take care, all of you. I hope you'll write and let me know when Beth's baby arrives. Actually, I just hope you'll write.

All the best, and, if I may, all affection,
Jim Lipton

EPILOGUE

JUNE 2011

The people carrier was full. Megan and Bill in the front. Molly and the three boys in the back. It was one of those sad June days that bore no relation to the fantasy of June brought to mind during the winter months. They were listening to Radio One, "Moves Like Jagger" by Maroon 5. And like some advertisers" dream of a modern, relaxed family they were all singing along together, especially to the moo-oo-oo-oo-oo parts. They tumbled out of the car a few minutes later and onto the pavement outside the Bird House, halfway laughing, full of pent-up energy and gladness in the moment. The boys immediately started punching each other and chasing each other up and down the narrow pavement. Megan called at them to be careful. That the cars drove through the village way too fast. From the back of the car she and Bill pulled out three matching bags and numerous gifts wrapped in pink. They were, as ever, the traveling circus, creating havoc and noise wherever they went.

"Why is my family so *loud*?" Megan complained, bringing down the back door, checking there were no heads or fingers in the way first.

Stanley shrugged. "Because *you* made us," he said.

"Right, well, listen, when we get inside there is going to be a very, very tiny little baby and a very nervous first-time mother who will think that loud noises can kill babies, so I want you *all*, and that includes you, Stanley, to behave in a reasonable and sensible manner. Okay?"

"Okay!" they replied in union, less out of obedience than from the knowledge that feigning obedience got their mother off their backs for a minute.

Megan appraised the house. It still took her aback, even on this, her third visit since Easter. Such a pretty house. Bethan had bought planters in beautiful Cotswolds shades of duck egg and sage and there was now a display of lavender and thyme on the sills. (They'd be nicked in under an hour on her London street, she mused.) Rory had fixed the garden gate and painted it white. (It should have been sage, Megan thought to herself, or soft dove gray. But she left the thought firmly where it belonged, inside her head.)

She took Bill's hand in hers and together she and her traveling circus headed up the garden path. Rory answered the door. He'd grown his shaved hair out, and it suited him.

"Come in, come in," he said. "Welcome to the house of shitty nappies. Excuse my language," he apologized to the boys, who all shrugged, unfazed.

Rory was living in Colin's side of the house. He'd replaced the stud wall himself. Megan had no idea how or when her brother had picked up so many manly skills; she assumed it was during his time on the commune in Spain. And Bethan was living on Lorelei's side, with four bedrooms to herself. And her baby.

"Where is she? Where is she?" she asked, aching at some very deep, fundamental level to meet this new person.

"She's in bed," said Rory. "*They're* in bed. She's having a babymoon."

"A what?"

"It was my idea," he said. "Well, actually, it was one of the women at the commune. She was trying to persuade Kayleigh into doing it when she was having Tia. But Kayleigh wasn't having any of that. *'What, lying about in bed on my skinny arse all day with a baby, I'd go nuts!'* But I always thought it sounded like a great idea. So I talked Beth into it." He held out his hands for bags and led everyone through the house. The kitchen was so cozy: the sun was shining through the leaded windows and casting rainbows about the place; there was a half-read newspaper on the table, mugs in the sink, a pot of yellow butter open on the counter, Babygros drying on the Aga; and the scrubbed flagstones were warm underfoot. Beth had put pink gingham curtains at the windows and the room smelled of toast and coffee.

The boys raced upstairs to their room. (It was Rhys's old room, finally exorcised, finally just a room again. Megan had bought two sets of bunks and paid for the room to be painted Farrow & Ball Cook's Blue.) Bill stayed downstairs to help Rory make tea for everyone, and Molly and Megan squirted Milton antibacterial hand gel into their palms and tiptoed quietly up the stairs to the room that had once been Lorelei and Colin's and then Lorelei and Vicky's and then just Lorelei's. Bethan had gone to town on this room once it had finally been emptied. She'd papered it with baby-pink rosebuds and curtained it with cream silk. She'd bought a brass bed from a local auction and clothed it with antique lace and satin eiderdowns. She'd painted all her mother's wardrobes and her dressing table in cream and carpeted the floorboards with pastel sheepskins and shag-pile rugs. But she'd left some of Lorelei's touches too: the trio of cameos of fat-bottomed cherubs in porcelain frames, a few gilt-framed oil paintings of indeterminate heritage, a couple of fussy bugle-bead-trimmed table lamps. Megan could not have stood for it. She'd have wanted it gone, every last shred of the hellhole that this room had once been. But it wasn't her room. It was Bethan's room. And it was lovely.

She'd been so proud of it. "My first real room," she'd said, last time Megan had visited.

"What about your room in Sydney?"

Bethan had sighed, her hand touching a small Perspex cabinet on the windowsill which housed a small pink pebble and the handwritten note from Vicky. "That wasn't a room. It was a stage set. A doll's house. It was where I lived when I was pretending to be a person."

Now Megan knocked gently on the door.

"Come in!"

She and Molly exchanged a small smile and then they stepped inside.

And there she was.

The newest Bird.

She was tiny—under seven pounds—much smaller than she'd looked in the photos Beth had been texting her, and with a full head of dark hair. Beth sat cross-legged on the bed in a cream embroidered smock that Megan recognized as one of Lorelei's, unearthed during the clear-out, and gray leggings. The baby lay in the nest created between her legs, in a pale-gray Babygro with pink spots on it. She was wide awake and the two of them were just staring at each other.

Bethan looked up at Megan and Molly and smiled. "Look," she said, "look at her. Isn't she amazing?"

They moved closer, barely making a sound. The whole tableau was so excruciatingly, mesmerizingly perfect, Megan could not bear to mar it in any way.

"Oh, my God," she whispered, resting the palm of her

germ-free hand against the baby's crown. "Oh, Beth. She is beautiful!"

Molly stared down at the baby, awestruck. "Oh, *God*," she said, "she's so *tiny*! She's so *precious*!"

"I know," said Beth. "I know."

Megan felt that familiar ache in her lower abdomen, that keening and calling of parts of herself over which she had no control. But no, she thought. No. No more babies. Here they were now. Here they all were.

Beth was surrounded by all the things she needed during her babymoon: liter bottles of water, muslins, nappies, wipes, creams, cards, flowers, clothes, books, a laptop and a phone. She had that aura of glorious tiredness of the first-time mother, the mother who has nobody else to care for but her baby and herself. She looked beautiful.

"You look amazing," Meg said, cradling the baby in her arms, perched on the edge of the bed. "Are you getting any sleep?"

"Tons," said Beth. "I'm feeding her in my sleep. I just roll over when she grizzles. Bam. Boob in mouth."

Molly shuddered gently and smiled grimly.

Megan said, "Oh, you're co-sleeping?"

Beth said, "Yes. I mean, where else would she sleep?"

And Megan said nothing because none of her babies had ever slept in her bed because that would have been *a bed made to lie in*. She smiled instead and said, "Have you got a name yet?"

The baby had been "the baby" for three days now and Megan was growing impatient.

"Yes!" said Beth. "I do."

Molly and Megan looked at her expectantly.

"Elsa Athena Rose," she said. "What do you think?"

"Athena for Mum's sister?"

Beth nodded.

"I love it," she said.

There was a knock at the door and Rory and Bill came in with trays of tea and the cookies that Megan and Molly had made together that morning in Tufnell Park. Rory sat on the other side of the bed and stroked Elsa's hair. Bill stood by Megan's side and smiled down at her. "Well done, Beth," he said, "well done. She's absolutely superb. Really."

Then the three boys came in, primed by someone, Bill she assumed, to be very quiet indeed. They tiptoed in, one behind the other, and then the room was full of them. Her family. She heard a car pull up outside and handed the baby back to Beth so she could peer from the window. It was a taxi, and as she watched she saw her father step out and pass a £10 note to the driver. From the other side of the taxi she saw the thin, pale legs of Kayleigh and the even thinner legs of Tia and the bottom of a suitcase and the handles of a pink gift bag. She pushed open the window and she hung over the ledge.

"Dad!" she called. "Kayleigh! Come up to Mum's room. Come straight up! We're all here."

ACKNOWLEDGMENTS

Thank you, Selina Walker. This was our first writer/editor collaboration and I have enjoyed every moment of working with you. Every writer should be so lucky.

Thank you, Najma Finlay, for publicizing. Jen Doyle for marketing and Richard Ogle for putting up with my bombarding you with ideas for covers while you were quietly trying to get on with it.

Thank you to everyone else at Random House; to Susan Sandon, Georgina Hawtrey-Woore, the sales team and everybody who has worked so hard on my behalf.

Thank you to my wondrous agent, Jonny Geller, and his amazing assistant, Lisa Babalis.

In the U.S. I would like to thank my incredible editor at Atria, Sarah Branham, such a true and loyal supporter of my work—one day maybe we might meet! I would also like to thank Daniella Wexler for patiently navigating me through all the nuts and bolts from the other side of the big pond. And lastly, thank you to the remarkable and legendary Deborah Schneider of Gelfman Schneider, who looks after my U.S. interests so well.

Thank you to the staff at Apostrophe, my "office." Thank you for the coffee, and, Maya—good luck with that film role!

Thank you to Mary Chamberlain, my copy editor, for painstaking attention to detail. I challenge anyone to find one single date out of alignment in here.

Thank you to my flesh-and-blood friends on the Board. Fourteen years and counting. I'd be lost without you. And thank you also to my virtual friends on Twitter and Facebook. You're all so supportive and wonderful. I'd be lost without you too.

And lastly, as ever, thank you to my people; to Jascha, Amelie and Evie, to my sisters and my father and my in-laws, my nieces, my nephews and my incredible friends. How blessed I am.

∽

The name "Stella Richards" was given to me by Sarah Richards, who won a character name in an auction raising money for Camille's Appeal. Camille's Appeal is a charity focused on supporting the recovery of children diagnosed with brain tumors. Working in partnership with other charities and the NHS, they are funding specialized rehabilitation units to allow children to access the support and therapy they need to help them reach their full potential. You can find out more about Camille's Appeal here: http://www.camillesappeal.co.uk/. It's a brilliant cause and I hope Sarah's daughter, Stella, whose name I have used, enjoys her fictional turn as a Cotswolds coroner!

THE HOUSE
WE GREW UP IN

LISA JEWELL

A READERS CLUB GUIDE

This reading group guide for **The House We Grew Up In**
*includes discussion questions for your book club. The suggested
questions are intended to help your reading group find new
and interesting angles and topics for your discussion. We hope
that these ideas will enrich your conversation and increase
your enjoyment of the book.*

TOPICS AND QUESTIONS FOR DISCUSSION

1. Jim and Lorelei meet on the Internet and form a close relationship. Do you think that the Internet is a helpful social tool for people who find themselves isolated, or do you think it can make them more vulnerable?

2. Lorelei and Vicky's relationship comes as a shock to the family. How would you describe the dynamic between them? Do you think they are both in the relationship for the same reasons?

3. Rory travels to Spain and then to Thailand. Do you think he is traveling to try to escape his problems? Why do you think he finds it so hard to face what happened?

4. Beth travels to Australia and starts a new life. In what ways do you think this decision to move abroad is similar to Rory's? What do you think triggers her subsequent breakdown?

5. Molly is quite open-minded and accepting of Colin and Kayleigh's relationship. Do you think she demonstrates a more modern outlook of a younger generation? How would you feel about it? Do you think Colin or Kayleigh is at fault?

6. Beth and Bill's affair puts a lot of the relationships in the family at risk. Why do you think Beth embarks on a relationship with Bill? Do you think the motivation for the relationship is the same for both?

7. Beth describes her room in Sydney as "a stage set . . . where I lived when I was pretending to be a person" (page 384). What do you think she means by that? Do you think it was important for her to live independently away from her family before returning home?

8. Why do you think Colin and Lorelei's marriage breaks down? How much do you think Rhys's death plays a part? And Lorelei's illness? Do you think the problems lie deeper than that?

9. All of the Bird family members feel guilt to some extent about Rhys's death. Do you think this guilt is the main factor behind the gradual breakup of the family? What other factors do you think are involved?

10. Colin and Rory discuss Lorelei and her tendency to live in denial. Why do you think she refuses to accept that she is unhappy?

11. Lorelei's hoarding problem becomes worse over time. Why do you think some people begin hoarding? Do you think only a certain type of person is susceptible, or could anyone become a hoarder?

12. Colin, Vicky, Meg, and Beth all have different approaches when confronting Lorelei about her hoarding. When Colin and Vicky try to help Lorelei clear out some of her house, she reacts very angrily. Why do you think she responds so strongly? How do you think you would try to help Lorelei? What do you think would be the best way to deal with it?

13. The members of the Bird family are affected in different ways by Lorelei's hoarding. What repercussions do you think hoarding can have on a person's family and friends?

14. Lorelei collects used candy wrappers and old wrapping paper. Why do you think hoarding often focuses on collecting items others would see as worthless?

15. Eventually Lorelei can no longer sleep in her bed or cook in her kitchen because of the severity of her hoarding. As a compulsive disorder, do you think it has anything in common with other addictions, such as alcoholism? Do you think it would affect family members in a similar way?

16. Did reading this book make you reconsider your relationship with your family? In what ways did each family member's romantic relationships mirror their relationship with Rhys?

17. What scene in *The House We Grew Up In* had the biggest impact on you? Why?

To find out more about compulsive hoarding disorder, read:

Dirty Secret: A Daughter Comes Clean About Her Mother's Compulsive Hoarding by Jessie Sholl

Stuff: Compulsive Hoarding and the Meaning of Things by Randy O. Frost and Gail Steketee

ATRIA BOOKS
PROUDLY PRESENTS

THE THIRD WIFE

LISA JEWELL

Coming soon from Atria Books

Turn the page for a preview of
The Third Wife . . .

1

APRIL 2011

They might have been fireworks, the splashes, bursts, storms of color that exploded in front of her eyes. They might have been the northern lights, her own personal aurora borealis. But they weren't, they were just neon lights and streetlights rendered blurred and prismatic by vodka. Maya blinked, trying to dislodge the colors from her field of vision. But they were stuck, as though someone had been scribbling on her eyeballs. She closed her eyes for a moment, but without vision, her balance went and she could feel herself begin to sway. She grabbed something. She did not realize until the sharp bark and shrug that accompanied her action that it was a human being.

"Shit," Maya said, "I'm really sorry."

The person tutted and backed away from her. "Don't worry about it."

Maya took exaggerated offense to the person's lack of kindness.

"Jesus," she said to the outline of the person, whose gender she had failed to ascertain. "What's your problem?"

"Er," said the person, looking Maya up and down, "I think you'll find you're the one with the problem." Then the person, a woman, yes, in red shoes, tutted again and walked away, her heels issuing a mocking clack-clack against the pavement as she went.

Maya watched her blurred figure recede. She found a lamppost and leaned against it, looking into the oncoming traffic. The headlights turned into more fireworks. Or one of those toys she'd had as a child: tube, full of colored beads, you shook it, looked through the hole, lovely patterns—what was it called? She couldn't remember. Whatever. She didn't know anymore. She didn't know what time it was. She didn't know where she was. Adrian had called. She'd spoken to him. Tried to sound sober. He'd asked her if she needed him to come and get her. She couldn't remember what she'd said. Or how long ago that had been. Lovely Adrian. So lovely. She couldn't go home. Go home and do what she needed to do. He was too nice. She remembered the pub. She'd talked to that woman. Promised her she was going home. That was hours ago. Where had she been since then? Walking. Sitting somewhere, on a bench, with a bottle of vodka, talking to strangers. Hahaha! That bit had been fun. Those people had been fun. They'd said she could come back with them, to their flat, have a party. She'd been tempted, but she was glad now, glad she'd said no.

She closed her eyes, gripped the lamppost tighter as she felt her balance slip away from her. She smiled to herself. This was nice. This was nice. All this color and darkness and noise and all these fascinating people. She should do this more often, she really should. Get out of it. Live a little. Go a bit nuts. A group of women were walking towards her. She stared at them greedily. She could see each woman in triplicate. They were all so young, so pretty. She closed her eyes again as they passed by, her senses unable to contain their image any longer. Once they'd passed she opened her eyes.

She saw a bus bearing down, bouncy and keen. She squinted into the white light on the front, looking for a number. It slowed as it neared her and she turned and saw that there was a bus stop to her left, with people standing at it.

Dear Bitch. Why can't you just disappear?

The words passed through her mind, clear and concise in their meaning, like a sober person leading her home. And then those other words, the words from earlier.

I hate her too.

She took a step forward.